CHOOSER OF THE SLAIN

BOOK I OF THE WATERS OF WYRD SERIES
E.S. OLIVER

SHADY GROVE
CREATIVE

CONTENTS

About the Author

E.S. Oliver lives in the northern Colorado Rockies with her husband, a gaggle of rescue dogs, alpacas, and *exceedingly* noisy ducks. She's a deeply spiritual person who spends a lot of time in nature and meditating.

Her work has appeared in: *The Las Vegas Sun, Beyond Words Literary Magazine, The Dillydoun Review, Liminal Spaces Magazine, Line of Advance Literary Journal, Alien Buddha Zine,* and the anthology, *"This Book is a Work"*

She also won honorable mention in L. Ron Hubbard's prestigious *Writers of the Future* contest.

Dedicated to my Cole.

Without him, this book would cease to exist.

One

Unknown Blood, Unknown Dreams

A ntje's strawberry-blonde hair dripped with the blood of the unknown, cascading down her tall, slender frame like melted snow after a morbid spring thaw. As deafening screams mingled with whizzing bullets and rapid gunshots, the unmistakable stench of fear and blood collided within her nose. Nausea and tinnitus set in as Antje turned around, witnessing musicians abandon their instruments and sprint offstage as gun-wielding attackers shouted orders to each other in a language alien to Antje.

To the left of her, a young woman whose chest had been perforated by a large-caliber bullet was bleeding out on a floor littered with handbags, phones, spilled cups of beer, and the bodies of individuals, most of whom were not yet half a century old. The woman's hands uncontrollably convulsed as she attempted to apply pressure to her wound, her very last moments spent gurgling and gasping for air.

To Antje's right, were the remains of a man, maybe nineteen, who had been shot square in the head; his lifeless eyes bulging as his mouth hung agape. Succumbing to complete chaos, hordes of people rushed multiple exit doors which were too narrow to accommodate the onslaught of bodies attempting to squeeze through them. The poor souls toward the back of the throng—the ones who just hours before had thought themselves lucky to be closest to the stage—were now being picked off one after another by a barrage of seemingly never-ending gunfire emanating from assailants on either side of the stage.

On the rear fringe of the crowd, a man who had been protecting a tanned young woman in frayed jean shorts and a slinky tank top, turned with unabashed rage and began to charge one of the executioners, only to be instantaneously focus-fired by several gunmen. He dropped to his knees less than three feet from Antje; she watched in horror as the life drained from his pained eyes, his limp upper body falling to the crimson-stained wood floor. Antje glanced at the exit door with her tear-laden blue-green eyes, only to see it slam shut behind the woman in the frayed shorts. The thunderous salvo continued as Antje stood in the center of the concert venue, trembling and frozen with fright.

The frenetic honking of a car horn replaced the popping of gunshots. It was then that Antje opened her eyes to find her car drifting into oncoming traffic. Swerving, Antje regained her position in her lane, her face wet with tears, the whole of her body quivering with anxiety. Antje had escaped from the surreal terror she'd witnessed in what felt like a complete loss of mental sovereignty. As her daily commute progressed and she readied herself for the drudgery of bureaucratic meetings ahead, she simply couldn't shake the uneasiness of the events that had nearly concluded her life with a head-on collision.

Antje arrived at the office, absentmindedly taking a seat in her drab half-cubicle, which doubled as an eight-hour-prison every weekday. With a half-turn of her poorly machined, creaking chair, Antje's meddling cubicle-mate, Sarah, encroached upon her personal bubble and now stood a measly six inches from her startled, pallid face. Bending down with her elbows on Antje's desk, Sarah perched her face on her palms, cocked her head with curiosity, and examined Antje's face.

"Good morning, Antje. You look like you've seen a ghost." Sarah often went on information-gathering missions only to have cannon fodder for gossip during her next book club meeting, where nary a book could be found. Typically, Antje cautiously filtered what she revealed to Sarah, but on this specific morning, the prolonged existential terror she experienced overrode her desire to not be the topic of derision amongst a group of bored middle-aged busybodies.

"Morning. Yeah, I had something strange happen this morning, and it's lingering."

"Something strange? What does that mean? Did you have another one of your 'I-can-predict-death' dreams? Ooh, which celebrity is going to die this time?" Sarah said hungrily, grabbing the seat-back of her office chair and rolling it under herself without giving Antje the reprieve of space she so desperately desired. Sarah seated herself and clutched her coffee with both hands, her bubblegum pink acrylic nails clacking against the ceramic mug.

"This one wasn't a dream. It was more like... I went into some time-bending trance while driving and had a vision or something. One second I was driving, and the next, I was basically trapped in the middle of a mass shooting at a concert. I have no idea who any of the people in my vision were, and I couldn't understand anything they were saying—I don't even think they were speaking English. The people being shot at were speaking several different languages, and the people shooting were yelling to each other in another language. It was just so... real. I could smell, hear, and feel everything. I can't get the image of one of the people dying right in front of me out of my head—I stared him straight in the eyes as his soul left his body," Antje lamented.

"Oh." Sarah's tepid reaction was typical, as it didn't involve celebrities or Sarah herself. "I bet you didn't eat breakfast this morning, did you? Low blood sugar really messes me up too," Sarah said, rolling her chair back to her desk with her feet before setting her coffee cup next to her keyboard and carefully placing her headset so as to not undo the hard work of her extra-strength hairspray. "Time to get to work—hello, thank you for calling the Middle Park County Forestry Service, how may I help you?" Antje understood who Sarah was and found no revelation in receiving such a vapid response, but it saddened her nonetheless.

Antje often struggled with facing a harsh truth: her reality was different from most people's. She was persistently disappointed as it became apparent that everyone around her failed to notice the synchronicity and everyday magic that was so obvious in her eyes. They brushed fate off as coincidence and explained the unexplainable by accepting such things as statistically implausible happenstances. The herd focused on the latest shoes and cars, obsessed over pop culture—none of which was the least bit important to Antje. She knew the iceberg of reality spanned immeasurable depths beneath the surface of the mass-delusion humanity participated in daily. It was as if she saw in color, and the rest of the world, sans her uncle, saw existence in shades of gray. It was isolating for her; she often longed for an intimate relationship with someone who had the ability to peek through the veil as she did—a best friend, a boyfriend, someone she could fully connect with for once. In a world full of Sarahs, she relentlessly pined for the day she crossed paths with another Antje, or even Antje adjacent.

The rest of the day's meetings were an unrelenting slog of, "How do we get the general public to stop setting the forest on fire?" Despite wall-to-wall meetings, somehow Antje just couldn't shake her overwhelming feeling of impending doom. As the day came to a close, she traversed the penitentiary-gray hallways of her cinderblock office building before rushing through the front door. A long pause and massive inhale of crisp outdoor air never failed to reset her mood; suddenly she had a single blissful moment of serenity—albeit a fleeting one.

Unlocking her car with the key fob and climbing inside, she caught a glimpse of a smudge in the rearview mirror. Upon further examination, it appeared to be some sort of ancient symbol loosely resembling the letter "F," except the short lines were at a downward trajectory. Antje did a double-take, but her second glance in the rearview offered something far more perplexing: a one-eyed elderly man with a surly grey beard, gnarled teeth, raggedy clothes, and a dirty, large-brimmed hat stared back at her, his good eye piercing through her as if he somehow could see her soul in its entirety.

"The Dark Army is assembling, Antje. It is time. Wake up!" The man's Scandinavian accent was unlike any she had ever heard before—not quite Icelandic, and not quite Norwegian, but somewhere in between. She swung around, readied for close-quarters hand-to-hand combat, but instead was left in shock as there was no one in her backseat. Antje returned her gaze forward, blinking her eyes twice, intending to reset her clearly malfunctioning vision. Another deep inhale and a slow exhale with her eyes closed soothed her racing heart. As she cracked one eye open, a raven on the hood of her car let out a loud "Grooooooonk!" Involuntarily jumping in her seat, Antje's arm accidentally hit the horn. The raven fled in reciprocal fright. Antje rubbed her eyes and shook her head, as if to rattle it back into functioning order, but as she again looked to her rearview, the symbol was still there in the bottom left corner. Antje wasn't always the tidiest of humans, but she certainly kept her mirrors clean. Using her smartphone to take a photo of the symbol, she pulled up an informational guide to runes.

A rune from Proto-Germanic times used to communicate the word "God."

This rune is associated with the deity known as Odin or the Norse All-Father.

Slack-jawed, Antje stared at the screen before setting the phone on the passenger seat and driving home. Two by two, thoughts raced through her head until she arrived home and dialed her Uncle Isaac, which proved to be difficult with her jittery hands.

Uncle Isaac was an ex-corporate CEO turned yogi; he was often Antje's mentor when she sought counsel, even though he was half a country away. The phone rang once and then connected.

"Hello?"

"Hey, Uncle Isaac. It's Antje. How are you doing?" Antje felt a tsunami of relief as he answered the phone; Isaac's baritone voice and gentle demeanor were soothing for her—like a large glass of wine at the end of a rough day.

"Antje! I'm doing well. So good to hear from you, but...what's wrong? You sound panicked."

"Well, think I had a vision on the way to work today and it totally freaked me out... I was in some sort of daydream or trance state and I almost hit someone head-on. It shook me to the core and then something bizarre happened when I got in my car after work; I hallucinated a man in the backseat, and then this raven was on my hood and—"

"Oh, Antje. I bet that was terrifying—I'm glad you're okay. Tell me about your vision... Was it a family member or a public figure like your dream premonitions have been?"

"No, this time was different. This time, it was people I didn't know..." Antje explained her waking nightmare in great detail. Isaac reassured her that it was merely a trick of her brain brought on by the banality of her morning commute, and while she quite often had dreams that carried premonitions of death, they typically involved people she knew or public figures—not random strangers. A renewed sense of safety washed over Antje as she poured herself a glass of wine. After the first refreshing sip, Antje began to share her bizarre hallucinatory experience with Isaac, but he interrupted her.

"Turn on the TV, Antje! Turn on the news!"

"Why the—"

"Just turn it on. Your vision is happening as we speak!"

Antje turned on the TV and heard the female news anchor painstakingly narrating the day's events. "As you can see from the footage we've obtained, several people were forced to flee into the alleyway. Just a horrible sight, Jim. Absolutely horrific. Our thoughts and prayers go out to the families of those affected."

Footage of injured people escaping from a building in Rotterdam filled the pixels on Antje's wall. Falling to her knees with the phone still pressed to her ear, Antje watched with tears streaming down her face. She recognized several people from her premonition by their outfits as they poured from the exit doors. *They lived. They escaped. The brave man in my vision did not. Why was this shown to me?*

"Antje? Are you alright?" Isaac gently asked.

"Sorry, Uncle Isaac. I just—I don't know what to say."

"Antje, your gifts are growing stronger. Tell me about this man you saw in the car... Did he speak to you?"

"He was old and had a bum eye... He said something about a dark army assembling and told me to wake up."

"I see." Isaac paused. "I think it's time."

"Wait—he said that too. He said, 'It's time', but...time for what? If it's time for more death premonitions, I don't want this godforsaken gift! These people are dead. I watched them die before it happened! I almost died!" Antje's voice intensified, her mourning now mingling with a tone of righteous indignation.

"I know, Antje, but I believe the reason your gifts are only related to death is because it is such a huge disturbance in the energy matrix of the universe that it comes through clearly. You're probably getting all sorts of other messages, like the man in your backseat and the raven on the hood of your car, but they just aren't as clear, and you're probably not even perceiving them as messages."

Antje paused and attempted to reel in her emotions. "Time for what, Uncle Isaac?"

"Time to visit the Cisterne. It's a school in Copenhagen for spiritually gifted kids. I have a friend who is a school counselor there."

"A school for gifted kids? I'm 27 years old. What am I going to do? Make macaroni art and learn a spell to tie my shoes?"

"No, of course not. I want you to visit and see what these gifts look like when they're nurtured. You don't have to participate, but I would highly suggest visiting and learning a little more about your gifts. I have to warn you, though, the things you will see at the Cisterne... they don't follow science or common logic. It's a school of mysticism, and the laws of nature and man don't apply there. So, be very careful while you observe. Are you open to this? I'll make an introduction if you are."

"I guess it couldn't hurt. I'm so tired of living this way, wondering why I don't ever feel like I belong anywhere in this world... Other than with you, obviously. Maybe someone at this school can explain why my dreams are always premonitions of death and why I had no control over my mind this morning."

"Antje, it will explain so much more than that. I went after I decided that being a CEO wasn't for me. It changed my life—and seeing as you're the only other family member who was given the gift of providence, I think it's imperative you go, but I understand if you need time to process everything."

"Alright. Only because I trust you implicitly, and I saw the change in you after your visit—I'll think about it. Let's say I do go visit... what's your friend's name, and where is this school?"

"Antje, here's where it gets weird, so please keep that faith in me... The school is literally in the cisterns under Copenhagen."

"What?" Antje questioned with a breathy laugh.

"Exactly what I said. It's called 'The Cisterne' because it's literally located in the cisterns. My friend will meet you there and escort you to the hidden entrance. A lot of tourists like to visit, so it will be easy to slip in unnoticed until they give you your permanent pass. My friend's name is Kari. She just had a baby, but she should be back at work by now, and I know she would love to meet you."

"I'll let you know. Thank you for everything, Uncle Isaac. I appreciate you more than you know."

"Anytime, Antje. I love you. You know... I think of you as my other daughter, and I want you to live a life of enlightenment—one where you aren't scared to close your eyes at night."

In only two days' time, Antje became resolute in finding the answers to the questions that plagued her. No amount of internet searches or videos could explain the bizarre and impossible experiences she'd lived through. Antje accepted Isaac's proposition via email and began correspondence about her upcoming journey to Denmark.

Antje lived outside a small town in Colorado, at the top of a mountain. She lived for the sound of aspen leaves rustling in the cascading winds, like waves crashing on a beach. But above all, she loved the sound-dampening peace of Colorado's snow-packed winters. Snow brought her a type of silence and insulation from the chaos and cruelty of the world that was invaluable to her. Friends and family persistently questioned her desire to live so solitarily, deep within the forest, but it was her isolation that allowed her to be sociable when she did venture out into the world she despised so fervently. Antje was empathetic to a fault, or perhaps extremely sensitive to the energy shifts around her. In public, she felt bombarded by the internalized feelings and energies of others. Oftentimes, she would leave the sanctuary of her mountain to visit with friends at the bar situated on the end of the 15-mile dirt trail leading to her home. Upon entering the watering hole, her temperament would change—sometimes into frenzied happiness, and other times into the depths of misery. Uncontrollable and consuming, it left Antje drained and wanting to retreat—especially because the people whose energy she was channeling were drawn to her for advice and emotional healing. Antje didn't mind being used as a free therapist, although she often found herself embarrassingly blurting out random things—things the advice-seekers typically embraced her for and thanked her for sharing, things she still had no understanding of how, or even why, they popped into her head and out of her mouth. Nonetheless, her solitude allowed for such encounters without draining her spirit to the point of nihilistic exhaustion.

Her existence at 11,000-foot elevation was more than simply a respite from society—she felt closest to creation, to the universe, to existence there. It was where she felt at peace internally, and where she felt convinced of something more to the world than working, eating, sleeping, and procreating. There was a reason for existing, and although the reason eluded her, something about the high country convinced her there was one.

As she watched the snow begin to fade off the peak to the far east of her cabin, she heard a ping emit from her laptop. It was an email from The Cisterne. As Antje opened it, she found a rather short message:

"Third of July. 8:00. Wear blue jeans, a black shirt, and carry a selfie stick. See you soon. - Kari."

July 3rd was merely days away. Over the next few days, Antje spent her time preparing for a trip that was essentially one enormous mystery to her. She had no idea what to expect, and while titillating from an adventure standpoint, it was also unnerving for her. *Will I see ghosts... or goblins... or gnomes? Will I find out that it's just a bunch of strange people standing in an old water cistern talking about their drug-induced hallucinations? What could this possibly be, that was so enlightening for Uncle Isaac?*

As she took her uncomfortably small seat on the plane, the smell of sanitizer and heady floral perfume burned through her olfactory system. Attempting to quell the sensory attack, she twisted and turned the bulbous air nozzle until stale refrigerated air cleansed her airways. Lulled into a quasi-state of relaxation by the continuous hum of the engines, she watched the runway gradually fall beneath the aircraft. The plots of land transformed from sprawling lush green meadows to tidy green boxes with the occasional crop circle carved into them. She stared at the sky with headphones on, listening to classical music. The rays of sun beaming through the small window port gently warmed Antje's face, finally pulling her deeper into the state of relaxation she had previously only dipped her toe into; it was now easy for Antje to settle in for her long voyage. She began to doze... Not quite asleep, not quite awake, she attempted to talk with creation.

Will I really learn anything on this trip? Blurred visions of a man flashed before her eyes along with images of an immaculate garden. *I'm going to meet a man and go to a garden? Is this seriously something important for me to know?*

"Yes!" a stern female voice from behind her left ear bellowed with such force that it jolted Antje awake. She awoke with a jerk that startled her elderly seat mate: a small, hunched woman with silver-gray hair and knobby-knuckled hands.

"Are you okay?" the old lady questioned. She had tired blue eyes and a kind smile that peeled her well-earned wrinkles back like velvet curtains folding into each other at showtime.

"Yes, sorry to disturb you. I just had a bad dream," Antje sheepishly replied.

"Well, life seems like a bad dream lately, so maybe you were actually awake. What happened in the Netherlands... I just can't even talk about it," the woman quietly moaned while her age-spotted hands turned the pages of the newspaper she was reading. The front page read "TERROR IN ROTTERDAM: 50 dead, 100 wounded in concert attack." Antje cringed.

"It's very sad. The way those kids died and the memories the survivors will have to live with... No one should have to go through that," Antje said, sinking down into her seat as a surge of depression crashed down on her like an avalanche.

"My grandson... He was killed. According to his girlfriend, he tried to stop the terrorists but was shot."

Antje's heart sank even further. "He is a hero. Acts of bravery like what your grandson did are superhuman. He went out a hero on his own term s... but I am so very sorry for your loss."

Antje embraced the elderly woman as she started to weep. "I am sorry for crying. I just can't imagine the suffering my poor grandson went through. I'm on my way to Amsterdam for his funeral. His girlfriend lives in the Netherlands, and they had been searching for their first flat to move into together. He was living with me, but was so excited to start his life abroad." She continued to sob.

"I am sure he didn't suffer. He had a quick death and likely saved a lot of lives in the process because it diverted their attention." Antje paused and then blurted out, "Gam Zu L'Tova."

The elderly lady stopped crying and stared at Antje in astonishment. "You speak Hebrew?"

"Not that I know of. I don't know why I said that. I'm sorry—sometimes things just fly out of my mouth," Antje nervously backpedaled.

"No! Do not apologize! Thank you for telling me that. I'm Jewish, as was my grandson, and whenever something bad was happening, he used to remind me 'Gam Zu L'tova.' In Hebrew, that means 'this is for the good.' It was his favorite principle to live by. How did you know?" she marveled.

Antje smiled and replied, "You'll think I am crazy if I tell you."

"I won't. Please tell me," the woman pleaded.

Antje proceeded over the next several hours to share everything she saw with the old lady, including her lengthy history of premonitions and unexplainable experiences. The old lady remained silent, mostly blotting her tears away and occasionally breaking down until Antje stopped speaking and simply hugged her.

The aged woman grabbed Antje's hand and cupped it between hers. "Thank you. You do not know what a mitzvah you've just done. You're a real mensch. I'll share with the rest of our family at his funeral, and I know it will bring much needed healing."

As the plane landed in Copenhagen and Antje readied herself to exit the plane, the elderly woman again smiled at her and warmly said, "Thank you. This meeting was kismet."

"I really am so sorry for your loss, but I'm grateful I was here to give you some closure." Antje embraced the woman one last time before stepping into the aisle and exiting the plane—unsure of what the journey ahead would bring.

TWO

THE CHAOS OF SHADOWS

It was a sunny, cloudless day in Copenhagen. A warm solar floodlight blanketed the well-manicured, emerald park in which Antje patiently waited. With a large latte in one hand and the required selfie stick in the other, she sat on the edge of a seal-grey fountain, staring at two aesthetically pleasing, angled glass pyramids on either side of her field of vision; the irregular panes of glass connecting in an interesting geometric pattern. Antje delighted in the architectural creativity of balancing the triangular structures on their square concrete foundations with one point veering toward the green blades of grass below. Antje sipped her latte, unaware of how rare still moments like these would become.

The sun's reflection flickered and danced on the ripples of the fountain's water and beamed from the two crystalline buildings, momentarily blinding Antje as she hadn't had the foresight to bring sunglasses. Even still, she couldn't help but succumb to her inner voyeur, stealing glimpses of parents with their young children in tow as they entered the glass pyramids one family after another. Antje was sure to keep a safe enough distance to shield herself from the inevitable energetic assault emanating from the crowd. A gentle, heavily Danish voice called out her name from a few feet away.

"Antje! So nice to meet you!"

Antje turned to find what looked like a seven-foot-tall woman with pale skin and pitch-black hair. Her light blue eyes were piercing, yet beautiful, and her perfectly aligned teeth complemented her severe and sharp bone structure.

"Hello, Kari! It's nice to meet you too," Antje warmly replied, standing up and putting her latte on the edge of the fountain, freeing a hand to shake Kari's. Kari bypassed her extended hand and leaned in for an uncomfortably long hug. Kari felt different than most people Antje encountered, and her energy felt balanced and contained, unlike the sloppy spillage of others.

"Your uncle is a splendid man. I've never known someone to be quite so mellow, yet so formidable and kind all at the same time. He says you are searching for some answers. Come with me, and don't forget your kaffe!" Kari happily chirped while approaching the glass entrances. Antje consumed the last of her latte in one gulp and threw the empty paper cup into the recycling bin to the right of the entrance inside one of the pyramids.

Antje and Kari descended a concrete flight of stairs into the heart of the cavernous cisterns; Antje mindfully focused on each footstep in order to block out the overwhelming energies around her. The scent of stagnant water in combination with the stark temperature drop upon entering hit Antje like a one-two punch. The walls on either side of the path most taken were sloped with water runoff in mind, and the sounds of trickling water and falling droplets ricocheted throughout the cisterns. Jarring entrance aside, Antje found herself feeling genuinely sentimental, as it reminded her of the cave tours she'd attended during school field trips—the echoing laughter of children lending to the memory's authenticity. A lover of all things unique, Antje also marveled at the ingenuity of using old water cisterns as a tourism destination. The many stone-carved statues thoughtfully placed about the tunnels beckoned her to examine them—and she would have, had Kari not led the way rapidly. Antje struggled to keep pace with Kari's long strides.

Quickly stepping off the damp walkway and deviating from the crowd, they trudged through a foot of water, navigating a series of arched doorways until they stopped right in front of an unexceptional column in one of the cistern's' dome-shaped rooms. Not a soul in sight, Kari then reached for Antje's selfie stick and placed a card where the phone would normally go.

"And now, the fun begins! Turn away from the corner and hold up your selfie stick like you are about to take a photo of yourself," Kari said, beaming. Antje did as instructed, and nothing seemed to happen.

"Okay? What now?" Antje asked.

"Step backward three steps and don't freak out," Kari told her with a giggle. The stone column that was once almost pressed up against Antje's back had mechanically receded and transformed into what was now an elevator barely big enough for two people.

"We had to modify our entrance because this has become a popular spot for tourists, and waving a wand wasn't exactly inconspicuous," Kari said with a laugh, joining Antje in the lift, the rickety box shaking and bouncing with each step she took. The elevator seemed to lower itself for 10 minutes before finally stopping. The doors opened from the center, and much to Antje's disappointment, it was merely a claustrophobic room with an old desk and a single unremarkable door to the right of it. Behind the desk sat a wrinkly, bald old man who appeared to be at least in his late 90s. He wore large round reading glasses and held a newspaper in one hand, and a coffee cup in the other.

"Security." Kari winked with a smirk.

"Oh, he's terrifying, that's for sure!" Antje joked back.

"No seriously—he is our security and probably the last person I would ever want to make angry. That man has been practicing offensive spellcasting for at least a century, maybe two," Kari whispered and grinned. Antje raised one eyebrow and stared at the man, attempting to imagine how someone so unassuming could be so formidable—and apparently immortal.

"Welcome to the Cisterne! Remember, this is a school for mystics. You can't trust your eyes to show you the whole picture here," Kari reminded Antje.

Kari nodded at the old man, who continued to ignore her, setting down his cup and waving her over to the door without ever looking up from his paper. Antje's jaw dropped as Kari opened the door. Behind this tiny, insignificant door lived cathedral-height ceilings, adorned with beautiful artwork displaying mythical creatures and beings such as dragons, unicorns, goblins, ancient wizards, and fairies. The walls were castle-like in their stone construction, and even though the school was deep underground, bright sunlight beamed intensely through skylights—exposing specks of dust that glittered throughout each and every ray. Antje's eyes widened to their limits when a statue moved as she walked past, revealing a glimmering silver sword with intricate copper designs inlaid on the blade. Antje stopped dead in her tracks and stared at it.

"Is...is that a real sword?!" Antje marveled.

"Yes, yes, it is. Though, no one but this statue has ever been able to hold it. You know the story of 'The Sword and The Stone'? Same principle. Except, in this case, the stone is our living statue. His name is Gudbrand," Kari replied.

"Hello, Gudbrand." Antje waved, nervously. The statue remained still and unresponsive.

"Don't be offended, Antje—he doesn't really interact with anyone usually." Antje smiled at the statue and nodded.

"Wait here. I had to leave Karl, my son, with one of the other counselors. In exchange, I said I would welcome this new student for her this morning. It won't take but a few minutes."

Antje nodded and continued delving into her surroundings. Kari walked into a tight alcove with a desk where her baby's bassinet rested on the table. A child of no more than nine patiently awaited her with his book bag in his lap, feet swinging as he sat in an adult-sized chair.

Out of seemingly thin air, a scarlet-haired woman clad in maroon, tightly fitting robes appeared. Her long, wavy, thick hair shimmered like fiery embers against her flawless alabaster skin, which accentuated her citrine-green eyes and pursed rose-colored lips. The woman cocked her head slightly, extended her hand toward Antje, and said, "Headmistress Paulson, but you can call me Rebekah. Nice to meet you." Antje shook her hand, and as their skin made contact, the hostile and borderline envious energy being exuded by Rebekah sent literal chills throughout her body.

"Nice to meet you, Headmistress Paulson, I mean, Rebekah. I'm Antje Valason," Antje replied with a nervous smile as Rebekah circled her as a shark circles chum. Rebekah was unusually zaftig and walked with a slinking gait. Antje decided to deescalate the situation.

"I'm eager to learn about mysticism. I have things—things I can't explain, and I'm here to find answers. Do you think I may be able to find them here?" Antje questioned genteelly.

"You'll find some answers here, but mostly what you'll find are a lot more questions," a smooth baritone voice spoke with an echoing chuckle; every atom in Antje's body responded with titillation. Antje turned around to see a man with supple olive skin, broad shoulders, and curled silver-threaded black hair approaching Rebekah. As he stopped at her side, Rebekah smirked and slowly turned her head, presenting her almost surrealistically beautiful profile to Antje. The way Rebekah eyed this man was conflicted, to say the least. It was like peering into the psyche of someone who wanted to melt effortlessly into his hands, but also simultaneously wanted to see him come to a gruesome and violent end. He stretched out an uncommonly rough, large-knuckled hand toward Antje; his honest smile and warm chestnut-brown eyes welcoming, and a bit alluring.

"Hi, I'm Cole Stalvey. I didn't think they let other Americans in here!" he said cheekily, almost crushing her hand. "Oops, sorry. I don't know my own strength sometimes!" he apologized, quickly loosening his grip. As Antje opened her mouth to reply, Rebekah hastily interjected, "This is Antje. Her uncle is one of our most prized scholars, Cole. He sent her here to become acquainted with her abilities."

"I see. Very nice to meet you, Antje. I hope you find everything you're looking for. I'm here on business. A child was murdered yesterday in Marseille, and we have good intelligence that the culprit, Kitt, has sought refuge here—apparently unbeknownst to school officials," Cole said, playfully glaring at Rebekah. Antje admired Cole's unusual scar above his eyebrow and his thick, but well-kept beard. His nose was pronounced, and in combination with his skin tone, Antje wondered if his lineage was Greek, Italian, or perhaps even Armenian.

"I think we would know if we had a murderous wraith under our care, dear," Rebekah said. "As I told you, we banished her last week. I'm starting to believe you're simply concocting reasons to see me."

"It's like you don't know me at all. If I want to see you, I don't need to make up an excuse," he said, lifting her hand to his mouth and gently planting a kiss upon it. Antje felt an unparalleled level of discomfort, her body tightening as she shifted her weight from one foot to the next, desperately attempting to ground herself. There was an intimate familiarity with Cole she had never felt before. If someone were to ask her to explain "love at first sight," this would be it—but clearly, and unsurprisingly, he was enamored with Rebekah and her impeccable gothic charm. Cole grinned at Antje with a tinge of affection, Antje reciprocating his friendly gesture before he walked down one of the many hallways leading to and from the atrium.

"Excuse me, Ms. Valason. I need to tend to my intensely nosy boyfriend and the gaggle of insufferably hyper children under my charge. Don't get into any trouble while I am gone," Rebekah requested in an oddly serious tone. Antje gave a sincere nod in response. With a wave of her hand, Rebekah vanished in a sudden onset of shadowy vapors, leaving Antje standing in the atrium by her lonesome. Antje glanced over at Kari, only to confirm she was still occupied with onboarding the new student. Clueless as to what her schedule was for the day, Antje feared she might not have the time to fully take in the exquisite beauty of the Cisterne at a later date. As such, she allowed herself to become engrossed in the elaborate design of the underground relic in which she found herself.

While absorbing every minuscule detail of the delightfully ornate architecture, she noticed what appeared to be an opaque shadow, marked by chaotic and erratic movements. It spastically juked across the atrium, landing next to Karl's bassinet. She spun around only to find the shadow had transformed into a disheveled child with ratty tar-soaked hair, deeply bruised circles under her eyes, and a mouthful of razor-sharp, rotted teeth. The embodied nightmare was now looming over the bassinet, snarling and dripping thick, stringy saliva onto the infant's head. With a crazed look and a maniacal grin, she grabbed the baby from his bassinet. Kari's eyes now affixed on her child, she instructed the nine-year-old to hide under the desk with one hand.

"No! Kitt, please no! Please, I am begging you! Put her down!" Kari shrieked, desperately pleading with the wraith as the baby fussed, his tiny fists and feet kicking and clawing to free himself from the creature's grasp. Kitt growled a little, looked Antje dead in the face, and eviscerated the baby—splattering blood and entrails everywhere. Kari let out a soul-shattering cry and collapsed to her knees, clawing and grabbing at the pool of viscera, attempting to piece her little love back together again. Antje's heart abounded with her pain. Kitt released what remained of the baby from her grasp, dropping it into Kari's trembling hands with complete disaffection.

Eyes still locked on Antje, Kitt slowly stepped over Karl's bloody remains. Juking and jutting toward Antje, Kitt's head glitched and jerked with deliberate wickedness that could only be described as psychopathic rage. Antje began to panic. Not knowing what this incarnation of evil was, or what it was capable of, Antje relied on the martial arts training she had completed as a teenager and searched around her for available weaponry. The only weapon within range was Gudbrand's sword. By this time, Kitt was within arm's reach of Antje, and for a split second, time stopped for Antje. It froze long enough for her to reach over to Gudbrand's arm and utter one simple word: "Please." Gudbrand's hands released the sword, Antje swiftly unsheathing and swinging it with all her might at Kitt's head. Her hands throbbed with the intoxicating power of the sword. Gliding effortlessly through the air with a type of authority Antje had never felt in an inanimate object before, she struck Kitt with suspiciously perfect aim, nearly beheading her. Kitt let out a monstrous bellow that was simultaneously shrill and demonically deep. The pained outburst was discordant and excruciating to everyone's ears. In response, everyone except Antje clasped their hands over their ears. Antje was still in a tense standoff with Kitt, whose head was now hanging upside-down against her chest—only held on by a literal thread of greyish-white skin. Kitt, scowling at Antje with unbridled hate, reverted back into a shadowy cyclone of chaos and bolted through one of the Cisterne's solid limestone walls.

Antje looked at the sword—there was no blood anywhere to be found. She looked at the ground. No blood there either. What was Kitt?! She began to hyperventilate as she looked to Kari, seeing her hysterically sobbing while clutching what looked more like a pile of blood and remains, and less like what was once a human child. A groundswell of sorrow overtook Antje as she placed the sword back into its rightful place: Gudbrand's marble hands. Rushing to Kari's side, Antje attempted to comfort her by wrapping her arms around Kari's blood-drenched body, cradling her while she wailed to the heavens and clutched what was left of Karl's remains.

Rebekah again appeared out of thin air, this time with several teachers in velvet hunter-green robes behind her. Rebekah walked over to Kari and gracefully placed her hand on Kari's head. Instantaneously going limp in Antje's arms, Kari was thrust into a dreamlike state. Rebekah motioned for a few of the teachers and demanded, "Take Kari to her chambers, and the baby to the medical chamber after Cole has taken an account of the scene. Let's see what we can do for them. I believe the child is gone, but still, we must try." She turned and looked at Antje. "What you did was impressive—and borderline implausible. Gudbrand never relinquishes his sword to anyone."

With her hands shaking, still in shock from what had just occurred, Antje stared at the pool of blood on the ground and stammered, "It was like time stood still, and he let go of the sword and gave it to me. I don't know."

"Well, what the hell happened here?" Cole's voice rang out as he entered the atrium. "Let me guess, Kitt?" Cole's glare, aimed at Rebekah, was an accusatory one.

"Yes, dear. It was indeed Kitt. Our new guest somehow managed to use Gudbrand's sword and scared off Kitt with quite the impressive display of swordsmanship. She nearly cut Kitt's head off," Rebekah explained, with a tone of academic distrust. "I'll leave you to question Antje and continue your investigation, Cole. I have a traumatized counselor I need to tend to." Rebekah handed her card to Antje, who stood up, weak-kneed, to receive it. "Here's my card. We need to schedule a private meeting. It's not often someone graces my academy on their first day with such a... bang," she said, waving her hand in the air. Once again, vanishing, she left Cole and Antje face to face, staring at each other.

"Antje, you couldn't have actually beheaded Kitt and saved me all the trouble?" Cole chided. "I'm kidding—but not really. Kitt has left a bloody trail of calamity behind her at every turn, terrorizing everyone in her wake for weeks now. That little demon is an absolute fucking nightmare."

"She was terrifying," Antje said, blank-eyed and trembling as she fixated on the pool of Karl's dismembered appendages and blood.

"They usually are. Don't worry, at some point, you get numb to it," he said while picking up a piece of small intestine with his pen and putting it back down. Standing up, Cole wiped his hands on his pants and grabbed hold of Antje's shoulders, redirecting her attention from the carnage to his face. "You're incredible. Wraiths are nearly impossible to kill and are immune to the magical powers possessed by most of the people in this building. I don't know what you're here searching for, but if it's a new fan of yours... you've made one. An expert swordswoman, and a beautiful one at that—you don't see that every day." He smiled. Antje reciprocated his smile, feeling her heart palpitate. Unsure if it was the adrenaline from the fight or the pheromones she was drowning in, Antje pulled back and nervously tucked a piece of her hair behind her ear—focusing her vision on a random wall.

"I appreciate the flattery, but she still got away. She could be murdering more kids as we speak. We should probably go find her, no?"

"I doubt she's doing anything but hiding at the moment, seeing as she's been partially beheaded, thanks to you. That, and she has every teacher in the Cisterne hunting her at the moment. However, I agree. We should probably split up to search for her as we are probably the only two in this building that can actually do anything to stop her," Cole said, turning and walking down one of the hallways with a laser-sighted pistol in hand. Antje was very well-versed in guns, from growing up and living where owning and using firearms is a necessity to survive, but this was unlike any gun she had ever laid eyes on. The tip of the brushed steel barrel glowed bright blue, and in front of the trigger sat a recess that contained a blue luminescent liquid—it had all the makings of a military test weapon.

As Antje stood in the atrium, again staring into the pool of blood, questioning the life decisions she'd made that had landed her in the Cisterne in the first place, a first-year student tugged on her shirt. Looking down, she saw a tiny freckled face, nervously looking back at her. Antje felt the same energy coming from this child that she'd once felt when she stumbled across a fox with its foot caught in a fur trapper's snare. It was the unmistakable static of animalistic fear. Antje squatted down.

"What are you doing here? You shouldn't be around all of this. Let's get you back to your classroom," Antje said, slowly grabbing the boy's hand. The boy started to cry.

"I need you to come to my classroom or else my friend will be in big trouble. Please help her!" he sobbed.

"Okay, okay! It's going to be alright," she promised the child, hugging him and frantically searching over his shoulder for Cole. With no such luck, she decided time was of the essence and headed to the classroom. On the way, she stopped by Gudbrand and asked, "May I borrow this again?" Only this time, Gudbrand tightened his grasp on the sword. "Okay, understood. Thank you for lending it to me in the first place," Antje said, bowing her head and slightly panicking. Gudbrand nodded and went back to the pole position. There was no time to waste, but she was absolutely sure she was entering a trap, with no weapon. She desperately combed the hallway for anything that could be used as a weapon as they briskly navigated the halls. There were no fire extinguishers, nothing. In a school of people with a full command of magic, there was simply no need, and the barren walls reflected this.

Arriving at the doorway, she instructed the boy, "Run. Run and get the silver-and-black-haired man with the gun. Tell him where I am, but do not come back without him, no matter what you hear coming from this room." Antje motioned to the child to go. He nodded, tears leaking from his eyes, and took off down the hallway in a full-blown sprint. Opening the classroom door carefully, Antje walked through the threshold, one deliberate step at a time. There stood Kitt, scowling at Antje, her head dangling like a lopsided pendulum. Another small child sat curled up in the corner of the room, trembling and weeping, with her knees pressed to her chest.

"It's okay, sweetheart. Thank you for being brave. I'm here. No one is going to hurt you," Antje assured the little girl.

"Not if you do what I say!" growled Kitt, opening a black vortex in the floor. The treacherous charcoal-colored vortex swirled with arcs of electricity snapping and crackling within, while the resulting windstorm began to consume the room, launching papers and debris in all different directions. Kitt angrily pointed at the tumultuous portal. "Get in there, or I'll end her!"

Antje looked at the terrified little girl and nodded at Kitt. "Okay, Kitt. You win. I'm going," she conceded. Antje's hands raised as she slowly walked in the direction of both the little girl and the vortex. "I need you to let her leave before I go in. Those are my conditions."

Kitt paused for a moment, furiously shook her head, and roared, "GO!" at the young girl. The girl, frozen in fear, looked to Antje for permission. Antje dropped her hands slowly and slipped one hand in her pocket, searching for anything to attack Kitt with; her other hand outreached to the little girl.

"How do I know that you won't just go through the walls again and kill another person, Kitt?"

"You don't! But you can save this girl by DOING WHAT I SAY!" she roared once more, shaking the very floor on which they stood. The little girl hurriedly made her way over to Antje, who turned her body and led the child toward the door, letting go of her hand and motioning for her to leave. As soon as she watched the door close behind the little girl, she turned her entire body and, with all her focused intention, flung the headmistress's business card. Soaring through the tornadic winds that now encircled the room, the card sliced through the turbulence as if it were nonexistent. The unlikely projectile targeted Kitt's only remaining strand of skin with the precision of a surgeon's steady hand, severing it. Kitt let out a heinous shriek as her head fell to the floor, shattering all the glass in the room as if her mouth had detonated an auditory grenade, her lifeless body tumbling toward the antique tile. The vortex collapsed into itself, returning the floor to its original structure with debris crashing down onto it. As the room fell eerily silent, Antje let out a huge sigh of relief and fell to her knees, Kitt's body disintegrating into a pile of dirt-brown dust right before her very eyes.

"What in the actual hell have I gotten myself into?" she wondered as the door burst open. Standing in the doorway was a slack-jawed Cole, gun drawn. Beside him stood the wide-eyed messenger boy, who took one look at the room's minefield of broken glass and raced back down the hallway; Cole and Antje were left alone.

"What in the—how?!" he questioned, holstering his gun.

"With Rebekah's business card," Antje replied.

"You...killed a wraith...with a business card. That is insane!" The whites of his eyes doubled in size as he stared at the pile of dust that was once a gruesome creature.

"Yes. I had no other weapons, and she was forcing me to go into this black hole, and I was freaking out, and I literally just grabbed the only thing in my pocket and just willed it to work and..." she rambled in shaky, borderline hysterics. Cole gently helped Antje to her feet and hugged her. He tenderly framed her face with both hands, his fingers intertwined with strands of her strawberry-blonde hair.

"You're safe now. Take a deep breath—breathe. In.... Out... Very good. I have something to show you—something that will help your nerves. Follow me," he said, releasing her face and grabbing her hand.

Exiting the classroom, Cole led Antje to a pair of walnut-framed French doors not far down the hall. Upon opening the doors, a garden unlike any other revealed itself. Sun beamed through the clouds in distinct columns of light, every blossom permanently in full bloom as if heaven was descending upon Earth. The ozonic smell of a cooling mid-summer rain mingled with various leafy green notes, lingering in the air like a fragrant perfume. Her eyes and mouth agape, Antje attempted to take in the full breadth of the garden. Cole gently led her by the hand to an overlook with an arched cedar trellis overhead; the trellis was inexplicably blanketed in blush-colored peonies, which are not a vining flower. From this vantage point were multiple acres of various plants—all boasting their most spectacular showing.

"This is the Cisterne's garden of Eden. It stays in bloom year-round. Most of these flowers have side effects when smelled," he explained, looking down and plucking a long sprig of English lavender from the ground. "Smell this. It's the mystic equivalent of taking a muscle relaxer—only better." Antje deeply inhaled the aroma emitted from the lavender sprig and immediately felt all of her tension, anxiety, and adrenaline start to fade—leaving her energy feeling balanced and calm.

"Wow—that is incredible," she said, awestruck.

"You think that's incredible? I just found out that you can kill a wraith with a business card! You are incredible; these are just some charmed flowers."

"So, what do the rest of these flowers do?" Antje's curiosity and wonder now fully in charge, the traumatic events of the morning felt more like yesterday's memory.

"Well, I don't know all of them, but I know sunflowers make you happy, peonies make you feel romantic, thistles make you feel confident, and I believe poppies distort your image to the point where the other person feels like they are hallucinating when they look directly at you or something—it's effectively an invisibility cloak from what I understand. I think if you dry them and grind them up, they still work. I've seen them added into liquids with other ingredients to make potions that have multiple long-lasting effects. That's all I know. I'm one of the only normies they let in here, but the mystics still aren't totally forthcoming with the information."

"Normies?" Antje raised one eyebrow.

"Non-mystics—normal people."

"Oh. I guess I'm kind of a normie—I just have crazy dreams."

"What? Are you kidding? You killed a wraith with a business card and had a sword given to you by an animated statue who has ignored literally everyone else for centuries. You are not a normie, Antje." Cole chuckled at the ridiculousness of her statement.

"Fair enough. I guess I don't really know who or what I am," she admitted. "Should we call your girlfriend and let her know what happened? I hope she doesn't boot me. This is my first day here, and I already feel like she hates me."

"Nah. My guess is, she already knows. It's not like these kids are bastions of secrecy," he said, leaning into Antje. "I don't think she likes you, either. Keep your distance from her. Rebekah is one of the most powerful mystics in the world, and I'm not entirely sure she hasn't been tainted by an organization that I've deemed 'The Dark Queen's Army,'" he whispered in her ear. The sensation of his breath on her skin sent shivers down Antje's spine, triggering a scintillating wave of goosebumps along the length of her body. Antje's eyes widened once more.

"Army of... wait—who—or what are you?" Antje stammered, backing up and looking into his eyes while brushing a stray strand of hair behind her right ear.

"I truly wish I could tell you, but I'm not at liberty to do so. I really want to tell you every single little thing, I just can't until I've gotten the okay," Cole said, taking his hand and tenderly brushing Antje's hair back behind her left ear. "I don't know if I am standing too close to these peonies or what, but being around you feels . . . different. I feel like I've known you forever. I feel like I want to know everything about you—it's a little terrifying, if I'm being honest."

"It's not the peonies. I felt it in the atrium, but I didn't think the right time to examine that was while I stood over the remains of a disemboweled baby," Antje laughed awkwardly, her trauma jabbing through the effects of the lavender.

"Well, at least we have our inappropriate timing in common. I don't think having this discussion after you just killed someone, for what I'm assuming is the first time, is appropriate either," he said, leaning in to kiss her forehead.

Antje began to melt, until her conscience slapped the sense back into her. "Timing isn't the only thing inappropriate about this. You have a girlfriend too..." she lamented. Cole's phone rang in his pocket. Pulling it out with an aggravated sigh, he looked at the screen and slipped it back into his pants. Clasping her hands and pulling her intimately close to his body, he quietly said, "I know—and that, I may be able to explain at some point soon. I am so sorry, but I have to go. My work is calling me, and it's urgent. Until next time?" he grinned, kissing the top of her right hand and slowly walking away, turning back to steal one last glance at the delicate features of her face over his shoulder.

"But you don't even have my phone number—or any way to find me if I leave..." Antje trailed off, her heart sinking at the thought of not exploring these bizarrely intense feelings that churned inside.

"I know how to find you. Don't you worry, we'll meet again." His smile was flirtatious as the door quietly closed behind him. Antje took a mental inventory of the wide array of flora in the garden. "Poppies are effectively invisibility cloaks," she heard Cole's voice repeat in her head.

I guess I'll just pick a few flowers while I'm here. If today is any indication, I'm in a world that is way out of my depth, and I need all the help I can get.

THREE

FRAPPES, FOES, AND FIGHTS

After returning to her rental flat, Antje ruminated on the day's surreal series of events. Needing some form of normalcy to help ground herself, she refreshed her work email three consecutive times, only to groan as not a single email graced her inbox. In less than a day's time, her world had transformed into a brave new one, full of excitement—and horror. Having transitioned from an incredulous view of magic to watching a baby being murdered viciously by a wraith, which then led to Antje killing it with a piece of paper—her mind spun like a fishing reel struggling to rein in a defiant marlin. The reeling was further complicated by the uncharacteristic catching of feelings for a taken man, and the realization that she was indeed capable of killing a sentient being with absolutely no remorse. It was a lot to process.

As she soaked her tightened body in a steaming charmed-lavender-infused milk bath, she sipped on a chilled glass of akvavit and began to ponder the purpose of her visit to the Cisterne. Had Uncle Isaac had the same experience? Had he also ended up killing someone, or had he just learned potions and spells? Was he a mystic too? If so, why hadn't she ever seen him use his powers? Was this the same Cisterne he had been to, or had she been thrust into a part of that world that even he wasn't privy to?

One thing about being isolated in the mountains of Colorado is it afforded Antje a lot of time to herself, which resulted in Antje developing the skills of an expert researcher. She was prone to nearly obsessive re-searching when something caught her interest, diving deep into the rabbit hole before resurfacing. This school was no different, but when she'd attempted said research prior to her trip, the usual search methods had returned nothing other than information on the cisterns being used as a venue for art shows.

Antje's thoughts wandered through the day's events as her glass emp-tied and couldn't quite detach from Cole's warning about Rebekah. Surely if she was that dangerous, she wouldn't oversee a school full of children—and surely Cole, whose energy felt protective and stalwart, wouldn't be dating her? Unable to answer her deluge of questions, Antje threw on some clothes, refilled her glass of akvavit, and sat in front of the fireplace with her laptop in hand. Rebekah was a relative technological ghost with absolutely no presence to be found on any social media. Un-successful once more, she rang Uncle Isaac. Half asleep, he answered the phone.

"H-heh-ahem, hello?"

"Uncle Isaac, it's Antje. I'm sorry I woke you up, but I had a disturbing day at the Cisterne with a wraith, the headmistress, some guy who makes me feel some kind of way, and I just have one question: Where do I go to learn about all of this stuff? Is there a search engine for the mystic world, or something?" she fired off, rapidly.

"I'll ask you more when I'm awake," Isaac said, "but there's an internet café in Copenhagen called 'The Wired Wizard.' They're open 24/7. Ask for Mathias and tell him that you want to watch the 1918 documentary on Nessie. You'll have access to everything at that point. That's all I can say over the phone. He's a little unorthodox, but tell him I said hi, and that you're my niece. I spent a lot of time there, and we're buddies. Is that all? I was in the middle of a nice visit with your grandma. We'll talk later."

"Thank you so much, Uncle Isaac. I love you. Sweet dreams." Antje hung up the phone, downed the last of the akvavit in one swallow, and hurried out the door.

Antje arrived at the internet café after a short cab ride. To her surprise, nothing seemed out of the ordinary. Despite the name, there was nothing related to magic or mysticism in sight, other than a sign on the counter that translated to: "Wi-Fi not working? Mathias is our wired wizard of all things wireless. Ask for help, and you shall receive it." An exceptionally tall man behind the bar, with the most glorious, braided beard Antje had ever seen, approached her in an ogre-like manner.

"Kaffe?" he asked, in Danish.

"Sure—do you have anything iced?" Antje replied in English.

"Oh. We have an American! I suppose you're looking for a frappe, or something equally as unrefined and terribly bastardized," he said, rolling his eyes as he dried a glass with a bleached-white rag.

"You must be Mathias. I'm here to watch some documentary about Nessie?"

"Oh, you are, yah? What year?" he aggressively questioned.

"19...18? I'm Isaac Valason's niece. He says hello."

"Well—why didn't you say so!" Mathias exclaimed, hopping over the bar and hugging Antje. "Any family of Isaac is also my family. What can I help you with, my dear niece? Oh, right. Frappes and the fancy internet. I've got it! Follow me," he said, releasing her from his bear hug and unwittingly knocking the wind out of Antje as he patted her back far too exuberantly. Mathias led her into the back storage room, where to her surprise, there was absolutely nothing of interest, with the exception of a Nordic axe carved with ancient runes and symbols hanging on the wall. Antje admired it from across the room.

"You like my axe! Its name is Økse."

"You named your axe... 'Axe'?" Antje giggled.

"Well, what else would I name it? It's a damn axe! That's the only sensible name for it!" he chortled, picking it up and flinging it toward the wall. In the spot where the axe embedded itself, a white portal developed.

"Come, niece. Nessie is through there." Grabbing her hand, they entered the portal. On the other side was a black sand beach surrounded by golden basalt cliffs. Frigid cerulean waves crashed on the shore, pushing and pulling grains of volcanic remnants back and forth in a sort of lulling sequence.

"I didn't literally mean Nessie. I'm looking for information on the Cisterne and its Headmistress, Rebekah," Antje explained, as a huge leather-bound book rose from the waters, levitating through the air and landing in her hands as if it were programmed to do so.

"Looks like Nessie found you anyway. If you want to leave, just blow this horn, and the portal will open to the stockroom. Nessie'll show you what you're supposed to know. She may even show you things that I can't see. That's how this all works, magic nonsense and all. Oh, and do not go in the water. Every year, some poor fool tries, and every single time, they become consumed by magic, walk into the waters, and are never seen again. Back to barkeepin'!" he said, blowing the horn and laying it down on a nearby boulder.

After Mathias exited, Antje sat down on the beach, digging her pale heels into the black sand. She began combing through the colossal book one page at a time. Most of it was written in a language Antje didn't understand. Frustrated, she asked, "How am I supposed to read this? Do you have one in English?" Suddenly, a swift wind barreled through the enclave, rearranging her hair and copious grains of sand; the letters of the book also rearranged and morphed into the Roman alphabet right before her very eyes. On the first page was the physical history of the cisterns. Pressed for time, she flipped through the pages until a headline caught her attention.

> 'Darkness is infecting the Cisterne!' claims Headmaster Vogel.

Upon reading the details that followed, Antje gathered that the headmaster predating Rebekah supposedly became overcome with paranoia and accidentally killed himself while trying to cast a banishing spell on the entirety of the Cisterne. The book went on to say the headmaster ranted and raved in the months leading up to the unfortunate event, claiming an 'invisible dragon in crimson robes' once attempted to murder him as he slept. He surmised the perpetrator couldn't be seen because it utilized a spell to obscure his vision during the attack; in addition, the mysterious villain had cast a spell encompassing the Cisterne, rendering any dispel he attempted completely useless. The mystic community dismissed his claims, and he was asked to step down as headmaster, but refused. After his death, the Council for Mystic Education then elected Headmistress Rebekah Paulson on a split-decision vote, where nearly half the council vehemently opposed her appointment, Paulson's critics citing deep concern around her previous explorations into the world of the dark arts.

Sensing a deeper thread of foul play afoot, Antje sifted and sorted through the following 500 pages of Cisterne-related news meticulously. Since Rebekah's reign, several children had perished under mysterious circumstances, and non-school personnel were regularly reported as being seen on the grounds after hours, often accompanied by Rebekah herself. The surveillance videos of each death revealed the victim was attacked by something invisible, each victim welcoming the evil with their arms outstretched as if they were bewitched.

Hmm. Peonies and sunflowers. It would be easy enough to slip that into their meals.

As Antje further flipped through the book, she stopped on a page outlining all of Headmaster Vogel's claims. The moment her finger lifted the page to turn it, a high-pitched bell sounded as a card with charred edges slid from within the book's pages, landing upon the sand next to her foot. Inscribed on the card in cursive were three words: "Onde Spiritus, København."

"Nessie, please translate this to English for me." A gust of wind once again revealed the meaning of the words: 'Wicked Liquors, Copenhagen.' Antje pulled her phone out to search for an address but, rather predictably, had no signal. Pocketing the card and returning the book back to the waters from whence it came, she walked over to the boulder where Mathias had left the horn-of-return and with a deep exhale, blew. The sound of a struggling gazelle emitted from the horn. Despite Antje's lack of horn-blowing abilities, a portal that looked as if someone had excised a human-sized hole through two realms with a scalpel appeared directly in front of her. Two steps forward returned Antje to Mathias' stockroom at the internet café. Upon exiting the room into the main bar area, she grinned at Mathias, who meticulously wiped down his beer steins, his enormous club hands remarkably nimble as they navigated the ridges of each glass.

"Antje! Did you watch the documentary?" Mathias asked with a mischievous smirk.

"Oh yes, it was very informative! Do you know where Onde Spiritus is?" Upon hearing the words 'Onde Spiritus', Mathias's light-hearted energy quickly shifted to anxious concern; Antje was hit by the shift as if it were a truck.

"Yes, but I don't think you want to go there, my dear niece. I don't think Isaac would want you going there either. There's a lot of, um, hooligans at that bar," Isaac explained, his face stern and his brow furrowed. Quieting himself and leaning forward over the bar, he gave Antje a warning: "It's a perilous place."

"I figured. Maybe I'll just head back home, then. Thank you for everything, Mathias. I really appreciate you," Antje said a little too easily, wrapping her arms around his neck.

"That is Uncle Mathias to you! And—I am serious. You know not what lurks in that bar, Antje. I do, and I don't want to have to come rescue you or explain to Isaac that you've disappeared. Many people go in that bar and never come back out. You are here to go to school and learn, niece. You should focus your energies there."

"Yes—but I'm not so sure that the Cisterne is all that safe anymore," Antje mumbled. "Thanks again, Mathias! See you later!" she chirped, three octaves higher than usual. Mathias squinted.

"Oh, it's like that, eh? Come with me one more time," he said begrudgingly, sighing as he set his rag and glass down on the bar before motioning for her to follow him into the stockroom once more. Shutting the door behind them, Mathias pulled Antje close to him and lowered his face to meet hers. Antje felt his breath on her face. "I worry you are saying one thing but will do another, Antje. I know your uncle, and if you are anything like him—you have no intention of leaving that bar alone." Antje looked down at the ground. "That's what I thought. Well, niece, you leave me no choice. This would have been better if you had done this the wise way, but I am not going to have your death on my conscience. I don't know what Isaac told you, but I am well-versed in mysticism, and if you are going to walk into hell, you will need all of your powers at your disposal. I must warn you—you are not likely to be in control of them at first. You may end up accidentally doing damage or even killing yourself if you don't quickly learn how to keep them within your spiritual restraints; very few mystics are intuitives that can control their powers immediately. The odds of you being able to skip The Cisterne and three years of schooling are not in your favor, Antje. With that disclaimer: do you really want your full powers? If so, I need you to say it out loud."

Antje mulled over the risk versus reward silently. She simply couldn't stomach the thought of any more children dying and became resolute in the decision that she would stop another tragedy from occurring—or die trying. Flashes of Karl's dismembered body reverberated through her mind's eye like a hurricane of carnage, and at that moment, Antje shook her head and looked Mathias dead in the face.

"Yes, I want all of my powers at my disposal. I'll continue at the Cisterne, but I'll learn faster if I have access to all of them—I think," Antje reasoned aloud for both herself and Mathias. Mathias sighed once more and nodded, putting his hands together with a loud clap, then raising them above his head while inhaling to the very limits of his lungs. He violently flung his hands back down, exhaling loudly, and as his hands reached chest height, a golden flame appeared around them. He then separated his hands, leaving a blinding golden marble of light levitating between his palms.

"A man of war, a woman of learning, give this family what she's yearning!" Mathias chanted as the golden ball proceeded to disperse itself into the air, transforming from a spherical object to an opaque cloud of swirling golden particles that swayed and twirled toward Antje.

"Breathe a nice deep breath, niece—the deepest one you've ever taken. Breathe in until your lungs feel as if they will explode." Antje nodded and inhaled as deeply as she could, taking in the entirety of the cloud, and gaining a golden glow, which then burst out of her eyes, ears, mouth, fingers, toes, and every pore in between. When the supernova-like burst subsided, Antje's body slumped a bit with exhaustion.

"What just happened?" Antje asked with hesitance, examining her hands and arms.

"I asked our ancestors to give you your powers. Turns out, you're a woman of war! I am a man of war, and that means your powers should be a little more manageable as I've imparted my knowledge of control unto you. I had no way to know who you are until I called upon our ancestors. What a glorious surprise! We should fight!" Mathias exuberantly suggested, tossing his axe to Antje.

"What? No! I can't fight you. You're like five times my size, and mystical!" Antje moaned.

"Nonsense! Fight me!" Mathias proclaimed, swinging his big hands at her head. At that moment, time once again slowed as it had in the moments leading up to her altercation with Kitt. Antje's grip on the axe tightened. As she dodged Mathias's attacks, she swung the axe as if she had swung one since birth, the axe nailing Mathias in the center of his chest, burying itself so deeply in his skeletal structure she felt the cracking of his ribs and the severing of his spinal cord through the wooden handle. Absolutely mortified, Antje promptly released the axe. As his body plummeted to the floor, she concurrently dropped to her knees, crying. A hand touched her shoulder as the sound of hearty, boisterous laughter rang in her ears; it was Mathias—in the flesh. In disbelief, her head jerked back to the axe as it dropped to the ground—Antje now witnessing what she thought was Mathias's body disappear completely.

"What the fuck, Mathias! I thought I killed you!" she yelled, leaping to her feet and slugging his shoulder out of both anger and relief.

"Sorry, niece. You didn't actually think I was going to put my real body in front of a newly crowned valkyrie, did you? That would be stupid and reckless. I may be reckless, but I am not stupid," he declared, laughing. "Here—you are going to need this, now that you've answered your destiny." Mathias handed Antje a shiny dagger with a deadly-sharp tip and an ivory bone handle. "This is my favorite dagger. I would never give this to anyone I didn't find worthy of it. Goodbye, Daggert, you have been a steadfast weapon, and now you have been promoted to serving the newest valkyrie in Midgard. May you be drenched in the blood of evil and taste the spoils of your victories with honor, old friend!"

"I mean, thanks for the dagger but—what? A valkyrie? As in, the Norse angels of death who decide who wins or loses in battle and who then goes to Valhalla?" she fervently questioned.

"Yes, but it is not like you think. Who will live, and who will die, is already fated. You are connected to death, and if someone lives when they are meant to die, or if someone is about to die who is meant to live, you will be called by fate to serve its will. I mean, it's not going to call you on your phone or SMS you, but you will just know—like you knew to be there during Kitt's attack. The Gods do not just kill babies, Antje." Antje stared at Mathias, mouth agape. "Yes, I know all about how you killed Kitt. News travels fast in the mystic community, my dear niece—especially when someone new shows promise. They are going to lose their minds when I tell them you are a valkyrie! Anyhow, the whole of it is crazy and I am bad with words—but good at bashing in skulls. The Cisterne will be better at showing you how all of this works, but if you need battle tips, I will help. Come to think of it, you being a valkyrie, I should probably ask you for battle tips!" Mathias joked, ruffling her hair. "Now get out of my cafe. I have normie work to do. Have to keep up appearances, you know?"

A warm, breezy night welcomed Antje on a long stroll back to her rental flat. She admired the bright moon in the clear sky—the evenings were short in Denmark, and it allowed her to appreciate the dark of night more than she had before. She relished in the ambiance of the cobblestone streets, and even the raucous laughter of drunks, who spilled from the bars, carrying the aroma of stale beer and bile into the paths of unsuspecting passersby. About halfway home, the sensation of encroaching danger began to consume her. It was heightened to levels Antje couldn't dismiss—like an alarm going off inside, warning her of something nefarious in the alley to her left. Now acutely aware of the peril she was in, it was replaced by an entirely new feeling—a calling inside of her. It was a visceral, primordial call to action she couldn't resist, despite the fear that was borderline paralyzing. She turned and walked directly into the pitch-black alley, scouring the walls of the surrounding buildings, looking for any sign of danger. A female voice hailed her from the abyss.

"Hello, Antje." It was Rebekah. "I see you've made a trip to Nessie. I hope it was enlightening," she sneered, crossing her arms.

"Oh, Rebekah. It's just you. Yeah, I was just curious about some of the dreams I've been having. How did you know I went to see Nessie?" Antje's head cocked with suspicion.

"I know everything, Antje. I know you are out of your depth. I know you killed Kitt. I know you have a thing for stealing forbidden moments with people's boyfriends in their own gardens. I know it all!"

"It's not what you think. Yes, I feel a very strange attraction to him, but if you actually knew everything, you would know I brought you up and said it was inappropriate, Rebekah."

"No need to explain, Antje. I really don't care. I knew from the moment you set foot into the Cisterne that you were going to be a nuisance. Your uncle was one of Headmaster Vogel's prized disciples, and I was happy he left before he became a real problem. You, on the other hand, wasted no time at all, and it's time to rid myself of this vexing inconvenience."

"You mean the headmaster that you somehow killed, so you could take his place, taught my uncle everything he knows?" Antje took a few steps towards Rebekah, signaling her courage.

Rebekah's eyebrow raised. "Who told you I killed him? And yes—your uncle returned to his normie life because he knew he was no match for me, and knew I would kill every single member of his family if he didn't retreat back into his meaningless life in America. He's a coward, and now I'm going to kill one of them anyway," she boasted.

"I assumed you were the 'dragon in crimson robes.' It was pretty obvious when you ended up taking his spot as the head of the Cisterne, Rebekah. My uncle is no coward, you evil piece of shit. Take that back!"

"Or what? So, Nessie let you see the full history of the Cisterne. Oh no! What else could you possibly have hidden up your sleeves? Let me show you why Vogel called me the dragon in crimson robes, and why that old fool and his pet pupil were no match for me!" Rebekah cackled, throwing down a potion that instantaneously made Antje feel like she was on a heroin bender. The walls of the surrounding buildings now oscillated as streetlights turned to starbursts, and her vision blurred—making Rebekah's humanoid form much harder to discern. Despite Rebekah turning practically translucent, Antje could still see her outline enough to follow her movement. Levitating and bouncing off the walls of the buildings, Rebekah shot hissing spheres of red light at Antje.

Time once again slowed as the orbs approached, and Antje dove behind a large trash bin, which immediately dematerialized once the red blast made contact with it. Antje began to panic, thinking she would meet the same fate if one of Rebekah's spells actually landed. Antje hopped to her feet and pulled out the dagger given to her by Mathias, holding it in her right hand, her knuckles white with tension. Rebekah sniggered.

"Hiding behind trash cans! How normie of you!" she scoffed, flicking her hand to the right and slamming Antje into the brick wall from 20 feet away. The bone in Antje's right arm shattered upon impact, causing her to drop the dagger onto the cobblestones. Landing face down on the ground, Antje reached with all her might to retrieve the dagger. It was her only hope of escaping. As she grasped the tip of the handle with her left hand, Rebekah again tossed Antje into mid-air and slammed her into the opposing brick building like a rag doll. Antje heard the cracking of several bones fracturing and snapping as the unmistakable metallic taste of blood flooded her mouth, triggering an inner fury she did not know existed within herself. Barely able to stand up on a now broken leg and ankle, she scrambled to her feet, seething with newfound wrath.

Rebekah slowly descended from the air, haughtily sauntering toward Antje to finish her off. Antje, bloodied and broken, huffed and puffed through her grinding teeth, blood dribbling down her chin and dripping from various parts of her body.

"Well, well, Antje—I guess you needed more than just one day at the Cisterne after all. It's a shame. I thought you'd put up more of a fight, seeing what you did to my hench-wraith and all. Ahh, I so hate being disappointed like this," she nonchalantly declared while glancing down at Antje's dagger with a snicker. "Oh, that's cute. You thought you were going to defeat me—with a dagger!" Rebekah erupted in hysterical cackling. "You are clueless and pathetic. Give me that."

As Rebekah reached for the dagger, Antje headbutted her, momentarily dazing Rebekah. Pulling her left hand backward, Antje swung her arm up and plunged the dagger into Rebekah's chest. In utter disbelief, Rebekah stared down at the dagger, stumbling backward a step.

"A—a dagger? Impossible. Daggers—they can't... hurt me. Unless—" she choked out, falling to her knees, as her blood gradually navigated the recessed channels of the cobblestone beneath her. Now involuntarily bobbing her head as she coughed and gurgled from the blood obstructing her airways, Rebekah managed to lift her head, looking wide-eyed at Antje, who now stood above her, wavering in pain. "Unless—you're... you're... a valkyrie?"

"Yes, I am, you heinous bitch—and I just had all of my powers given to me. You've killed your last child, your last Headmaster—your last victim, and you're about to breathe your last breath," Antje said, spitting blood onto Rebekah's face, and ripping the dagger from her chest. "Time to meet your maker and atone for your evil deeds. On behalf of Isaac—go to hell," Antje viciously preached before plunging the dagger through the center of Rebekah's skull, pressing down through the bone and sinking the tip into her brain. Antje let go of the dagger, stumbling back a few steps and collapsing on the ground from the massive loss of blood.

FOUR

PENS AND NEEDLES

With her legs crossed and eyes shut, Antje's palms rested on the smooth boulder she sat upon, the sun kissing her cheeks as her hair danced on the wind. With each breath, her body gave way to the frigid caress of the persistent gusts of high-country air. Enveloped in complete and total peace, it was as if Antje's life had never actually existed.

A familiar male voice stroked her ears, his tone less harsh than before. "It is beautiful here, is it not?" The voice was remarkably audible considering the raucous whooshing of the steady squalls. Antje opened her eyes, revealing an elderly man standing to her left. He stared straight ahead at the mountaintops which peeked through a solid blanket of clouds, his hands clasped behind his back, gently pressing against the wolf hide draped clumsily over his shoulders. Antje marveled at his brilliant white beard and the scarring on his face as he began to lower himself, crossing his legs to match Antje's posture before reaching for her hand and tenderly holding it on his knee.

"You were in my car—who are you? Are you Odin?" Antje inquired, feeling curiously affectionate toward the old man. Antje was surprisingly unconcerned with how she'd ended up on a mountaintop holding hands with a strange old man who had previously been raptured from her back seat—and was very likely a god.

"That's not important right now. Consider me family, Antje," the man answered calmly. "What is important is that you wake up. Spend time here as often as you like, but today you must go back. Tell me when you're ready."

Antje's mind shifted from her newfound nirvana as flashes of her earthly existence began to return to her. "You're right, I have to go back—but, where are we?"

"Your home, Antje. We are where your soul calls home," he replied, grinning.

"Am I dead?"

"No—just here temporarily. Your friends are working on your body in Midgard as we speak. It took you longer than expected to visit, child. You have guided so many people here, and you never stop to say hello. It has been nice to see you, Antje. Ready to go back? Your body is waiting."

Antje sighed. A pause from the anxiety-laced pain of existence was a welcome reprieve, yet she knew she belonged back in Midgard, in the midst of complete chaos. "Yes. I guess I'm ready," Antje acquiesced. The man released Antje's hand and hovered his palm above Antje's.

"Touch your palm to mine. Until next time, Antje." A loving smile crept across his wrinkled lips as Antje placed her hand on his, the world around her fading into black.

The vibratory notes of Tibetan singing bowls ran through her body like an electric current. The aches and pains, which had not plagued her on the mountain, returned in a deluge of misery.

"Oh-ho, Jinpa! You've done it!" a loud recognizable voice rang out.

"Mathias?" Antje weakly questioned, struggling to open her eyes. Mathias bent down until his face became level with Antje's. Mathias visually resisted his urge to hug her, as there were hundreds of acupuncture needles protruding from her body.

"I knew you wouldn't quit on me! Taking down one of the greatest mystics in history on your first day—what a shield maiden!" Mathias boisterously praised, his face maniacally gleeful.

"H...how did you? Wh...where am I?" Antje feebly eked out, taking in her surroundings. She was in someone's dark and very sparsely decorated flat, which felt more like a model home than a residence.

"Oh, right!" Mathias pulled up a chair and sat next to the makeshift operating table. "When I gave you your powers, I also bound us in an unbreakable bond between warriors. When you were injured, I felt it deep in my bones, and the gods called me to retrieve you. I found you unconscious on the ground next to Rebekah, who still had Daggert sticking straight from her skull—that's a brutal way to kill, Antje! I like your style. Yah, so—I brought you to Jinpa. You are very lucky, Antje. Jinpa only comes from Tibet to visit the Cisterne for a month or two out of the entire year, and he's the best healer I know. You'll be back to normal in a few hours—he is the master of expedited healing. Be patient and still, niece."

Antje turned her head, her eyes searching for who Mathias was talking about. A middle-aged Tibetan ngakpa with a top knot made of dreadlocks sat on a floor cushion with a bronze bowl in hand, moving the striker around in slow, deliberate circles, exuding an intense sound that changed each time he added water to the bowl. The smell of herbs lingered in the air, mixing with aromatic incense and the metallic scent of Antje's blood. The man's gentle eyes met with Antje's; she mouthed 'thank you' to him as he silently bowed his head and returned his deep focus to the singing bowl in his hand.

"Jinpa doesn't speak much English. You really need to learn more Danish if you're going to stay here, Antje. Jinpa! Hun siger tak!" Mathias hollered jovially. Jinpa smiled at Antje, again lowering his head. "So, while Jinpa was fixing you, a dark-skinned man in a black suit came to the door and gave me a pen to give to you. He said his address is in your pocket, and then said something bizarre like, 'when you meet the crows, stand in the rainbow and click the pen twice'—oh, and make sure no one is around. I have no idea what it was all about; it makes no sense to me—but he was definitely American government. Your government is always nosing around the mystics—you guys have no finesse!" Mathias rambled.

"She done," Jinpa interjected. "Sit up now."

Antje sat up slowly, expecting her broken ribs to be excruciating—but the pain had dulled to more of an annoyance.

"That's incredible. I'm just sore like after a workout. I could have sworn I broke a bunch of bones..." she trailed off.

"Yes. All them. You fixed now. No payment," Jinpa informed Antje, packing up his singing bowl into a beautifully embroidered silk pouch.

Leaning toward Antje, Mathias whispered, "I saved his son's life one time, and now he won't let me pay for anything." Mathias sat back in his chair, turning to Jinpa. "We're even, Jinpa! You don't have to keep giving away your healing for free!" Mathias heartily slapped Jinpa's shoulder and launched the man forward a couple of feet.

"No. My son life precious. She precious. I heal for free. I go now. You leave when ready. Careful, Antje—you not made of stone," Jinpa warned, wagging his index finger at Antje.

Antje chuckled. Knowing she was getting a much-deserved scolding, she bowed her head to Jinpa with respect. "Takk fyrir, Jinpa." Both men erupted with laughter.

"That's Icelandic, Antje. Say 'mange tak,'" Mathias corrected.

"Mange tak, Jinpa." Antje's face flushed with embarrassment as the words left her lips.

"You welcome," Jinpa replied with a cool smirk before exiting the room.

Mathias handed Antje the pen, motioning to look inside her pocket. Slowly reaching down with her right hand, she removed a card that contained an address: Ørn Kunsthal- Colbjørnsensgade 6-15, 1253 København

"Eagle art gallery? This guy must really love birds," Mathias surmised, ripping open a package of cookies and shoving several of them into his mouth. "What? I was hungry!" Mathias confessed, crumbs spilling out of his mouth. "I'm not sharing if that's why you're looking at me like that," he warned, tucking the package under his elbow and dusting his hands off. Antje chortled, realizing all her discomfort had completely subsided. "Oh, before I forget, here's Daggert back. I cleaned him for you." Mathias handed Antje's dagger over, handle first. "Also, I don't think you need those needles anymore." Mathias began plucking the acupuncture needles from her skin, one by one, like an ape cleaning a family member.

It was mid-morning as Antje left Jinpa's flat, parting ways with Mathias as she ventured to the address on the card. Antje opened the hulking wooden door and entered the vacant art gallery where simplistic, yet dark paintings hung from the stark white walls. At the far end of the gallery, a sizable mobile of hand-carved wooden crows hung from varied lengths of fishing line. As she approached, a rainbow projecting from a stained-glass window revealed itself beneath where the crows hung. Antje stepped into the rainbow-tinted light beam. Looking around to confirm she was alone, she clicked the silver tab at the top of the pen twice. Nothing happened. Examining the pen to see if perhaps it was user error, she waited a few more seconds before giving the pen two additional clicks. Again, nothing happened.

Exasperated and beyond drained from the previous evening's brawl, she began to think this was an ill-timed prank on Mathias' behalf. Not one foot had left the rainbow-tinged light when a man in a black suit appeared from the back room. He was tall and well-built with smooth sable skin and an immaculately coiffed beard. With each step, the clanging of metal against the concrete floor of the gallery became more apparent to Antje. Looking at his feet, she realized one foot was made entirely of steel.

"Hello, Antje. Sorry for the wait. I'm not quite as fast as I used to be—I was hit by an IED in Afghanistan, and my right leg has never quite been the same," he explained, knocking his closed fist against his right leg, which emitted a metallic ringing. Upon seeing Antje's eyes widen at the realization that he had a cybernetic leg, the man flashed an amused smile before motioning with his heavily tattooed hand for Antje to follow him into the back.

"I'm going to need more than that before I follow you," Antje tersely stated.

"Understandable considering what you've been through. I wanna to you about a job offer. I'm American too...we've got a mutual friend."

Sizing him up, she assumed that to be the truth, agreeing in her head that he reeked of three-letter-agency personnel, or at the very least, high-ranking military. With a quick nod, she followed the man into an unexceptional office with nothing but a desk and two chairs inside.

"Please, take a seat," the man requested, slightly pulling back the chair in front of his desk.

"I'll stand. I've had a really long night, and stretching my legs feels good."

"Ah, yeah. You were at the acupuncturist. That makes sense. You aren't the easiest to find, by the way. It took fifteen informants to piece together where you went. Anyway—I'm Special Agent Kenny Davis with the CIA. We know what you've been through in the past few days, and I want you to know that you have a friend in us—and hell, we're impressed. So impressed, we wanted to offer you a position with the agency as a consultant." Antje moved her hair back behind her ear—a self-soothing mechanism she had developed during childhood. Antje always had a deep-seated aversion to government agencies and an equally deep mistrust of authority, often avoiding any reason to step foot in even the most menial of government buildings.

"I appreciate the offer, but no, thank you. I just kind of fell into all of this, and I'm really just trying to live my life," Antje coldly declined, turning toward the door.

"That's a shame, Antje. We could use your help. Our country could use your help—the world could use your help... and your powers."

Antje stopped dead in her tracks. "My powers? How did you know about my powers?" Antje inquired, with her back to Special Agent Davis.

"You don't think anyone still believes you're a normie, do you? You killed a wraith with a business card. According to his report, Cole was dumbfounded and has never seen anything like it in the entire time he's been with the agency."

Antje whipped around, her face flushed with rage. "Of course, Cole is CIA. Son-of-a-bitch! The whole 'us in the garden' thing was part of some operation to gather information on mystics. I get it now." Antje seethed. Although, most of her ire was aimed at herself for falling into such an obvious honeypot.

"Well, yes. He's CIA, but no, that was not part of an operation. You were a complete surprise to Cole—a pleasant one that took out a foot soldier for him. He's thankful, you know."

Antje turned back around and headed toward the door. "Still not interested, Special Agent. Don't contact me again."

"Understood, but we are still your ally—the enemy of my enemy, you know? Keep the pen. If you get into a situation you can't get out of and need help, click the pen quickly three times. There's a small beacon inside that is dormant but will transmit a signal once activated with three successive clicks."

"I won't need it. Oh... and tell Cole I killed his girlfriend," Antje apathetically stated, closing the door behind her.

Special Agent Davis laughed out loud and mumbled to himself, "Man, Cole sure knows how to pick 'em."

FIVE

STONES AND POTIONS

Antje once again stood in the waterlogged cisterns, searching for the pillar that would grant her entry to the academy below. Confident in her choice of pillars, she raised her selfie stick, which triggered the transformative mechanism behind her. She began to take three steps back into the elevator when her name rang out, followed by the sound of rapid, sloshing footsteps.

"Antje, wait!" Cole yelled, his voice echoing through the cisterns while his pace quickened to a full-on sprint. Antje took the last step back into the elevator as Cole approached. "Wait!" he yelled once more, now doubled over and out of breath. "We need to talk."

"No, Cole, we really don't. I know all about you being CIA. I know I was probably a mark of some sort. No need to explain. I feel stupid enough for thinking that there was something real there already." Antje dismissed Cole and pushed the button for the door to close. Grabbing the end of

Antje's selfie stick and placing it between the closing doors, Cole forced the elevator doors to retract. Antje rolled her eyes, both of their right hands still holding onto each end of the selfie stick. "What, Cole?"

"Look, it's not what you think. Yes—I am with the CIA, but no, I did not know anything about you, and what I felt was absolutely real. All of it. Do you really think I would risk a mission to warn you about Rebekah if I wasn't interested in you? This isn't some game. I can't explain why I feel this strongly about you—in fact, I've spent my entire life using women for sex to avoid catching feelings exactly like these... But, this—this is different. This is real, and aside from us, we're onto something big, Antje. Uh, shit—I probably shouldn't have told you most of that. I'm going to shut up now."

The elevator doors attempted to close, once more retracting as they tapped against the collectively held obstruction. Antje squinted and curled her lips inward. "What about your girlfriend, Cole? Was that real?"

Cole sighed and shook his head. "No. No, it wasn't. If it was, I never would have come onto you. She was a mark. Nothing more. I was investigating her role in the disappearances of a bunch of kids, and a lot of other sinister happenings around Europe as of late," he paused and a smile crept to his lips. "Did you actually kill her? I got reports this morning that she was found in an alley with head and chest wounds, but no murder weapon to be found. Special Agent Davis said you told him it was you, and that our informants had tracked you to Jinpa's home, where they assumed you were being healed. But—how the hell did you do that? Rebekah was an expert in warding, and other than my gun, I don't even think the agency has a weapon that could have taken her down," he probed.

Antje let out another irritated laugh—her eyes rolling again. "So that's why you're here? To gather intel?"

"No. Step out of that elevator, and I will show you why I am here, Antje." "Why should I?"

"Because you want to know if this is real, and deep down, you want me just as badly as I want you." He wasn't wrong. Antje had a bizarre, visceral yearning to be with Cole. Since the moment she'd laid eyes on him, he had occupied every thought that wasn't fixated on survival or death. Cole flirtatiously stared into Antje's eyes, pulling the selfie stick toward him, one hand after another. Refusing to let go of the selfie stick, Antje begrudgingly allowed herself to be pulled from the elevator. As both parties synchronously released the selfie stick, it plummeted into the water with a splash that diverted Antje's attention. Looking back at Cole's face, their eyes locked, triggering a fervent chemical reaction in both of their bodies. After a brief pause, Cole pulled her close to his broad chest, leaving Antje breathless, just inches from his face, their noses nearly grazing one another's.

"You really are beautiful, Antje." Cole brushed the hair back from Antje's cheek with his hand, just as he had done during their last spirited rendezvous. Once more, Antje had a visceral reaction that sent butterflies into her stomach, and chills throughout her entire body.

Her face flushed as Cole asked, "Can I kiss you? A real kiss this time? It's all I've been able to think about since the garden." Antje, impassioned and abandoning all inhibition, leaned in and took his lower lip between hers, intermingling their mouths. Cole pulled her in ever so tightly, wrapping one arm around her waist, and the other reaching up her back; his stout hand cupped her neck tenderly. It was as if the current world melted away around them. The damp cisterns gave way to a cliffside in the high desert, overlooking a large canyon with geological wonders in every direction, as far as the eye could see. The unmistakable perfume of sagebrush and sediment swirled in the cool, arid air as Antje opened her eyes, still ensconced in her kiss with Cole. Bewildered, Antje took a step back from Cole.

"What's wrong? Was that too fast?" Cole worried as the desert scene dissipated back into the cisterns right before Antje's very eyes.

"Th—the desert. Did we go to the desert?" Antje stammered.

Cole, brushing her hair back behind her ear with his finger, said, "What are you talking about, darling? We're in the cisterns. Is that what you're seeing?"

"Well, yeah—now. But before, we were on a cliff, and I could smell the sagebrush and... never mind. I guess I did suffer some pretty severe wounds last night," she said, shrugging her metaphysical transport off as a head injury.

"Are you sure you're okay? Special Agent Davis said you were at Jinpa's this morning. It had to be bad if you were there."

Antje cringed a little, remembering that Cole was CIA. "Yeah, Rebekah definitely did a number on me—I almost died. You promise you're not manipulating me for work? Look me in the eyes and tell me," Antje demanded. Looking into her eyes, Cole ran his fingers through her hair, his hands resting on either side of her head; Antje's ears gently rested in the cradle between his thumbs and index fingers as Cole assured her, "This, right here, has nothing to do with work. I promise. I think I...love you. I think, I love you? I know—it doesn't make sense and it's way too soon... But, I honestly think I loved you at first sight. I don't believe in soulmates, but if I did—hell, you're mine," he confessed, pulling a jadestone silver necklace from his pocket. "Here, I want you to have this. I bought this during my time in Afghanistan, and I've been holding onto it for the right woman. I came here today to tell you—you're that woman."

After kissing her forehead, Cole walked behind Antje and brushed her hair from her shoulders, placing the token of his affection delicately around her neck. Antje's body warmed with the genuine nature of Cole's confession, and her mind calmed itself as she clutched the jadestone necklace. Cole gently arranged her hair back as it had been, and Antje turned around, carefully studying his face. Antje was skilled in the art of lie detecting. One of her obsessive research sessions had led down a two-year rabbit hole on the study of using facial tics and behavioral abnormalities to distinguish lies from the truth in others. If Cole was lying to her, he was also lying to himself.

Antje grabbed Cole's hands with her own. "It's beautiful. Thank you. I can't believe I'm about to say this, but..." Antje took in a deep sigh. "I think I love you too, Cole. I don't even know why yet—but that's how I feel. Anyway, uhhh, I hate to ruin this sweet moment, but my anxiety just kicked in, and I have to tell you that I found something big. Nessie gave me the name of an apparently scary bar that has something to do with these dead kids and the Cisterne. I'm headed below because I really need some potions, and lessons on how to use my powers before I go investigate; I really don't want a repeat of last night."

"A scary bar? As in Wicked Liquors?" Cole's demeanor flipped from enamored to concerned as he tightened his grip on her hands. "No, Antje.

You can't go in there alone. That's like walking into a lion's den wearing a meat suit—you'll never come back out."

"Well, lucky for me, my new boyfriend is a super badass special agent with some futuristic monster-killing gun." Antje giggled. To disarm the panic emanating from Cole, she swung his hand—attempting to play it off as insouciantly as she could.

"Boyfriend? Oh? Is that what we're doing now?" he teased.

"It depends. Are you going to meet me at the bar for backup, or not?" Antje fired back.

"Of course. It's a date. See you at 10? Does that give you enough time to get what you need from the Cisterne?"

"It does." Antje leaned in to kiss him once more. "And don't forget to bring that gun," she half-joked, tapping the concealed firearm on Cole's hip.

"Where I go, it goes. Don't forget to bring that cute butt of yours, ok?" he retorted, grinning like a teenage boy who'd just seen breasts for the very first time.

Antje stepped backward into the elevator. "Where I go, it goes." Antje locked eyes with a sly grin on her face, as the doors closed.

"Kari!" Antje yelled, rushing to her with open arms and tenderly embracing her. "How are you holding up? I am so very sorry about Karl." Kari smiled warmly at Antje's somber face.

"Don't be. He's fine because of you."

Antje stared at Kari, clearly perplexed. "Oh, thank the gods! How? What have I missed?"

Kari pointed at the bassinet where a teeny-tiny foot crested the edge of the basket, sounds of giggling bouncing joyously on the air above it. "The rules of magic, Antje. You killed Kitt. The rule is: if a wraith kills, and the wraith itself is killed before midnight that night, the life it last took is restored."

Exhaling a sigh of relief, Antje beamed as she once again girthed her arms around Kari, squeezing tightly. "That is literally the best news I have ever heard! I hate to ask you a favor so soon after such a traumatic event—But..." Antje hushed her tone. "There is evil at play in the Cisterne, and I need help."

Kari leaned back, an alarmed look in her eyes. A raspy, aged woman's voice interjected, "Come child. I see all, and I know what ye need."

Antje turned around to find a silver-haired woman of short stature in an oversized hooded white robe—the kind a Druid priestess would wear. "Yeh yeh, yer surprised. I'll tell ye who I am while we work. We've nae time to waste. Let's go," the old lady barked, fixing the crown of mistletoe that sat upon her wild, silken locks. Kari immediately bowed to the woman with great respect, her head and body stooping conjointly.

"Good morning, Professor Scawen." Kari's greeting was laced with reverence. Professor Scawen gave a quick bow of her head and took hold of Antje's hand.

"We'd better crack on. Time's wastin'." The professor hurried, essentially dragging Antje down the hallway and into her botany lab.

Upon entering the lab, Antje gazed in awe at the sheer volume of plants hanging from the ceiling to dry, not an inch of ceiling left bare. "I can dry 'em with a spell, but they're more potent if ye let nature take its course," the professor explained.

"Professor Scawen—"

"Ah, please, call me Philomena, er Phil fer short." She began ardently gathering bottles, each bottle containing liquids of various hues. "I know why yer here. I know all about Rebekah. Good riddance! That evil walkin' pair of teets shoulda never have even been allowed in the place! Anyhoo, Nessie told me everything. I also know about the card in yer pocket, and what ye plan to do. Mathias is lookin' out fer ye. In a bit, we'll be joined by our Defensive Arts Master, Professor Ultingaard. He'll teach ye how to 'unleash the Kraken' if ye know what I mean." Philomena cackled vociferously. "Sorry. Can't help meself at times."

Antje felt taken aback by Philomena's candidness and wry humor, as she had come off somewhat curt just minutes before. "Grab me some ghost peppers, will ye?" Philomena pointed to a rack of baskets, filled to the brim with every pepper and fruit imaginable. Antje plucked three ghost peppers from the jute-covered bin and placed them on the oversized pinewood table, where Philomena stood with a pile of greens and several bottles in front of her.

"Peppers of hot, and bodies of rot. Show yerself for what ye are, not fer what yer not!" As Philomena chanted, the ingredients began levitating into mid-air, interweaving themselves into a mass like freshly sheared wool. Once all combined, Philomena snapped her fingers, freezing the formed mixture in mid-air. Reaching down, she grabbed a bottle from the table that contained a light-infused blue elixir of some sort. "In ye go!" Philomena declared, wafting her hand toward the bottle. Antje observed Philomena's magical prowess in complete captivation as the mass of ingredients unraveled into a single thread; flowing into the bottle as if it were a liquid. With a glance at Antje and an impish grin, Philomena pointed at the bottle. "Watch the top." As the remainder of the ingredients trickled into the bottle, a pale plume exited the top in the shape of a rose, which then wilted into a ghoulish face. "That's how ye know ye made it right!" Philomena proclaimed with pride.

Antje, new to all forms of magic, began to ponder if she too had the ability to craft such enchanting chemistry. "Can any mystic brew potions?" Antje asked, inspecting the bottle.

"Yes and no. Ye could make some simple potions. Fer example, a calmin' potion er a happiness potion. But, potions like what ye just saw take years of trainin' and if they're made by someone who don't know what they're doin', they're likely to transform themselves into a flower er somethin'. Besides, ye need'nt know how to do potions—that's what ye got me fer. Ye focus on sending those bastards back to the deep abyss from whence they came," Philomena lectured as the heavy wooden door to her lab opened with a groan. "Ah, Professor Ultingaard, ye dosser! What took ye so long? Time fer yer defense lesson, Antje!"

Professor Ultingaard was a colossal specimen of a man, who barely fit through the doorway. Clean-shaven, his intense features and striking coloring presented as if he was not actually a man, but an animated marble sculpture. His wavy, walnut-brown hair was pulled back in a braided ponytail, and the warmth of his hazel eyes popped against his pale, scar-covered skin.

"Ye'd think with all the scars on his face that he's not real adept at defense, wouldn't ye?" Philomena ribbed, jabbing her elbow into his hip, due to the extensive height difference.

"Very funny, Phil. I'll take her from here. Antje, you can call me Ragnar. I will be teaching you a quick lesson in using your powers, as well as how to defend yourself this afternoon," Ragnar outlined, his gaze zeroing in on her necklace and pointing at it. "Where did you get that?"

"Oh, this? It's new. My—b-boyfriend gave it to me," she stammered. It had been several years since Antje had taken a boyfriend, and the very word leaving her lips felt entirely alien to her. Ragnar grinned with delight. "Is Cole your boyfriend?"

"Yes. How did you know?" Antje blushed.

"I would know that necklace anywhere. I was with him in Afghanistan when he got it. He had to fight a damned evil Sahira to keep her from draining the life out of a villager's 14-year-old daughter. That Sahira was one of the fiercest mystics I've ever seen. Of course, the fiercest ones always want immortality. Thank Odin that he stopped her. Anyway, that necklace was a gift from the daughter in exchange for saving her life. The daughter was a good Sahira who used her powers to heal the village's collateral damage during the war. Cole was in the right place at the right time, but that necklace means that our lesson will be quite short today. It is enchanted with a protection spell, stronger than anything I could teach you to cast. Mathias told us you're a valkyrie. That means the necklace's power is magnified by more than I can fathom—even a nuclear bomb would not be able to singe a hair on your head. It also means that the power will drain more quickly, though," Ragnar elaborated. "Want to see something? I promise it won't hurt."

"Sure?" Antje apprehensively replied.

Ragnar clapped his hands together, summoning a fuchsia and lime green flame in his palms. Separating his hands pulled the flame into the shape of an arrow, which materialized in his right hand. "This arrow is called a 'sure-shot arrow'; that means wherever I envision is where it lands. I am envisioning your throat. Go!" he yelled, the bass harmonics of his voice sending vibrations through the air as the arrow launched itself straight at Antje, stopping a mere inch from her. Antje quickly ducked behind a table, only to have nothing follow. She poked her head up, her eyes just peering over the table, with only her fingertips holding onto the tabletop. Ragnar and Philomena chuckled in unison.

"I told you, you can't get hurt. Here's the best part— that necklace allows you to now control whatever has been launched at you. Envision where you want that arrow to go and launch it. Just—don't launch it at me or Phil, please?" he chortled. Antje stared at the arrow, which was only a few inches from where she had been standing. Focusing on a small bottle on one of the shelves, Antje yelled, "Go!" Suddenly, the arrow launched itself, zipping through the air before hitting its mark, the bottle shattering into thousands of tiny shards of glass upon contact.

"Oh shit!" Philomena proclaimed. "She shot the bottle of guckle-juice!" Philomena bawled, now bent over, and snorting uncontrollably. A neon-yellow plume of powder danced around the room like silly string. Ragnar fell to the floor on his hands and knees, tears rolling down his cheeks and guffawing to the point where his ribs ached. Antje, unaffected, knew she had unleashed some sort of laughing potion into the room. Philomena, clutching her side with one hand, pointed with her other to a bundle of dried sage hanging in the window.

"Burn it!" Philomena squeaked, still drowning in hysterics. Antje lit the bundle on fire, wafting it through the room as she had once seen on a house-hunting show on TV. As the smoke overcame the plume, it solidified into a yellow ball, which Ragnar managed to grab with one hand, still belly-laughing to the point of unrestrained slobbering. Ragnar shoved the ball into an empty bottle, wiping his eyes and mouth as he rose to his feet.

"Well, that was eventful. Masterfully done, Antje!" he praised, attempting to catch his breath.

"Masterfully done? This is why we don't do lessons in my lab, ye dumb oaf!" Philomena scolded, kicking him in the butt. "Not to worry, Antje. A good laugh never hurt nobody. We'll get yer arsenal of potions sorted straight away—I've already packed up a freezin' potion fer ye. It creates an easy escape if ye should need it."

Six

Bawling and Brawling

It was a humid summer evening as Antje arrived at the bar across town from her residence. She checked her phone. "Shit, I'm 30 minutes late! 'Ride a bike,' they said; 'it's charming,' they said! Ugh!" Antje muttered. Leaning her bike against the bike rack and walking down the front steps, she opened a narrow red door which revealed a suspiciously desolate watering hole. The bar itself sprawled through the center of the claustrophobic room, lined with merely half a dozen barstools in various states of disrepair. To each side of the bar were pub-height tables sans chairs, the bases of the tables involuntarily glued to the dirt-encrusted, sticky floor. A pool table, which had seen better days, sat in the far back right corner, illuminated by the flickering fluorescent light that hung lopsidedly above it. The stench of stale cigarette smoke and turned beer mingled with the obnoxiously intense scent of the bartender's clove cigarillo.

The bartender was a lanky young female with over-processed fluorescent green hair, an overwhelmingly thick layer of makeup, and an immodest top that ironically highlighted her unimpressive cleavage. The visual assault would have been incomplete had she not also made the daring decision to squeeze herself into a pair of black leather pants. With the half-burned cigarillo hanging from her lips, she dubiously scanned Antje from head to toe. Antje was never one to dress up for bar hopping as she felt it was a waste of time and energy, but for her first date with Cole, she was resolved to appear palatable. Wearing her favorite pair of stretchy skinny jeans, a pair of worn black leather high-heeled boots, and a blousy, collarless top; Antje felt feminine as ever. The icing on her femme fatale cake: her jadestone necklace and cherry-red lipstick.

"Ugly Americans. Tsk. You look lost. The fast-food chain you are looking for is down the street," the bartender snarked with a Russian accent. Antje rolled her eyes, confidently strolling toward the bar, each foot sticking to the floor as she walked. Slamming her bag on the bar top, Antje sat down on one of the only fully intact stools and responded, "Nope. This is where I was headed. Get me a shot of vodka with a lime—and not the cheap shit. I'm meeting my boyfriend here. Salt and pepper hair, broad shoulders, a glorious dark-brown beard—ring a bell?"

The bartender became visibly uncomfortable, fidgeting while pouring Antje's drink. She slid the shot glass across the bar and leaned in toward Antje's face. "Yeah. I've seen him. You're in the wrong part of the bar. Go to the hallway where the jukebox is and play 'Lullaby' by The Cure. A door will open in the floor. It's downstairs—but, I really don't think you should go. I think you should just leave," the bartender sternly warned.

"Luckily for me, I don't really care what you think, ultra-Natasha. That's the charm of being an 'ugly American'. We don't give a shit what anyone thinks—especially not some bartender working in a smelly shithole like this one," Antje snapped, downing the vodka in one gulp before slamming the empty glass down on the bar and biting into the slice of lime. "But thanks." Tossing a few euros on the bar and slinging her bag over her shoulder, Antje hopped off the stool and headed down the hallway to the jukebox. "The Cure. That's clever," she mumbled to herself while sliding a bill into the machine and pressing the correlating buttons.

A trapdoor opened in the checkered floor, revealing a stairway leading to a smoky, neon-red-lit room below. The entire bar came to a standstill as Antje's heel hit the last step. Turning their heads en masse, most of the room was now staring at Antje. The sea of sweaty bodies parted, filled with whispers and glares as she passed through, the hair on Antje's neck rising to attention. Finally, she spotted Cole at the bar with a collection of empty highball glasses in front of him. He waved her over and playfully patted the empty seat next to him with a wink.

"You made it. You're a little late, so I started drinking. It's been a long week—I hope you don't mind," he confessed with a slight slur.

"I see that," Antje replied, eyeing the graveyard of glasses alongside his current mostly empty glass. Antje quieted herself. "Slow down. I thought we were here on business?"

Cole smiled, drunkenly. "Can't we be here for both, Antje? Can't I enjoy a little rum and some even better company while I work? It's not like I get actual days off or anything. All work and no play makes Cole a grumpy guy," he said in a sing-song tone, kissing her cheek with an inebriated grin.

"Of course, but slow down on the booze there, pirate boy."

"Pirate?! I'm not a pirate, yarrrr a pirate! Boop!" he light-heartedly joked, tapping the tip of her nose before his smile rapidly faded to a very solemn expression. "I have something to tell you, Antje."

"Oh yeah? What's that?"

"I really like you. I would never do anything to hurt you, and that necklace..." he trailed off, his foot nervously bouncing on the barstool's footrest.

"I know, I learned all about it from Ragnar."

Taking the last sip of his rum, Cole tipped his glass to signal a refill and sighed. "That necklace is supposed to help keep you safe, but you can't rely on it, Antje. Who knows how well it works or how long it will work for. Most of this magical shit is unpredictable as hell—especially for normies and new mystics." Cole welcomed another glass of rum, quickly taking a sip before grinning at Antje. "That's cool you met Ragnar. I love that fucking guy. He's a beast!"

"I had a lesson with him today. Candidly, he's a little intimidating. Noted on the necklace—I won't rely on it. I still need to get my full training done at the Cisterne; I honestly don't know what my powers are, or how to use them, but I feel like I've been thrown into the deep end of the pool and I need to figure it all out—like, yesterday. I don't think Rebekah's departure is going to stop the disappearing kids, though. All of this is giving me a good amount of anxiety, to be honest." The bartender approached, pointing to Antje, who gave a nod and said, "A shot of vodka, please." Moments later, an overflowing shot glass arrived before her.

"Anxiety, huh? I can relate. I need—I need to tell you the truth about me. I owe that to you at least," Cole bemoaned, staring down at his glass. "I'm kind of an asshole—but, it's not on purpose. I just have to make the decisions that no one else wants to make, and they never end well."

"Like what?" Antje replied.

Cole took a sizable swig of rum. "Like, you met Special Agent Davis. His leg—his leg is my fault."

"How was an IED in Afghanistan your fault, Cole?"

"I knew I was endangering my team, but I also knew thousands of people were going to die if we didn't hunt down that evil fuckin' sahira—sorry, an evil witch. They call them sahiras in Afghanistan. If I didn't hunt her down and kill her, she was gonna kill an innocent 14-year-old girl—and then thousands of people afterward. And when I tell you the girl was kind, oh god, she was so kind, Antje. She dedicated her whole life to helping the villagers while she lived in abject poverty with them. If I hadn't done something, she was going to die a terrible, painful death."

Cole ran his index finger in circles around the lip of his glass. "There were two ways to get there: one way that I knew had a very high possibility of IEDs, or the other way, which was less dangerous, but would have tipped off the sahira and taken us 3 hours longer. I chose the faster route, and the tank behind us hit one. Davis lost his leg, and two—two of my men... they died. One of them had a newborn son who he never got to meet because of me—because I chose the wrong path."

Emptying his glass, Cole slammed it onto the bar top, his foot vibrating the stool as it rapidly shook. "I watched his wife fall apart as they put his casket into the ground. I see her pain every night as I try to fall asleep," Cole confided, a tear rolling down his cheek. "And now you—I've dragged you into this shit, and I'm so worried I'm going to lead you right into another

IED." Cole's head hung so low that his forehead almost touched the top of the bar. Antje ran her hand down his thigh to his knee and squeezed it, his unexpected vulnerability endearing him even further to Antje.

Cole was like a closed book, and every time you tried to pry it open, you could read maybe a paragraph before the cover would snap shut again. But on this night, he opened the book to one of the darkest chapters of his story and allowed Antje to read it with impunity. Antje's head and heart finally converged on the feelings around Cole. He was a good man, albeit tortured, and she simply couldn't let him live with the burden of guilt he carried.

"Cole, you made the right decision. You saved that 14-year-old girl and thousands of people. War is an ugly, horrific evil in this world that ends the lives of many people who do not deserve to make that sacrifice; But—what happened is not your fault. There could have just as easily been an IED elsewhere. It's my turn to tell you something." Antje slugged back her entire shot and turned, facing Cole.

"This week, I found out that I'm a valkyrie. When I found that out, I also found out that life and death are not what we think they are. Everyone's death is fated, and the Gods will intervene when it's not someone's time to leave. After that fight with Rebekah, I almost died. I was in some place that I don't think exists on Earth, but was sent back because he, who I'm pretty sure was Odin, said it wasn't my time. As much as I know you still grieve the loss of your brothers, their deaths were fated—with or without your choices. It was their time. We all have an exit date, and there is nothing you could have done to make that any different." Cole's head rose during Antje's monologue, his eyes now wide as saucers. "And Cole, as far as I go: I walked straight into Kitt within my first half-hour at the Cisterne. I ended up in this with you, not because of you. It's you and me now—and somehow, I know that it's meant to be this way, Cole. You don't have to make those decisions alone anymore, but you have to let go of the guilt. Second-guessing yourself isn't helping anything. Your instinct was right. You're not an accidental asshole—you're just someone who has had to make choices where there were no good options."

"Wait, did you just say you're a fucking valkyrie?!" Cole slapped the bar with his hand. "Well, that explains a lot of things. Killing Kitt with a business card, for one—and then how you killed Rebekah... Oh, it makes so much more sense now! A fucking valkyrie. That is wild, Antje. I've heard about valkyries, but never actually met one. So, you do the bidding of fate and stuff, huh? Do you hear a voice or something? Holy shit. I'm dating a valkyrie. A valkyrie and me versus evil! Who would have thought—this shit is insane. Did you know I have a valkyrie tattooed on my arm? How weird is that? No—of course not, because you haven't seen me with my shirt off yet, but I doooo. I have you tattooed on me!" As Cole continued his speak-singing to Antje, she noticed people were no longer shying away from her, but were now actively closing in on her and Cole.

"Cole," Antje spoke out of the side of her mouth while slowly grabbing her bag. Cole didn't respond and took another sip of rum. "Cole!" she said a little louder, catching his attention before again hushing her voice to a whisper. "Are all of these people in the army of darkness? I think—I think they may have overheard us talking about how I killed Rebekah." Cole looked around and instantaneously began to sober up as his adrenaline and killer instincts overrode his blood alcohol content.

"No. Some are, but I'm pretty sure some aren't. They're wearing concealment spells to blend in. They always do," he explained in a muted tone. "I'm going to the bathroom. Hopefully, a fire alarm doesn't go off while I'm in there. Normies tend to run when the alarm goes off. Get ready to test out that necklace, Madam Valkyrie," he chuckled, with a sly wink.

"Yes—go to the bathroom. I'm ready. It's you and me, babe." Antje squeezed his hand and kissed his cheek as Cole stood up, smiling. Letting her hand go, he stumbled haphazardly through the crowd, playing up his now diluted drunkenness by apologizing in an exaggerated slur to each and every person he bumped into. Bouncing off a girthy gentleman in a bomber jacket, Cole slammed into the wall with the fire alarm lever pressed into his back, which he impressively managed to activate without using his hands. "Ild! Ild! Fire! Run! Everybody get out of here!" Cole yelled as a stampede of intoxicated people charged up the stairs. A crowd of thirty or so people remained, staring at Antje as another ten glared at Cole. "Well, that did the trick," Cole said, quickly unholstering his gun.

Antje reached into her bag, pulling out the glowing, sky-blue potion Philomena had made in her lab and lobbed it at the blades of a fan that hung from the dead center of the ceiling. The bottle exploded, releasing the contents and spraying them throughout the entire room. People began the rapid deterioration from beautiful, chic club-goers to their true, putrid forms. Before Antje was a wide array of beings ranging from humanoid, to goblins, to animal hybrids, to rancid, wart-covered, unimaginably rotten creatures, some of which sent chills down Antje's spine with solely a glance. Time slowed once more for Antje, allowing her to pull Daggert from the back of her jeans and another potion from her bag, this one marked "freezing potion." Not knowing if this would only freeze one person, or the whole room, Cole included—Antje surmised that this was a worst-case scenario solution and wedged the vial in her bra for later use. Hurrying to where Cole stood, time returned to its normal speed for Antje.

Humanoid hands began to raise and clap around the couple, as the army of darkness conjured their magic in chorus. The summoning methods of the non-humanoid mystics differed widely, and Antje's stomach dropped as she witnessed the vocal sac of an enormous toad-creature filling with blue light. Out of the corner of her eye, she caught the furious spinning of a tail attached to a creature resembling a Chupacabra, its tail whipping up an orange ball of light that grew in size with each rotation. Flicking the safety off on his gun, Cole began to pick off their enemies one by one, prioritizing his targets by the level of their magical prowess.

"Take them out in order of the colors of their spells. Order of the rainbow, ROY-G-BIV, Antje!" he yelled, pulling the trigger several times. Each gunshot broke his speech pattern into fragments, effectively punctuating each of his words. Antje nodded in response.

Dust rained down from the ceiling as ricocheting bullets and spells gone awry blasted through the plaster. This effectively created a glowing red dust cloud with flashes of multi-colored light balls filling the room, the scene reminiscent of a rave boasting superior special effects. Antje used a fallen barstool to launch herself into the air, one foot after the other, before plunging her dagger into the face of an undead, wart-covered woman in the middle of a healing chant. As Antje pushed the blade in deeper, a geyser of thick onyx goop erupted from between the creature's dead eyes. While quickly removing the dagger, a spell landed on her necklace's protection shield, freezing in place. With a flick of her hand, Antje launched the captured spell back at the small, chartreuse goblin from whence it came. The goblin stared in disbelief at Antje, slack-jawed and wide-eyed as the spell landed, killing him upon impact. Antje immediately spun around, smoothly slitting the throat of another casting mystic—soaking herself and everyone in the immediate vicinity in blood splatter. Antje was slicing through the crowd without much conscious activity in her head. Killing was now becoming second nature to Antje, and her fighting skills had rapidly surpassed her martial arts instructor's, practically overnight—if he could only see her now.

The carnage continued for merely one minute more as Cole and Antje rapidly picked off members of the Dark Army, one by one. Cole expertly ducked spells, virtually acrobatic in his escape of debris as the spell-sprayed walls crumbled around him and launched shrapnel in every direction. Meanwhile, Antje used the bar furniture as a sort of second level in which to maneuver around the room. She leaped from table to table, ending lives with a precision and quickness unassociated with any known hand-to-hand combat weapon before. Vaulting across the grouping of tables to the bar, she ran down the last standing mystic who was poised to unleash a purple fireball on Cole while he reloaded his pistol. Snapping the mystic's neck like a dry twig, Antje hopped from the bar and ran to Cole, putting her back against his and taking a defensive fighting stance. They both gasped for air, in complete enervation.

In a matter of five minutes, which seemed as though it were a lifetime, everyone aside from Cole and Antje had perished. Plastered in blood, mystic viscera, soot, and debris, they smiled at each other—exhausted. Antje hugged Cole before stiffening and pulling away from Cole's reciprocal embrace.

"What's that noise?" Antje asked, on edge.

"Shit. Short-lived victory—it sounds like another fifty or so coming from upstairs. I know this is a bad time to tell you this, but I am out of bullets, and while I'm excellent at hand-to-hand combat for a normie—I'm not as good as you are and would prefer not to test out my skills on fifty dark mystics at once," Cole admitted. "I have a freezing potion. Do you know how big the area of effect is for this potion?" she asked.

"I don't know, but if I freeze, just drag my ass out of here on a rug or something. Those potions take a while to wear off—like at least 10 minutes. Use it when the last of the mystics start descending the stairway. Area of effect potions work best when the enemy is tightly grouped because it reaches more people, and if you can get them in a choke point like the stairwell—even better. We may have to fight the first few that exit the stairwell and thin the herd," Cole explained, staring at his empty magazines and the last bullet in the chamber of his gun. "I've got one in the chamber. That's it, Antje."

"We'll get out of here, together. I promise," Antje swore to Cole, squeezing his hand once more. As the horde descended the stairwell, the first mystics approached; Antje braced herself and hurled the freezing potion. It landed dead center in the crowd, just inside of the stairwell—freezing their aggressors where they stood. Simultaneously, a stinging burst of glacial air knocked Antje sideways into one of the stone walls, her head bashing into it as all of the breath left her lungs. Antje, briefly rendered unconscious, awoke less than five seconds later, her shoulder slumped against the wall, sitting on the floor where she had landed. Her eyes opened to a throng of petrified evil mystics, with Cole nowhere to be found.

"Cole? Cole! Where the fuck are you?! We have to leave! Let's go!" Antje screamed desperately, hoping he would answer at any moment. She looked to the floor where Cole had stood before the blast, only to find his gun and two empty magazines—nothing more. Antje noted a trail in the dust leading toward the direction of the frigid blast, as if someone had dragged his body to obscure their footprints. Antje followed the dusty path down a side hallway, the trail vanishing under a small basement window on the exterior wall; the window was unlatched and slightly ajar. Antje frantically searched for any sign of Cole: blood, hair, cloth—anything that could give her a clue as to where he had gone, but there was no trace in sight.

Antje continued her meticulous investigation of the building for any signs of Cole, crying his name repeatedly, to no avail. Cole had been kidnapped somehow, and Antje was beside herself with grief and guilt. She had failed to protect the man standing right next to her; the realization that Cole could be getting tortured—or murdered—as she stood there, clueless, absolutely gutted her. Antje stood on the bar top, attempting to secure a view from above to see if there was possibly some clue she was missing. Glancing at the cracked façade of a clock that hung crookedly on the wall, Antje knew she needed to escape before the freezing spell wore off and she found herself in another impossible situation. Hurdling herself from the bar like a gymnast, her feet planted squarely on the shoulders of a frozen mystic. Using the horde's heads as stepping-stones, she made her way upstairs.

There stood the female bartender, frozen in place—but no longer the thin, humanoid trollop Antje had previously encountered. The bartender was now bulky and hideously troll-like, her clothes squeezing ample fatty tissue like a can of busted biscuits as a thick string of drool clung to her chin.

Who's ugly now? Antje thought to herself, as the flames of seething rage burned inside her. Looking at the ogre face-to-face, Antje desperately wanted to drive Daggert through the bartender's heart, as she was likely the one who had called in the dark cavalry—but to her surprise, she was physically unable to. It was as if her subconscious rendered her incapable of disobeying the wishes of fate. Antje walked behind the bar. Leering at the ogre, whose cigarillo now had several inches of ash hanging from it, Antje was perplexed by the conflict bubbling within. If she couldn't kill her, she was sure as hell going to make her suffer.

"I'm pretty sure you can hear me. You called the Dark Queen and got my boyfriend kidnapped, didn't you? I wish I could snap that fat neck of yours right now, you evil piece of shit. But for some reason, the gods are keeping you alive, at least for now. If I ever cross paths with you again, I will make you suffer so badly that you will beg me for death."

Antje kicked the bartender's knee with the heel of her boot as hard as she could, snapping it and causing the fossilized troll to fall over like a dead tree. Antje stepped over the motionless body, leaned down to the troll's face, and whispered, "Timber." Standing back up, she grabbed an entire bottle of akvavit, flicked the top off, and ran out of the bar, chugging it. Antje needed something—anything—to calm her nerves and extinguish the flames of rage that grew with each passing moment. Antje was in the throes of a full-blown frenzy of panic-laced wrath that could only be temporarily numbed, as Cole was the only cure.

How could this fucking happen? I thought that necklace completely protected me. He warned me not to rely on it. Stupid, Antje! My first boyfriend in forever literally just vanished into thin air on our first date. I swear to all that is good in this world, I am going to find him, and I am going to murder whoever took him.

Antje hailed a taxi and opened the car door. "W-w-where do you want to...?" the driver trailed off nervously as he stared at Antje's blood-drenched face, her stringy, dust-caked hair, and her blouse saturated in various hues of bodily fluids.

"Oh, relax. I went to see the band GWAR in concert tonight. It's fake blood," Antje fibbed. The driver sighed with relief, nodded, and turned on the meter. Antje got into the taxi and shut the door. "Take me to the cisterns, quickly, please."

SEVEN

A VINDICTIVE VALKYRIE AND VINDICATED VICTIMS

A ntje burst through the security door and into the atrium of the Cisterne, with the ancient security guard following closely behind her,
his wrinkled face riddled with alarm. She began yelling, "Philomena! Ragnar! Kari! Literally fucking anyone! Help! They took Cole!" she wailed. It
was almost midnight, and the Cisterne was dark, minus a few wall sconces
that were permanently lit, including the one above Gudbrand. Gudbrand
began to move, walking toward Antje with the sword in hand. His smooth
marble hand reached out to Antje with the palm facing upward. Antje
placed her hand in his as he spoke to her in Danish before handing her his
sword. "Thanks, Gudbrand—but I have no idea what you just said to me,"
she admitted sheepishly, receiving the sword with both hands.

"He says he's sorry for not giving you ze sword before, but ze gods are
saying you are finally ready to meet your fate," a voice with a Germanic

accent interpreted for her. From the shadows emerged a hunched, time-worn man. The tapping of his warped wooden staff, which served as his cane, echoed as it hit the stone floor with each step. The man's face was disfigured, drooping on one side, with a clouded eye, and an impressive collection of scars scattered across it. His face was unsightly, but improved by his kind smile. "Hello, Antje. My name is Headmaster Vogel," he informed, shuffling toward her and waiving security back to his post.

"Headmaster Vogel—I thought, I thought you were dead?!" Antje marveled.

"As good as," he lightly chuckled. "Rebekah told everyone it was my failed banishing spell that was responsible for my disappearance, but it wasn't. She snuck into my room in ze middle of ze night and cast a spell that exiled me to ze Underworld. There, I fought every bit of evil you can imagine—until you killed her. When you killed her, I woke up in ze same bed that I had been shanghaied from 3 years ago. Quite terrifying for ze staff to see me roaming ze halls, I am sure. Indeed, Professor Scawen nearly passed out from ze shock of it all!" he chuckled. "Right under my nose, ze Dark Queen infiltrated our academy with Rebekah, and I failed every student and staff member by not taking a stronger stance in opposition to ze ones in alliance with ze Dark Queen that sit on ze board. Things change now. Killing Rebekah was ze first step, but ze threat is much more sinister than just Rebekah and our board members. This is not only about our academy anymore. It is about ze entire world as we know it. We are under threat on all sides, Antje. Ze Dark Mystics want to eradicate us because we are ze only living beings capable of keeping them contained in the Underworld. They mustn't kill Cole, Antje. He is ze bridge that unites ze two worlds of normies and mystics, and without him, I fear that normies will find our very existence a threat. They outnumber us. This is all a part of ze Dark Queen's plan. If she manages to turn ze normies against us, they will weaken us to ze point where ze Dark Army will easily defeat us in a battle. Please, let us help you find him and take care of ze Dark Queen. You can't do this alone—while that necklace helps to protect you, it is also easily dispelled by any mystic with a higher skill level. You will need ze support and ze training our professors can provide." As Headmaster Vogel ended his impassioned speech, professors and staff began to appear one by one in the atrium, some in a cloud of vapor, others enlarging themselves from a much smaller form, and a few joined simply by exiting one of the many hallways leading to the atrium.

"Ze Cisterne pledges our allegiance to Antje Valason, chooser of ze slain, and keeper of ze fates of men!" Headmaster Vogel declared, raising his staff and teetering a bit. "We will stand with you and fight by your side, always." Antje looked around to see the entire staff kneeling around her. Dumbfounded, and not knowing how to respond, she finally piped up after a few seconds of gob-smacked silence.

"Thank you, Headmaster Vogel—and thank you, everyone. We will get Cole back—but I do know that I am going to need your help. I'm new to all of this. In fact, as Professor Scawen and Professor Ultingaard will tell you, I am comically bad at this mystic stuff. But—what I lack in experience, I make up for in vindictiveness. These cretins have killed our children, they've terrorized these halls, and now they've kidnapped Cole in an attempt to start a war between you all and the world I grew up in. I think I am not alone in saying that it's time to rid our world of these heinous creatures of evil. It's time to undo Rebekah's influence on this school, and it's time to take back mysticism for the sake of every being on this planet!" Antje ardently advocated. Her speech was met with resounding cheers from the group as they came to their feet. Philomena scurried out from the crowd and linked arms with Antje, Ragnar trailing behind her and silently coming to stand behind the two.

"Yeh! What she said. Pull yer socks up! Sleep is fer the dead and havin' a go at these cans of piss is gonna be as rough as a bear's arse if we don't get Antje sorted out straight away. We need ta make a team fer Antje's speedy mystical education. Who'll join me and Ragnar?" Philomena aggressively asked, eyeing the staff. One by one, a total of four people stepped forward.

"I'll join," said an athletic tan-skinned man in his 20s with bleach-tipped hair and bright green eyes. "I teach mystic martial arts. My name is Misha Avraham. I will teach you the art of Krav Maga mixed with mystic weaponry and offensive spell-casting."

"I too will help," a mousy voice with a thick Japanese accent interjected. It came from a short but striking woman with shimmering black hair who was so small in stature that everything she wore seemed to swallow her whole. Pushing her oversized glasses back up to the narrow bridge of her nose, she took another step forward. "Mikono Kobayashi. I will teach you how to speak and bond with animals who will protect and serve you."

"And I as well." A prim-and-proper English gentleman in his early fifties stepped forward proudly, his posture and gait impeccable. "William Henry the Sixth, at your service. I am the Professor of Deception here at the Cisterne. I will be teaching you how to use mystic deception skills not only to blend in but also to manipulate your foes. I look forward to working with you, Miss," William Henry said with a bow, his perfectly coiffed, wavy hair unwavering in the battle with gravity.

The last person to step forward wasn't actually a person at all. She was a large creature with a moose's head, the torso and arms of a muscular woman, and the legs and wings of an eagle. Her voice was soothing and felt wise. Antje noted that the creature's energy reminded her of the same energy she felt in geothermal hot springs—calming, but frenetic under the surface.

"And I, Takhi Pamola, will show you how to call upon the gods to unleash weather upon your foes. I also offer to teach you how to fly." Takhi's wings fluttered a bit behind as she looked to Antje, her demeanor softening some once their eyes locked. Antje smiled warmly at her team of four advisers, her hands clasped at her chest. "Thank you! Sincerely, thank you. I am more than ready to get started, and truly appreciate every single one of you."

"First, you are going to need some understanding of ze Dark Queen. Antje, Mikono, Misha, Phil, William Henry, Takhi, Ragnar... Please meet me in my office," Headmaster Vogel instructed, raising his staff. With a quick flash of amber-yellow light emanating from the ends of his staff, the Headmaster vanished.

"Don't ye worry, Antje. This be the best group ye could possibly ask fer," Philomena assured, waddling forward and dragging Antje along with her. She then lessened her voice to a whisper and got close to Antje's ear. "Takhi likely could kill the so-called Queen of Darkness on 'er own, but alas, she's a peace-lovin' mystic. She's the daughter of the chief of her tribe. Supposedly he's kinda a murderous wanker, and she vowed to never be like him after he killed her husband. She be a little standoffish at first, but she warms up."

Inside Headmaster Vogel's office, Antje marveled at the display of magic her eyes beheld. Floating several feet above her head was a live nebula, constantly in mercurial motion. Dots of crystal-white light sparked and waned through the opaque clouds of pink and purple against the dark black abyss of the ceiling. Antje's sight slowly meandered just under the nebula, where candles and plants floated effortlessly in mid-air, Headmaster Vogel's pet cat batting and pawing at them as she levitated and somersaulted playfully.

"Friends, we find ourselves at a serious crossroads between good and evil prevailing. I've been to ze abyss; I've seen and fought through what these wayward mystics are capable of. I must say, everyone here needs to understand—there is a very real risk of losing this fight. With Cole missing, the clock ticks quickly. If ze Dark Queen wakes Cole's lower self, and manages to empower it and weaken his higher self, or if she murders Cole and convinces ze normies it was us...we are all in for the worst battle you can imagine. We must truly understand ze evil we are up against," Headmaster Vogel warned. "Antje's necklace won't protect her against ze Dark Queen—her magic is far too strong and even some of her higher-level minions may have powers strong enough to dispel ze necklace. So, her training needs to go forward under ze impression that ze necklace is not a factor we can rely on in any fight. Ze Dark Queen believes this world we live in belongs to her and her kin and that good mystics are heretics that go against the word of ze one and only true Goddess, Hel. She sees normies as a scourge that has infested ze planet and believes that ze world will be a better place if normies and good mystics are all exterminated. She considers herself to be ze direct descendent of ze Goddess Hel, and because ze power of Hel runs through her veins, no one will win against her. Whether or not that is true is debatable, but we do know that she plagiarizes ze power of every being she bewitches to follow her, and her power is unmatched by any mystic I know, other than perhaps Takhi as she can channel ze Gods."

Takhi looked down at her talons, guilt-ridden. "I'm sorry, Headmaster, but you know I can't break my promise to myself. If I kill, I may turn into..." she trailed off, the pain of her inner demons palpable to the whole of the room. Headmaster Vogel slowly raised himself from his desk chair and hobbled over to Takhi, who leaned against the wall next to the door. He put his frail, liver-spotted hand on her wing, tenderly.

"I know, Takhi. No one is expecting you to betray yourself. We are all in this together. We are all here to support and educate Antje so that she is prepared for literally anything that comes at her next. She was not born into this world like most of us, so we have our work cut out for us as we bring her up to speed. We have maybe two to three weeks, maximum, before ze Dark Queen decides whether or not Cole is of use to her after he inevitably rejects her as his leader. I met a soul in ze Underworld who I befriended. He now reports what he sees and hears to me. I cannot tell you who it is, but I trust him—he has saved my life before. This friend told me that she has taken Cole in an attempt to lure us into a battle. Ze one thing we have going for us, is that she believes Antje is just a low-level good mystic that Cole has taken a liking to. I believe she has no idea that Antje is a valkyrie, with ze power of the Norse Gods flowing through her. Does anyone have any questions?" Headmaster Vogel asked, looking to the small group scattered throughout his office.

"I do," Misha said. "How do we train Antje in two or three weeks when a normal mystic takes years and years to master just one of these skills?!"

Grinning, Headmaster Vogel replied, "Antje is no normal mystic. Aside from her being a valkyrie—Mathias, the Guardian of Nessie, has unlocked her powers for us. We just need to instruct her on how to use them, and from what I know of valkyries, they already possess an inherent level of knowledge... Otherwise, Antje wouldn't be standing here alive today after her encounter with Rebekah."

Ragnar straightened his shoulders. "Yes, valkyries are born knowing how to kill from their very first breath. Antje has already slain more evil mystics in the past week than any other person in this room—other than myself and Headmaster Vogel. You know she killed a wraith with a business card, right?" Ragnar chimed in, as Mikono raised her hand slowly.

"Excuse me. I would like to get started with Antje today. We have a shisa about to give birth in the stables, and I would like for one of them to imprint on Antje when they are born, so we can train it to protect her. I expect these shisas to be larger than normal, thanks to the pedigree," Mikono explained.

"Of course. Any other questions?" Headmaster Vogel asked. Met with total silence, he continued, "Great, let's get started. Antje, head to ze stables with Mikono." Antje nodded at the Headmaster and dutifully followed Mikono out of the office.

"Arigato gozaimasu, Mikono," Antje said quietly, bowing her head. Mikono smiled gently, nodding her head slightly at Antje, and motioned for her to follow.

As they entered the stables, Antje's eyes swelled with awe; the many mythical creatures freely roaming the colossal building were inconceivable to Antje. Baby dragons coughed small flames from their mouths while chasing down crickets for a late-night snack, griffins soared through the air, and she even witnessed an airavata summon a small rain cloud. The rain cloud hovered over a small group of joyous baby krakens who frolicked in the pool of collected rainwater. Antje watched with childlike glee as the krakens changed into a symphony of colors while roughhousing on the liquid playground.

At the end of the amphitheater-sized structure lay a gigantic creature that was part-dog, part-lion with a swollen belly that looked as if it were about to explode at any moment.

"This is the pregnant shisa I was telling you about. Her name is Nima," Mikono said, stroking Nima's head affectionately. "You are a very good girl. Not long now until you can rest comfortably, sweet Nima. This is Antje. She is here because I hope one of your babies may imprint on her. She needs our help, and with your temperament, I think one of your pups could be a most suitable guardian for Antje." Nima, too tired and pregnant to get up, nuzzled her head into Antje's side and made a light guttural noise with her mouth shut to express her affection.

"She likes you, and she approves. Perhaps you should spend some time bonding with her so that your shisa can hear your voice before it is born. It will also be good for Nima to get to know you while I collect the necessary items for her impending birth. I estimate it should be about 2 hours until we see the first pup. You will know she is ready when she stands up and roars repeatedly. I'd teach you how to hear her communications, but she's already exhausted and I don't want to pressure her to communicate," Mikono whispered with a smile.

Over the next two hours, Antje stroked Nima's fur and rubbed her belly, talking to her and sharing the background on why she would need one of her pups. Nima listened attentively and enjoyed her massage. Nuzzling her head into Antje one last time, Nima then stood up abruptly and roared so loudly that every animal in the stable returned to their living quarters in silence. Antje took several steps back and covered her ears as the roars boomed and rattled the windows. Mikono arrived in the nick of time to lay down a series of heated blankets. Nima's labor was expedient, and as the last pup dropped onto the blanket, Mikono's eyes lit up with a level of excitement that didn't seem plausible to come from such an unexcitable and reserved woman.

"A blue-gray shisa is extraordinarily rare and an omen of great power!" she squealed, watching the baby shisa stand up. Shaking out its matted-down fur, which instantly became fluffy once it finished, the mastiff-sized fluffball stumbled toward Antje. Just learning to walk, it swayed and warbled before haphazardly plopping down at her feet like a loyal guardian. Mikono beamed, "He has imprinted on you voluntarily. This is excellent. You will need to name him to solidify the imprint." Mikono patted Nima's head and made eye contact with her. "Thank you, Nima. Yes, I agree. Antje will love and cherish him. I think this is fated too."

Antje thought about it intensely. He was a huge pup, the size of a full-grown adult mastiff at only a few minutes old. He also seemed alarmingly aware of everything happening around him for a newborn. "I'll have to think on it a bit more; nothing fitting is coming to mind at the moment... But, is this about how big he will stay, or will he grow?" Antje asked Mikono.

Mikono smiled and giggled a bit, covering her mouth in a polite way as not to shame Antje for her lack of knowledge. "Shisas can grow to be the size of a large lion. He will likely be bigger than that, because I have never seen a pup quite this big. They're all born with an adult sense of intellect and emotional ability. He will still need to be trained, which I will do over the next two weeks while you are also receiving your training—but for a quick lesson to help you name him, let me teach you how to communicate with him, and all of the animal kingdom. We do not start this spell with a clap as you've seen previously. Interacting with nature's creatures requires a gentle but confident sense of self, and a quiet approach," Mikono explained, gently clasping her hands together as if she were to commence singing a gospel. "Go ahead, clasp your hands like mine," Mikono instructed as Nima curled up with the rest of her litter and closed her eyes, absolutely drained. Antje nodded and followed suit. "Okay, now take a very deep breath and focus on the sound of the shisa's breathing."

Antje could now hear the very distinct sound of his breathing, and also his heartbeat. "Can you hear his heartbeat, Antje?" Antje nodded at Mikono. "Very good. Now, envision yourself opening up your heart and mind to him. Picture yourself in nature where you feel at peace, and visualize your hand reaching out to him, inviting him to come home with you." Antje nodded again, only this time she heard a loud, squeaky, boyish voice instead of Mikono's. "HUNGRY! FOOD. WANT FOOD. HUNGRY!" the voice said vociferously. Antje's eyes jolted open, and she saw the shisa staring straight at her. With her eyes still open, a second round of pre-pubescent boy voice cascaded through her ears.

"HUNGRY! STILL HUNGRY. VERY HUNGRY!"

Squatting down to eye level with the shisa, Antje asked, "Are you telling me you're hungry?" The shisa's tail wagged furiously as he quickly stood, climbing on her shoulders, knocking Antje to the ground, and licking her face.

"HUNGRY! YES! SO HUNGRY. FOOD, FOOD, FOOD! HUNGRY!" he exclaimed as Antje looked to Mikono while struggling to hold his gargantuan head back with her hands.

"You can hear him, Antje, can't you? On your first try—how impressive! Let's get him some food. Tell him to go to Nima and latch onto her nipple."

With a nod and a turn of her head, Antje stared the shisa in the eyes and instructed, "Go to Nima, your mom. She will feed you if you latch onto one of her nipples just like your siblings."

"HAPPY! OKAY. GO EAT. SO HAPPY!" he chirped while turning around and prancing over to Nima excitedly, his head flopping about as he tripped over his enormous paws.

"Oh! I have to name you. Who are you?" Antje asked him.

"LOYAL. PROTECT YOU! LOYAL." He latched onto Nima's nipple along with his siblings and began gulping away, his body vibrating with excitement. Antje looked at Mikono.

"I'm going to name him Shields," Antje informed Mikono, who smiled at Antje with absolute approval.

"Shields... I like it. Now, let's continue your training with some slightly more hostile creatures." Mikono pointed to a giant worm creature whose head was nothing more than a round hole with a series of razor-sharp teeth encircling said hole. It looked like something out of a nightmare. "That's a Mongolian Death Worm. Their venom will instantly kill any living being that it touches, but don't be scared, he's really just misunderstood." Mikono petted the giant worm as it pressed itself into her hand, slithering and writhing in place.

"O-okay," Antje said tepidly, closing her eyes. She envisioned herself in her aspen grove back home, peacefully sitting as the breeze rustled the green, coin-shaped leaves above her, the shadows cast from the intense sun above dancing on the forest floor around her. She watched the Mongolian Death Worm slither toward her through a colorful patch of wildflowers before outstretching her hand to it.

"I know, I know, I'm ugly and terrifying," the worm said. Antje opened her eyes.

"I didn't say that!" Antje insisted.

"You didn't have to. I've seen my reflection in the pond. I'm terrifying. I know, a self-aware worm; it's bizarre. Truly, it's fine. My delightful exterior keeps the Phoenix from trying to eat me. So, you're new here. I've never seen you... but you're different. I can taste it." The worm's mouth opened and rings of flesh behind its teeth undulated.

"You can taste it?"

"Yes, this giant mouth of mine allows me to taste people without touching them... and then I spit venom at them if they taste bad. Call it a millennium of evolution. Predators taste bad. You taste sweet. Like candy. I like you," the worm fondly informed Antje.

"Why didn't you tell me that I taste like candy?" Mikono asked the death worm, smiling cheekily.

"Because you don't. Don't get jealous, Mikono. It's a bad taste on you," it teased; Mikono giggling and rolling her eyes.

"Wait, you can hear it too?" Antje said inquisitively, flipping her head to look at Mikono.

"Yes, of course. I can hear every creature in here, except for the new pups. I haven't invited them into my heart and mind yet... Well, that and the Cerberus. No one can get them to communicate, it seems. Rebekah was the only one he would talk to, and she's gone now, as you know." Mikono motioned to a solitary creature in the corner with three chillingly monstrous dog heads. "They can deny your invitation, although it doesn't happen often with any other creature in my experience. The Cerberus is not a friendly creature, though. They have been known to lunge and growl at people they feel are a threat—and would likely kill people if they weren't restrained. But, as the guardian of the Greek Underworld, they possess great information about all of the underworlds and the people you will be fighting. With the Cerberus here, who knows what chaos is stirring that we do not know about. If you could speak to them, they might be helpful, not only for you but also for us to know what is coming. Do you want to try?"

"Well, if they won't talk to you, who can speak to almost everything, why would they talk to me?" Antje questioned, seriously.

"Because you have a connection to the Underworld, and so do they. I have a feeling they may speak to you," Mikono explained. Antje loudly gulped and followed Mikono over to the Cerberus. With a heavy enchant-ed chain around its necks and shackles on two of its four legs, it lunged at Mikono as she advanced. Mikono, completely unfazed, turned to Antje and gave her the nod to start the inviting process. Antje's eyes closed, and this time she was outside of her rough-cut log cabin, in two feet of glistening snow, with the view of mountain peaks in the background. The snarling Cerberus began its approach, hackles up; its body stiffened. It was at that moment, Antje felt something large knock her backward in the physical plane. Her eyes opened, only to watch the ceiling come into view as she landed on her back. Getting up quickly, she witnessed Shields in a defensive position in front of her.

"WORRIED. DO NOT LUNGE AND GROWL AT HER OR DIE. ANGRY!" Shields snarled at the Cerberus, who was now continuously lunging, slinging foaming spittle from all three of its heads while barking furiously and snapping its jaws.

"Stand down, Shields. It's okay. They don't know me, and I think they are just worried. They can't hurt me. Please let me try to talk to them," Antje requested, patting his back and petting him while consciously ex-uding soothing energy. As the Cerberus continued to act like a rabid pack of strays, Antje once again closed her eyes and found herself surrounded by chilled air and shimmering snow. She reached out her hand to the aggressive creature, whose three heads sniffed in unison; the creature in-stantaneously relaxed its posture and ceased the frenetic snapping and frothing of all three mouths.

"A valkyrie. That's odd," one of the heads said. The other sniffed again. "You killed Rebekah!? You are a friend!" it exclaimed, with its tail wagging swiftly. The third head tilted, "Your shisa desperately needs manners," it said, perfunctorily.

"Hi, yeah, sorry about that. He was literally just born and is acting purely on instinct. I am indeed a valkyrie. My name is Antje—what is yours?" she asked. All three heads looked at each other inquisitively.

"We don't have a name. We make sure no human goes into the Under-world... well, we tried. Until Rebekah imprisoned us here, so that she could send Headmaster Vogel to the Underworld, where he didn't belong!" one head proclaimed in angst.

"She tricked us!" one of the other heads howled.

"We don't belong here! I want to go home. I want to go back to the gate. Please set us free!" the third one lamented. Antje opened her eyes and looked at Mikono.

"The reason they're unfriendly is because they're being imprisoned here. They don't belong here. They belong at the gate of the Underworld. We have to unchain them immediately. This is beyond cruel, and I can actually feel their pain," Antje said seriously as Mikono cringed.

"Antje, those chains are the only thing keeping them from killing everything in here—you included, potentially," she warned.

"I will prove they aren't blood-thirsty; they're just sad and homesick," Antje reassured, turning her back to the Cerberus and walking backward toward them, in the ultimate display of trust. "Cerberus, if you want to go home, and you believe that you are being held prisoner because of Rebekah, show Mikono now that you aren't out to kill all of us."

The Cerberus sat down and poked the middle head through Antje's legs, allowing her to sit on its back. Standing up, Antje was now riding the Cerberus.

"Please, unshackle them. They are our allies, and Rebekah's victims just as much as the rest of us," she pleaded. Mikono, still hesitant, nodded and unlocked the Cerberus, who let Antje off its back and laid down once again.

"Cerberus, please talk to Mikono and tell her everything you know. We will get you back home as soon as we know where home is and how to get you there... But Mikono will have to be the one you guys communicate with until then because I have to go and train for the next two weeks. Please trust her. She is my friend, and she is on your side," Antje said, holding the middle head in her hands, stroking its face softly with her hands, their eyes locked on each other's. Slowly, the Cerberus walked toward Mikono, and the left head slipped under Mikono's hand, as a sign of trust. Mikono took a sigh of relief and looked at Antje.

"You truly are something different. I believe everything everyone has said now that I have seen it with my own eyes, Antje Valason, chooser of the slain." Mikono bowed her head with respect. "Don't worry about Shields. I will get him trained to perfection for you."

Antje glanced at Shields, who was now scratching behind his ears with one of his monstrously huge hind paws. "ITCHY. YOU GO. SHIELDS OKAY. SHIELDS ITCHY," he said as Antje headed toward the doorway and to her next lesson. Mikono smiled and nodded to her as she massaged the Cerberus's body, all three tongues hanging from their mouths as their jowls synchronously curled into joyful smiles.

EIGHT

SOARING, SPARRING, AND SHAPESHIFTING

Antje softly knocked on the door, so as not to spook William Henry. "Do come in, Antje," William Henry motioned without looking up, his glasses resting on the tip of his nose, as he used his index finger to skim the pages of the book he perused. Antje quietly entered before taking a seat in the chair opposite William Henry's, nothing but an ornate crotch-mahogany desk between them. The oversized windows of his office illuminated specks of dust, which drifted in the air as if it were enchanted glitter. The shelves behind William Henry's desk were a bibliophile's dream, filled with immaculately kept leather-bound books and the rarest of literary treasures. A large persimmon-colored Persian rug ran beneath the leather chair Antje was perched in, the pattern moving and changing like a kaleidoscope.

William Henry stood up, removing his spectacles and letting them hang from the small silver chain around his neck. Setting the book down,

William Henry pushed the chair out from underneath him, its clumsy metal wheels clinking against the legs they were attached to.

"Come over to the windows and look out of them, if you would please?" William Henry requested, gesturing toward the large wall of windows. Antje obliged. William Henry stood behind her, looking over her shoulder and out the window. "Now, close your eyes and feel the sunlight on your face. Take several deep breaths in through your nose, out through your mouth, controlling and noticing how each breath feels. Constrict your throat upon exhale—it should feel tight, almost like a yawn." Antje began the breathwork, struggling at first to get the exhale to feel like William Henry described.

"Almost, Antje. Open your mouth and put it in the position you would if you were going to say 'haaaaaaah'... Very good. Can you feel your body begin to relax, starting with your shoulders?" Antje, exhaling, nodded gently. This was the most relaxed she'd felt in years. "Allow all thoughts to spill from your mind until it goes completely blank. Do not try to control your thoughts or try to silence your brain. Just be, and let your brain empty itself like a shaken bottle of soda with the cap off. Eventually, it will calm, and your brain will be empty and silent, just like it would during meditation. Is it blank?" William Henry questioned in a whisper. Much to Antje's surprise, her mind was blank. As she stared at the back of her eyelids, she once again gave a subtle nod. William Henry put his hands on her shoulders. His energy coursed through her shoulders like a gentle warming sensation.

"Excellent. Now, see yourself in your mind's eye and really focus on the area of your shoulder blades where my hands are. Tell me, dear—how do you like your iridescent feathers? Can you see them?" William Henry asked with as much excitement as his reserved, prim-and-proper demeanor would allow. Releasing her shoulders, he took several steps to the side of Antje.

"Yes, I can see them," Antje mumbled, too relaxed to enunciate.

"Perfect. Now repeat this, verbatim: 'Light as a feather, strong as an ox, this body of mine now leaves its box. Take a new form, grow to new lengths, this body it joins the valkyrie ranks!'" William Henry chanted, with expert musicality and a rhythmic cadence. As Antje recited the chant, her body began to emit a white glow, beautiful wings sprouting from her back as though they'd been waiting decades to emerge.

"Open your eyes, Antje. Look at your reflection in the surrounding windowpanes."

Antje's eyes opened, instantly turning into saucers. "I have wings!" she proclaimed, turning quickly to face William Henry and displacing numerous items as her wings swept them off the windowsills and his desk. William Henry flicked his hands in a quick series of motions, stopping the litany of items from crashing onto the floor below. Letting out a polite chortle, William Henry levitated all of the displaced items, returning them to their rightful homes with a smile.

"Yes, and as a result, your body has gotten much bigger. It will take some getting used to. Takhi will have to teach you how to fly. My body doesn't have wings like yours, and I'm afraid you may plummet to an untimely death if you rely upon me for flying lessons. However, I will teach you how to conceal your wings and how to obscure the evil eye from seeing your true identity and intention. The evil eye is something dark mystics use for curses—it also helps them see through deception spells. In this case, the Dark Queen mustn't see your true form, or true desires when you come face to face with her. Are you ready to learn?" he asked, sliding one of the feathers on her wings between his index finger and his thumb. "Absolutely magnificent. What a pleasure to work with you, Antje. You are indeed the first valkyrie under my instruction, and it is truly an honor."

"Yes. How do I put these wings back before I break literally everything in your office?" Antje laughed, embarrassed.

"This is the easy part! Close your eyes again, take one deep inhale, and in your mind's eye, imagine your wings retreating back into your body. To deploy them again, you just need to close your eyes and exhale a long breath... Long enough to imagine them exiting your body," he instructed. Antje explicitly followed his instructions, and in a series of inhales and exhales, she opened and retracted her wings several times.

"Brilliant! I think you're ready to obscure your true self. Sit down on the floor with me, cross-legged." Lowering himself onto the floor, William Henry patted the spot directly in front of him. Antje sat down quietly and crossed her legs. "Keep your eyes open, but let them blur, almost like you've crossed your eyes. Now repeat after me: Evil eye, I won't show you why. Your vision field cannot penetrate this shield. Reality blurred; you will see not what I've obscured. My mind's eye will show you the truest lie." Antje felt a zing of electricity shoot through her body, as if she had dragged her wool-sock-covered feet along plush carpet before touching a metal doorknob.

"Did you get zapped?" he asked.

"Yes, I did."

"Fantastic! Are you ready to learn how to shape-shift?" William Henry said with a mischievous tone.

"Like there's even a question!" Antje exclaimed.

"Similarly to awakening your wings, you will start with the same chant, but replace it with whatever shape you want to shift into. Let me show you how it's done." William Henry explained as he began chanting with his eyes closed. "Light as a feather, strong as an ox, this body of mine now leaves its box. Take a new form, grow to new heights, make me Antje Valason, wearing pink tights!" Antje's eyes blinked, and from one blink to the next, William Henry changed from a dapper old Englishman to the spitting image of her. Her doppelganger grinned at her and slowly lifted her pant leg from her ankle, revealing hot pink tights. The doppelganger laughed and said, "Alright, I've had my fun." Closing her eyes, the doppelganger drew in a deep breath. In another blink, Antje found herself once again face to face with William Henry. "Your turn, Antje. Just like you grew wings, chant what I did, and come up with your own ending. If you fail the first time, don't worry—I can undo anything you might do in error."

Antje took a deep breath, closed her eyes, and began to chant. "Light as a feather, strong as an ox, this body of mine now leaves its box. Take a new form, grow to a new shape, make me something with a cape."

Laughter erupted from William Henry's mouth as Antje opened her eyes. "Too vague, Antje. You've turned yourself into a squirrel wearing a cape. Hilarious, but probably not what you were after. Close your eyes, inhale—now see your squirrel body returning to its normal shape. This is good practice for returning to your body, at least." Antje, nervous she would forever stay the superhero embodiment of a rodent, followed his instructions and returned to a life-sized human.

"Let's try that again, Antje. Instead of something with a cape, let's try something more specific... Maybe a silver ape?" Antje obliged and closed her eyes, starting the chant once more.

"Light as a feather, strong as an ox, this body of mine now leaves its box. Take a new form, grow to a new shape, make me a silver ape!" Antje's eyes opened to find silken tufts of silver hair peeking from the openings of her pant legs. Pulling her hands up toward her face to examine them, she observed that her slender hands had turned into the colossal mitts of a gorilla.

"Fantastic!" William Henry shouted, clapping his hands quickly. "Now let's phase into a form that will be helpful in your fight. Imagine a putrid creature like the ones you've been fighting in your mind's eye. Now, tweak the chant to fit it. Remember, specificity is key," he instructed. Antje grunted in a gorilla tone, surprising herself, and clenching her mouth as if she had just burped loudly in an expensive restaurant.

"My, oh my, Antje! You have even managed to change your voice. Hopefully, you can still speak in English. Let's try the chant. If not, you will have to phase into a human in-between shape shifts."

In a deeper voice than her own, but still a humanoid one, Antje began her chant. "Light as a feather, strong as an ox, this body of mine now leaves its box. Take a vile form, make me—orcish born."

William Henry's eyes beamed with childish delight as Antje transformed quickly into a giant green orc. "Masterfully done, Antje! What a creative and quite effective chant, I must say! Now, close your eyes and come back to your human form. Remember, deep inhale..." In one blink, Antje was back in her human form. "I'd like to say, Antje, that we need more time together, as this sadly has been the pinnacle of my teaching career, but somehow, in merely one session, you've mastered something that takes most mystics years to fully grasp. One can only hope for the sake of us all that your other training goes as smoothly! Also, here's a B12 tablet. Shifting—and also astral travel—both deplete your B12 levels. Be sure to keep some on you at all times. Too many shifts can cause you to pass out, which is not only dangerous from the level of wherever you land but also will leave you wide open to an assault by the Dark Queen. In fact, here's the whole bottle." William Henry handed Antje an amber glass bottle with golden gel capsules inside. "Hurry along. Misha and Ragnar are undoubtedly looking forward to beating up on you. Savage men, they are."

As Antje pushed open the doors of the gymnasium, the sound of clanging metal and grunting men echoed in her ears. The gymnasium sprawled for what seemed like miles; equally impressive was the collection of varying weaponry hanging from the walls. From seemingly medieval torture devices to modern high-tech military armaments, the options were plentiful. The scent of sweat and testosterone hung in the air like a thick blanket of primordial musk. As the door slammed shut, the sound bounced off the stone walls and shiny wooden floor, garnering the attention of both Misha and Ragnar. "There she is! The hero of the hour!" Misha exclaimed between labored breaths. Wiping the sweat from his brow, he walked up to Antje with a grin. "I hope you're ready for a workout—as you can see, Ragnar and I have been warming up in anticipation of your lesson."

Antje gulped, and both Misha and Ragnar burst into laughter. "Don't worry, Antje. The warmup was so that we don't get injured by you, not the other way around. You forget, I know what you're capable of. Remove your necklace, so we don't have another gucklejuice incident," Ragnar chided. Antje, a little relieved, smiled and removed her necklace, placing it in an inner pocket of her coat and zipping the pocket shut.

"Let's see what you can do. Hit me!" Misha taunted, stepping back and assuming a defensive position. Antje felt a rush of adrenaline and anxiety course through her veins. Blips of the fight with Cole flashed through her mind. She took three deep breaths and began to engage Misha in a rigorous spar. Missing a few hits and at times getting tapped by Misha's fists and feet, Antje soldiered through until the spar ended with her foot connecting to Misha's jaw, knocking him to the ground. Misha stood up, rubbing his jaw. "Not bad, Antje! But...I still have teeth. Now, let's try some grappling."

Antje, gasping for air, sweat dripping from every pore, groaned and put her fists back up. A heavy tap on her right shoulder caught her by surprise, and she swung behind her, the inertia of her swing spinning her around backward as Ragnar ducked the misadvised attack. "Whoa! Easy there, valkyrie. I'm only trying to give you some water," Ragnar exclaimed.

"Shit. Sorry, Ragnar! You caught me by surprise. I guess I'm a little on edge after everything I've been through lately." Ragnar nodded at her in a silent display of support while handing her a much-welcome bottle of chilled water.

As the hours passed, Antje learned her weaknesses and her surprising amount of strengths, one of which was that getting hit didn't impact her as it should. Ragnar had landed a blow that would have knocked any human flat on their back, but for Antje, it felt more like a sharp zap to her chest. The sensation subsided immediately. Ragnar mumbled under his breath, "Must be nice to be an angel of death, eh?" while locking eyes with Antje and smirking. Antje found herself exhausted and dropped her arms by her side. "Guys, I think I'm done with training for the day. See you tomorrow?"

"What...? You're quitting...? We were....we were just getting warmed up!" Ragnar said, panting at each break in his sentence. Misha was collapsed on the gymnasium floor and barely managed to raise his right hand to give her a thumbs up and a wave goodbye while murmuring something about the next lesson being weaponry.

As Antje exited the gym, the large doors latched loudly behind her. The golden sun beams poked through the dense velvet drapery that adorned sporadically placed windows with inlaid diamond metalwork. The school felt as though the days long since passed had seeped into every facet of its existence, but somehow also felt clean, and slightly cold—like an old Scottish castle.

"Antje. Are you ready for your lesson?" a gentle voice from the far-right side of the corridor she was now standing in asked.

"Yes! I've been looking forward to our lesson most of all." Antje smiled and approached Takhi.

"I was thinking today, we will go deep into the forest to sit and talk; that is...if it's okay with you?" Takhi confirmed, opening a large door that led outside.

"After the day I've had, nature and getting lost in the forest sounds amazing." Antje laughed. Takhi gave a friendly smile and motioned for Antje to follow her outside.

"Do you have enough energy to fly into the forest with me?" Takhi asked.

"Well, I've never flown before, but I can try!" Antje said, half laughing.

"You've been to William Henry's training, so—transform yourself into a raven. I'll teach you how to fly in your valkyrie form another time; it's a little more advanced. Go ahead!" Takhi backed up a bit as Antje nodded and took a deep breath, exhaling her nervous energy.

"Light as a feather, strong as an ox, this body of mine now leaves its human box. Take a new form, a new flying haven, my body is now a sizable raven." Antje lifted what used to be her arm, only to see beautifully black, iridescent feathers that shimmered in the sunlight like oil on wet pavement.

Takhi beamed with pride and began Antje's first lesson. "Spread your wings as far as you can. Really stretch them out and get a good feel for how to flap them—but gently."

Antje, feeling supremely weird in her new avian body, gave a gentle flap. As her talons began to lift off the ground slightly, a wave of adrenaline invigorated her tired body. "That's it, Antje. Very good. Now jump while flapping."

Antje took a deep breath, flapped her wings, and launched herself into the air. "Holy shit! I'm flying!" Antje croaked in a low, raspy tone. Takhi grinned as she lifted from the ground to join Antje. Antje felt free for the first time in a long while. The sense of peace and weightlessness she was experiencing was unlike any sensation she could have imagined. The forest was now within eyesight, and Takhi pulled up alongside Antje in the air. "Time for a lesson in landing. Change your trajectory and slow your flapping as you approach the ground. There's a meadow up ahead. Let's land there," Takhi instructed.

Antje, now feeling a bit nervous, began her descent as she spotted the meadow straight ahead. Lower and lower her body effortlessly glided until the ground was now close enough for her to see individual blades of grass. In a last-second panic, Antje flailed and crashed into the ground. Standing up, she shook her feathers out and surveyed the remarkable lack of damage.

"Are you okay?" Takhi asked, landing next to her with unparalleled grace and ease. "That wasn't bad for your first landing, believe it or not."

"I'm fine, Takhi. Just my pride is wounded." Antje laughed half-heartedly.

"Go ahead and change back to your human form, Antje."

Antje nodded. Closing her eyes, with a couple of deep breaths, she found herself back in human form, fully dressed. Takhi pointed at a small outcropping of rocks on the forest's edge, just above the meadow. "There. That's the spot. It's on top of a large quartz vein and should help replenish your energy. Quartz is like a battery, constantly recharged with the energy from the sky and the earth beneath it." They walked through a field, Antje relishing the sight of colorful wildflowers reaching toward the sun. Antje felt at peace in the forest; she always had, and was relieved that she was getting a reprieve from the Cisterne—but mostly the city.

"Where are we, exactly?" Antje questioned.

"The Cisterne is sort of its own realm, seated within the earth itself. These underground forests and natural spaces are sealed off to the world above."

"But—the sun?"

"Magic, Antje. Everything you see here is real, but not bound by the laws of the world you have always known. Trees and plants here need sunlight to grow, so Headmaster Vogel duplicated the sun. He also created a weather system that emulates exactly what happens above the Cisterne. Mother nature created the blueprint—the Headmaster simply applied the same blueprint to this environment," Takhi explained as a moment of silence overtook Antje's overawed mind. "How are you doing, Antje—internally?" Takhi lowered herself onto a flat boulder.

"Good, I suppose. It's just been a lot, and I'm still kind of processing the killing that I've had to take part in. I rarely even kill bugs in my home, so the persistent bloodshed and violence... It's been hard for me to wrap my head around," Antje admitted, tears welling up despite her best efforts to suppress them.

"That's why I asked. Antje, I see part of me in you. I too have great power, but I have seen what that power can do when used in a way that isn't altruistic. My father..." Takhi trailed off and looked to the ground.

"I heard what he did to you and your husband, Takhi. Philomena shared it with me. I am so sorry," Antje said, placing her hand on the upper part of Takhi's wing. Takhi wiped a tear from her eye.

"It's important that you only use your powers for the protection of the innocent, Antje. A piece of your soul is damaged every time you engage in killing and is only replaced by the joy of seeing another spared. You must keep the balance," Takhi warned.

"Understood. Candidly, I probably have some form of PTSD that I am coping with right now, but I am also starting to identify with a darker side of me who feels compelled to kill at times. It's kind of terrifying. I see flashes of these fights in my dreams every night, and I wake up shaking, sweating, and sometimes crying. The only thing that helps is reminding myself that if I hadn't killed these beings, they would have killed others—and that if I don't kill them, they might kill Cole." Antje sighed and paused her words, rolling her eyes upward to thwart any further tear production. "Cole, who I don't even really know, but has somehow captured my heart in the few hours we've spent together. I just have this like, compulsion to be with him... A compulsion that my brain and heart are at complete and total war over. My brain is like, 'this makes no sense, you're going to get hurt', but my heart is like, 'this is the love of your life and you know it'. The fact that he feels the same is somewhat comforting, but is also making me wonder if this is a spell or something? I don't know, nothing makes any sense to me right now, and I honestly feel like I'm going insane." Antje gulped, feeling a lump rising in her throat. Takhi extended her right wing out and wrapped it around Antje.

"You have the ability to keep the balance, Antje. We will get Cole back. Don't fret. As far as your feelings go—I've known Cole for a while, and he's never shown interest in anyone like how he has with you. Soulmates are a tricky thing, and usually hit you when you least expect it."

"Like over a dead baby's body?" Antje cheekily replied through her tears, tucking her hair behind her ear.

Takhi laughed heartily and nodded. "Like over a dead baby's body. Follow your heart; in time, it will all make sense. Trust that the gods are guiding you where you need to be to meet your fate. Now, would you like to attempt calling one of your gods to control the weather today?"

"I thought I wanted to rest, but I'm realizing there is no time for rest right now. I can't, in good conscience, take a break while Cole is in the clutches of the Dark Queen." Antje wiped the tears from her eyes and sat up straight, as if she had flipped her emotional switch off.

"Very well. As you are a valkyrie, our best bet is to call upon the Norse gods. Your connection with them is fortified by your higher self, and they will be inclined to help with little to no questions asked—which is important when you're in battle. There are two that I recommend calling upon: Thor, God of thunder, and Skaði, Goddess of snow and the hunt. Be forewarned though, both Gods are interesting characters. Skaði prefers those who speak bluntly and to the point, and Thor—well, he's a bit of what the normies would call a 'bro'. He's playful and almost childish at times, but do not be fooled—Thor has a heart of gold, and is quite a formidable opponent. Gaining his help will give you a weapon that even the Dark Queen cannot match. Let's get you acquainted with Thor and Skaði today. I brought two bottles of mead with me as an offering, should they need one."

"What's mead?" Antje questioned.

"It's a honey wine that the Norse Gods cherish," Takhi answered, sliding the bottle across the rock with her clawed foot. Antje picked up the bottle and looked at it.

"So, in exchange for a lethal weapon, they require wine? These gods sound like my people!" Antje laughed.

"They are your people, Antje. How familiar are you with Norse mythology?" Takhi asked, plucking some yarrow from the hillside.

"I'm not really, past what I've seen in the movies and some light internet searching." Antje looked at her feet, somewhat ashamed.

"Have you seen a one-eyed man in your dreams at all?" Takhi asked, pausing to look Antje in the eyes.

"Not in my dreams, but right after I had a premonition about a terrorist attack, he appeared in the back seat of my car, and I saw him again after I fought Rebekah. I found myself on the top of a mountain with the old man with one eye, who felt almost like a father to me."

"That was indeed Odin, the Norse all-father. He is the god of war, knowledge, and death. The valkyries are known to work for him and Freya, the Norse Goddess of wealth and love. She is also a fearsome warrior. Since you have met Odin, you may also be able to call upon him... But be warned, Odin is a tricky god. He can see the future and will do whatever needs to be done for the greater good, even if it means sacrificing his own. If you saw him in the space close to death, chances are, you'll be hearing from him again at some point. Today, we will keep things less complicated and stick to Thor and Skaði. Stand up, close your eyes, and stare at the back of your eyelids," Takhi ordered mildly. Antje obliged, rising to her feet.

"Antje, can you see what looks like stars, spinning around you?" Antje focused her eyes a bit and, sure enough, saw stars spinning around her as if she was standing stationary in the middle of a tilt-o-whirl, with the sides of the room rotating around her.

"Yes!" Antje exclaimed excitedly.

"Good. Now say 'Thor, God of Thunder' as if you were paging him, then empty your mind immediately. No thought, nothing should be in your brain. It should be absolute stillness inside your mind."

Antje nodded with her eyes closed. "Thor, God of Thunder," she said confidently, and then wiped her mind clean as if a mute button had been pushed. A few seconds went by before Antje heard a loud, booming voice from behind her left ear.

"About time! I was wondering when you were going to say hello," Thor teased with a loud chortle that startled Antje. Antje's eyes sprung open, but there was no one in the forest with her and Takhi. Takhi leaned her head in toward Antje's face a bit.

"Can you hear him, Antje?"

"Can you not!?" Antje replied, surprised.

"No. This is your own personal 'call' with him. Ask him for help. Tell him what you're up against. Close your eyes. The connection is easier to hear that way, as you must concentrate all of your focus and energy on holding the energy frequency he is in."

Antje closed her eyes and began to speak but was interrupted, "Th—"

"No need!" The booming voice replied. "Odin has explained all. I will help you whenever you need, but for now, take this Mjolnir. It was crafted for Freya, who has decided that your service to the side of good deserves a special protective talisman. When you need me, wrap your hand around this Mjolnir and say my name. Wear this with the necklace that boyfriend of yours gave you, and you should have little issue in any fight. You sure decided to wake up and enter our world with a bang, Antje!" Thor exclaimed, again chuckling loudly. "Good to hear from you. Call upon me anytime—I will strike down your opponents with lightning."

Antje heard Takhi gasp with delight. "Antje! Look at what I found hanging on the branch next to me—a gift, I'm sure." Antje opened her eyes to see Takhi turn around while holding a golden necklace in the shape of Thor's hammer. It was encrusted in blue gems and was quite large. Takhi examined it a bit before placing it in Antje's hand.

"An Elgiz rune is engraved on the back. That's a rune of protection, associated with a great protector animal: the elk, or as Americans call it—the moose. I take it Thor has agreed to help you?" Takhi said in a joyous tone.

"Yeah, he said that Odin had brought him up to speed, and he's happy to help. He also said Freya is giving me this necklace as protection, and a way of quickly calling him if I am in need," Antje explained, in a slightly muted tone. Antje was overtaken by the concept of gods being real and knowing who she was, but was mostly mind-blown at the thought of being able to communicate with them. "Sorry. I'm a little shell-shocked right now, but what did you mean by 'what the Americans call the moose'? Elk are a different animal."

Takhi giggled. "What Americans call elk are actually not elk. They're wapiti. In Europe, moose are called elk, and when settlers came to America, they landed in areas that didn't have moose. So, when they encountered wapiti, they called them elk because of their resemblance to their European counterparts. Anyway, it's understandable that you're in shock, but try not to take interacting with other realms so seriously. One of the things that will keep you sane in this world of magic, is understanding that this realm we live in—it's not the only realm. There are countless realms out there, and this one is just a pit stop for your soul; one which you might choose to come back to again, or not." Takhi realized that she was unleashing another chapter of a book that Antje was unprepared to read at the moment, and changed the subject quickly. "Let's contact Skaði. The same way you called Thor."

Antje took a deep breath and called Skaði. A curt female voice with a thick Norse accent trickled through her head. "So, you're the valkyrie that just woke up. I'll help you and unleash a blizzard of massive proportion unto your foes. Call me as you just did, and I will be at your side, valkyrie." The connection was immediately severed; the energy around Antje quickly changing back to the status quo. She opened her eyes and looked at Takhi.

"She's in. You weren't kidding when you said she liked straight-to-the-point."

Takhi laughed and replied, "The Norse Gods—they all have quite specific personalities. You'll get used to them, and even learn to love some of them. They're all unique and interesting characters. The sun is setting. We should make our way back to the Cistern. Flying at dusk is an advanced technique, and after your crash landing, I think we should probably leave that for another lesson," Takhi chided, playfully.

"I can always transform into a bat," Antje lightheartedly proclaimed.

"There you go. That's what I meant about not taking things so seriously. You're quite the quick study, Antje!"

Nine

Undercover and Unconscious Underpinnings

Two weeks had passed, and Antje was feeling delightfully comfortable in her new abilities. She outperformed most of her instructors at this point and could even shapeshift without saying a word aloud.

"Yer bang on with yer lessons there, Antje! Quite the specimen there, aren'tcha?" Philomena hollered, her voice echoing down the corridor where Antje thought she was walking alone.

"Philomena! I am...certainly progressing. I'm getting antsy about finding Cole, though. The longer we wait..."

"Yeh, yeh! You two and yer undying love. If ye want to try a test run, I'll tell ye what... There's a small café in an area a wee bit from here. The patrons are small-time no good fer nothin' rat-arsed wankers, but some of 'em are low-level henchmen fer the Queen, and she'd never tell them feckin' cabbages nothin' about somethin' as big as a valkyrie bein' in town. Them eejits would talk the hind legs off a donkey about it! They won't know ye. Go have a run at 'em. I won't say nothin' to no one." Philomena smiled mischievously. "'Bout time someone put them rotten potatoes deep in the dirt where they belong!"

"What if the Headmaster finds out you knew? Won't you get in trouble?" Antje questioned, concerned, while simultaneously excited at the prospect of potentially getting one step closer to finding Cole and punishing his captors.

"Ahh, the Headmaster might act like he'll eat my head, but he knows well as I do that yer gonna do what yer gonna do, and it's better we start ye off slow. Go have at 'em!"

"Have at who?" a deep voice bellowed from a distance down the hall. Turning the corner was Ragnar, who was closing the gap between himself and Philomena quite quickly.

"Oh, cop onto yerself, Ragnar. What do ye think we're talkin' 'bout?" Philomena said, as her lips peeled back, revealing the same mischievous grin that had appeared merely moments before.

"So, I was right then? She's ready to draw blood? What a valkyrie!" Ragnar exclaimed.

"Wait, what? You guys knew I'd want to go to this place?" Antje questioned, curiously. Philomena and Ragnar looked at each other and burst out laughing.

"Knew it? We want ye to!" Philomena called out, still laughing.

"You see, Antje. A few months back, we had a little gathering at the café after work. Well, Phil here, indulged in a little too much whiskey and entered a game of Daldøs, where she got her proverbial ass handed to her, and lost all her money." Ragnar chuckled while stumbling around, mocking Philomena.

"Jesus, Mary, and Joseph, Ragnar! If ye don't houl yer whisht, I'll burst ye!" Philomena put up her fists and jabbed them in the air toward Ragnar. "I might've been pissed as a fart, but really—who takes money from a poor old woman?" Philomena said, shrinking in stature.

"Oh yes, Phil, everyone definitely sees you as some poor old woman!" Ragnar chortled, leisurely holding Philomena by her forehead with one arm, as she continued her non-connecting jabs.

"So, you want revenge, then?" Antje asked.

"No, we want to see what you can do in the field, Antje. I speak for Misha and myself when we say that we're a bit worn out from your lessons and would like to see what you'll do to some of the dark mystics if the reins are removed," Ragnar replied, dropping his hand from Philomena's forehead as she doubled over with her hands on her knees, struggling to catch her breath.

"I'll get ye one day, ye big muppet! Ye forget—I've a potion that'll even make yer fearsome jotuns run once they see me!" Philomena said, in between gasps. Ragnar looked at Antje, with a giant grin and rolled his eyes.

"You okay there, Phil? Need some water? If you give me the keys to your lab, I'll go get you some," Ragnar offered, bending down to talk to her like a small child. Philomena reached up and grabbed Ragnar's nose between her thumb and pointer finger while replying, "Give you the keys I will, yeh? Stop slaggin' me before I kick ye in the bollocks. I might be short, but my legs have carried me fer this long and mockin' is catchin'!" Philomena let go of Ragnar's nose as Ragnar stood upright, rubbing it a little.

"What does 'mocking is catching' mean?" Antje questioned, with a confused look on her face. Trying to keep up with Philomena's colorful Irish-isms was a full-time job, it seemed.

"She's telling me, 'Karma's a bitch' as you Americans say," Ragnar explained, still rubbing the tip of his nose. "Be flattered. She only speaks in tongues around people she really likes."

"Anyhoo. Time to suit up, Antje! Ye got yer necklace that Cole gave ye?" Philomena asked, reaching for the necklace around Antje's neck. "Oh, would ye look at that! That's not the necklace I was expectin'! Ragnar, she's got a fancy mjolnir!" Philomena exclaimed, running the hammer charm through her fingers and admiring it intensely. "No wonder she's been kickin' yer arse to hell and back!"

Ragnar looked to the side to avoid making eye contact and scratched the side of his head while mumbling, "We make her remove her jewelry before sparring, and that one's new."

Philomena heard what he said and got a tickled look on her face. "Oh, I'm sorry, my ooooold ears didn't hear that! What did ye say?" she mocked, shuffling closer to Ragnar.

"You heard me, Phil. Anyway—we should get going, so Antje can go beat the daylights out of some bad guys, no?" Ragnar replied, grabbing Philomena's hand and walking back down the dimly lit corridor toward the exit. Philomena begrudgingly walked with him, turning around to yell at Antje, "Beat the piss out of 'em, Antje! Ye tell them I want my coin purse back!"

Antje, back at her flat, removed the necklace Cole gave her from the box it was stowed in. She admired how intricate the silverwork of the inlay was, and delighted in the smoothness of the jade between her fingers as she rubbed it. Cole's absence stung. This was an unusual sensation for her, as her addiction to solitude rarely afforded her the desire to be with someone for longer than a few hours; he was different, as though Antje had read an unfinished book, and Cole was the conclusion she'd longed for.

Pulling her black skinny jeans over her plump derrière, Antje threw on her most cherished, yet tattered, metal band tee. The nostalgia of the borderline illegible white text coupled with the well-earned holes was comforting to her as she looked in the mirror. Finishing the look with a charcoal-black leather jacket and thick eyeliner, she felt she'd accomplished blending in as best she could—although she knew her American accent would draw some attention regardless of her fashion choices. Antje slipped each foot into her combat boots and pulled the laces tight, double knotting, just in case she was made, and the evening devolved into another acrobatic brawl for her.

Thoughtfully clasping the necklace that Cole gave her around her neck and arranging it behind Freya's mjolnir, Antje armed herself with Daggert and pulled up the address of the café on her phone. As it turned out, it was within walking distance. Antje exited her flat and began the brief trek to her first undercover operation. While Ragnar and Philomena may have had ulterior motives for sending her there, Antje's sole motive was discovering where Cole was being held, and she was resolved to avoid an altercation as best she could.

The walk to the café was uneventful, and Antje managed to enter it relatively unnoticed, but the moment she ordered an espresso, heads swiveled, turning in concert before locking onto her. The barista slowly slid the espresso cup and saucer across the bar, sizing up Antje with suspicion. Clearly not a tourist spot, Antje was the only non-Dane in the entire room. It reeked of cigar smoke and the smell of over-roasted coffee, but most pungent of all was the cloying stench of death, which lingered in the soupy air. Wallpaper peeled from around the many window frames like a failed paper-mâché project, and the furniture was reminiscent of what you'd find at an estate sale in the less affluent part of town. It was dark, dank, and a place no sane person would willingly choose to patronize.

Knowing she was in the right spot by the redolence of decay, Antje sat down at a bistro table with only one chair, a strategically sound choice in the event she needed to make a quick escape, as it provided an unobstructed view of the entrance and was near a large window facing the alley. Onlookers began whispering as a gaunt man with dark brown hair and a pronounced jawline approached Antje, pulling up a chair from an empty adjacent table.

"Hej, taler du Dansk?" he asked, slightly amused. Antje was pretty sure he knew her answer but chose to play along to keep up the façade.

"Nej. English?" she answered with a sultry smile.

"I do speak English. That's an American accent, correct?"

"Yes. You caught me. It is indeed an American accent. I'm here on vacation and decided to explore the city. I heard this place has good mead, but I got overwhelmed when I saw the menu in Danish, so I just stuck with some coffee." Antje was really playing up the dumb American stereotype, and it seemed to be working—the man leaned in closer and closer to her, his body obscuring half of the table.

"My name is Lucas. What name should I call you by?" His affected tone made Antje's skin crawl. She could physically feel the predatory energy oozing from his pores, like a greasy construction worker grabbing their crotch and pursuing anything with a pulse.

"Anna. My name is Anna," she coyly replied, sipping her espresso, attempting to disguise her look of disgust.

"Well, Anna. You smell delicious. What is that scent you are wearing?"

Antje cringed internally. "Deodorant," she replied, again sipping her espresso as her patience dangerously waned. "Hey, have you seen an American guy named Cole anywhere? I met him at a bar nearby and he accidentally took my phone instead of his. I tried calling my phone from the hotel, but it's dead and goes straight to voicemail. I need my phone back. I know it's a long shot, but..." As she asked, the man's body stiffened; sitting upright, his brows furrowed.

"An American man, with wavy salt and pepper hair?" he asked, his demeanor changing from a slimy used-car salesman to an aggressive interrogator. Antje noticed the hushed whispers fade, and people began rearranging themselves in the room—each one positioning themselves to pounce, like a mountain lion stalking its prey.

"Yeah, I suppose you could say salt and pepper." Antje's hand slid down to her thigh where Daggert was concealed when movement in the alley window caught her eye. In the window were familiar faces: Philomena, Ragnar, Misha, Takhi, and William Henry; their heads all ducked below the window as soon as they were spotted. Only Philomena dared to poke her head back above the windowsill for a second glance.

"That's a very special American you swapped phones with," the man answered, pushing his chair back some, readying himself to stand up. At this point, Antje knew her diplomatic mission had been blown; her trainers were about to receive the show they had desired.

"Aren't we all special Americans, though?" Antje snidely snapped. With a piercing gaze attached, she launched a potion bottle as high as she could into the air. The bottle collided with the water-stained ceiling above, releasing a mist of royal-blue fog. Every being in the café, including the barista, reverted to their true form. Snarling, snapping, and foaming at the mouth, the dark mystics began to summon spells and ready their weapons as they rapidly encroached upon Antje. Now with her back against a wall, she saw Ragnar and Misha through the window. Misha gave her a thumbs up and pointed at his chest to communicate that Antje still had protective talismans, and to take a deep breath—a stark contrast to Ragnar, who looked like a teenage boy sneaking into a peep show. Antje inhaled deeply and clasped her hand around both the Mjolnir and her jade pendant. Her anxiety was through the roof, in an alarmingly unusual way; her heart pounded as if it would explode straight from her chest if she didn't regain control soon.

No longer in the form of a mere man, the sexual predator reverted back to a ghoulish undead creature called a draugr and was now priming himself for a vicious physical attack. In her previous late-night research quests for all things Norse, following her embarrassing confession to Takhi about how little she knew of Norse mythology, Antje had discovered that draugrs possessed supernatural strength. The level of reverence that the other patrons had for him now made sense to Antje. His greasy human appearance also now made sense to Antje, as putrid slime dripped from every orifice of his necrotic, blue-black skin. Adorned in old Viking gear, he pulled a long sword out from nowhere.

"Your Mjolnir...it's mine!" he snarled, as a thick, mucosal drool spattered from his decayed lips and pushed through his blackened teeth. Draugrs were known for being envious of the wealth of the living, but it was rare to find one away from their village or their burial mound, as most souls that became draugrs were infinitely greedy and fiercely guarded their treasure trove. It became apparent that while this particular draugr had some typical motivations, he was not otherwise typical. Although they were known to possess superhuman strength and mystical abilities, they tended to be fairly zombie-like in their intelligence level. This draugr had not only caught onto Antje's somewhat poorly disguised recon mission, but was also silently directing the tipsy group of monstrosities into a military formation. With each step toward Antje, the clanging of his metal boots and the sound of his long sword dragging across the well-worn floor elevated Antje's already skyrocketing anxiety to unimaginable heights.

"What a nice draugr you'll make!" he barked, spit flinging onto the table between them. The table now looked like a Jackson Pollock painting, and Antje realized that draugrs, like zombies, could turn the living into their own. Antje began to hyperventilate—her hands trembling. The draugr began a fearsome offensive as he effortlessly swung his sword, creating a shockwave that was visible to the naked human eye as it sliced through the air. Antje's body, against every desire of her heart and soul, betrayed her; completely frozen, Antje was unable to defend or attack.

Through the window, Antje saw Ragnar's face switch from a joyous grin of anticipation to the heavy eyes of concern. As Ragnar began to steady himself, with the intent of joining in on the fight, Takhi's large wing curled around him. She motioned for him to stay and gave a nod in Antje's direction, which Antje interpreted as, "Conquer your fear. You can do this."

In that very second, the draugr's sword narrowly missed Antje—the power of her jade necklace sending the weapon's momentum back toward the draugr himself. The field of force emitted from the sword was enough to knock Antje to the ground, the sword lodging itself deep inside the draugr's head, landing so perfectly perpendicular, it was almost comical—like a cheap Halloween costume. The draugr's body clumsily dropped to the floor. Simultaneously, Antje felt one of the necklaces around her neck fall into her hand. It was Cole's necklace, and the jade stone had shattered, leaving it drained of all magic and protection. Antje tightly gripped the necklace, her rage enabling her to stand up once more. Sliding the necklace into her inner coat pocket, she gripped Daggert with renewed wrath and locked eyes with the closest dark mystic, who was stunned and terrified after seeing their otherwise impervious commander fall.

Antje lunged, stabbing the toad-like creature in the neck, releasing a stream of viscous green fluid like a water balloon with a small puncture. She carved her way through several dark mystics with intuitive ease. Stopping midway through the crowd, blood dripping from the hand that held Daggert, she wrapped her other hand around the Mjolnir and confidently said, "Thor." A blue bolt of electricity emanated from her hand, zapping several dark mystics; sizzling and smoking, their bodies promptly dropped to the floor. The remaining dark mystics began to flee for their lives like cockroaches in the light. Standing alone in a wake of misshapen, vile bodies, Antje finally began to catch her breath. Outside the window, her instructors gleefully celebrated, minus Philomena, who had now entered through the front door and was rummaging through the pockets of the deceased.

"Ye didn't even ask about my coin-purse! Nevertheless, ye were spot on, Antje! I got a wee bit worried there fer a second, but ye managed to pull it together! Thank ye lucky stars that ye necklace had a charge left in it, or we'd be dealin' with the worst draugr this world had ever seen! Can 'ye even imagine? A valkyrie draugr," Philomena yammered, stuffing the pockets of her floor-length skirt to the point of overflowing.

"I didn't find out anything about Cole, except that even these guys knew who he was, and I'm guessing, how important he is," Antje grieved, pulling her necklace from her coat pocket and running her fingers around the silver inlay, her eyes glossy with tears. Takhi and the gang entered through the front door, admiring the damage done as they approached.

"Don't worry, Antje. The survivors are no doubt running to report to the Dark Queen that you are searching for Cole. Knowing what we know about her love for power, my guess is, she will come to you now that you've taken out a draugr—whether it was on purpose or not. Are you alright? It looked like you disassociated for a split second," Takhi asked, enveloping Antje in her wings like a warm blanket.

"I...I had a flashback of the last brawl with Cole, where he was taken from me, and I just— I...I was paralyzed," Antje stammered, tears flowing down her cheeks. The rest of the instructors pulled in close, surrounding Antje.

"Your rage about your necklace being destroyed guided you through it though, no?" Misha questioned in a leading manner. "Antje, as you know, I'm Jewish. The only thing that keeps my people alive, after almost having been wiped off the face of the planet multiple times, is the ability to tap into the pain created by profound loss. Use it to fuel your fire, not to extinguish it. When you feel that fear and pain start to creep in, remind yourself that past losses hold no meaning if you too are lost in the end. In some cases, it only takes one or two people to win the war, and that one person in this case is you. Give it your all, and know we are here to help guide you, not just physically, but emotionally and mentally as well."

Ragnar wrapped his freakishly long arms around everyone. "You did good, Antje. I am very pleased that your field test proved successful, even if you lost your necklace in the process. You've been training without the necklace this whole time, so although I know the sentimental value of it means a lot to you—you don't actually need it to survive. Soon, we will find Cole, and that's way better than the necklace anyway, is it not?" Ragnar reasoned.

William Henry quickly ducked under Ragnar's arm, freeing himself from the physically intimate circle, and changed the subject. "Now, dear Antje, why did you not shape-shift into a draugr yourself? You can mirror any opponent, and while your abilities will still be your own, the mental warfare that mirroring provides is a stunning improvement over your adversary. Remember your training, dear." Philomena slapped William Henry's back, making him recoil with a cringe.

"Now, we all know that ye childhood has made ye uncomfortable with emotions and touchin', but wait until ye get back in the classroom fer yer lectures, ye old stick in the mud!" Philomena harangued, pulling at the waistband of her skirt as it sagged from the weight of the items she'd pilfered from the dead. "Antje, I'll make ye some more potions when we get back to the Cisterne. Expert aim ye have though! They never saw it comin'!"

Takhi smiled at Antje and quietly spoke into her ear, "Masterfully done with the lightning, Antje. Try to be kind to yourself about the fear you experienced. I think this was the perfect timing for you to overcome your fear—better now, than when you are face to face with the Dark Queen. To quote one of your presidents, 'The only thing we have to fear is fear itself'."

TEN

MIMOSAS AND MADDENING MEDDLING

Antje woke from a much-needed deep sleep to the sound of her phone vibrating on the nightstand. Since the first day she'd set foot in the Cisterne, her sleep cycle had been spotty at best, and the previous night's escapades left her energy massively depleted—she would have slept the entire day, given her druthers. Tapping the answer icon without looking to see who it was, Antje groggily answered the phone.

"Ughem. Heh...hello?"

"Rise and shine, kiddo!" a male voice chirped. Antje was still too sleep-logged to figure out who it was. Pulling the phone away from her face and squinting at the screen, she realized it was her older brother, Dirk. Antje groaned internally. Her brother was five years older, yet constantly called her "kiddo," even as an adult. His constant infantilization of her never seemed to cease, and no matter how much Antje grew as a person, or how many wrinkles she earned, Dirk would only ever see her as his kid sister.

"Hey, Dirk. What's up?" Antje replied, sitting up and yawning.

"Guess where we are?"

"Where? And who is 'we'?" Antje's blood pressure rose with each word leaving her mouth.

"Me and Mom! We're at the Copenhagen airport! We thought we'd surprise you since you just disappeared. After you ignored our calls for the fifth time, I called Uncle Isaac. He informed us that you took a leave of absence from your job and ran off to Denmark—how could you do that to Mom? Do you have any idea what that was like for her?" Dirk scolded.

Antje wasn't close with her immediate family. The only person in her birth family that she had ever truly connected with on a deeper level had been her father, who had passed away a few years ago. Often away on business, the stress of providing financially for his family had inflamed an already explosive temper. However, he truly attempted to understand and encourage Antje, which made her feel loved—even if their relationship was strained at times.

When the power dynamic of the family had shifted with his departure into the afterlife, she had found herself less and less interested in maintaining the façade that had once held her family together. Antje was always the nail that stuck out, and rather than being constantly hammered for who she was, she decided to quietly remove herself from the board altogether.

Dirk and her mother were a tag team, joined at the hip, and would often take a united offensive against Antje—while simultaneously playing the victims. Antje coped with the family dysfunction as a kid by spending her days in the woods alone, building forts, and fantasizing about the day she could leave home to live in a forest of her own.

In a full-blown panic at this point, Antje cleared her throat and stood up, tensely running her hand across the top of her hair—tightening her forehead as though she'd just had a facelift.

"You guys shouldn't have come, Dirk, this really isn't a good time. I've got a lot of exams and…"

"Exams? Isn't that place like a day camp for kids who believe magic is real?" he interrupted. Antje's face throbbed, and her ears burned, but she silently convinced herself that he may have been told that by their uncle to keep things from getting too complicated. "At least meet us for brunch at the hotel after we check-in, Antje. You owe Mom that, at least," Dirk demanded.

Against every grain of self-respect in her body, Antje agreed. She figured that by meeting them for brunch, they'd be predictably self-centered, leaving her to go off and do whatever tourist activity piqued their interest—and she could go back to her training. Taking a few quiet deep breaths, Antje regained her center.

"Okay. Brunch it is. I'll meet you at your hotel at 11. Text me the details," she tepidly confirmed.

"Don't sound so excited, kiddo!" he joked. "Hey, Mom is really hurt that you haven't been answering the phone or calling her. You should pick up a small gift for her or something before you come..."

Antje promptly hung up the phone, her jaw clenched, and her nostrils flaring. After a blisteringly hot shower and thirty minutes of meditation, her phone rang once more. A pit formed in her stomach as she thought it was her brother—or worse, her mother calling with an ever-present laundry list of complaints. She looked at the phone. It was Isaac. Antje sighed a deep sigh of relief and picked up the phone.

"Antje, I'm sorry to call so early, but your bro..." Isaac couldn't even finish his sentence before Antje replied, "Ugh. They're already here. Thank you for trying to warn me, though, Isaac."

"Remember what we talked about, Antje. You didn't choose to be born into a family with them, so don't take anything they say to heart any more than you would any random stranger," Isaac reminded her lovingly.

"Thank you. I needed to hear that today," Antje replied. "I've got to go get ready for brunch with them, in the midst of my boyfriend being kidnapped and training to fight an army of evil to get him back."

"Wait, what?" Isaac was understandably alarmed.

"A lot has happened very quickly here. CliffsNotes: I'm a valkyrie. I met a CIA agent. Much to my chagrin, it was basically love at first sight, and now he's been kidnapped by some evil mystic army, and I have to go retrieve him. I'm pretty sure I have post-traumatic stress disorder, and I'm going to have to take out a second mortgage for therapy when I get home, Uncle Isaac," Antje quickly rambled.

"Oh, Antje," Isaac bemoaned empathetically.

"Yeah. So, now on top of this, I have to play clapping monkey for my family. This is so typical. I'm going through something beyond traumatic—not that they would even care if I told them—and now they've flown here to guilt trip me for not centering my world around my mother's desires. By the way, did you tell them that I am at a day camp for kids who believe magic is real?"

"What? No! I told them that you were spending time at a school for mystics, and while you weren't actually going to school, you were learning about your abilities. Is that what they told you?" Isaac questioned, deeply concerned.

"No. It's just Dirk being... Dirk. Never mind that I asked. If you don't hear from me in the next week, call Mathias, please. Just know—I've found out that I am more capable than I ever could have imagined, and that I feel confident I'll be okay... If I can only get through brunch."

"Be safe, daughter of mine. I love you, and I'm petitioning the great spirit for your safety and success in retrieving your boyfriend. I hope to meet him soon," Isaac said tenderly.

"I love you so much, Uncle Isaac. Thank you for sending me on this journey. It might be scary as fuck, but for the first time in my entire life, I feel like I'm fulfilling my purpose for existing. We'll talk soon." Antje hung up the phone and glanced at the clock. It was time. She would now have to face her biggest obstacle yet: brunch.

Antje entered the restaurant at the base of the historic hotel, which was smack-dab in the midst of the tourist district. A rather stark departure from American brunches, where white dominated the entire occasion, the room was warm, antique, and inviting. Admiring the wood-trimmed walls and the shimmering chandeliers, which hung from the ceiling like designer earrings, Antje heard her mother's voice from behind.

"Antje! Oh, thank goodness. I was so worried! How are you, my only daughter?" her mother projected in a high-pitched, overacted manner, as if she was auditioning for a daytime soap opera. Antje's mother liked to put on a show of the ever-doting mother in front of people—Dirk included—but was a very different mother when they were alone. She was often aggressive, accusatory, and argumentative. That made her public displays even less palatable for Antje. Physically recoiling as her mother leaned in for a hug, Antje went limp and stared dead ahead.

Typical Mom—just get through brunch.

Dirk was preoccupied with surveying the buffet's spread, and as Antje was released from her mother's death grip, she turned to walk up to the maître d', spotting a man who looked suspiciously like Cole from behind. Staring, Antje bumped into a chair directly in front of her.

"Oh, goodness. I'm so sorry about her!" her mother exclaimed, leaning down to the affected restaurant-goer. Antje flushed with embarrassment, bowed her head apologetically, and smiled at the man. The man, who clearly didn't speak English, shook his head and hands back and forth to communicate, "It's okay, no big deal." Antje quietly continued to walk toward the table but not before her mother caught up and quietly whispered to her, "I've been saying you need to work on your weight problem. You nearly knocked that guy out of his chair with your belly."

Antje had always been lean, but muscular, and never worried about her weight. Her mother, however, was obsessed with it—constantly making remarks about the size of her body, even during some of Antje's darkest hours. Antje's jaw clenched as Dirk and her mother began to lower themselves into their chairs. On the table in front of them were three champagne glasses filled with champagne and orange juice. Antje snatched one of the flutes, slamming the mimosa like a shot before setting the empty glass down.

"I guess I should skip brunch then, to watch my weight. Enjoy your mother-son date," Antje tersely announced before heading toward the man who looked like Cole. Her brother sat slack-jawed and in shock by

Antje's slight, but her mother took this as the perfect opportunity and leaned into her victim complex, turning the theatrics up a few notches.

"We flew all the way here to see you! It was such a long journey! Oh! My heart! My heart!" her mother exclaimed, clutching her heart and falling back into her chair as if she was having a heart attack. A smirk grew across Antje's lips as she mumbled under her breath, "Ah yes, it's your heart this time. What was it last time, again? Oh—your non-existent brain tumor, that's right. The time before that, I triggered your sciatica. Before that, your broken thumb."

Restaurant staff swarmed the table out of concern for the non-existent medical crisis that had now usurped the attention of everyone in the room. The upside of her mother's gratuitous performance was that it caused the man in question to turn, revealing his face. Antje's heart exploded with joy and dropped, all at the same time. It was Cole.

What the fuck is Cole doing at a brunch buffet? How did he escape? Why hasn't he called? Is this actually unrequited love that I feel? Antje's mind raced through a rat's nest of emotional tripwires.

As her mother's caterwauling continued, Cole signed his receipt and exited the restaurant. Antje proceeded to follow Cole from a safe distance and immediately texted Headmaster Vogel.

> *ANTJE: I'm not sure how this happened, but I think I've found Cole. He's alive and well. I'm secretly following him.*

> *VOGEL: Be careful. The Dark Queen's magic is strong and that may not be Cole. Come back to The Cisterne. Your training hasn't been completed yet. You're no match for the Dark Queen after two weeks of training, Antje. It's dangerous.*

> ANTJE: I know, but I don't want to lose him if it is actually him. We can't afford to be fighting Cole AND the Dark Queen. I'll stay out of sight and report back soon with a location.

Antje's phone rang—it was Headmaster Vogel. Antje, conflicted as to whether she should answer or follow her intuition, looked up from her phone and found herself face to face with Cole's irresistibly handsome smile.

"You found me." Cole said, playfully.

"Where the fuck have you been?" Tears began to flood Antje's eyes as Cole continued to give her the swoon-worthy grin that had caused her to fall in love with him at first sight.

"I'll explain everything. This war you're fighting is not what it seems. I want to introduce you to the Queen. She just wants to share her side of the story. She's not the villain she was painted to be, and I now see that," he replied, reaching for her hand.

"Be careful. Ze Dark Queen's magic is strong, and that may not be Cole." The headmaster's warning echoed through her mind. Had a surprise family invasion not just triggered decades of repressed childhood damage, Antje likely would have attempted to bring him back the Cisterne to confirm the headmaster's suspicions—suspicions which she now shared. However, Antje had another idea that innately felt right. Her simmering rage was begging to be unleashed, and she was unwavering in the pursuit of rescuing the real Cole; *her plan* would satiate both of these desires, concurrently.

"I trust you," Antje assured, squeezing his hand. "Let's go meet her—but, I have to go pick up my pet from the Cisterne first."

"You have a pet?" Cole asked, surprised.

"Yes. A shisa. He's my emotional support shisa," she said, forcing a playful smile.

Cole flashed a warm grin in return. "Okay. How about, while you're there, I run back to your place and mine and pack us some weekend bags?"

Antje paused for a moment, assessing the risk of letting a member of the Dark Army into her flat. "That would be great—I've been living out of my suitcase, so just grab it with whatever's in it. Oh—and my bag of toiletries off the bathroom counter."

Cole smiled, "Whatever you need, sweetie. When I'm done, I'll wait for you above ground in the car—I don't want to be swarmed by the professors, you know? Also, please don't tell them that you've found me. They won't understand why I've had such a change of heart," Cole replied. Antje nodded, relieved that she now knew with absolute certainty that this was some dark perversion of Cole— because ultimately, knowing someone is truly your enemy isn't always the easiest feat.

Eleven

Preparations, Pep Talks, and a Precious Pup

As Antje strolled down the Cisterne's corridors on the way to procure Shields from Mikono, Headmaster Vogel materialized in front of her.

"Headmaster Vogel! I was going to come to your office after grabbing my shisa."

"Yes, I figured. So, you know for a fact now that Cole isn't actually Cole, and is a trap set by ze Dark Queen, yah?"

Antje nodded. "One hundred percent, a trap. But—I have to know where Cole is. I can't believe I'm going to say this, but I plan to contact the CIA office and enlist their help. My goal is to have her hideout surrounded, so she has nowhere to escape to. If the CIA can keep the Dark Queen and her minions busy, I can go find Cole, and then both of us can take her down together," Antje laid her plan out methodically, sans emotion.

"Antje, I heard about last night. Psychologically, are you sure this is ze best timing to walk headlong into a trap?"

"They could kill him, Headmaster Vogel. You told me we didn't have much time before she would deem him an unnecessary risk and dispose of him. She needs to believe that I am walking straight into her trap. Or—better yet, she believes I don't know that isn't Cole, and she thinks that somehow, she has managed to flip me. If I can infiltrate her organization, I can dismantle it with a lot less collateral damage than if we just go straight to war with her. The Dark Queen's Cole is in a car above ground waiting for me. He says the Dark Queen is really just misunderstood, and that you guys are actually the bad guys here. I made it seem like my emotional connection to Cole left me vulnerable to having empathy for her—you know, lovesick, desperate teenage girl schtick, and all that. I genuinely believe neither of them know that I am onto them—and I intend to keep it that way."

"Okay. If you say you are ready, I trust your judgment, Antje. Do not be afraid to call on your Gods for help if things get too intense for you. I do have a little trick that I used while fighting my way through ze underworld, if you would like some guidance should another panic attack happen to you like last night?" Headmaster Vogel's tone was gentle, like the guidance you would receive from a grandparent, and Antje could physically feel the warmth emanating from his altruistic concern.

"I am all ears." Antje grabbed his hands and tenderly held them between hers. "Thank you for volunteering your wisdom. Anything to avoid a repeat of last night is more than appreciated."

"Convince yourself that they cannot hurt you. Tell yourself that good always prevails, and that this is a test from your gods to see if you are ze valkyrie we all know you are. When I was in ze underworld, I saw and fought all sorts of terrifying beings. But, ze one thing that stopped me from collapsing and giving into my fears was knowing that on ze other side of this nightmare, was new knowledge and wisdom that could only be provided through ze vulnerability and forced adaptation that trauma provides. I only had to survive ze trauma in order to receive ze learnings. If you want ze knowledge, and want ze truth bad enough, you *will* prevail. I know you will prevail." The sincerity in his voice inculcated a stillness within Antje. She too, now knew she'd prevail. If a man who had literally defeated death, and every creature associated with it, believed in her—there was no reason for her not to do the same. She leaned in and hugged Headmaster Vogel.

"I won't let you down, but I do have to go get Shields before Dark Cole gets suspicious."

"I will see you soon, Antje. Believe in yourself. Ze rest of us do. Again, reach out to your gods. They will always protect and guide you."

Antje removed her shoes and entered Mikono's office through the delicate rice-paper sliding door, her bare feet compressing the immaculately woven tatami mat beneath them; the scent of rush grass meandered through the room.

"Please enter, Antje. I heard you had a very eventful night last night." Mikono whisked matcha powder into a shallow cup of hot water and placed two small candies on a hand-painted dish. "The candy pairs well with the earthy bitterness of the matcha. Balance, in everything." Mikono smiled. "I have been working on commands with Shields, but I have to be honest—I think you will find he will protect you without any command at all. He was ready to fight a large serpent just for sticking its tongue out at me." Mikono grinned once more, handing Antje the cup of matcha and offering her a piece of candy. Shields was asleep on a mat in the corner on his back, his legs outstretched, with the pinks of his jowls curled outward as he gently snored with each inhale.

"That's really good to hear. I'm walking into a known trap, and I need a weapon in disguise. What can we do to make him less threatening in stature?" Antje sipped her matcha. Her eyes brightened a bit after the first sip. "This is an absolutely delicious matcha, Mikono!"

Mikono quietly replied, "Thank you, Antje. My family has a tea farm in Aichi. It is grown with lots of love and care, and the candy is full of sweetness. Both, I felt you needed right now. Can I share a technique for conquering fear and anxiety with you?"

Normally, Antje would have felt embarrassed by the barrage of people trying to fix her, but after the events of the last forty-eight hours, the flood of love and support was much needed, and she was grateful.

"Please do, Mikono."

"It is called the Jin Shin Jyutsu method. Each finger on your hand is associated with an emotion: the thumb, anxiety and worry; the index finger, fear; the middle finger, anger and resentment; the ring finger, depression, sadness, and indecisiveness; and the pinky, anxiety, pessimism, and lack of confidence. To combat any of these feelings, you simply wrap your hand around that finger until you feel a pulsating in the finger. When you release the finger, the emotions release with the pressure. How are you feeling after last night?" Mikono asked, demonstrating the technique on her thumb.

"I feel calm now, thanks to a pep talk from Headmaster Vogel, but I will definitely use this. Last night's episode had a ramping-up period before I basically became petrified, so this will be really helpful. Thank you so much, Mikono."

"My absolute pleasure, Antje. About Shields: I worked with Headmaster Vogel on a spell to make his communications audible to anyone you trust, but silent to anyone he deems a threat. This way, he may serve your allies as well. Oh, I also had a monk from my hometown write a talisman of good fortune on his collar. I hope it brings you a glorious victory." Mikono embraced Antje gently, and then motioned Antje toward Shields. "You go wake him up. He will be so excited to see you."

Antje walked over to Shields and gently stroked his face with her hand. His eyes opened slowly at first, until he saw Antje's face, and in one haphazard motion, he flipped himself onto his legs, knocking Antje onto her back and zealously licking her face. In between each lick, Shields proclaimed his love for Antje. "HAPPY! ANTJE BACK! HAPPY! LOVE ANTJE! HAPPY, HAPPY, HAPPY!"

Antje laughed and pushed Shields back with her forearm. "Easy, boy. Sit," she commanded. Like a switch was flipped, Shields became instantly obedient and sat at attention, awaiting Antje's next command. "Wow. You really did train him, Mikono!"

"He was the easiest shisa I've ever trained—truly a gift from the gods, Antje," Mikono replied.

"Well, easy or not, you are a miracle worker. Thank you again. About my question earlier though..."

"Oh, yes. The intimidating stature issue—did Phil provide you with potions yet? If not, I'll send a message quickly and ask her to add a transformative potion into your cache." Mikono quietly pulled her phone out and began to tap on the screen.

"Not yet. That would be great, though."

"HAPPY. NO LEAVE SHIELDS! NEED ANTJE. SHIELDS HAPPY!" Shields barked cheerfully as Antje and Mikono both giggled.

"Okay, Shields. We're going to go on an adventure together. Would you like that?" Antje asked, playfully scratching behind his ear. He raised his hind leg and itched under his armpit as a smile of sheer delight peeled his drooping jowls back.

"YES! SHIELDS LOVE ADVENTURE. SHIELDS LOVE ANTJE!" Antje and Mikono again laughed.

"Okay, buddy. We're gonna go fight some bad guys, but I need you to not attack anyone until I say so, okay?"

Shields sat back down at attention with a stern look on his face. "NO ATTACK. SHIELDS GOOD BOY. SHIELDS LISTEN TO ANTJE."

With Shields dutifully walking by her side, Antje headed toward the front atrium at the entrance of the Cisterne. Gathered there were all of the professors, Headmaster Vogel, and Kari. Philomena, as usual, was the first to greet Antje with a small satchel of potions.

"I got yer message and put two transformative potions in yer bag. Just pour the green one over yer shisa and say whatcha want him to be, and to turn him back, pour the white one over him. Yer gonna beat the pants off 'em, Antje. Don't ye worry about a thing." Philomena handed her the satchel and grabbed Antje's face on both sides. Standing on the tips of her toes, she kissed Antje's forehead before releasing her face and dropping back down on her heels.

"Thank you, Philomena!" Antje poured the green potion over the top of Shields' shoulder and spoke the word 'Pomeranian'. As the liquid hit Shields, he shrank into a diminutive fluff-ball, his massive muzzle now small enough for a toddler to wrap their hand around.

"SHIELDS SAD. SHIELDS FEEL LIKE SAD BABY. SHIELDS NO LIKE." The sound of boisterous laughter echoed through the atrium as Antje picked up Shields from the ground, holding him under her arm like a football.

"Don't worry buddy, you'll only be in this body for a little while. I promise you'll be back to normal in no time," Antje comforted him, stroking his tiny head.

"SHIELDS TRUST ANTJE. SHIELDS OKAY." Shields' tiny tongue gently licked Antje's hand.

Every member of the staff took turns hugging Antje and giving her words of encouragement. William Henry, who had been hanging in the wings, finally stepped up.

"Remember, Antje. Mirroring. It's psychological warfare that wins a battle before it has started." Antje smiled at William Henry and forced a one-armed hug on him, Shields cradled in the other. Every muscle in William Henry's body visibly tightened until Antje reasoned with him. "You've already shifted into my body, William Henry, so why be so uptight about a hug?"

William Henry saw her logic and turned, hugging her with both arms, before whispering into her ear, "Well done, you. Go knock their knickers off." William Henry released Antje from his hug, straightened his posture, and fixed his clothes, clearing his throat. Ragnar gave a shoulder-slap of approval, almost knocking William Henry off his feet.

"Well, everyone, this is it. Wish me luck." Antje proclaimed, waving at her mystical family as she exited the Cisterne's entry door. With a nod to the guard and Gudbrand, she stepped into the elevator and savored what she knew were the last moments of silence to be had for a while. The doors opened, and she exited into the actual cisterns above the school. Water dripped from the ceiling around her, and in her head, she heard Misha's advice about soldiering through loss to make the previous loss meaningful. She ruminated on how the pain of Cole being ripped from her could be used to her advantage over the next coming days, and finally emerged above ground.

Dark Cole exited a British-racing-green compact car, and Antje psychologically prepared to feign ignorance about what he really was. Hurrying around the front end of the car, Dark Cole opened the passenger door for Antje. Cole looked at Shields and let out a gasp, attempting to pet him. "What a cute dog!" Shields let out a ferocious growl and snapped at his hand. Dark Cole's hand recoiled quickly, and he looked at Antje, his dismay plastered all over his stolen face.

"Bad boy, Shields. Remember what I told you? Be nice!" Antje scolded. Shields calmed down and whimpered a little. "That's right. Good boy." Sitting down in the passenger seat of the car, Antje looked up at Dark Cole. "Sorry, he hasn't had a lot of socialization. I've been a little busy with my family in town and searching for you, and all."

Dark Cole smiled a nervous smile and replied, "That's okay, but he'll have to get used to me since I'm your boyfriend," and closed the door. Antje screamed internally and gritted her teeth as he walked back around the front of the car to the driver's side. "He'll get used to the taste of your ankle," Antje mumbled before he opened the door. Shield's tail started to wag furiously. "Not yet, Shields. Good boy for being quiet, though. Soon."

TWELVE

CAR RIDES AND DEEP DIVES

T he rolling hills seemed to appear and vanish the same as molasses poured from the jar—it was a tediously long car ride. As Antje dreamt up a multitude of inventive ways to kill him, Dark Cole yammered on about menial nonsense with a remarkable lack of self-awareness. The pattern of Shield's snoring would have lulled Antje to sleep if it weren't for the flames of anxiety and rage burning within her. In between her murderous fantasies, flashes of her confrontation with the draugr pushed their way through, triggering heart palpitations.

What if I freeze again? This time, no one is with me, and I don't have the jade necklace to protect me. What if, what if, what if...

"Are you okay?" Dark Cole asked, looking at her with a warm smile.

"Yeah, sorry—just a little nervous about meeting the Queen," Antje answered candidly, trying to ground herself by gently massaging Shields' back with her fingers as he slept.

"Why don't you relax and get some rest?" he suggested. Antje decided to sustain the appearance of being amiable, and with zero intention of actually napping, she closed her eyes with a nod. As she stared at the back of her eyelids, stars began to twinkle through the black of her vision. The stars twirled around her like a cosmic carnival ride, and suddenly she found herself sitting cross-legged in the ethers, surrounded by nothing but darkness and stars. The sound of Shield's snoring began to wane as she was no longer aware of her physical body.

"Antje!" she heard a deep male voice call from a distance.

"Hello?" she telepathically replied.

"Antje, turn around," the voice instructed with a thick Scandinavian accent.

In her mind's eye, Antje turned her head to the left only to see the same man who she'd met on the cliffside during her near-death experience, and in the back seat of her car. Odin motioned for her to follow.

"Come, Antje. Let us talk," he said, opening a portal that materialized in the blink of an eye. Peering through the doorway, Antje realized it was the mountaintop where she had last seen Odin. "Come. We do not have much time."

Antje followed him through the portal. Two thrones sat side-by-side on the edge of the cliff overlooking a sea of clouds with mountaintops peeking through. Odin sat on the throne to the left, and patted the one to his right. "Sit," he quietly commanded. Antje sat down, observing the eye patch that hadn't been present during their previous meetings.

"You're the Norse God Odin," Antje stated, beleaguered in processing her current situation.

"The one and only," he said with a stoic face and a haughty tone. "You will get the whole picture soon, but for now, you have a task that must be executed—for the safety of all the realms. You are a valkyrie, Antje. Surely you know this by now?" His deep voice ricocheted off the walls of the shallow cave behind them.

"So I'm told," Antje replied, her mind still consumed with disbelief and confusion as to what was happening.

"So you are told? You are one of my most cherished warriors, Antje. This is why I have entrusted you with such a sacred task. The power to change the threads of fate is yours." He grabbed her left hand, which sat on her thigh, and with a squeeze, he brought both of their arms up to the abutted armrests, where he didn't let go. "You must kill Cole."

Antje tried to pull her hand away, but Odin's vice grip held strong. "I know you have already conjured ways to kill the shell of a man next to your body in Midgard, but do not lose focus when the time is at hand—that is not your Cole."

Antje sighed, her shoulders rolling forward a bit. "Oh, you're talking about the imposter?" she confirmed. The tension that had contracted every muscle in her body at the thought of killing Cole, was now released in a single wave of relief.

"Yes, but his characteristics are the same. You must maintain your truth and rid yourself of fear." He squeezed her hand again. "For mortals, fear is useful at times. It protects them. For valkyries, it is a death sentence. I witnessed the coffee shop, Antje. That will not happen again."

Antje felt pangs of shame and regret bounce around her body like electric sparks between Tesla coils.

"You are a valkyrie, Antje. Fear is not a part of your existence. To accept the path of the valkyrie, fear must be eliminated. Stand up." Rising from his throne, he gently pulled Antje's arm, guiding her into a standing position beside him. They then moved to the edge of the cliff in unison. Looking down, Antje could see the tips of trees poking through areas of lesser cloud cover. Odin let go of her hand, and with his index finger, lifted up his eyepatch and plucked his eyeball from his eye socket before placing his eyeball into the palm of her hand. Antje was shockingly unfazed and simply observed the eyeball and its grey-blue iris as if it were a bouncy ball.

"With this eye, you will gain passage to a fearsome part of Helheim—one of the nine realms. Leave this cliff by diving into the Depths of Despair. There, you will leave your fear with the keeper of the realm, and return as the fearless valkyrie you are fated to be." Odin finally released her hand and faced Antje as she tucked the eyeball into the breast pocket of her coat. Odin's hands tenderly held Antje's face as he lovingly kissed her forehead and touched his brow to hers. Antje felt a paternal familiarity with Odin, and now understood why he was referred to as 'The All-Father'. His parental tenderness halted abruptly as he turned Antje toward the edge of the cliff and shoved her off without any notice. Free-falling, but oddly not in a state of panic, Antje heard Odin's voice from above.

"Dive, Antje!" His voice echoed for miles, cutting through the deafening whooshing of air. Antje reoriented herself mid-air, and with her arms tightly pressed to her sides, she was now diving head-first toward the ground. Piercing the clouds, she began to make out a large river stone well below, its age-patinaed fascia blanketed in a velvety moss carpet. Antje knew it was the gateway to The Depths of Despair, and her body approached the well with magnetic precision.

Drawing in a deep breath to hold, she entered the well—realizing it was not filled with water, but a more viscous substance that pushed against her as though it were solid. The resistance of this fluid slowed Antje's movement to a crawl, until she gently landed face-first on a semi-solid, vaporous surface. Scrambling to her feet, Antje lifted her foot and gently placed it onto the fog-like surface beneath her, pushing but never breaking through the surface. Repeating the motion several times, she marveled at the discovery of matter behaving in a way not bound by the laws of physics. Antje scanned her surroundings with childlike curiosity, her observations revealing human figures gliding effortlessly through the realm as if they were in a state of trance.

Antje was directly in the path of a wandering woman in a white chiffon nightgown, which trailed behind her, flowing as though she were walking underwater. In a panic, Antje immediately grabbed the eyeball from her coat and presented it to the woman, who paid no mind to her as she passed right in front of Antje, repeatedly mumbling an unintelligible mantra. The muffled cacophony of ghoulish moans and muttering from the thousands of souls sent a chill down Antje's spine. The entire realm felt claustrophobic to her, and there was a deep sense of hopelessness that permeated every being, vapor, and shadow in it. Antje turned her head to the left, only to see a half-undead woman staring straight at her. This woman differed from the other souls in this reality—she was sentient and engaging. The woman's piercing eyes locked with Antje's. A tsunami of intense energy crashed into Antje as she apprehensively approached the woman.

"Hi... can you... see me?" Antje asked, tucking her chin in a little and cocking her head.

"Yes, Antje. You have something for me," the eerie woman apathetically stated.

"Oh, yes. Sorry!" Antje handed the eyeball to the woman. Suddenly remembering a description she'd read of a half undead woman, it dawned on Antje that she was speaking to the Norse goddess of the dead. "Are you... Hel?", she asked.

"Yes, I am sometimes called by that, but I prefer Hela. The Christians and Jesuits of your existence have sullied my name by associating it with eternal suffering," she explained while receiving the eyeball into her bony hand. Hela placed her other hand on Antje's forehead. Viscous strands of shiny black goop pushed themselves from Antje's pores, filling in the gaps between Hela's fingers and clinging to them. Pulling her hand from Antje's forehead, Hela flung burnished gunk from her hand into the mist around her, where it slowly sublimated. "You're cured." Hela's monotone and sarcastic proclamation triggered a giggle in Antje, but unsure of the goddess's reaction to laughter, Antje held it in out of respect.

"The Dark Queen—she says she's your bloodline, but why are you helping me if that's true?" Antje questioned, sincerely confused.

Hela groaned and rolled her eyes. "The Dark Queen...some of my followers are such self-deluded simpletons at times. She is powerful, but she is no Queen—and certainly no kin of mine. I understand how delicate the balance of the nine realms is, no matter how infuriating it may be, and I would never endeavor to purposefully disrupt it, out of concern for my people and the integrity of my realm. The Dark Queen is a broken mystic who chose power and wrath over healing her trauma. That choice has now galvanized into terroristic power and unchecked rage—both will ultimately be her downfall."

"I mean, why can't you gods just cut her off and be done with it?" Antje asked, watching the last of the viscous yuck disappear.

"You don't think I've tried? She's in Midgard, and none of our incarnations other than my father's are awake yet. You, however, are now fully awake and the perfect incarnation to do it."

"Why am I the perfect incarnation?"

"You ask too many questions. I'm growing bored of this conversation," Hela dully replied, looking at the back of her skeletal hand.

"One... quick one, if you don't mind?" Antje humbly requested. Hela nodded, as she motioned with her hand for Antje to hurry up.

"Are we in the Shore of Corpses... err, Náströnd? Are all these people murderers and cheaters?" Antje questioned, as her eyes followed another entranced passerby.

"It's part of Náströnd, but this section is solely where people who commit suicide, the ultimate expression of fear, end up. Most of these souls have been down here for centuries, trapped in a loop of the exact point in their lives where they succumbed to fear, and it derailed their fate," Hela elaborated.

"So, they're replaying the same traumatic memory over and over in their head for centuries? But, Odin said that fear was helpful for mortals..." Antje trailed off, cocking her head and crossing her arms across her chest.

"Odin," Hela sighed. "He never gives the full story, does he? Fear is useful for self-preservation purposes. Fear is meant to keep them from dying a death that isn't fated for them—but just like anything, when fear becomes unbalanced, it allows the inner demons, or lower self to take over, and the human ceases to be in control of their reactions or perspectives. Completely unchecked, it leads to suicide, and they come here. There are only two exits from this realm: either they must conquer their fear or be rescued."

"Rescued? By who?"

"By one of the Gods of their pantheon, or by a member of their lineage who has laid their ancestral trauma to rest." Hela ran her skeletal fingers through the mist, shaping it as a sculptor would soft clay. "None of this is of concern to you. You got what you came for, now leave. You do not belong here," Hela demanded coldly.

"Okay. Heard. Thank you for your help," Antje smiled, bowing her head momentarily. As Antje's head lifted, Hela placed her hand on Antje's forehead once more.

Antje's eyes shot open. Finding herself back in the car with Shields fast asleep on her lap, she lightly ran her hand the length of his back—more thankful for his stalwart companionship than ever. The vibrations of the gravel road Dark Cole was poorly maneuvering were intense, and Antje felt as though she had been dropped into complete chaos physically. Straightening herself in the seat, she looked out the window.

"You're finally awake! We're almost to our rental cabin," Dark Cole said cheerfully. Antje rubbed her eyes and pulled her cellphone from her bag, only to find she had zero signal.

"Where are we?" Putting her phone away, her eyes absorbed the dense forest that now lined each side of the road's edge.

"About halfway there—Swedish Lapland. Our meeting with the Queen isn't until tomorrow. I figured we could both use some rest, good food, and maybe a few drinks?" Cole turned his head and grinned at Antje before centering his attention back onto the pothole-riddled road.

"The last time we got drinks, you disappeared on me. We can skip that part." Antje noticed her anxiety around walking into a trap was no longer there, as if the live wire that repeatedly sparked in her chest had now been replaced by a grounding mechanism. Hela really had removed her fear, and Antje felt a sense of calm that she couldn't have previously fathomed.

She examined Dark Cole's profile. This creature's transformation was impressive, as every line, curve, and hair was identical to Cole's. Antje's gaze halted at his lips, instantly recalling the out-of-body experience she'd felt during their only kiss. She longed for Cole as she longed for a steaming cup of coffee on a blustery winter morning. Something about Cole made Antje feel like the world wasn't the unkind place she grew up in, and although Antje could clearly handle herself, Cole gave her a sense of security she unknowingly lacked. Antje still couldn't comprehend why she felt so deeply for Cole, but that didn't stop her from persistently analyzing her feelings in an attempt to make sense of it all. She had heard tales of love at first sight and soulmates—but promptly brushed them off as idealism expressed by hopeless romantics whose discontentment stemmed from unrealistic expectations of what love was. Antje was reevaluating her assessment of these concepts and began to ponder if both were the driving force behind her and Cole's unlikely romance.

Dark Cole hit a deep pothole, and the thudding of the wheel well colliding with the edge of it spooked Shields. Springing from a dead sleep to attention, Shields was now barking and growling, with his hackles spiking from his shoulders.

"It's okay, Shields. We're almost there," Antje assured, petting him gently and patting his head. Shields gave Dark Cole a quick side-eye and let out a small rumble before circling a few times and laying back down on her lap. Antje giggled to herself, admiring her adorable companion. "He's grumpy when you wake him up," she said to Dark Cole, who let out a nervous chuckle as they passed a large, occupied house nestled in the woods. A traditional, Swedish guest hut appeared at the end of the road in a small clearing with dog kennels to one side, and a small out-building on the other.

"There are dogs in those kennels!" Dark Cole exclaimed, jutting his head forward over the steering wheel, before turning to look at Shields, who had rolled onto his back and nestled himself into the crevice between Antje's closed legs. His tiny paws pitter-pattered in the air. "I hope they don't eat him," Dark Cole sneered. Realizing his jab was out of character, he chuckled nervously. "Kidding! I'd never let anything happen to that little guy."

"Somehow, I think he can hold his own." Antje smiled at Cole as he parked the car. Five Siberian huskies sprinted from their doghouses, charging the tall, chain-link fence while barking and whining. Antje gently woke Shields and rolled him onto his feet. His ears perked as the symphony of barks became thunderous with the car door now ajar. With zero hesitation, Shields hopped from her lap and ran to the fence where the huskies stood on their hind legs, jumping against the chain link. Instantaneously, every husky lowered themselves and rolled onto their backs, silently submitting to Shields, who turned with his head held high and pranced up onto the small deck of the hut.

"What the?" Dark Cole mumbled, jerking suitcases from the back of the car before slamming the hatchback down. Dark Cole stared at the huskies, who had now returned to jumping on the fence, greeting him with a face full of teeth and ominous growls. He walked around the other side of the car, effectively using it as a shield, and set the bags on the deck as he searched for any sign of a hidden house key. Antje followed, laughing to herself silently at the impressive emotional intelligence of dogs.

The hut was charming in its simplicity. The exterior façade was composed of worn, grey, squared logs, and a black metal roof with a matching chimney. The front door felt inviting, with its large window which offered a peek into the idyllic abode, and the Swedish flag to the left of it was an affirmation that Dark Cole had told the truth—they were indeed in Swedish Lapland.

Dark Cole opened the door, motioning for Antje to go in. The interior of the cabin was small, but the floor-to-ceiling wood panels, hand-carved furniture, and antique wood-burning stove created a delightfully cozy atmosphere. As Antje explored the cabin, she realized the auxiliary building she'd noted on the way in was actually the bathhouse. This cabin felt like the bungalows from deep within the Colorado wilderness where Antje had spent many nights during her childhood, and for the first time since the onset of this unpredictable adventure, she felt somewhat at home.

Upon entering the only bedroom, Antje's comfort was betrayed by the sight of a single queen-sized bed, and she began formulating a plan to maneuver the situation without raising suspicion. Antje would rather spend an eternity with Hela in the Depths of Despair than sleep next to the glorified body-snatcher who approached.

"Hey, so I'm going to take Shields outside and let him run around, and also go find the bathroom," Antje told Dark Cole, heading toward the front door as he placed the bags in a corner of the bedroom.

"Wait, Antje! I'll come with you!"

"To the bathroom? We aren't at that point in our relationship yet, Cole. Relax, I'll be back before you know it," she replied playfully, closing the door. It dawned on Antje that this would be the perfect time to contact the CIA and bring them up to speed. As Antje walked to the bathhouse, she searched her coat pockets for the pen that Special Agent Davis had given her. Opening the door to the bathhouse, Antje's eyes widened. This wasn't like the outhouses in Colorado, where one's butt cheeks fused themselves to the seat during wintertime—this was a truly modern bathhouse, complete with heated floors. Antje noted the sleek porcelain toilet that stood next to a glass-encased freestanding shower and the designer vanity with a custom marble sink on top.

"Problem solved—I'm going to sleep in here tonight," she mumbled.

Antje poked her head from the bathhouse door frame and spotted Shields prancing back and forth in front of the huskies, his chin pointed toward the heavens.

"Shields! Come here!"

He immediately turned and bolted to Antje, sitting at her feet with his eyes locked on hers. "Keep watch for that asshole, okay? If he's coming toward us, let me know, and don't stop barking until he gets to the door, okay?"

"WILL STAND GUARD. GUARDING!" Shields replied.

"Shh. Good boy. I promise we will get you back into your body soon enough." Antje replied, bending down to pat his head and scratch under his chin.

"NOT UNHAPPY ANYMORE. BODY SMALL BUT SHIELDS HAPPY," he replied with a tail wag. Antje giggled, went back into the bathhouse, and shut the door. She examined the pen carefully.

"How the hell does this work?" Antje clicked the pen three times and waited ten minutes before trying again. Nothing happened. Antje began to reassess her plan of contacting the CIA after leaving town. "Shit. I didn't really think this through. What am I going to do? It's not like I can ask Dark Cole for his phone. Hell—I don't even know if his phone has service. We are in the middle of nowhere. I guess maybe I could try the house down the road, but what reason do I have to go down there? Ugh. Leave it to the CIA to give me a pen as a failsafe."

Shields began to bark and yip. She slid the pen back into her coat pocket and opened the bathhouse door with the dread of having to face Dark Cole once more. But, to Antje's surprise, it wasn't Dark Cole—it was a burly man in his early forties, with sun-kissed brown hair, and tanned, weathered skin.

"For you," he said in a thick Swedish accent, handing over a cell phone. He tipped his chin up and raised both his eyebrows, motioning for her to take it.

Antje took the phone and replied, "Thank you?" while not really understanding what was happening. The man motioned for Antje to put the phone to her ear. She did, and he immediately turned around and walked off.

"Antje?" asked a familiar male voice on the phone.

"Who is this?" Antje rapidly questioned, suspicious.

"We don't have a lot of time. It's Special Agent Davis. You activated the pen; we got your location, contacted the property owner, and bought his phone for you since your phone has no signal. He's been instructed to speak to no one but you about this. Keep it on your person, but if you can't use it and you're in danger, click the pen three times, and we will send a team to your location. What are you doing in Swedish Lapland, and why did you activate the pen?" he rapid-fired.

"Of course, you geolocated me with a pen, and you've been tracking my phone; you're the CIA. What was I thinking? Anyway, long story short—I am walking into a trap to find Cole. I'm with a guy who looks like him and is pretending to be him, but isn't him. He said we are halfway to our rendezvous point with the Dark Queen tomorrow. I'll send up a flare with the pen as soon as I find Cole, now that I know it works." Antje opened the bathhouse door, and with the phone still pressed to her ear, she ensured that Dark Cole wasn't anywhere in earshot. Looking down, she saw Shields, sitting at attention with his ears perked as if they were satellite beacons.

"No, don't wait until you find him. Three times when you get there, and I'll have my team surround the place. You guys are going to need all the help you can get, Antje."

"Okay, fine. I'll signal you when I get there. But do not have them come in guns blazing. Tell them to lay low—if I can get him out without a fight, I'd prefer that. There's no need to put a bunch of people in harm's way," she countered. "We'll wait until you guys start fighting before we start shooting—we'll have drones cover the entire area...and Antje? Be safe. Cole will never forgive me if anything happens to you."

Antje was taken aback a bit, as she was surprised that Cole had clearly spoken about her affectionately to Special Agent Davis, but her silence was short-lived as Shields began to sound the alarm and claw at the door.

"I've gotta go. If you don't get a signal from me tomorrow, send a team the next day," Antje instructed, hanging up the phone and tucking it into her bra. Shields suddenly stopped barking, and Antje lunged toward the toilet and flushed it.

"Antje? Are you okay in there?" Dark Cole called out.

"Yes—coming out shortly!" Antje surveyed the bathroom to see what was provided and noticed a bar of soap on the counter. "The owner came and dropped off a bar of soap for us and I think he told me if we needed anything to reach out. I really had to go, so I wasn't paying much attention!" she rambled, opening the door to see Dark Cole's face immediately. Antje noticed that Dark Cole's arms were folded behind his back. He grinned and pulled out a small bouquet of wildflowers, presenting them to Antje like a four-year-old presenting to his neighborhood crush. Antje cringed inside. The real Cole was a level of cool that this charlatan could never achieve, and his attempt angered her. She forced an insincere smile, put her hand over her mouth, and mimicked every romantic comedy she'd ever seen.

"For me!? You shouldn't have! You're so sweet!" she sappily chirped, kissing him on the cheek and closing the door behind her. "I was thinking about the sleeping arrangements—I don't know if I am ready to share a bed yet, but there's not really anywhere else to sleep." She looked down at her shoes, playing the coy, demure woman she had never been.

"Oh, honey, it's okay. I'll sleep on the floor." Dark Cole was clearly disappointed.

"Thank you, darling. The sun is getting low. Let's go in." Antje again kissed his repulsive cheek.

"Sure thing." Dark Cole turned, attempting to hide his crestfallen face.

Antje scooped up Shields with her left arm and carried him as though he were a football. Once inside the cabin, Antje stopped at the bedroom door, turned, and smiled at Dark Cole with insincerity unrivaled by anyone except for high-level politicians; she closed the door before collapsing on the bed with a loud sigh. Shields hopped into bed with her, coiling himself to fit like a puzzle piece into the crook of her stomach as she lay on her side.

Antje attempted to rest, and as she drifted into the state of not-quite-awake, yet not-quite-asleep, she heard the alarming sound of a woman's voice inside her head. Antje didn't have an inner monologue comprised of sound; her thoughts arrived in the form of images, feelings, and inner-knowing, rather than hearing, so the unfamiliar sensation of hearing a voice jolted her awake.

"Who are you?" Antje whispered out loud.

"I'll explain soon. Go outside through the window. Bring the dog," the voice sternly commanded.

"Not before I know who this is." Antje sat up in bed, feeling violated by the intrusiveness of an unknown presence in her head.

"It's Freya. Go. Outside. Now." The voice became increasingly irritated.

Antje's clairsentience confirmed that this was indeed Freya. The energy around Antje now felt very similar to when she had spoken with Thor and spent time with Odin during her out-of-body experience. It was like being wrapped in a warm, weighted blanket. Antje opened the window and placed Shields on the sill of the single-story hut, which he leapt off of, landing in the grass below. Antje climbed through and followed Shields as he confidently walked into the woods with his tail furiously wagging; it was apparent that Shields had also received a communication, and knew exactly where to go. Shields abruptly stopped and sat under a large pine tree, his tail sweeping the soil like a child making snow angels. Antje heard Freya's voice once more.

"Lay your hands flat on the tree and envision a green glow being pulled from it and absorbed into you. You need energy for us to continue," Freya instructed. Antje let out a slight scoff and shook her head slightly, sighing in the theme of "Why not?" and placed her hands on the pine tree. The tips of her fingers freed small flecks of the wrinkled bark as she tried to get her hands as flat as possible against the trunk. With her eyes now shut, she envisioned pulling green energy from the tree. A soothing warmth surrounded her hands, then gradually migrated through her entire body. The feeling was pleasantly electrifying at first, but all of a sudden, Antje became so uncomfortable that she felt the desire to claw her own skin off to free herself from it. She recoiled from the tree as if it were electrocuting her.

"You overcharged, Antje. Now you know. The feeling will pass. Give it 15 minutes. In the meantime, sit down and go to the stars."

"Go to the stars?" Antje rubbed her hands and shook them out, trying to discharge some of the excess energy.

"Yes. Like you did before. Get calm, relax your body, and stare at the back of your eyelids until the stars encircle you and begin to spin," Freya clarified. Antje sat with her back against the tree, closed her eyes, and took three intensely deep breaths, in through her nose, and slowly out through her mouth, when sure enough, the stars once again began to spin in her mind's eye. A woman approached from Antje's left peripheral and extended a hand, each finger adorned in gold rings. Antje could now see her own body and subsequently, her hand reaching out to Freya's. Antje grasped her hand as Freya turned and walked toward a door that seemingly appeared out of thin air. The ivory door's golden handle shimmered, accented by matching gold adornments and light blue hand-painted detail work; Antje could have spent hours appreciating the beauty of this particular door. Within fractions of a second, the door swung open, and Antje's eyes felt the sting of the concentrated luminescence beaming from the other side of the ornately decorated portal. Antje placed her right hand above her eyes and squinted. Following Freya through the doorway, Antje was agog to explore the entirely different kind of world now unfurling before her very eyes. As the last inch of Antje's body passed through the portal, the door slammed shut and vanished behind her.

Beneath her feet were large slabs of marble adjoined with expert precision. Her gaze drifted from the immaculate stonework to reveal a dreamy skyline of striking white buildings and shimmering golden rooftops that varied from thatched, pointed ones, to dome-like structures. Freya beckoned Antje to follow with a wave of her hand, and walked up the inclined path. Antje's lungs were sapped of breath as they turned the corner, which unveiled an opulent, sprawling palace embellished with the same ivory, gold, and cyan flourishes as the portal door. Guards and townspeople stopped dead in their tracks to honor Freya as she and Antje strolled by, Antje spastically bowing her head at each person; clueless as to whether or not she should bow— she opted to bow to everyone.

"Stop that." Freya turned to Antje with her brows furrowed. "You're a valkyrie. You bow to no one, understand? Welcome to Fólkvangr."

Antje nodded, the corners of her lips turning downward as her shoulders touched the bottom of her earlobes in embarrassment. Nearing the prominent entrance of the citadel, Antje's eyes were hypnotically drawn to the groups of buxom, Amazonian-like women who engaged in sparring matches about ten yards to her left. The grunts and growls emitted by the shield-maidens were fearsome and barbaric, but combined with the clashing and clanging of their metal swords and axes, it became musical in nature, as if they were an orchestra playing a symphony of death. Antje halted and stared, her eyes unable to part from the women.

"Ah. You recognize your kind. That's interesting." Freya was delighted, and her demeanor drastically changed to a far warmer one.

"My kind—valkyries?" Antje replied, still staring at the duels. Antje was fixated on two warriors in particular: a brawny redhead with a severe jaw-line, and her opponent, a relatively lean woman with platinum-blonde hair and the fairest skin one had ever seen. Antje's eyes finally disengaged from the duo when a third woman, dressed in a gold-embroidered emerald-green gown, entered the sparring area and sat upon a stout wooden bench that could have sustained the weight of a giant. A smile crept to her pale pink lips and curled into a most curious facial expression. Antje once again felt her eyes magnetically drawn to this woman in a way that was visceral and all-consuming; her gawking only ended by a howl of pain echoing through the plaza like a primordial distress call. The platinum-blonde shield-maid-en had been knocked backward and fallen onto her wrist, which now had several small bones protruding from the skin.

"Sigr!" the burly redhead shouted, towering over the blonde and raising her axe in celebration, suspiciously unfazed by the bellowing of her man-gled counterpart.

"Watch," Freya chimed in with a smile, now also attentively observing the scene that unfolded before them. The woman in the green dress stood up, her strawberry blond hair illuminated by the sun, each strand resem-bling filaments of spun rose gold. The woman's hands began to glow the same hue of green that Antje saw when she visualized pulling energy from the tree in Midgard. The woman sauntered over to the injured valkyrie and nodded at her. Reclining, the battered valkyrie lay her body flat on the matte-finished marble beneath her.

"Who is that?" Antje asked Freya, her eyes again locked on the mystery woman.

"That's Eír. She's a little different from the other valkyries. Keep watch-ing."

Eír knelt down and hovered her hands over her patient's body, anesthetizing the injured valkyrie, whose body immediately went limp. The green energy that now enveloped her hands like gloves slowly extended in green strands from her fingertips to the patient below. Antje watched in total disbelief as the threads began to vertically pull what looked like a glowing green hologram of the woman from her body. The opaque, green replication of the valkyrie's body was now statically hovering above her. Antje squinted as she noticed a red glow coming from the wrist of the floating, chartreuse body. Eír fluidly moved her hands with intentional tenderness as she pinched the red energy between her pointer finger and thumb—pulling and winding it into a ball as if it were energetic yarn. The last of the red energy filament snapped into her hand like a broken guitar string. Holding the red ball of energy in her right hand, Eír pressed it slowly into the marble, palm down, until it was absorbed in its entirety. Lifting her hands back above the unconscious valkyrie, she gradually pressed the energy print back into its physical body. The valkyrie began to stir, rolling her wrist around and rubbing it.

"Thank you, Eír! Good as new!" The blonde valkyrie said before turning to glare at her much larger opponent. "Sigr, my ass—you can't claim victory yet!"

Eír helped the valkyrie to her feet and playfully slapped the redhead on her sinewy shoulder with a cheeky nod. The scarlet-headed valkyrie sighed with angst and gestured her discontentment with both hands outstretched to Freya. Freya laughed, grabbed Antje's hand, and continued walking toward the palace doors.

"Wait here," Freya commanded of Antje as she approached one of the many guards standing at attention in front of the palace doors. Now standing face to face with a guard who bore a scraggly, yet impressively long beard adorned with metal beads, Freya unfolded her hand, revealing only her palm. Silently, the guard unsheathed one of his swords and handed it, handle-first, to Freya. Turning around and returning to Antje, she stopped directly in front of her, closed her eyes, and chanted in Old Norse. As Freya opened her eyes, glowing molten runes engraved themselves in the blood groove of the blade, which turned black as they cooled.

"Here." Freya handed Antje the sword. "This sword will kill anything other than a god with one hit. The Dark Queen is powerful, but she is no god. It has been bound to you and will only be a mere sword to anyone else if they attempt to use it."

Antje received the sword and examined it, using her arms as a shelf. "Thank you, Freya. This is incredible," she said, enthralled by the craftsmanship of the weapon.

Antje felt herself being pulled up and backward, watching Freya and the palace quickly diminish and fade away. Antje once more found herself surrounded by nothing but stars. Among the stars, she heard muffled barking in the distance, and as she gradually became aware of her body again, she felt the sensation of Shields jumping on her lap.

"LIGHT ON. LIGHT ON!" Shields barked, turning his tiny body and pointing it toward the cabin as Antje's eyelids slowly peeled open. Looking to her side, Antje saw the hilt of a sword next to her hand and ran her fingers along the blade, her fingertips reading the ridges of the engraved runes as if they were braille. Antje stood up, sword still in hand, and motioned for Shields to head for the bathhouse; she could get there without being seen from the cabin window. Antje and Shields made a beeline for the outbuilding and entered the bathhouse, unseen. Sliding the sword's blade between the rear of the vanity and the wall, Antje placed a small trashcan in the corner to obscure the hilt of the sword.

"I'll get it in the morning when I go to shower. How am I going to hide this after that, though?" Antje ruminated aloud.

"POTION. USE POTION."

"Oh, you're right, Shields! I bet there's a potion that can shrink this or change it into something else. That seems like something Philomena would slip into my arsenal of potions." Appreciative of his help, Antje patted Shields on the head, when they both heard the sound of a twig snapping outside. Composing herself, Antje opened the bathhouse door.

"There you are! Are you okay?" Dark Cole questioned, standing too close to her for comfort.

"Oh, yes. I couldn't sleep, and we both had to pee," Antje sheepishly replied, looking down at Shields who simply barked and wagged his tail in agreement.

"I'll walk you back to the cabin. How did you get out?" Dark Cole asked, scratching the top of his head and turning to walk back to the cabin.

"I went out the window—I didn't want to wake you up by walking on those creaky old floors while you were trying to sleep on them. Aren't I the most thoughtful girlfriend ever?" Antje bumped her shoulder into him playfully as they strolled. He chuckled quietly.

"You didn't have to do that, Antje."

"Oh, but I did. What can I say? I'm thoughtfully sneaky." Antje turned her head toward Dark Cole and flashed a sincere grin while playfully bringing her shoulder to her chin.

Thirteen

Fylgias & Jotuns

Antje's strawberry-blonde hair splayed across the flannel pillowcase like a hand fan as the warm rays of sun kissed her porcelain-skinned cheek. Rubbing the sleep from her eyes, Antje rose from her bed. Awoken by Antje's movement, Shields stretched his tiny body to its limits, his tongue unfurling as he opened his miniature jaws and released a squeaky yawn. Shields' morning ritual was interrupted by the loud creak of foot-steps on the other side of the bedroom door; his hackles stiffened.

"Today's the day, buddy. You ready for this?" Antje asked, gently scratching Shields' cheek with her index finger. His rear-end wiggled, and his woolly ears perked up. "That's what I thought. Let's go find Cole."

Antje dressed herself and sifted through her bag for an answer to her sword dilemma, finding a small vial with a label that read:

Transmutation Potion
Anoint non-sentient item with three drops of potion. Close eyes and visualize end result of transmutation in the mind's eye. To reverse, wipe potion off.

"Phil, you've done it again, you beautiful, wild woman," she whispered to herself, with a sigh and a smile. Antje pocketed the potion and exited the bedroom. Dark Cole was searching through the main living space like a dog on a bone.

"Hey, babe. Whatcha lookin' for?" Antje questioned with one eyebrow raised.

"Water. How is there no water in here?" he replied with disdain, while rapidly opening and slamming every cabinet door in the kitchen. Antje giggled as she identified an opportunity to solve her quandary of transmuting the sword without arousing suspicion.

"It's a dry cabin, silly. See that white jug? It has to be filled in the bathhouse. Give it to me. Shields needs to go potty, and I need to brush my teeth. We'll be in tight quarters all day—I'm basically doing you two favors."

"Oh. I didn't see that on the reservation. That's stupid," he grumbled, slamming his closed fist on the kitchen countertop. Antje grabbed the water container and exited the cabin with Shields tight on her heels. Nearing the bathhouse, something large caught her eye on the edge of the forest. A large, snow-white moose stood in the exact spot where she and Shields had entered the forest previously. Antje froze as the moose was within charging distance, and she knew the dangers of moose all too well from her encounters with them back home. Much to her surprise, Shields launched himself at full speed toward the moose, his tail oscillating as though it were a propeller. Antje's heart pounded, and as soon as she opened her mouth to recall Shields, she witnessed a most unusual event: the moose lowered its head and allowed Shields to lick its nose. Shields whipped around and casually trotted toward Antje. Slowly raising its head, the moose followed suit.

"FRIEND! FRIENDLY FRIEND!" Shields barked. Stopping directly in front of Antje, the moose's nostrils flared as his neck stretched to sniff her face. Following a couple of deep whiffs, the moose gently nuzzled its gigantic head into the crook of Antje's neck. Relieved and amazed, she reached up and gently stroked the moose's taut, strong neck. As its coarse fur ran through her fingers, she felt an electric charge zap her fingers—like when one walks through carpet in freshly dried wool socks. The moose gradually pulled away from Antje and disappeared into the forest.

Antje analyzed the tips of her fingers, curious as to what they'd just been charged with, her mind still struggling to grasp the concept of snuggling a wild moose, let alone a white one—the rarest of all. Shields barked to remind Antje of the mission looming in the bathhouse.

"Right—the sword. Good boy, Shields.," Antje loudly exhaled, took a few steps forward, and entered the bathhouse. Scooting the small trash can to the side with her right foot, she found the sword, exactly as she'd left it. Antje set the jug in the sink and turned the faucet on—the sound of running water would mask any noise that could occur from the transmutation process. Picking up the sword with her right hand, she reached into her front left coat pocket and grasped the vial between her thumb and index fingers.

As instructed, she poured three drops on the blade of the sword, closed her eyes, and envisioned the sword shrinking and bending into a wearable ring. The hilt shrank rapidly in her hand, and as she opened her eyes, nothing lay in her hand but a small, silver ring, fashioned from a tiny sword. Antje ensured it was safe to wear by running her finger along the ring's edges—her mind's eye had seen them as blunted; therefore, the ring had rounded edges. Antje slipped it onto her right ring finger and shut off the tap.

Exiting the bathhouse, Antje found the property owner, who had gifted her the phone, marching down the driveway toward her.

"The rare elk..." he said, pointing at the forest line with his mouth agape. Antje approached the man, water jug in tow.

"You saw that? It was surreal. I've never even seen a white moose before, let alone had one press its face into me."

"They're called elk here. The elk is a sign of protection from my...gods..." he trailed off, still gaping at the tree line. Suddenly, his head whipped to the right, his eyes now locked with Antje's.

"What are you?" the man bluntly questioned, now looking down at the Mjolnir around her neck.

"I'm Antje."

"I did not say who; I said what. The day before you arrive, I have a dream of the All-Father telling me to give a cellphone to a woman with a Mjolnir. You arrive, and a man offers to pay me thousands of kronor for a phone that I would have to pay someone to buy from me—and now, the white elk, it touches you. What are you?" he questioned, stepping closer to Antje and examining her, his head tilting curiously.

"Are you a mys...tic?" Antje asked, uncomfortable with her bubble being invaded.

"No. I am a Norse heathen, just like my ancestors," he boasted.

Antje's lips curled with amusement. Hushing her voice, Antje leaned in toward him while looking toward the cabin. "You're never going to believe this, but—I'm a valkyrie. Also, that guy with me is a body-snatching monster who thinks I don't know what he is, and the element of surprise is really my only upper hand right now—so, please don't tell him anything about the phone or the elk if he comes out."

"A valkyrie—what an honor! I'm Leif Sarlsson." He grabbed Antje's hand and shook it enthusiastically. "The elk was a communication from the Gods that you are protected. You will be victorious! I will come and help you fight." Leif puffed his chest and widened his stance.

"Nice to meet you too, Leif. Unfortunately, I think I have to do this one on my own. But, thanks for the phone, your bravery—and for your silence. You're a good man." Antje reached out and shook Leif's hand, clasping it with both of hers and flashing a genuine smile.

"Well, at least let me send you to your victory with a bottle of my homebrewed mead. It's not every day I get the honor of meeting a valkyrie," he demanded, turning and speedily heading back toward his home.

As Shields took one last walk of hubris past the huskies, Dark Cole exited the cabin with bags in hand. "What did he want?" he asked, packing the bags into the back of the car and slamming the hatch shut.

"Oh, nothing, we just got to talking about the history of Sweden and our ancestors. He's really interesting. He brews mead and ran home to grab us some for the road. What a nice guy! You're all packed up—do you still need the water?" she asked, eyeballing the bags in the back of the car and lifting the water jug slightly.

"Yeah—I still need coffee and to brush my teeth, too. I can't be trusted to drive without coffee, and I don't want to greet the queen with bad breath." Dark Cole wafted the air in front of his mouth with his hand and gave a cheeky grin.

"Well then—I'll take it inside." Antje chuckled as she walked to the cabin and set the jug down on the kitchen counter. She headed to the bedroom to see if anything had been left behind. As her eyes scanned the room, the edge of the forest caught her eyes through the window once more. There it was, the white elk, watching her from the trees. Antje ran outside toward the white elk and the bathhouse.

"Where are you going?" Dark Cole hollered at her, as she sprinted past him.

"I left the water running!" she yelled back. As Antje advanced on the bathhouse, she had a clear view of where the elk had stood previously, but saw nothing except the pristine forest edge. Disappointed, Antje entered the bathhouse and turned on the hot water. Splashing her face several times, she mellowed herself before embarking on yet another lengthy drive with Dark Cole and his obnoxiously cheerful antics. After patting her face dry with a towel, she looked into the foggy mirror and saw a three-pronged rune in the dead center of it. The longer she looked at it, the more she recognized it as the elgiz rune, and flipped her Mjolnir over to compare—the runes were identical. Antje turned off the hot water and laughed to herself, straightening the sword on her ring finger.

"Alright, gods—I hear you. I'm protected," she said, leaning forward, and staring herself in the eyes. "Let's go kill the Bitch Queen."

The tires hummed on the pavement, lulling Antje into a state of tranquility. With her fear having been removed, or at least massively subdued, Antje found herself able to slip into a peaceful state of being rather quickly. She heard a woman's voice in her head that sounded nothing like Freya. The voice was tender, but the energy that now surrounded Antje was strong.

"Hello, Antje."

"Who is this?" Antje inquired in her head.

"That elk you saw. That is your fylgia," the woman answered.

"My feel...gyuh? What?" Antje's head involuntarily cocked with confusion.

"Come see me in the stars. I will meet you there."

"Not until you tell me who this is," Antje demanded—these intrusions were becoming increasingly irritating for her. The woman gently laughed.

"A temper like your father's—of course. I'm Frigg. Now, come."

Antje closed her eyes, mortified that she'd caught an attitude with Odin's wife. Within thirty seconds of closing her eyes, she saw the revolving star space in her mind's eye. A beautiful woman in a fitted royal blue, silken dress, detailed with elaborate golden embroidery approached from her left. The woman's matching cape dragged behind her like a train of an expensive wedding gown, its intricately embellished clasp resting against her flawless ivory chest. The woman extended her delicate hand to Antje.

"Come. Your fylgia is waiting." Frigg locked her kind eyes with Antje's. There was a deep sense of familiarity, reverence, and adoration of this woman for Antje. Taking her hand, Frigg used a key enrobed in white light to open a door that appeared in the ether. The door resembled something more akin to a tall garden gate, the blackened vertical planks held together only by two horizontal iron strips—it was remarkably plain in comparison to the others Antje had seen thus far.

Stepping through the gateway, Antje felt her first footstep sink into the ground. As her second foot landed, she looked down at both feet, rubbing her eyes—these transitions were always disorienting and a tad blinding. Her feet rested upon black sand, and the unmistakable scent of salty ocean air hit her olfactory receptors in perfect synchronization with the sensation of sea spray kissing the back of her neck and arms. Antje looked over her shoulder to see a choppy ocean performing its daily tidal dance with the beach. The sounds and smells of this realm were hypnotizing, and Antje again felt oddly at home—considering there were no oceans in Colorado.

Turning back around, Antje watched as Frigg headed toward a small outcropping of trees lining the far edge of the beach. Antje followed, awestruck by the white-capped mountains in the backdrop. Frigg climbed the chiseled stone stairs that led into the forest, stopping a few steps in and beckoning for Antje to join her. As Antje ascended the stairs, a secret outcropping unfurled; the tree-shrouded enclave was not more than maybe ten feet wide. Flames flickered from a stone-lined fire pit in the center of the clearing, with a bench on either side. Bottles, animal pelts, feathers, rocks, and bowls neatly sat upon rough-hewn shelves, which were mounted to the surrounding trees and created the appearance of walls. It was an intimate and magical space. Frigg motioned Antje to sit on the opposite bench from the one she lowered herself onto. Settling onto the bench, Antje heard a rustling behind her and instinctively reached for Daggert, which was now eternally concealed inside her boot.

Frigg laughed. "Relax, dear one. It is a friend behind you. Turn around."

Antje lessened her grip on Daggert and slowly turned her upper body, finding herself face-to-face with the white elk.

"This is your fylgia." Frigg's face beamed with fondness when she looked at Antje. As the elk pressed its forehead against Antje's, she instinctively raised her hands and placed them on either side of its face. The elk let out a sigh, turned, and stepped back into the forest. As Antje watched its body slowly disappear into the forest, she turned to Frigg, wide-eyed.

"I know. You want to know what this is all about. A fylgia is a spirit who guides you in life—a guardian of sorts. A mortal seeing their fylgia is an omen of death, but the incarnation of a valkyrie is no mortal, is it, dear?" Frigg walked through the fire and seated herself on the bench next to Antje, taking Antje's hands into her own and clasping them gently. "Your fylgia will show you where your path leads. Trust it. But this is not the full reason you are here with me now." Frigg kissed Antje on the forehead, leaned back, and turned her head toward the forest behind them. "Eír!" Frigg's voice rang out like a melody. Frigg smiled and patted the top of Antje's hands with her right hand. "You have to be whole before you face the Dark Queen, my love."

"Whole?" Antje's eyebrows raised.

"Whole. You will see." As Frigg finished her sentence, the strawberry-blonde valkyrie she had witnessed with Freya entered the outcropping. "Ahh. Here she is. This, Antje, is your higher self."

Antje blinked, gawking at Eír, who was now sitting on the bench opposite Frigg and Antje, with joy exuding from every pore of her face.

"Finally, we meet in my realm." Eír's glow continued to flourish.

"Hi. I'm... you're... my.... higher self?" Antje stammered.

"You are my incarnation, Antje—there to help keep the balance in Midgard; that's your life path. It always has been. That's why you've seen death your entire life, that's why everyone comes to you for healing—because you carry a piece of me, and I am the valkyrie of healing. We have a formidable adversary in the Dark Queen, Antje. Odin has told me you will need to learn your healing powers before you meet her." Eír closed her eyes and placed them palm-down on the wooden bench. "Our healing energy is provided by nature. Trees, our best energy allies, will give energy to you freely, and without limits." Eír's hands began to glow with the same green energy Antje had overcharged herself with in the woodlands of Swedish Lapland. Frigg's eyes twinkled with excitement as she squeezed Antje's hands, which were still enveloped her own.

"I've seen you do this before," Antje interjected. "Outside of Freya's palace— you healed the other valkyrie."

"Hah. Right!" Eír laughed, the green glow in her hands now fading on command. "Now, it is your turn to try," Eír instructed, rising to her feet. Frigg too stood, and they positioned themselves around the flames between them. Frigg held onto Antje's left hand as she stood and reached out to Eír with the other. Antje joined them in standing around the fire.

"Grab my other hand, and close your eyes," Eír instructed, extending her slender, pale-white fingers to Antje, who obliged. Eyes now closed, Antje heard chanting in Old Norse and felt an encouraging squeeze from Frigg before both women let go of her hands. Antje opened her left eye first, hesitant to find what new absurdity loomed over her. She found herself and her two Norse companions in a lush green meadow, surrounded by snow-capped mountains, a stream trickling behind her. In the middle of the paddock stood nothing but a wooden table lined with two benches. Antje caught movement out of her peripheral vision and turned her head to find a gargantuan teenage boy carried by two equally enormous elders.

"Antje, this is Bjarke. His legs do not work," Eír explained. "He and his parents are jotuns—giants as you in Midgard call them. Bjarke visited Lyf-jaberg, where I live, to seek the help of the jotun healing goddess, Menglod. I am one of her handmaidens, and after looking at his legs, she decided he is ours to heal." Eír turned and motioned for Bjarke to lay down on the table. Antje was awestruck by the enormity of the family. As his parents carried him to the table, Frigg linked arms with Antje, again grasping her hand and clasping it between hers.

"You will be spectacular, Antje. Do not doubt yourself," Frigg encouraged. Antje took great comfort in this statement for some reason unbeknownst to herself, and stood a little taller. She gave a nod and let go of Frigg's hands before approaching Bjarke.

"Please, get as comfortable as you can, Bjarke. My name is Antje. I'm from Midgard, and we will get you sorted out shortly," she assured him, gently gripping one of his willowy legs. She looked to Eír, who pointed with her chin at the bench that was touching Antje's knees. Antje placed her hands on the bench and closed her eyes, visualizing energy being pulled from it. Once her body was sufficiently electrified, she removed her hands from the bench and opened her eyes to see green light sheathing both hands.

"Now, put them above him and let the energy flow from your hands down to his body. When it connects, you will feel a shift in your energy as it mingles with his. Think of it like fishing—you will know when a fish has taken your bait, because there is resistance. Same feeling here, and just as when you fish, you have to pull it toward your hands, slowly." Eír's comparison made complete sense to Antje, and she felt confidence swelling within her.

Antje took two deep breaths in through her nose and out through her mouth to center and calm her energy. As her hands hovered above Bjarke's body, she began to feel resistance. She gradually pulled her hands upward, extracting the chartreuse energetic body from Bjarke. His parents gasped, Bjarke's father pulling his mother into his arms as she buried her head into his chest. His energy hologram now hung right below Antje's hands.

"Very good, Antje. Now, see the large, glowing red ball at the base of his spine? Grab ahold of it with your fingers and gently pull—again, like you are carefully reeling in a fish." Eír used her hands to demonstrate in the air.

Antje complied, pinching the red orb with her right index finger and the pad of her thumb. As she drew her hand back toward her, the crimson energy sphere began to unravel like a ball of yarn. The red strand burned and pulsed between her fingers as if she had hit them with a hammer. Antje continued in spite of the discomfort and began to wind it around her left hand. Several minutes of winding the energetic filament passed, and the fiery orb at the base of Bjarke's energetic spine had now shrunk to the size of a pea before Eír once again chimed in.

"Very slowly now. The last bit will have extra resistance and will pop as it exits the body. It is far less painful for the patient if you do this as carefully as you can."

Antje looked down at Bjarke, whose hands had literally cracked the wood of the table from clutching it so tightly.

"I will be gentle, Bjarke. You're doing great. We're almost done," Antje reassured him. Bjarke's eyes were squeezed shut, and he anxiously nodded his head in affirmation. Antje slowly pulled the thread until she felt the aforementioned pop; Bjarke released the table and took a huge sigh, his entire body collapsing from exhaustion as chunks of wood fell to the grass below.

"Now, Antje, place the ball into the ground. The ground will absorb and disperse it," Eír mentioned, lowering onto her knees and tapping the soil with her pointer finger. Antje followed suit and pulled the red strands from her left hand, pressing them into the soil where they dissipated quickly. Her hands felt numb from the sustained pain she had endured. Antje jumped to her feet and asked Bjarke to wiggle his toes. Bjarke gave his parents a concerned look, his mother rushing to his side and grabbing his hand, with

Dad not too far behind. Bjarke's face lit up with delight as he witnessed the wiggle of his toes. His mother let out a loud sob as joyous smiles crept to everyone's lips.

"Now, lift your legs, please. One at a time," Antje requested. Bjarke struggled, grunting and groaning as his left leg scarcely lifted from the table, only a small glimpse of daylight to be had between the wood and his calf. His attempt to lift the right leg, no different. Antje shot Eír a glance of concern. Eír grinned and gave a quick nod.

"His muscles have atrophied, Antje. It will take him time to have full range of motion—but he is no longer paralyzed."

Bjarke sighed once more in relief, his mother draped herself across his chest, still sobbing. "It's okay, Mom. I'll work hard, and I'll be able to help with the farm in no time." Bjarke patted his Mom's head and looked up at his father, whose glassy-eyed smile warmed Antje's heart.

"I feel exhausted." Antje flopped onto one of the benches.

"Replenish your energy. You're sitting on a battery," Eír replied, pointing to the bench. Antje once again closed her eyes and siphoned energy from her seat. "Very good, Antje. I think this is sufficient training for what is coming." Eír looked to Frigg for corroboration.

"It is," Frigg confirmed, beaming with pride. "You are magnificent, my dear Antje. Rejoin your shisa in Midgard. Time is closing in on you," she warned, clapping her hands once.

Antje's eyes jolted open. The road ahead twisted and turned. Shields licked her hand twice, his tail wagging excitedly.

"You're awake! You nodded off for several hours. I guess you didn't sleep well after your midnight pee break, huh?" Dark Cole teased, turning his head to look at her before fixing his eyes back on the open road.

"Yeah, sorry. Where are we?" Antje rubbed her eyes and cracked the window for some fresh air.

"We're an hour out from the Queen. Don't go back to sleep."

Antje examined her hands. They felt different than before. They felt heavier but energized, as though she was full of low-voltage electricity. "I won't. I'm ready to meet the Queen," she replied, spinning the sword-ring on her hand with her thumb.

FOURTEEN

KILLS AND CATCHES

The remainder of the drive proved to be uneventful, and Antje spent most of it reflecting on the Norse realms, along with what had been shared with her about her life path and her abilities.

"Here we are!" Dark Cole announced, turning onto a forest-lined dirt road. Antje glanced at the clock; it was almost midnight, but the sun still poked through the forest's leaves, printing a pattern on the road ahead that danced erratically with each gust of wind.

"Where exactly is here?" Antje asked, shielding her eyes as the sunlight strobed through the forest canopy.

"Northern Finland—still in Lapland."

As the road exited the trees, a clearing appeared, revealing an ice castle surrounded by a winter wonderland, a most peculiar sight in the midst of summer. The castle towered over the surrounding woodlands, its intricate ice block carvings and statues woven into the architecture.

"What the–?" Antje trailed off. Straightening herself in the seat, she leaned forward, her nose nearly touching the windshield as the boundaries of the frosted road began to vanish under several inches of compacted snow. Shields stirred with her movement, now standing with his tiny paws on the passenger door, staring out the window.

"You didn't think she'd be in some shack in the woods, did you?" Dark Cole playfully patted Antje's knee.

"Yeah, but—an ice castle? Isn't that a little on the nose, and—impossible in the middle of summer?" Antje's head cocked, her left eyebrow furrowing as she tried to make sense of the gratuitous display of magic before her.

"I told you—she's powerful!" Dark Cole grinned, turning the steering wheel and parking the car. "Here, I noticed you didn't bring a jacket. Take mine." He handed Antje an oversized black coat. Slipping into the coat, she stepped out of the car with Shields and covertly searched the pockets with her fingertips for anything nefarious, coming up literally empty-handed. Glistening snowflakes floated delicately through the air, a few alighting on her nose, others liquefying between her eyelashes. Shields' tiny mouth snapped at random snowflakes as he hopped on his hind legs, barking.

Antje glared at the arctic castle, lording over the land. The guards perched on either side of the entryway stiffened simultaneously as Antje, Shields, and Dark Cole advanced, each guard opening their respective side of the carved ice doors. Antje felt the energetic maelstrom surrounding her—dark and cloying, like the air was made of tar. The stench of death permeated the air, inciting Shields' nose to work overtime. Antje struggled to suppress her nausea, until entering the snow castle, when she immediately realized why the Dark Queen had chosen a magical ice castle as her headquarters—it dulled the stink of her cohorts.

Dark Cole motioned to close the doors and nodded at a droopy-eared, crocodile-green goblin who stood at the base of an icy staircase—its banister adorned with icicles, as a runner of compressed snow carpeted each step. The goblin nervously bowed to Dark Cole and hurried up the stairs. While waiting, Antje and Shields methodically examined every iota of the atrium in which they stood. Imposing depictions of dragons and trolls were carved with meticulous detail into the outer walls, clumps of hoarfrost acted as valances and lined the upper frames of the building's tall, ice-paned windows. Had this not been a perilous situation, Antje would have delighted in the whimsy of the castle and its creative, wintry embellishments.

Not moments later, a ghoulish apparition sashayed down the stairs, slipping through time and space as though it ceased to exist.

"My Queen." Dark Cole fell to his knees and bowed his head. A low growl escaped Shields' bared teeth as he positioned himself in front of Antje, lunging at the ghastly being. With a snap of her fingers, Antje heeled Shields, who promptly sat by her side, dutifully awaiting her next command.

Antje straightened her spine and pulled her shoulders back before scoffing at the apparition. "I traveled all the way here and you're... you're what? A ghost?"

"Foolish child!" the Dark Queen bellowed, sending bone-chilling terror through her servants, who instantly made themselves small—hiding in the nooks and shadows of the frozen fortress. "You really think I would show myself to you, a valkyrie, upon first meeting you? Hah!" The Dark Queen's voice was shrill and grating.

"For being the infamously evil Dark Queen, that's pretty cowardly—but smart, I suppose. Why am I here?" Antje asked, plainly.

"Well, Antje...I brought you here to ask one thing of you: join your precious lover and help me right the wrongs of the stupid, meddling gods."

Antje brought her hand to her chin and folded her opposite arm underneath, as if she was pondering something profound. "The wrongs of the gods—explain."

"Light always thinks it is superior to dark, and it keeps us locked up, hidden away like some shameful secret to be kept! We are not shameful, and we will not be held hostage by the gods' skewed sense of morality any longer!" the Dark Queen erupted. The righteous indignation and the panache with which she expressed it was an intoxicating combination, and Antje finally understood the appeal.

"Okay. So, suppose you're no longer in hiding. What of the normies? How do you see this playing out?" Antje tilted her head.

"The way it is supposed to play out. My goddess—Hel, her blood runs through my veins, and she believes the time has come for the underworld to rule Midgard."

Antje dropped her hand from her chin, which slapped against her forearm as it landed. With her arms now crossed, Antje sighed and tepidly responded, "So, Ragnarok is your plan, then? That's so—uninspired."

"Ragnarok is a tale of Odin," the Dark Queen growled. "He says all will be destroyed because it is he who is vying for supreme power—but he lies! Only the light will be destroyed!" The apparition glitched, her flawless face momentarily phasing into a gnarled one, with a vertical line of puckered scar tissue that ran from her forehead down to her chin. As the Dark Queen composed herself, the apparition returned to its previous porcelain-like perfection.

Antje's eyebrows raised, and her chin dipped toward her chest. "Right. So, I'm part of the light, am I not? You want me to join a side that will ultimately destroy me?"

"Not if you join me. Valkyries were never meant to do the bidding of the Aesir and Vanir Gods. They are meant to be dealers of death! It does not get darker than that, you foolish child."

Another small growl vibrated in Shields' chest, and Antje glanced down at him. "It's alright, boy. We're just chatting." Antje's attention returned to the Dark Queen's eerie projection. "Okay, fair point. Let's say I join you—what's expected of me?" Antje asked, dropping her hands to her hips.

"Fight alongside me—lead my army with your lover as your second. If you can manage to inspire the same loyalty and obedience in my men as you do in that furry little rat of yours, we will easily restore all as it should be!"

"If I lead this army for you, I want to rule all of the Norse realms. All of them."

"Never!" the Dark Queen shrieked like a banshee. "I will never give you my goddess's precious underworld. The rest of the realms—do with them what you like." The apparition floated back and forth in mid-air, jutting toward Antje to gauge her reaction. Antje didn't flinch.

"Fine. But I get to call the shots for my army. You give me an objective, and it's my call on how we deliver on it. Deal?" Antje negotiated. A few moments of tense silence overtook the atrium.

"Deal. But know this, girl: if you turn on me, I will wipe everyone you have ever cared about off the face of this planet–mystics and normies alike."

A wry smirk grew on Antje's lips. "I would expect no less." Antje tapped Dark Cole's shoulder as he continued to kneel beside her. "Get up. I need to see what kind of shape our army is in," Antje snidely demanded. "Wait—when do I get to meet you in person, my Queen?" The words "my Queen" left the putrid taste of expired sushi on Antje's tongue.

"In due time. Once you've proven yourself to be loyal, we shall have tea in my ice garden together. Until then, don't fuck things up, valkyrie." The ghoulish specter dissipated.

Antje turned to Dark Cole. "Well? Show me around."

The snowy abode sprawled like a frost-bitten maze, ripe for getting lost in. Thankfully, the Arctic Circle's twenty-four-hour sun kept the castle bathed in light, and after about an hour, Antje got the lay of the land.

At the conclusion of their tour, Dark Cole opened a heavy wooden door, revealing a spacious bedroom—one that eclipsed the size of her entire cabin back home. Shields charged through the doorway, scouring every inch of the room with his sniffer. An oversized four-poster bed adorned with velvety, merlot-colored curtains sat next to an inglenook fireplace, comprised of stones carved from snow. The black flame within the colossal fireplace burned hot, yet did not melt the structure encasing it.

"Her powers are incredible," Antje said, her mouth agape. "Black flames that don't melt snow but heat the room somehow... now I've really seen it all."

Dark Cole chuckled and put two more logs on the fire. He flashed a warm smile at Antje as he walked toward the two large windows to the right of the fireplace and pulled each set of thick, damask curtains to a close, the rime ice fringe of the curtains twinkling in the moonlight as they met in the middle and interlocked like a zipper.

"Get some rest. We will get started early tomorrow, General Antje. I don't suppose you're ready to share a bed yet?" He stopped mid-step and flashed a coy grin at her.

"You suppose correctly. I am not ready—although this place is a bit spooky and some company would be nice. I'll just have to make do with Shields." Antje patted the bed and winked at Shields, who jumped onto the bed, circling several times before lying down.

"I had to ask. Goodnight... sleep tight... don't let the bedbugs bite," he trailed off, closing the bedroom door behind him. Antje's eyes rolled as she pulled Daggert from her boot before kicking both of them off. She slid Daggert underneath the fluffy goose-down pillow—not even releasing the hilt before the shifting of shadowy footsteps through the crack beneath the door caught Antje's attention. Quickly retracting Daggert from under her pillow, she silently crept across the floor, her hand gently wrapping around the frigid door handle before slowly pulling down it. Motioning for Shields to follow, Antje swiftly opened the door with Daggert in hand—ready to strike. To her surprise, it was her fylgia slowly walking down the hallway—its hooves making nary a sound.

Frigg's voice rang like a bell through her head. *"Your fylgia will show you where your path leads. Trust it."*

Antje noiselessly followed the moose down the hallway with Shields at her heels until it walked through a door to her right and dematerialized. Antje attempted to open the locked door, to no avail.

"I thought I told you to get some sleep," Dark Cole said. Surprised, Antje swung around, pointing Daggert at him before relaxing her stance and sighing with relief.

"You scared me! I was thirsty, and there was no glass in my room. Is this the kitchen? Why is it locked?" Antje casually pointed at the door as Shields sat down next to her left foot.

"No. The kitchen is down the hall and downstairs. This room is off-limits to everyone," Dark Cole grabbed Antje's shoulders and positioned her toward the direction of the kitchen.

"Oh, okay. Lead the way, will you? I'm parched." Antje motioned for him to walk ahead. As she followed, she turned around and stared at the door.

That must be where they're keeping Cole, or the Dark Queen. Either way, I need in.

After a short walk down a flight of glacial stairs, her socks sticking to each step slightly, Antje reached the kitchen. She sat on a wooden, spindled chair and pulled her knees up to her chest, placing her feet in her hands to keep them warm. Her breath was visible as her nose began to turn numb. Dark Cole retrieved her water and kissed her on the forehead before kneeling down and rubbing her feet furiously with his hands. Antje knew in her head that this wasn't her Cole, but her heart fluttered as his eyes met hers. Realizing her momentary lapse in judgment, Antje snapped herself out of it and shot up from the chair.

"Thanks, babe! You're the best!" she said quickly, following with a fake yawn and an exaggerated stretch. "Oh, I'm pooped. I better get to bed. I can find my way back if you're tired of playing tour guide." Antje kissed Dark Cole on the cheek and exited the room. She wasn't more than ten feet up the stairs before she heard a loud ruckus and a man screaming bloody murder.

Antje turned her head over her shoulder. "Cole...what was that?" She hollered, frozen in place on the stairs for several seconds. Cole came running to the base of the stairwell, looking up at her.

"It's the weird landlord from Sweden—why the hell is he here?" he replied.

Antje cringed. "Go find him and stop the guards from doing whatever they're doing. I'm sure this is just a misunderstanding—we don't need to draw any unnecessary attention. I'm going to put my boots on, and I'll be right down to handle it."

Antje ran to her room with Shields tight on her heels, slipped her boots on, and slid Daggert back into the right one, along the outside of her ankle. Antje rifled through her potions, looking for anything to help, when she spotted one with a label that said:

Undeath Potion

Anoint sentient being with one drop on neck. It will not have any effect if put on skin anywhere else.
Choke being until unconscious, where all bodily functions will be frozen, giving the appearance of death.
To reverse, tap between the eyes of the affected being three times while chanting: "Once dead. Twice alive. Three times, you survive!"

A plan promptly unfurled in Antje's head, and she placed one drop on the inside of her right thumb. Hiding the bag of vials under the sink in her bathroom, behind a pile of toiletries, Antje ran down the hallway and bounded to the edge of the stairs where she regained her poise. Chin lifted and chest puffed, she looked over the edge of the stairwell to see a bloodied and battered Leif, being held by two large guards, unable to stand on his own two feet with his head hanging low.

"What is this?" Antje yelled, angrily descending the stairs.

"An intruder, General. He says he knows you," one of the guards snarled. Antje walked to Leif, and with her index finger under his chin, pulled his head up until his swollen, bloodshot eyes were level with hers.

"Stupid normies! Why would you follow us? Who do you work for?" she demanded an answer, using her eyes to motion toward her Mjolnir to signal "protection" to Leif.

"I... I work for no one. You left your mead." Leif barely finished his sentence through his split lips, blood dripping from his mouth and pooling on the floor as the dark soldiers around him salivated at the smell of it. Antje turned around and walked a couple of feet away, her back to Leif.

"You followed us for ten hours to give us mead? Lies!" Antje yelled, turning around, running at him, and strangling him with both hands. The guards released him and stepped back. Antje continued to choke Leif until he collapsed, lifeless on the floor. Out of breath, she stumbled back from Leif's motionless body and charged one of the guards, her finger a mere half-inch from his nose. "And you—the incompetency! Why was this man even allowed in the castle's boundaries! I had to kill him! Do you have any idea of the mess you've made? There are cameras on the roads, you idiots! They know where his car has gone. Not a good start—not good at all!" she continued, rearing around and backhanding the other guard across the face. "Put him in his car—I saw a lake coming in. I will handle this, as apparently none of you are capable of handling anything on your own. Tomorrow, after I wake up from this nightmare you troglodytes have created, I am going through this army one by one, and anyone who doesn't meet my standards is gone. Shape up, do you hear me? Get him the car." Antje glared at the terrified guards. "What are you waiting for?" she screamed, turning and yelling at everyone in the atrium. The voyeuristic servants and shamed guards scurried like cockroaches as Dark Cole walked up to her. "Wow. I didn't know you had that in you. I think I'm turned on right now," he said lasciviously.

"There's a lot of things you don't know about me, Cole. This is your fault too—how did you not notice him in the rearview? Can I trust no one? This is my first day here, and the Dark Queen is undoubtedly going to have my head over this. Go make sure the guards are ready for my inspection tomorrow. Punish them. I'm sure you'll think of something harrowing for them to do."

Dark Cole's face shifted from a state of arousal to that of a kicked puppy. "Yes, General," he replied in a dejected tone, bowing his head and exiting the room.

Antje returned to her room and bundled up. "I need you to stay here, Shields. I need to go save this sweet idiot's life, and I can't risk you getting hurt. Stand guard over my bag in the bathroom, please?"

Shields let out a small yip and sat in front of the bathroom door. Antje smiled and scratched behind his ear before exiting the room. Antje made her way through the ice castle's corridors outside to Leif's car where his motionless body sat slumped over in the passenger seat. She shooed the guards away, motioning with visible irritation for them to go back inside. Closing the driver's side door, she turned the key in the ignition and drove down the road before stopping in the woods—just out of sight from the castle.

Turning her entire body and reaching over the center console with her right hand, she tapped Leif's forehead once. "Once dead." She tapped again. "Twice alive." She tapped a third time. "Three taps. You survive!" Leif took a gasp of air and jumped away from Antje, pancaking himself against the passenger door.

"Calm down, I won't hurt you. It's okay, Leif, it's okay. You're safe—but I need you to calm down and listen carefully to what I'm about to say," she said, gently grasping his hand.

"What the fuck!" he sobbed, his entire body trembling with adrenaline and confusion.

"I'm so sorry, Leif. I had to put you under so I could get you out of there safely. You're alive, but you're injured and if I take you to a normal hospital, it will end up blowing my entire mission and getting innocent people, and me, killed. I need you to go deep into the forest and find a safe place to rest." Antje handed shell-shocked Leif the pen Special Agent Davis had given to her. "Take this pen with you, and when you've reached safety—click it three times. It's a GPS transmitter. A team of CIA agents will show up and get you additional medical care. Explain what happened and tell them that I've found the Dark Queen's fortress, but not Cole yet. Tell them to set up in the woods and await my signal."

"I...I was dead. I could hear everything, but I couldn't move..." Leif stuttered, eyes bugging from his head as he blankly stared past Antje and laid the pen on the center console.

"Leif! I don't have much time. Do you understand what I've just told you?" she questioned, squeezing his hand gently. Leif shook his head and blinked a few times.

"Can't go to hospital. Go into the forest, three clicks of the pen. CIA team. Help. Dark Queen's fortress found. Tell them to wait for call when Cole is found. Yes. I've got it," he rattled, still in shock.

Antje squeezed his hand once more before letting go. "Good. I told you not to help, Leif. I'm so sorry you got hurt. Be careful and take care—I have to go drive your car into a lake to make it look like I got rid of your body. Tell the CIA you need a replacement vehicle."

"Mead. I have mead in the car. Take it back with you." Leif coughed, wincing, and clutching his left side with his right hand while wiping the blood from his lip with the other.

"Great idea, Leif. They'll think you were just some lovesick guy who followed me to give me mead. I've got it—a love note. Can you hold that pen well enough to write something, and do you have any paper in here?" Antje questioned, nodding her head at the pen she handed him.

"Yes. In the glove box," he answered, attempting to lean forward and open it, but recoiling in pain instead. "I have a broken rib. I know that feeling from previous bar fights." Leif leaned back into the passenger seat and tried to take a deep breath before shivering with pain. "Definitely broken."

"I can help you. You know how I said I'm the incarnation of a valkyrie? Well, it's the healing valkyrie."

Leif's eyes widened. "You are the incarnation of Eír?" he let out a slightly amused chuckle before wincing in pain again. "What an honor to be healed by Frigg's handmaiden!"

"Menglöð, not Frigg, I don't think anyway—but that's all for another time. Get out of the car and lay on your back in the forest. I'll grab the paper for you," she instructed, reaching across to open the door for him. Leif nodded, grabbed the pen from the console, and tensed up, quietly groaning with each small movement. As Antje retrieved the paper, Leif collapsed onto the forest floor, his breathing now labored and shallow. Leif watched with awe as Antje placed her hands on a nearby tree and transferred the glowing green energy to her hands. Hovering above him, she pulled his energetic body up and out of his physical one. Leif stared up at his hologram, slack-jawed. Antje observed small, red orbs of light in several areas across the energetic body, but where Leif had been clutching was a large, bright red orb that spanned three ribs.

"You didn't just break one rib, you broke three. Overachiever," Antje said, smiling at him as she grasped the orb and separated out a strand gently between her thumb and index finger. Leif grimaced, and his fingers dug into the earth, deeper and deeper with each pull of the glowing, red filament. Finally, the end of the thread exited his body with a pop. After dispersing the energy into the soil, Antje reached her hands back over his body and slowly pushed down on his spirit body until it absorbed itself back into his physical one. She snapped her hands shut. "How do you feel, Leif?"

Leif rubbed his rib, preparing for excruciating pain, but was pleasantly surprised when there was only a mild soreness left. "Incredible!" Leif stood up, stretching and poking at his ribs.

"Great—now write a note." Antje shoved the pad of paper into his hand. "Where's the pen?" Antje asked, looking around.

"It's uh... it's..." Leif frantically searched his pockets before eyeing the ground beneath him. "It's right here!" He bent down and snatched the pen up.

Antje turned around and gave him her back. "Sorry to be so curt, but this has taken longer than expected, and I need to get back before it seems suspicious. Write what I tell you, please. You ready?"

"Yes. I'm ready," he replied, placing the notepad on her back and positioning the pen.

"Beautiful, Antje, I couldn't stop thinking of you after the conversation about our ancestors. You are as lovely as you are wise. I hope to share this bottle of mead with you. If you feel the same, come back to my rental... alone. Yours, Leif."

"I wouldn't write that!" Leif replied.

"It doesn't matter. Just write it," she snapped.

"Okay, okay!" Leif scribbled away, feverishly. "Done." Leif reached around and handed Antje the notepad—who quickly read it and hugged him in return.

"Take care and be safe. Do not let yourself get spotted by anything other than Americans in black-ops type armor, okay?"

"Well, that's something I never expected to hear!" he replied with a chortle. Antje smiled and waved as she walked back to the car. Leif waved in return and began his covert hike into the forest. Antje removed the bottle of mead from the backseat and placed it on the ground along the forest's edge, with the love note pinned beneath it.

She closed the car door and drove a kilometer down the desolate road. Antje passed the lake and made a U-turn as it sat at the bottom of a steep hill when driving from the opposite direction. With the car perched at the top of the hill, Antje depressed the clutch and pushed the gear shift into neutral. Turning the wheel as far to the left as it would allow, she closed the driver's side door and placed herself at the rear of the car—pushing it over the crest of the hill and allowing gravity to work its magic. Speeding down the hill, the car crashed into the lake, muddy waters flooding the vehicle as large bubbles emerged between ripples in the lake's surface. Antje watched the car slowly sink, nose down—taking a photo once the vehicle's taillights were partially submerged.

Antje walked a quarter of the way back to the castle, playing out the events she'd encounter once she returned in her head.

Shit, this is a long walk.

She looked around and realized she was still alone—not a single car in sight. Transforming herself into a raven, Antje flew back to where she had bid Leif adieu and picked up the bottle of mead; pocketing the note, she walked down the driveway. Right at the line of delineation between winter and summer, Antje spotted Dark Cole, anxiously pacing.

"Oh, thank Hel, you're okay! How did it go? I made the guards who screwed up drink shrinking potions, and then sent the cats after them. I think they've learned their lesson—if they're still alive by the time it wears off," he proudly shared.

"I want to go to sleep. He was innocent and not a part of any of this," Antje snarled, slamming the bottle of mead into his chest and pulling the love note out of her pocket. She grabbed his free hand and slapped the note into it. "Hopefully the normies buy that he fell asleep at the wheel and drove into the lake," she added, pulling her phone out and showing him the photo. He leaned in toward her to look at her phone.

"You're so quick on your feet, Antje. I love it. Sometimes, I wonder how I got so lucky," he said, turning his head and sniffing her neck.

"I'm still pissed at you. Don't press your luck," she sniped, briskly walking off.

The door to the snow castle opened, and a corporeal Dark Queen stood in the doorway; her spindly, blue-hued hands expelled a slow, echoing clap. She lowered her hands into the clasped position, pressing them against the bodice of her ornate white lace gown. Antje couldn't help but think of the irony of the Dark Queen being so...white. From her borderline translucent skin, to her platinum-white blonde eyelashes and hair, the Dark Queen exuded an intense energetic frigidness that was devoid of all joy and warmth.

"Well done, Antje. This is why I chose you—quick on your feet and brutal. I saw what you did to Rebekah, but this...this was inspired."

"How do you know what happened? I just got back," Antje replied, exhausted.

"My cats were chasing my miniaturized guards. I asked your boy toy what was happening. Speaking of..." The Dark Queen leaned to her right and looked over Antje's shoulder. "What is that you have, Cole?"

"Mead and a love note. The trespasser was telling the truth," he replied, scurrying and handing the note to the Dark Queen, who immediately flicked it open and read it.

"Hilarious! Like a valkyrie would want anything to do with a hut-dwelling, backwoods simpleton. Hah!" she cackled, callously releasing the note from her fingers, which floated away on the wind. "Come, Antje. Tomorrow, let's have some of lover boy's special mead in my garden. But—for now, do get some sleep, dear. You look absolutely ragged. Besides, you will need as much energy as you can muster for what awaits you in the morning."

Fifteen

Witnessing the White Witch

Haphazardly falling backward onto her pillow, Antje stared at the canopy of drapes overhead. Shields bounded onto the bed and commenced his evening ritual of circling and pawing at the bedspread until the perfect sleeping nook was achieved. As Antje sank into a hypnagogic state, the sound of Odin's voice reverberated through the room as if he were standing directly behind her left ear. "Antje," his voice boomed. Startled, her eyes sprang open.

"Antje—close your eyes, clear your mind, and wait until the stars surround you. There, I will meet you and take you to Helheim. Clarity awaits."

Antje closed her eyes and began her breathwork. After the third mindful breath, she felt the tension in her body release. By her fourth breath, the tension was replaced by the bizarre sensation of floating while simultaneously submerged underwater—a sensation that felt all-consuming, yet supremely comforting. In her mind's eye, the stars began to form a curved wall that looped back on itself, rotating around her astral body like a carnival ride encircling the operator. From her left, a static entryway into the revolving room appeared. Stepping through the stationary portal, Odin approached Antje and stopped directly in front of her, silently offering his hand. Upon grasping his rough, mallet-like hand, Antje was instantly transported to the base of seemingly infinite stairs that led to a castle. As she stood with Odin, admiring the imposing patinaed-stone castle perched above, her eyes were once again drawn back to the mountainous steps as Hela gracefully descended them.

"Shall we?" Hela drolly questioned. With a nod, Antje and Odin followed behind Hela as she leisurely strolled toward the edge of the forest to the left of the castle. An old, birch door shrouded in the chaotic overgrowth of vines emerged. Hela pulled a brass skeleton key out of thin air and opened the door, stepping through the doorway and entering a black sand desert that sprawled for eons. With Antje and Odin crossing the threshold, the portal behind them collapsed in on itself. Antje trailed behind Hela and Odin, taking in the foreboding realm with relative unease.

Off in the distance were countless scenes dispersed across the desolate landscape. As the group approached the scattered vignettes, Antje noticed each setting was vastly different from the next. To her left, a woman in a hospital bed with a litany of tubes protruding from her fragile frame. To her right, a child clutching a dead puppy as a woman stood over him menacingly. Each tableau contained a soul whose attachment to the traumatic memory created an unending loop of misery. The suffering of this realm seemed infinite to Antje, and as searing winds trundled through the ash-hued dunes, it carried the black sand in miniature haboobs that stung and sand-blasted her skin as she trudged through them.

Off in the distance, she noticed a man who looked a lot like her father sitting in a worn, stained, leather recliner with a flimsy wooden tray table in front of him. His glassy-eyed stare affixed on a comically antique TV set, complete with a large antenna and dial knobs on the front.

"Dad!" Antje yelled to her non-responsive father, lunging forward a few steps. Without turning his head, Odin extended his arm, stopping Antje in her tracks.

"That is not the father you remember—that is a part of his shadow that has been trapped down here. You can retrieve him later, but for now, we need to focus on the task at hand, Antje." Still absorbed in the intense desire to run to her father, it took a few moments for Antje to completely grasp why Odin had stopped her. Regaining her composure, Antje gave Odin a quick nod of compliance. Lowering his arm, Odin grabbed her hand and affectionately squeezed it as they continued to tail Hela.

"Here she is," Hela said, coming to a halt in front of a small blonde girl with pale skin and gold-flecked eyes. The little girl was accompanied by an older woman with long, strikingly black hair and equally fair skin, her chiseled and severe facial structure softened by an inviting smile and her kind emerald-green eyes. "Just observe. Do not interact," Hela instructed.

Antje watched as the little girl and the woman carefully measured baking ingredients into a small cauldron that sat atop a worn butcher-block kitchen island. The woman stroked the girl's golden locks lovingly with her delicate hand; the little girl's eyes lighting up like sparklers as she added the last ingredient into the cauldron. With a short, thoughtful pause, the woman gently pinched the girl's chin between her thumb and the middle knuckle of her index finger and stared into her honey-colored eyes.

"Do you know what your name means, Kjellgunn?" the woman asked, releasing her chin.

"No. What does it mean, Aunt Lofn?"

"Well, Kjell comes from the Old Norse word 'Ketill' which means black cauldron, just like the one we're using to make your favorite honey spice cookies." The woman dotted the tip of the girl's nose with a dollop of cookie dough and giggled.

"What... about... the... gunn...part?" the girl asked, jerking her head upward as she attempted to lick the cookie dough from her nose in between each word.

"Gunn also comes from Old Norse. It means 'battle' or 'fight'. But the thing is, Kjell, you must not fight unless it is the only path to peace. Even good people become monsters during battles and many give in to their darkness—some even lose themselves along the way and become unbalanced...and some never become balanced ever again. Always let the light guide you on when to fight and when to make peace, do you hear me?"

"Yes, Aunt Lofn," Kjellgunn replied in a somber tone.

"Good girl. Now, let's get these in the oven!" Lofn scooped the last of the cookie dough onto a baking sheet and placed it inside her large wood-burning oven as a scruffy man staggered into the kitchen through the doorway behind them.

"Where's my dinner?" the man loudly slurred, stumbling into Lofn. Lofn sighed and rolled her eyes before replying, "It's 3 pm. I'll make everyone's dinner in three hours—like I usually do." A drunken scowl swept over the man's face as he glared at Lofn with his piercing, bloodshot eyes. Uncomfortable, Kjellgunn grabbed her Dad's hand and hopped off her stool, tugging at his arm. The man's arm jerked as he looked down.

"Oh. Hi, Kjell. What do you need?" His demeanor somewhat softened with the realization that his daughter was in the room.

"We made cookies today while Mommy was at work, Daddy!"

"Cookies? Where? Daddy's hungry and wants to try one."

"Well—we just put them in the oven, so maybe in..." Kjellgunn trailed off, looking to Lofn for an answer.

"Maybe 10 minutes," Lofn answered, locking eyes with the drunkard.

"Don't stare at me like that, you judgmental bitch!" he growled, spit spewing from his lips.

"Dad!" Kjellgunn interjected.

"It's okay, Kjell. Go play with your toys—your dad and I need to have a talk. It's years overdue," Lofn assured, shooing her out of the room before turning around and approaching the man head-on. Kjellgunn picked up a doll from the living room floor and hid around the corner of the doorway into the kitchen, clutching it to her chest for some semblance of safety while eavesdropping.

"Listen—I've kept my mouth shut for long enough. You need to step up as a father and a husband, or do all of us a favor and just leave. I never should have married you and Gunhild. I fought for you! To the extent that my own family disowned me, just like they disowned both of you on the day of your wedding. I never would have sacrificed them if I had known you'd bring such misery and pain into the lives of your family. My sister and niece deserve so much better than you," Lofn ranted, leaning over the kitchen island to get closer to the man.

"Shut up, you stupid, stupid woman!" the man yelled, raising his fist and swinging it toward her with absolutely zero control. Lofn ducked the blow by leaning backward and caught his forearm in her hand as it narrowly passed by her nose.

"You're going to have to do better than that, you low-life, sad excuse for a man!" she snarled. The man jerked his hand back and slammed it on the kitchen island, kitchen tools and loose silverware tossed about as his anger undulated throughout the wood countertop.

"I knew it! I knew from the first moment I met you that you thought I was a drain on your precious sister. I knew you looked down on me then, just like you are now. You, with your goody-two-shoes bullshit—like you're better than me! Always lording over me like some sort of morally superior know-it-all. Screw you, Lofn!" The slurring began to diminish as the rage and adrenaline muted his inebriation. Kjellgunn poked her head around the doorway to see what was happening. Her dad's eyes shifted to a knife on the countertop behind Lofn. He began to make his way onto her side of the island, Lofn slowly retreating as he drew close. He lunged for the knife.

"Dad, no!" Kjellgunn shrieked as he grabbed the knife and raised it to stab Lofn in the chest. Lofn again caught his hand and was now engaged in a battle of strength with her much taller brother-in-law; struggling to keep her own kitchen knife from plunging deep into her heart. As the knife crept closer, Kjellgunn ran to her father, sobbing, and pulled on the pant leg of his stained jeans. "Dad, please! Put it down. Please don't!"

He kicked Kjellgunn, and as she fell to the ground, she witnessed the knife's blade slowly vanish into the center of her aunt's chest. Lofn's hands dropped to her sides, and as her eyes widened, she mouthed the word "run" to Kjellgunn. Her eyes still fixed on her beloved niece, Lofn coughed, and copious amounts of blood flooded from her mouth, dribbling down her chin.

Pulling the knife from her chest, Kjellgunn's father chaotically swung his arm back in preparation to stab Lofn a second time. Her body slowly slid down the oven door to the floor as the last of her life drained from her fading eyes. Kjellgunn jumped to her feet and attempted to grab her father's knife-wielding hand. During his haphazard telescoping, the man caught his blade on Kjellgunn's face, swiping it perfectly up the center of her face before raising his arm and plunging it down into Lofn's chest again, and again... and again. Kjellgunn fell to the floor and retreated in horror, the heels of her feet clawing at the floor until her back pressed against the wall; she attempted to blend into the kitchen corner by pulling her knees to her chest and minimizing herself. Her tiny hands shook uncontrollably as she attempted to hold her face together, blood flowing between her fingers onto the backs of her hands and into her eyes. Her tears cleared small trails through her blood-drenched cheeks before falling to the ground, drop by drop.

With a crazed look on his blood-spatter-covered face, her dad turned around, still wielding the murder weapon, and looked down at her. His chest heaving, he looked at his terrified, mangled daughter, and dropped the knife.

"Kjell. Oh, no. Oh, no, no, no, Kjell!" He dropped to his knees, bawling, and reached out to Kjellgunn, who recoiled in sheer terror. Her father stopped his crying as if his emotional connection to his daughter had been severed. Staring at her with dead, glassy eyes, he stood up and stolidly said, "I'm sorry." The sound of a car pulling up drew his attention away from Kjellgunn, and panic suddenly set in. Without a single word, he sprinted out the back door of the cottage.

"Kjell...I'm home...Lofn? Ooh, I smell cookies!" a woman's cheerful voice rang out.

"Ma—Mom!" Kjellgunn wailed, as her mother entered the room. Gunhild dropped both handfuls of grocery bags as she ran to Kjellgunn; a bottle of mead slowly rolled from one of the discarded bags into the crimson pool of blood surrounding Lofn's lifeless body, before halting right next to her hand. Looking at Kjellgunn's face with shock, Gunhild glanced over her shoulder to find her twin sister's limp body, slumped over with her back against the oven door. Turning her attention back to Kjellgunn, Gunhild cradled her and frantically stroked her hair.

"We need to get you to a hospital right now, Kjellgunn. Listen to me. Mommy is here. You are safe. You're safe. You're going to be okay. I promise my sweet, sweet, little girl."

The tragic scene slowly faded away before Antje's teary eyes, resetting itself into a static tableau. She looked to Hela, still processing the destruction they'd collectively observed.

"That poor little girl. Kjell..."

"Yes, that's the Dark Queen as a child. Her given name is Kjellgunn. This is only the beginning of the trauma she endures. Steel yourself." Hela began to walk toward another tableau diagonal to the one they had just witnessed. Odin and Antje again followed silently behind her, before stopping at the next scene.

Kjellgunn's face was covered in linear stitches, like a threaded zipper that connected both sides of her face in the middle. She tightly held a stuffed cat with both arms as she watched her mother pray to Loki for vengeance—begging him to fill her with his power. Suddenly, dark energy engulfed the room as charcoal-colored vapors crept through every crack in the wooden floors her mother kneeled upon, the shadowy billows surrounding her body and entering through her mouth. Kjellgunn retreated into the corner of the room as the whites of her mother's eyes filled with what resembled black ink. Once the sinister energy subsided, onyx-eyed Gunhild appeared to be frozen in place.

"Mom?" Kjellgunn asked, slowly rising from her corner and warily creeping toward Gunhild. "Mom?" she asked again, this time standing in front of her and peering into Gunhild's baleful eyes. As Kjellgunn stared, her body quivered with fear. It was then that she witnessed the shadows drain from her mother's eyes, leaving Gunhild with a completely blank stare. "Mom...talk to me. Please?"

Her mother let out a jarring, demented laugh that stopped just as abruptly as it had erupted. Silently, she rose from the floor, walked into the kitchen, turned a knob on a timer, and placed a blender inside the oven, leaving the door to the oven ajar.

"Mom, you're scaring me," Kjellgunn whimpered, tugging on her shirt. Gunhild looked down at Kjellgunn, although it was less at her and more through her. With a sweet smile, her mother replied, "Mommy's here.

You're safe." Once again, without a word, she turned away from Kjell-gunn—only this time, she went to the refrigerator, and with the doors still wide open, began to pour an entire carton of milk into the air. She cackled maniacally as the milk splashed onto the planks of the kitchen floor. Tears of disquiet rolled down Kjellgunn's increasingly dim face.

The scene again faded, and Antje's head swung as she looked to Hela and Odin. "What the hell happened to Gunhild?" Antje inquired, visibly shaken. Odin again grabbed her hand and squeezed, giving her a slight yet comforting smile as Hela turned to answer her.

"She overdosed on dark magic. Loki granted her wish, and she was filled with the deepest of dark magic—power born from vengeance. However, without her twin, Lofn, to be the yang to her yin, she sank into complete madness as there was now no light in Midgard to guide her, or keep her balanced." Hela began to drift toward the next tableau as Antje replied, "I feel so sad for the Dark Queen. No wonder she is so full of hatred and violence. She basically became an orphan at age—"

"Ten—she was only ten," Odin interrupted. "To make matters worse, Kjellgunn endlessly tried to find help for her mother, but no one ever helped. They took advantage of her and her mother—humans and mystics alike. The humans did what they do best—they imprison anything they do not understand. At the age of 15, Kjellgunn discovered that an orderly at the asylum where Gunhild was being held captive had hit her mother hard enough to break one of her teeth and ripped the locket with Kjellgunn's photo inside from her mother's neck. Kjellgunn, filled with rage, then kidnapped her mother to help her escape. Those facilities were terrible places back then. Kjellgunn was forced to live in a government shelter at the time because the bank foreclosed on their home. After rescuing Gunhild, Kjellgunn quit school to take care of her, and they lived in a tent in the woods for several years, surviving off the land. Kjellgunn is an excellent forager, and as I am sure you have noticed—she is a survivor. Eventually, they were found by a group of halfwit mystics who were in the woods for a ritual. These mystics took them in and gave Kjellgunn hope. However, after several months, Kjellgunn heard her mother's screams and walked in on a ritual where they had conducted a painful experiment on Gunhild to try and remove her powers and usurp them as their own. Kjellgunn stole all of the artifacts in the mystics' temple and again helped her mother escape their commune in the pitch black of night. Using the money from the rare artifacts, she bought a small cabin in an area of Lapland not too far from where your body currently rests in Midgard, Antje."

With each additional piece of Kjellgunn's tragic past exposed, Antje's empathy for the Dark Queen grew, and a pit developed in her stomach as they arrived at the next tableau. Antje recognized a familiar face in this vignette. Eír stood next to a gaunt man who sat with his shoulders hunched. They both faced Kjellgunn, who was now an adult; a raggedy, soot-bathed woman peered over her right shoulder. No one in the room, other than Eír, seemed to even acknowledge the woman's presence. Eír's eyes became intense and fixated on the foul vagrant.

The timorous man pleaded in a nasal tone, "Please, Kjellgunn. Listen to her. She's the valkyrie of healing, and she's here to help you—to help us."

"I don't want to think about what happened that day. I don't need to dredge that back up! I don't want to relive that fear and pain of my piece of shit father's devastation! Why is that so hard for you to understand? Have I not suffered enough already? Leave me alone, both of you!" Kjellgunn snarled. The raggedy old woman delighted in Kjellgunn's outburst and goaded her silently, putting both hands on the top of Kjellgunn's head.

The man frowned, the corners of his mouth turning inward as his eyes welled up. "But Kjellgunn, she's here to help you. You cannot wake up if you do not face your demons. You need her help! She's been sent to you by the gods—by Odin himself."

"I don't need help. What I need is power, so that I can protect myself and my mother from the horrible people in this shithole existence! I don't care if you're my so-called 'higher self'! I know what I need, and I don't need you or your helper!" Kjellgunn leered at the man as he feebly looked up at Eír.

The slovenly woman's gnarled hands dug into Kjellgunn's head as her crooked, blackened teeth began to expose themselves between her lips, revealing a disturbing grin. "Good, my sweet. You don't need them—you need me. Cling to your pain, let it drive you. Without your pain, you are nothing. You are nobody. You are your pain, and your pain is you. They are telling you that who you are is wrong. They're wrong! Show them—show them how powerful we are!" The ghastly woman's words slithered like a snake through Kjellgunn's head, and Antje could see the poisonous manipulations physically manifesting in Kjellgunn's body as it tightened; her jaw clenched, her gaze turned steely.

Eír looked to the man and empathetically explained, "The gods help those who help themselves. I've been given strict instructions by Odin—if she won't help herself, I can't help her heal."

"Please, Kjellgunn. I am begging you to wake up. With every day, I grow weaker. You must wake up—for both of us," the man pleaded.

"You know what? I don't like how you're telling me that I need fixing. I am fine the way I am. How about both of you just fuck off, stop lording over me, and I'll continue living my life how I see fit, okay? What do you know anyway? Just look at you—you're pathetic and weak."

Kjellgunn stood, shadowed by the repulsive woman, and stormed out the front door of her cabin's modest living room onto an even smaller porch, where Gunhild sat—drooling on the quilt draped across her body, leaving only her head exposed. The vile woman mimicked Kjellgunn's every move like a shadow puppet. As Kjellgunn wiped the drool from Gunhild's mouth with the corner of the quilt, the despicable woman maliciously grinned, a mere half-inch from Gunhild's face, her head violently jerking as it twisted and turned. The woman's movement was glitchy and demonic in nature—as if she were an apparition that was connecting and disconnecting in cycles that only lasted for fractions of a second. Antje looked to Hela once more, flummoxed.

"That's her lower self," Hela whispered from the side of her mouth while motioning for Antje to continue observing.

Kjellgunn knelt in front of her mother and reached under the blanket, tenderly grasping her mother's limp hand. "I'm going to get the power to bring you back, Mom. I know I'm a witch, just like you, and I'm going to ask Hela to give me the power to help you, Mom."

Antje looked at Kjellgunn's higher self through the front doorway—his head in his hands, he sobbed as Eír placed her hand on his shoulder.

"I'm dead—aren't I? She won't do the work to wake up. Now, she's going to make the same mistake her mother did—and I can't stop her. Why is this my human incarnation? Where did I go wrong? Why won't she listen?" the man whinged.

"I'm sorry, Óstarki. Let us hope that Hela can help her to face her past before she does any further damage to both of you. This is all in her hands now," Eír sympathetically replied.

Kjellgunn released her mother's hand and pulled a jackknife from her back pocket, bowing her head in prayer before closing her hand around the blade. In one quick motion, she sliced the palm of her hand and made a fist. As her knuckles turned white, blood dripped from her hand onto the deck below, her seedy lower self bouncing around like a rabid animal, gyrating with anticipation while gnashing her teeth.

"Hela, Goddess of the Underworld, daughter of Loki, hear my plea. My mother was taken from me by the power of your father, and I need her back. Help me heal her wounds and give me the power I am entitled to." Storm clouds swiftly barreled through the sky as another familiar face appeared on the edge of the woods. It was Hela herself.

"I can help you. Come with me." Hela reached for Kjellgunn, who kissed her mother's forehead and advanced toward Hela. Taking Kjellgunn by the hand, they disappeared into the woods together, and the scene faded away.

"I don't get it—how did she become the Dark Queen if you helped her?" Antje asked, turning to Hela.

"Come," Hela said perfunctorily, walking to the next vignette, which looked practically identical to where they were currently standing. In the scene Antje observed, Hela and Kjellgunn were conversing before witnessing a memory of their own.

"You've done a lot of work on reclaiming power from your lower self, Kjellgunn. I am proud of you!" Past Hela was far more animated and warm than the Hela that stood beside Antje now.

"Thank you, Goddess Hela. I am ready to learn and grow more. I am ready to reclaim all of my power."

"I know. That's why I've brought you here. It is time for you to face your fears." Kjellgunn's body stiffened as the scene began to unfold. In the memory, baby Kjellgunn lay in a bassinet on her mother's lap while her mother sat in front of a drab, institutional desk with a forgettable man on the other side.

"Are you married?" the man monotonically asked, looking at Gunhild over the crest of his glasses, which slowly slid from the bridge of his nose.

"Not yet, but our wedding is next week!" Gunhild replied enthusiastically while rocking baby Kjellgunn in her arms.

"Congratulations. Will any other adults be living in the house with you?"

"Yes, my twin sister, Lofn. She loves kids and has a clean record."

The man scribbled his signature on several sheets of paper before turning the papers around on the desk and pointing with his pen to each space with an X preceding it. "Sign here, here, and here. When you're done, she's officially yours."

Adult Kjellgunn erupted in tears and screamed, "No! That is impossible!"

Hela reached for her hand and calmly replied, "Kjellgunn, you must keep your center. Remember, balance is the key to healing."

"No!" Kjellgunn screamed, rejecting Hela's hand. "This means she lied. They all lied! My entire life is a lie! She is the reason that piece of shit did this to my face!" Kjellgunn angrily flicked her wrist, pointing at her scar. "This wasn't my life, and she tricked me into living a life that has been nothing but pain and suffering. The things I sacrificed for this woman—she's not even my real mother! I'll kill her. I swear to every god in the entire universe that has ever existed, she will pay for making a mockery of me and my misplaced love!" Suddenly, Kjellgunn's body was sucked backward and up into the sky, quickly disappearing. Past Hela drew in a deep breath and shook her head as the vignette faded away and reset.

Antje looked to Odin and Hela. "Did she...?"

"Yes, she did," replied Odin, somberly.

"See for yourself." Hela pointed at the tableau behind them. Turning around, all three began to watch a most dreadful and heartbreaking ordeal. Catatonic Gunhild sat once more on the deck of their Lapland cottage, Kjellgunn's feet hammering the dirt as she aggressively approached, charging up the deck's steps and lunging toward Gunhild.

"How could you? You're not even my fucking mother and that monster wasn't even my fucking father! You couldn't have told me? I lived my entire life thinking that I was made of madness and evil, and you didn't think to be honest? Oh, Gunhild—I can't even call you 'Mom' anymore, and you—hah! You can't even reply! Why? Because you overdosed on dark magic out of vengeance, not even thinking about your fucking child who had no choice but to be brought up in this absolute nightmare!" Spit flung from Kjellgunn's rabid mouth as Óstarki appeared to her right.

"You! Fuck off! You're here to lecture me more on growing and healing—well guess what? You don't know what it's like to find out you've lived a life that is nothing but lies!" Kjellgunn pulled out her pocket knife and leaned in toward Gunhild. "I should have put you out of your misery long ago!"

"Kjellgunn, no!" Óstarki bellowed, leaping toward her. It was too late. Her lower self rose from behind Gunhild's chair, her dirt-caked hand grabbed Kjellgunn's, and swept the blade across Gunhild's throat. The frail woman's eyes looked up at Kjellgunn and a single tear rolled down her face as Kjellgunn was overcome with shock and dropped the knife.

"What have I done?!" Kjellgunn shrieked, her eyes rapidly darting between her quivering hands and her mother's lifeless body. Gunhild's head was slumped over, and her chin rested on her chest as two cascades of blood flowed from either side, joining together like ruby-red tributaries merging into a single river. Dark energy began to exit Gunhild's corpse, encircling Kjellgunn like an unholy tornado before entering her body. Kjellgunn's lower self jumped and clapped giddily. Óstarki's complexion became increasingly pallid and he withered into nothingness, until a light wind carried him away on the winds like ash poured from an urn over a gentle ocean breeze. The scene once again faded away and reset itself.

"Is he...dead?" Antje questioned, frantically turning to her companions once more.

Solemnly, Hela replied, "Yes. He was already weak, and the dark power she consumed, combined with the killing of her mother–it was the death blow. This is how she became the Dark Queen, and how she descended into such delusional madness. I tried several times to reach her after this event, but between the dark energy and her lower self being in control, I was never able to get through to her again. Kjellgunn's lower self convinced her that it was actually me who empowered her, and it didn't take much for Kjellgunn to convince herself that she was receiving instructions and guidance from me. Obviously, none of that is accurate, and Kjellgunn is so ruled by her lower self that she doesn't even question it. She has the power that she so desired, and her lower self wants for nothing but the complete death and destruction of the world around her—she wants for her pain to be everyone's pain."

Antje gulped and stared at Kjellgunn's pain-infused face in the frozen tableau before her. "Can she be reasoned with? Is there a way to kill the lower self rather than kill her?"

"You can try, but the lower self has been in control for so long that I am not even sure it would make a difference. It takes a rare and extremely strong incarnation to free themselves from the clutches of a lower self. With Óstarki dead, she will have no guidance even if you do manage to help rid her of the lower self." Hela looked to Odin. "Unless you have a way I'm not privy to?" Odin shook his head and grimaced a bit.

"Why did you two shown me all of this?" Antje asked, her gaze now glued to Gunhild.

"To defeat your enemy, you must know what drives them, Antje. This is one of the first tenets of being a warrior. You must understand your opponent in ways they do not even understand themselves. Only then can you find their weakness and exploit it. Now that you know why and how she became the Dark Queen, you understand how to appeal to her and gain her trust," Odin clarified, placing his hand on her shoulder.

"You also now understand that my father's power courses through her veins. She will not be an easy win for you—and your team of mystics—they are vastly outpowered other than the winged one who can call on the gods but won't," Hela added.

"But, if she's got Loki's power running through her, can he not just take it back? I mean, Odin, he is your blood brother. If this is literally impacting the balance and fate of the nine realms, why are we not getting Loki involved?" Antje asked as both Hela and Odin glanced at each other with amusement.

"You've never met my father, have you, Antje? The Dark Queen is chaos and mischief embodied—he finds endless entertainment in her and will not intervene."

"There is a downside to her power. Her lower self has no access to the knowledge of the higher realms, and Hela, along with the collective gods of their respective underworlds, have no interest in aiding her—in fact, she has angered Hades by kidnapping Cerberus and disrupting the balance of his realm. Her powers, albeit impressive, are not all-encompassing—she has no help from the Gods other than the power she wields. She has no foresight, and no insight into the people and world around her. If one cannot be honest within, there is no honesty to call upon externally. She is a blind soul, armed with a weapon she does not fully grasp, and you must exploit that blindness to be victorious. The time has come, Antje. Wake up!" Odin said, grabbing her wrist. Antje's eyes jolted open to find herself lying in bed, with Dark Cole's hand wrapped around her wrist, shaking it.

"Antje, wake up! You're late. You have to meet the Queen in the garden. Get up!" Dark Cole rushed around the room, opening the curtains and throwing clothing at her as she sat up in bed. "Hurry, Antje—she *really* doesn't like to be kept waiting!"

SIXTEEN

MEAD AND MURDER

Antje's faded denim jeans and tattered Opeth t-shirt were a harsh divergence from the Dark Queen's glistening, ice-crystalline garden, located directly south of the castle. Antje entered the wrought iron garden gates to find the Dark Queen admiring a patch of burnt-orange flowers bearing a resemblance to tiger lilies.

"You're awake. Welcome to my garden, General Antje." The back of the Dark Queen's head was unexpressive as she spoke and matched the tone of her voice as she stroked the petals of her botanical interest with her pointed, long, white nails. The entire scene felt stark to Antje, from the Dark Queen's bleached appearance, to the inch-thick layer of ice that encased almost every plant in the perfectly coiffed garden, the only exception being the tiger lily doppelgängers.

"Beautiful, aren't they?" the Dark Queen questioned, finally turning to acknowledge her presence as Antje approached her left side. Antje stopped to join the Dark Queen in marveling at the peculiar flowers. As she continued to admire the blossoms, Antje couldn't shake the feeling of something being off about them—other than the curious lack of icy encasement.

"Watch this," the Dark Queen boasted, raising her arms as if she were a symphonic conductor. "Wake up, my pretties! Sing for Mama."

Antje's eyes and ears did not deceive her as the petals peeled back one by one, revealing a scarlet interior, each petal lined with two rows of ivory, hypodermic-needled teeth. One by one, the flower buds began to sing a most macabre melody. The Dark Queen swayed with each note, absorbing the haunting tune in absolute delight.

"They're spectacular," Antje murmured, awestruck.

"Aren't they? What good is power if you cannot make things as they should be, rather than as they are? When this war is over, I intend to sow seedlings across all of Midgard."

"Their teeth look like they'd take a finger off." Antje squinted, leaning toward the deadly yet harmonic plants for a closer look.

"By design, my sweet! If I hadn't given them teeth dipped in poison, these wretched humans would pluck every single one of these beauties from their homes and place them in a cheap plastic vase on their sticky kitchen countertops. They have no respect. No appreciation. No class at all," the Dark Queen sneered, her eyes still shut as she swayed in ecstasy to the melancholic harmonics.

"Yeah, I do agree with you there. Humans do tend to ruin everything." The Dark Queen's porcelain face bore a mischievous expression as her nude lips curled into an omen of evil. Her white eyelashes and alabaster locks were illuminated by the intense arctic sun, a stark contrast to the warmth of her striking, amber-gold irises.

"Speaking of humans—the male species—how could your feelings ever amount to adoration of those...beasts?" the Dark Queen's mischievous grin transformed into a grimace of disgust. "That man you disposed of last night–shall we see if his mead is worthy of two would-be goddesses?" Her eyebrow raised and the curl of her lips returned as she meandered to an ornate black iron table in the center of the garden.

"My kind of woman! Who doesn't like a little morning mead?" Antje complimented, trailing the Dark Queen and taking a seat at the bistro table.

"Cole!" The Dark Queen's shrill call sent goosebumps down Antje's spine, and ached in her ears, like nails dragged down a window in the dark of night. "Fetch the dead man's mead!" Dark Cole hurried from the chilled manor's side door into the garden with a bottle of mead in one hand and two drinking horns in the other hand.

The Dark Queen grabbed one of the horns from Dark Cole's unsteady hands and held it level with the top of her head to be filled. As the honey wine cascaded from the bottle into her horn, the Dark Queen smiled at Antje. "If you can't drink from the skulls of your enemy, horns are surely the next best thing." Antje took the other horn into her hand and mimicked the Dark Queen's body language.

"So, Antje. As impressive as last night was—I still need more proof. You can understand my predicament."

"Proof of...?" Antje trailed off, her head turning slightly to the side with her chin elevated.

"Proof that you can be entrusted with my army—with my life's work." The Dark Queen stared deeply into Antje's eyes, her gaze intense and fiery. Antje's eyebrows raised, and she gave a nod of comprehension to the Dark Queen as Dark Cole filled both horns with mead. As Dark Cole corked the bottle and attempted to walk back to the building, the Dark Queen snapped her fingers. "Not so fast, Cole. Come here, darling."

Dark Cole dropped to his knees and bowed his head before her. Lifting his chin with one finger and pulling his face upward toward hers, she demanded, "Get up, dear. Real men bow to no one." The Dark Queen sensually planted a kiss on Dark Cole's lips, who melted like wax from a candle. Frozen in place, his eyes were still closed as the Dark Queen continued to hold her finger on his chin; she slowly turned her head to Antje for a response—which was a look of bemusement.

The Dark Queen's gaze still locked on Antje, she asked, "Cole and I have become intimately acquainted since his arrival. What say you about that?"

Antje shrugged. "A powerful woman with unmatched beauty—he's a disloyal fuck, but I can't fault him for that."

The Dark Queen's face swelled with obvious enjoyment, and Dark Cole's eyes opened as the Dark Queen's death grip on his chin thwarted his attempt to look at Antje. "So, you're willing to share him with me?"

"Only if you promise it won't get in the way of my duties as your General," Antje answered plainly, matching the intensity of the Dark Queen's stare, sans any identifiable emotion.

"Well, now that you mention it, I am the jealous type, and I have been envious of Cole's affections for you." The Dark Queen's tone of indifference spooked Dark Cole, and he attempted to flee, only to be snatched by two of the Dark Queen's undead guards, who again forced him to his knees. "Cole...tsk tsk. Now she's going to have to kill you." The Dark Queen stroked his hair before giving him a light slap across his face and turning to Antje. "Prove it to me. Prove your allegiance. Prove to me that you will sacrifice your lover to serve my wishes."

Antje bottled her excitement, evading any detection of emotion. She had fantasized of millions of ways to kill Dark Cole, leading up to this very moment, but now faced with that task, and seeing the visceral, animalistic fear in Dark Cole's eyes, an aversion took over.

Nonetheless, Antje heard Odin's instructions in her head and silently tipped a single, unexcited nod at the Dark Queen. Casually, Antje wedged her mead horn into one of the many holes of the tabletop's wrought-iron design—creating a makeshift stand for it. Gripping the neck of the mead bottle, Antje smashed the bottom over the arched back of her wrought-iron chair, sending the mead in every direction. Antje grabbed a handful of Dark Cole's hair with her left hand and pulled his head back before using the jagged edge of the mead bottle to slit his exposed throat. Dark Cole's body fell face-down into the frosted grass with an eerie crunch, blood decanting from the large gash in his neck and instantly freezing into a morose skating rink for the garden's resident mice. Antje stared at her mead-drenched chair and coldly ripped a swath of fabric from the back of Dark Cole's shirt, using it to dry her seat. Tossing the booze-saturated rag onto Dark Cole's carcass with insouciance, she plucked her mead horn from the tabletop and looked at the Dark Queen while taking a long sip of mead.

"*Such drama!* I like your style, General." The Dark Queen clapped enthusiastically, her talon-like nails clacking together. Antje looked down into the horn of her mead.

"Such a waste of good mead," Antje said with a sigh.

"So, now that you have proven yourself, tell me more about your life, valkyrie. Let's get to know each other—girl chat, if you will." The Dark Queen glanced at the cadaver by her feet. "He will be a hard one to replace. He was so...attentive. Guards! Remove Cole from our sight and bring us another bottle of mead." As the guards lifted Dark Cole's limp body, his head flopped onto his chest and they dragged him away by his arms, the toes of his boots leaving an indented, blood-dotted trail across the frost-kissed lawn. Antje watched as one of the guards manhandled Dark Cole, throwing the flaccid body over his shoulder as though he were a baker gathering a sack of flour from the pantry. Her eyes returned to the Dark Queen's visual inquisition. Antje took another sip of mead.

"My father was an alcoholic who beat me. My mother was a histrionic mentally ill disaster, and my sibling—he's a kiss-ass who weaponized my naivety against me every chance he could. My childhood was unstable, and I never felt safe. So that's me, a supposed valkyrie who never believed in God, let alone multiple gods, feeling forever alone, like I don't belong in this existence—or any other for that matter. I don't belong with the mystics or the gods, because at the core of who I am, there's this searing fire of rage, and that's completely unacceptable to them. They keep trying to change what cannot be changed. My pain is who I am."

"And Cole? What role did he play in your terribly tragic saga?" The Dark Queen leaned forward and rested her elbows on the table, her demeanor softening considerably.

"Cole was the first man I thought I felt unconditional love from, but like everyone in my life, he turned out to be a disloyal, self-serving liar in the end. That's why I like dogs and brought mine here with me. They're loyal, honest, and easy to read."

Antje massaged the account of her life to fit the Dark Queen's own truth, although there were facets of truth in her tale—that *was* why she liked dogs, and her mother *was* histrionic at times. As a guard returned with a new bottle of mead and topped their vessels, a stern pensiveness washed the inquisitive mien from the Dark Queen's face.

"Well, Antje, it sounds like you and I are cut from the same cloth. We are both disillusioned with the reality of man and mystics. All are power-hungry and fearful. A toast, to us, the souls who have accepted our shadow and empowered it." The Dark Queen raised her horn.

Antje raised hers in kind before replying, "To us, Children of Hela, the dark mother who sees all with absolute clarity in the shadows, and to Loki who teaches us that there is bottomless enjoyment in the darkness of chaos and trickery."

"Yes. To Hela and Loki. This is the beginning of a beautiful partnership, Antje. I have a feeling our fates are intertwined permanently now." The Dark Queen smiled and sipped her mead in tandem with Antje.

"Our fates are most definitely intertwined," Antje replied, noting the unmistakable glint of a scope in the forest from over the Dark Queen's shoulder.

A smirk grew on the Dark Queen's face. "Do call me Kjell from now on."

SEVENTEEN

RECON AND RECHARGE

Nightfall approached as Antje retreated to her bedroom chambers with Shields following closely behind. The day felt insufferably long. Antje had learned the Dark Queen's army was far larger than anticipated, with at least a thousand of her soldiers living in nearby communes—all able to assemble on the castle grounds in a matter of minutes. All in all, one thing became painfully clear: the Dark Queen's army was going to be far more than a special ops team could handle.

Antje champed at the bit for the perfect moment to step away and call Agent Davis to warn him; they weren't dealing with a small uprising—it was a literal army of darkness. Closing the door, Antje stood with her ear pressed against it until she was sure no one lurked, eavesdropping. She pulled the phone from her pant leg, only to find the battery entirely depleted. With the realization that Leif hadn't supplied her with a charger, Antje collapsed against the wall and sighed. If only Dark Cole were still alive, she could send him for one without arousing much suspicion—he was nothing if not easy to manipulate. Antje found herself bemused by her desire to bring back from the dead someone whose death she'd fantasized about a hundred times over. She gazed out the window at the forest tops, exhaustion fully setting in as an epiphany struck.

"Wait, I can fly to where the scope was. I'm so dense sometimes," Antje muttered to herself as Shields settled in for a long gnaw session on a bone Antje had snatched from the kitchen. "I'll be right back, Shields."

Shields' eyes rolled upward at Antje, drool foaming and bubbling in the corners of his mouth as he continued to chomp on the bone. Antje opened the bedroom window and assessed the lengthy fall in store for her if she failed to shift and fly. She took a deep breath and relaxed her shoulders before carefully climbing onto the windowsill. Transforming herself into a raven, she effortlessly took flight. The cool evening air caressed her feathers like the tender stroke of a lover's fingertips. For a moment, Antje felt free from the insanity currently consuming her world. Scouring the landscape beneath the forest canopy from above, she meticulously searched for any sign of a special ops team. She caught a glimpse of a muted glow from between two trees and dove down to inspect further. The glow emanated from a drab olive-green tent, covered in camouflage netting. Antje knew she was in the correct location and landed, transforming back into her human body in the middle of the camp. Instantly, Antje found herself encircled by the cacophony of rifle safeties being disarmed.

"At ease, boys. That's Antje," Special Agent Davis stepped out of the tent, hunching over as not to hit his head. "My apologies, Antje. We can't be too careful, you know?" Following Special Agent Davis' exit from the tent was Leif, who all but tripped over himself to get to Antje. Leif spared no time in getting on his knees and bowing his head to her with overabundant veneration.

"I did as you requested," Leif said quickly with his eyes closed and his bruised head still bowed. Antje grabbed him by his shoulders and guided him to his feet.

"Thank you, Leif. It's so good to see you're on the mend. Don't bow to me from now on, okay? It's weird. We're equals." Antje smiled and embraced Leif. Special Agent Davis' shoulders bounced as he turned his head away, obscuring his silent laughter.

"I'm never going to get used to this job," Special Agent Davis said, amused. He turned and made eye contact with Antje. "While we're on the subject of making things less weird, call me Kenny." Kenny flashed his immaculate pearly whites and put his hand on Antje's shoulder. "I think we're past titles at this point."

"Will do... Kenny. So, in the interest of making sure my shisa isn't murdered by a broken child living in the body of a great sorceress, let's get to it. I think I know where Cole is being held—don't ask how. I just do. We have an issue though: the locked door is heavy and her guards are always in the hallways. In order for me to break down the door, I'm going to need some form of loud chaos for cover."

"Oh, I think we can provide that," Kenny replied with a mischievous smile, looking to his team, who nodded with excitement.

"So, here's the thing: we've underestimated her. As her 'General', I spent the day assessing 'my army' and it's huge—I'd say upward of a thousand mystics of various abilities in total. Your special ops team won't cut it—especially not with her powers in the mix."

"I've got you covered, Antje. Don't worry. I had to call in the military for this one. With my direct superior being held captive, this operation now has a lot of visibility, and we need as many bodies as possible. I requested fifteen hundred men, just to be safe. They should be here at 06:00 tomorrow. Are you ready for us to storm the castle tomorrow, or do you need more time?"

"You'd better call and make that two thousand, Kenny. There is no such thing as playing this one safe. We can only pray that the gods intervene to help. Tomorrow is preferable if we can swing it. If I am forced to ingratiate myself to her for one more day, I might actually go insane."

"Tomorrow it is. Do you have access to the Dark Queen's schedule?"

"I don't. I'll need to send you a signal whenever she goes out to the garden. I'll ask Skaði to aid us by creating freezing fog for cover. The army's quarters are all to the north of the castle, so approach from the south, east, and western sides. I think that's the best way to capitalize on the element of surprise without leaving ourselves open to being flanked. We have to get the drop on her, so that we split the encounter with her army into two waves, or tomorrow will be an absolute massacre. The first line of defense is around 500, and we can expect at least 500 more from the north. Where's the pen I gave Leif? When I signal you with it, start your approach—but wait for full fog cover before you get close enough to start the siege."

"Here it is," Leif replied, pulling it from his pocket and presenting it to Antje with both hands laid out flat like a serving platter. Antje giggled at Leif's dutiful demeanor coming from such a rough-and-tumble man.

"Thank you, Leif. You're a good one," Antje replied, grabbing the pen from his hands.

"And me? I want that bitch dead as much as the rest of you. She broke my ribs. Do I get to join in?" Leif questioned, looking ato both Antje and Kenny through his swollen black eyes.

"Well, that's not protocol..." Kenny trailed off before Antje chimed in.

"No, he deserves revenge. I take full responsibility for Leif." Antje pointed at a gun sitting on the folding table that abutted one of the tents and motioned toward Leif. "Arm him. He's faithful to our cause and will literally die in a blaze of glory if it means taking her out."

Leif beamed. "Thank you, Antje. I won't disappoint you, or the gods. To Valhalla!" Leif hollered, instantly hushed by Kenny and Antje.

"Fine. I'm assuming you know how to handle a gun?" Kenny questioned.

Leif answered in a hushed tone laced with bravado. "Of course. I live in Lapland. I was born with a gun in one hand and a horn of mead in the other!"

Antje giggled again and gave a nod of approval to Kenny, who begrudgingly acquiesced. With his eyes locked on Antje's, Kenny inquired, "So, you'll signal us with the pen. My teams will surround the compound and breach the doors. Once inside, there is no telling what hell will break loose, so we need a code word to know it's you. What word do you want to use?"

Antje mulled it over for a few seconds, thinking about Cole. "Sahira. It's a word Cole taught me. It means witch and seems fitting for this occasion."

"Sahira it is. Everyone hear that? Sah-hee-rah. Do not engage if that word is said," Kenny instructed his team. With nods of congruence, the platoon replied in unison, "Sir, yes, sir."

Kenny turned to Antje and put his hands on her shoulders, facing her. "Antje, be careful. We're all pulling for you. Bring Cole back to us in one piece, please. He's a real smartass at times, but he's family."

"I know the feeling. I'll find him and bring him back or die trying. You have my word," Antje replied, placing her hands on Kenny's shoulders in an interlocking embrace of solidarity. Synchronously, they both dropped their arms back at their sides.

"I need another cell phone, please. The one Leif gave me is dead, and I have no way to charge it."

"I knew it!" Leif exclaimed, catching how loud he was on his own this time. His hand raised to his mouth, and he quieted to a whisper. "I knew it. I brought you a charger." Leif pulled a small phone charger from his pocket, which was wrapped tightly with a rubber band, and handed it to Antje.

Pocketing it, Antje replied, "Leif, you are a godsend. Thank you. I'm gonna reach out to my teachers at the Cisterne and see if they'll join you in the fight tomorrow. This may be our only chance to capture the Queen, and just like with wildfire, sometimes you need fire to contain fire. They'll all know the safe word and will be instructed to tell you it immediately upon their arrival. Some of the professors aren't human, but I vouch for them. They're my mystical family, and I expect them to be treated with dignity and honor—no one is to touch a hair on their heads. I've got to get back to the castle. Wait for my signal."

Kenny gave one last nod of affirmation as Antje shifted into a raven and began to flap her wings, the phone charger in one talon, and the pen in the other.

"I'm here if you need me!" Leif yelled, looking up at Antje's ascending feathered body. Leif was immediately hushed by Kenny, whose hands turned outward in a display of, "Really?" Leif sheepishly smiled, and a playful grimace washed over his face as he shrugged his shoulders.

"Sorry," he whispered. "I'm a little excited that part of my fate is helping a valkyrie in a war against evil. I've lived a quiet life in the woods, and this is the most excitement I've ever seen."

Kenny's demeanor relaxed, and with a muted smirk developing, he nodded at Leif with one eyebrow raised. "I get it. Just don't get yourself killed tomorrow. If a civilian dies under my watch, it's *a lot* of paperwork."

As Antje traversed the skies, her wings ruffled and flickered in the pale sunlight reflecting from the stratiform clouds. The feeling of coasting on the wind was reminiscent of snowboarding down freshly fallen powder, from the way her body was effortlessly carried by a power greater than her, to the lack of demarcation between where she ended and nature began.

The castle approached. At a side entrance stood her glowing white fylgia, his front right hoof pawing at the ground. Antje dove and landed next to it. Her fylgia quickly glanced at her and resumed pawing at a frozen block of stone beneath his hoof. Antje shifted back into her human form and walked deliberately toward him, softly putting her hand on the hump of his back.

"There's something under that stone for me, isn't there?" she whispered. Nodding his head gently, he stepped back from the stone. Antje attempted to pry the stonework apart with her thin fingers—a task that proved to be impossible. It was then that Antje realized she had a tool wrapped around her finger. Removing it from her finger and placing it in the palm of her hand, she wiped the potion from the ring and it transformed into a large sword once more. Grinning with satisfaction, Antje pried the large piece of loose stone from its resting place with the tip of the sword. She looked beneath it, only to find a smaller flat stone with the elgiz rune carved into it. Examining it closely, she turned to her fylgia and whispered, "This is the same symbol that is on my Mjolnir, and the same symbol I saw in the mirror when we first met. It's for protection, right?"

The fylgia nodded and exhaled a loud puff of air through his elongated nostrils before walking toward the woods. Antje took that as affirmation that she was to keep the rune and heaved the stone back into place. To disguise any signs of disturbance, she kicked dirt from the surrounding stonework onto the surface of the block and filled any crevices.

Antje quietly crept through the side door, stopping at every hallway intersection and peeking around the corner to confirm the coast was clear. Several times, she paused and waited for patrols to pass by before tiptoeing to her next stopping point. Reaching her bedroom chamber door, Antje sighed in relief, only to find Shields bum-rushing her with his teeth bared as she entered.

"Whoa! It's me. Calm down. Shhh." Antje flung her hands up, her palms facing him.

Shields sat, tail wagging. "SORRY. SCARED. SHIELDS SORRY."

"It's okay, buddy. Hey, so, tomorrow is the big day, and we're going to need you back in your normal form. Are you ready to be changed back to your big body?" Antje asked, plugging her phone into the wall to charge.

"SHIELDS READY. SO READY." Shields' already frenetic tail became supercharged.

Antje giggled and pointed at the bathroom. "Speaking of turning things back, I need to apply the potion to this sword to turn it into a ring again. I had to use it earlier. Can you go fetch the bottle for me?"

"FETCH. SHIELDS FETCH NOW." Antje giggled once more to herself, laying the sword on the bed as Shields disappeared into the bathroom. Moments later, he returned with his tiny mouth wrapped around the strap of her bag as it dragged on the floor beside him. Antje picked up the bag as Shields hopped onto the bed and perched himself next to the sword.

"Good boy. In all this darkness, there's you. You're my little fluff-ball of joy in the abyss of insanity, Shields. Thank you for being my trusty companion. I love you, buddy."

Shield's tail wagged furiously as he licked Antje's hand and barked, "HAPPY! SHIELDS LOVE ANTJE. ANTJE LOVE SHIELDS. HAPPY, HAPPY!"

Antje scratched behind Shields' ear before rifling through her satchel and uncorking the potion. Anointing the sword with three drops and visualizing it once again as a ring, she opened her eyes to find one of her most prized pieces of jewelry had returned. Antje slipped it onto her finger, placed the vial back into her bag, and checked her phone.

"Twenty percent. Bless that crazy heathen—he gave me a fast charger," Antje murmured to herself, picking up the phone and dialing Headmaster Vogel. The phone rang exactly once before the headmaster answered.

"Antje! Are you alright?" he questioned with intense concern.

"How did you—you know what, never mind. I need to make this quick. I'm in the Dark Queen's lair. She believes I'm on her side and today I found out that her army is massive. The CIA said they called in the military, but even so, we need mystics. Can you please round up anyone who is ready and able, and have them meet Special Agent Davis in the forest nearby? The code word is "Sahira." Make sure that is the first word out of everyone's mouth upon arrival, and they also need to immediately use it should they encounter any military or special ops members during the battle tomorrow. I can't lose anyone else—especially to friendly fire. Do you think anyone will help?"

"Oh, Antje. Of course, we will help. I knew you would be calling—call it ze gift of seeing. I've already assembled ze team, and all your professors will be joining. Ragnar has gone full-blown berserker and filed his will in preparation to meet Odin in Valhalla."

Antje paced the room. "I really hope it doesn't come to that, but thank you so much for gathering them. Be safe. I'm going to text you Special Agent Davis's number as soon as we get off; he'll send you coordinates. Oh, also, there's a heathen named Leif that might need some looking after—he's a great guy who has been amazingly helpful, but I have no idea what he will be like on the battlefield. Can you please have someone watch over him?"

"I will take care of it, Antje. Do not worry. We will be there."

As Antje hung up the phone and laid down on the bed, Shields began to snore, his belly exposed, and his legs splayed wide open.

"Cole, we are so close. Please hang in there and help me find you tomorrow," Antje whispered out loud, a solitary tear rolling down her temple and catching in her hair. "I love you. I'm coming to save you—or die trying."

Eighteen

The Unkindness of Battle

The previous night's rest was fractured at best. Antje soaked up a few fleeting moments of cuddling with Shields and pulled Cole's shattered necklace from her leather jacket, which had been sloppily hung on one of the bedposts. Running her fingers around the inlay where a smooth piece of jade had once been, she felt a pit growing in her stomach. It had only been a month since Cole's disappearance, but for Antje, it felt like an eternity. She had never felt a sense of home with anyone like she did with Cole, and the thought of never seeing him again was excruciating. The feelings she had only barely managed to push down deep within; were now mingling with intellectual anxiety around the events to come. With a large sigh, Antje dropped the necklace back into her coat pocket, her index finger grazing the stone she had pried from the castle's perimeter during the previous evening's outing. Antje removed it from her jacket and held it in her hand. Using her now fully charged phone, she captured a photo of the stone and texted it to Headmaster Vogel.

> Antje: Any idea why a stone with the elgiz rune would be buried along the side door entrance to the Dark Queen's castle?

> Headmaster Vogel: Protection spell. By removing it, you've disarmed her magical security system. We have arrived at the camp. All of your training team has come, as well as Mathias. Also, the military is here. I have a sinking feeling today. Be careful, please.

> Antje: Thank you, Headmaster. I truly appreciate everything you have done for me. I feel like this is my life's purpose, and I could not have prepared for this if it weren't for you and the Cisterne. I am forever indebted to all of you.

> Headmaster Vogel: We are the ones indebted to you. Without you on the inside, this would be impossible. See you when the dust settles, Antje. Remember your training, and do not underestimate the Dark Queen.

Antje darkened the phone screen with the press of a button and stood up from her bed. Shields stood at attention. "SHIELDS LIKE BIG BODY NOW."

"Oh buddy, I know. Hang in there just a little longer. You're my secret surprise, and we need to wait until the last possible second for them to figure out that you're not just some cute fluffball."

"SHIELDS UNDERSTAND," he replied, his head lowering in disappointment.

"Today, Shields. I promise. I need you to stay by my side at all times and watch my back, okay?"

Shields immediately stiffened, puffing his tiny chest out. "SHIELDS PROTECT ANTJE. SHIELDS LOVE ANTJE."

Antje smiled and kissed his petite muzzle. "Good boy. Let's go put on a good last act for this wretched and sad woman."

Suddenly, there was a knock on the bedroom door. Antje walked across the room and opened it, only to be met by the face of someone she never wanted to see again.

"*You!*" Antje snarled at the ogre-like bartender from Wicked Liquors.

"Nice to see you too. My knee still isn't the same thanks to that stunt you pulled. Anyway, the Dark Queen wants to see you in the garden. Get dressed and meet her there in 20 minutes," the green ogre instructed, turning and hobbling down the hallway.

Antje closed the door and quietly growled, "Unbelievable. She's going to be the first to die today."

Shields reacted as if he were a wind-up toy and his string had been pulled, every muscle in his body vibrated with excitement. "ANTJE HATE OGRE. SHIELDS HATE OGRE! SHIELDS BITE OGRE!"

The unconditional love of Shields snapped Antje from her sourness and her lips cracked a smile. "Maybe you'll like ogre bones. We'll see!" she replied, scratching his chin as his body's vibrating continued. Antje dressed herself, sliding Daggert into her boot once more. Looking in the mirror, she wrapped her hand around her Mjolnir and closed her eyes.

"Thor, God of Thunder, I call to you. Please protect me and mine today and help me should I need it."

A thunderous laugh filled her head. "As if you really needed to ask, Antje. Go show us what you're made of, valkyrie. I am here when you are ready," the male voice replied.

"Thor, is that you?" she questioned quietly, her eyes popping open as she turned her head slightly to the left.

"Yes—you called me!" His boisterous laughter rang through her head once more.

"Sorry. Still getting used to this whole 'spiritual telephone' thing." Antje smiled.

"It is okay, valkyrie. Go to battle. I am with you," Thor assured her—her mind again returning to silence.

Antje closed her eyes and took several deep breaths. "Skaði. I know you don't like a lot of chatter, so I'll be quick: I need a thick layer of freezing fog to surround the building I am currently in, starting in about ten minutes. Can you help me, please?"

"Done," a woman's gruff voice replied before Antje's eyes opened. Grabbing the pen she had reclaimed from Leif, Antje clicked it three times and texted Kenny.

> Antje: Fog cover ETA 10 minutes. Be ready. Heading to garden now.

> Kenny: All units ready for combat. Marine General in camp with access to air support. Good luck, Antje.

> Antje: Right back at you, Kenny. Don't die. Cole will be really disappointed.

> Kenny: Well, we don't want that.

Antje let out a little giggle before sliding the phone into her back pocket and heading to her bag. She removed the small kit of vials Philomena had sent with her and read each potion carefully, selecting a few and slipping them into her bra on each side.

"Guess what this potion does, Shields?" she asked as his head tilted with wonder. "It's the potion to transform you back to your normal body." Shields' tail flicked back and forth with the speed of dragonfly wings. "Okay, let's go to the garden, shall we?"

Antje exited the side door of the castle, her fingers sticking to the frosted metal doorknob slightly. As she peeled her hand from the knob and walked down the stone steps, the Dark Queen's shrill voice rang out. "Antje, dear! Do join me; it's a beautiful day for some tea!"

Antje smiled and replied, "I'm more of an espresso girl in the morning, but I'm up for anything caffeinated."

The Dark Queen cackled and gave a nod to one of her henchmen, who scurried inside like a rat. "Anything for the commander of my army. So, now that you've seen them all, what do you think?" The Dark Queen brought a white porcelain teacup up to her pale lips and sipped her tea, never breaking eye contact with Antje, and seemingly unbothered by the steam as it wafted into her face.

"I think we need more men. One thousand is great, but to win a war against normies and the mystics who have chosen the other side, we will need at least twice as many—and they will need to be trained to have maximum control of their abilities. Do you have someone who can train them in their own magical abilities?" Antje replied as the ratty henchman placed a small cup of espresso on a saucer in front of her, the porcelain rattling against itself on the way down. The Dark Queen lowered her cup with exasperation.

"Did I choose the wrong general for my army? Training falls under your jurisdiction; plus, I've passed some of my goddess's power to each and every one of them. Do we have a problem?"

"No, my Queen. I only asked in case you had someone you trusted. As you know, trusting the wrong person in battle can be deadly. I will find a mystic trainer for our army. Leave it to me."

"Better." The Dark Queen's head shook with irritation, and her lips curled into a half-smile.

"On to other business. I have assigned you a new assistant. Her name is Katya, and normally I have her guarding the bar where you and I first crossed paths—well, where I saw you first, at least. I know you two have an interesting past, but—make it work," the Dark Queen brusquely commanded.

"We're on the same side now. I look forward to getting to know her and her abilities."

"Good. How peculiar—there is dense fog rolling in." The Dark Queen barely finished her sentence before the groans of death and the thudding of bodies crashing onto dirt emanated from the perimeter of the woods around them. Shields let out several barks before retreating under Antje's chair.

"We're under attack! Sound the alarms!" Antje screamed to the henchman who had previously been playing waiter as she flipped the table onto its side for cover. "Get down, my Queen."

"I will do no such thing. I am the Dark Queen! Who do these brazen fools think they are?" The Dark Queen's hands began to glow red, and as men dressed in military fatigues began to appear along the edge of the clearing to the east of the garden, the Dark Queen shot black shadows from her hands, changing the men into putrid creatures upon contact. Within seconds, the men turned and fired on their own platoon. The Dark Queen smirked as she turned her head, spotting a dust cloud rising above the road leading to her fortress. Angrily, she trudged across the frosted lawn toward the road and intercepted three Humvees as they approached. As she levitated all of them with her hands, their tires spun, and several men bailed from the cars; falling to the road below, they scrambled to their feet. With a single flick of her hands, all three vehicles crashed into each other before dropping to the ground like crumpled soda cans— narrowly missing the ejected soldiers who had fled into the woods.

Still in the garden, Antje barked orders at the men around her as they assembled into formation. Shields, not more than inches from her heels at any given point in time, became her inseparable shadow. With the Dark Army at her rear, she raised her dagger and yelled, "For the Queen!" Sprinting toward the men in fatigues who approached from just south of the garden, she knocked them to the ground one by one as she quietly said, "Sahira." The soldiers stayed down as Antje stabbed to the sides of their bodies, the tip of her sword pushing into the earth and merely grazing their uniforms in the process. She looked up and found herself face-to-face with Mathias—a crazed look in his eyes.

"Hit me," she mouthed as Shields backed himself against a large tree and stood, barking. Mathias' fevered demeanor spread to his lips, where a maniacal grin formed. Mathias let out a guttural yell. "To Valhalla!" He lunged toward Antje, Antje parrying his blows each time and striking back—only to be parried in return.

"Is the Dark Queen behind me?" she mouthed again. Mathias glanced over Antje's shoulder and shook his head no as he swung his axe, which Antje ducked. "Fall down," she mouthed to him once more. Antje kicked Mathias square in the chest, knocking the air out of him, before retreating back to the garden, where more soldiers were arriving.

"For the Queen! Shield wall formation, then attack!" Antje yelled at the top of her lungs—the Dark Army following her every whim. "Where is the Queen? Protect the Queen!" Antje frantically looked around, relieved to find the Dark Queen was now out of eyesight. She ran quickly into the castle, shoving her way through members of the Dark Army, who rapidly exited the building before she collided with Katya.

"Katya, thank Hel, it's you. Look—we're on the same side and we are under attack, whatever happened before— I just need to know where the Dark Queen is."

Rolling her eyes, Katya replied, "Some general you are. You lost the Dark Queen but still managed to keep tabs on your little shit dog. I have no idea where she is. It doesn't matter. These normies are no match for us."

"I can't take that risk. Find her. That's an order. I will clear the top two levels. You search the first two floors," Antje said, out of breath and running toward the front door, grabbing the banister with her left hand before taking a sharp left turn. Antje's feet barely touched the stairs as she ascended. Running through the corridors, she continued to bark orders, Shields on her heels every step of the way—his tiny legs struggling to keep pace.

Entering the hallway with the locked door that her fylgia had previously walked through, Antje carefully checked each room to make sure she was indeed alone. The sound of gunfire mingling with screams and explosions could be heard through the castle walls, even from four stories above. In one of the rooms, Antje glanced out the window as she cleared it. Blasts of colored light could be seen as if flash grenades were being launched back and forth across the castle grounds. Antje exited the final room on the top floor before finding herself face to face with the impenetrable door. Antje held her mjolnir in her hand and closed her eyes. "Thor, give me your strength to open this door." Antje immediately felt electrified and backed up until her butt touched the opposing hallway wall. Sprinting at full speed, Antje hunched down and collided with the door, knocking it off its hinges. Before her lay Cole, comatose and pale, in an open casket of sorts.

"Cole! Oh, what has she done to you?" Antje cried out, running to the casket before feeling her body freeze in place, as if she'd entered a magnetic field. Her airways began to tighten as shadows engulfed the entire room, spreading across the walls and the ceilings like ghoulish tentacles.

"I knew you couldn't be trusted," the Dark Queen sneered. Her arms were raised, and her fingers were tensely spread apart, forming claws that orchestrated the magical bondage Antje was currently ensnared in. Antje's feet dangled as she levitated a few inches off the ground. Slowly, Antje's entire body was rotated to face the Dark Queen. Gasping for air as she was being choked out by The Dark Queen's death grip, Antje's sight began to grow dim from the lack of oxygen.

The Dark Queen sauntered closer to Antje, her hands still in the air. "You killed your lover too easily. It wasn't remotely believable—and now, because of your hubris, you'll die just like he will. I'll have no need for either of you once I wipe out this bothersome army you've brought to my door." Shields bit the Dark Queen's ankle as hard as he could with his miniature mouth—doing no significant damage. "Ow! You little shit!" The Dark Queen punted Shields across the room, his little body slapping against the wall, rendering him unconscious. As the room faded to black, the last thing Antje heard was Katya's spit-laden speech pattern in her ears.

"I brought the draugrs to guard her. I'll stand watch. Guards—bind her and the fleabag."

Outside, the battle raged on and those on the side of light found themselves questioning if they'd ever see their loved ones again. The mystics hung behind the first line of soldiers, shielding them when possible with magic and targeting key opponents who proved to be hard to kill with military-grade weaponry. In the forest to the southwest of the castle, at the base of a steep incline leading to camp, Philomena pulled up her sleeves, anointed her fingers with a potion, and pushed them deep into the earth, crouching.

"Roots of old, seeds of new, help us, friends, I summon you!" The ground beneath Philomena began to shake and rumble as roots unearthed themselves. The roots swung and whipped around the forest floor, wrapping themselves around the legs of dark mystics and pulling them into the ground violently, where their victims would suffocate in the dirt. Philomena cackled, "Teach 'ye to feck with a Druid!" before anointing her hands with the same potion and placing them on a large birch tree directly in front of her. "Spirit of the trees, hear my call: our opponents...kill them all!" The sound of creaking and cracking wood roared through the fog as every tree in the forest began to animate. The evergreen trees began to shiver. Like heat-seeking missiles, a slew of unopened pinecones whizzed through the air, pelting the dark mystics and interrupting their spells. Philomena giddily laughed as she threw potions at her foes, which exploded upon impact, like grenades. Philomena ducked as a branch swung over her head. Birch branches were transformed into flexible spears, impaling and flogging any members of the Dark Army within reach. Philomena sniggered with delight, until out of the corner of her eye, she caught a red ball of light heading straight toward her.

One of the Dark Army's treasured mystics had pinpointed where the botanical attack was originating from, and was now intent on taking her out. Philomena panicked, searching for her protection potion but was hit by the red blazing orb before she could manage. Knocked back several feet, her skin burned and her lungs ached. Philomena struggled to stand back up as the dark mystic's hands began to recharge with dark energy. Philomena again fumbled. Overcome with fright, she desperately tried to find the protection potion on her belt. Right as the dark mystic should have released the orb, Philomena witnessed his head fall clean off his neck. Where his head once rested was Ragnar's blood-drenched face, with a look of lunacy plastered across it.

"Get up, old woman! We're getting our asses kicked, and you're dirt napping!" Ragnar yelled, slicing through three more men as though they were merely mannequins standing in the way of his sword and axe.

"Aye ye big brute, I just woke up the entire forest to fight with us. Shut it." Philomena rose onto her feet, using the tree to pull herself up. Calmly finding the protection potion on her belt, she took the whole of the liquid into her mouth. Cautiously walking toward Ragnar, who was still slicing and dicing like a skilled butcher, she spit some of the potion at him—it landed on his arm as she swallowed the rest.

Phil held her side, wincing in pain and chanted, "Keep me safe, keep me sane. Do not let us be taken from this plane!" A white bubble of energetic light surrounded both Philomena and Ragnar.

"That'll do us fer fifteen minutes, dependin' on how long we manage not to get hit!" she yelled to Ragnar.

"Speak for yourself, Methuselah! You should have kept that potion for you. These 'soldiers' can hardly be called such!" Ragnar playfully retorted, burying his axe in the skull of a blue-skinned troll's head.

"Ragnar! Watch out!" Philomena screamed as a draugr raised its sword over Ragnar's head, only to be stopped in mid-swing as a birch branch impaled the draugr from behind. The draugr's body went limp as the branch punched its way through the undead heart and swiftly pulled itself out. Ragnar rapidly turned around only to witness the draugr falling face first onto the forest floor.

"Old lady he says. Methuselah, he says. Yer welcome ye overgrown boy!" she screamed to Ragnar as he turned around and looked at her with a giant smirk.

"You got a kill!" he hollered back, chuckling and continuing to carve a path of blood through a throng of dark mystics.

To the southwest of the castle, a sea of putrid creatures continued their onslaught, and the military losses mounted at a staggering rate. Normies were no match for the powers of dark mystics, and friendly fire began to chip away at their numbers, as it was hard to tell who had been turned to darkness by the Dark Queen and who was still in control of their own consciousness. Bullets whirred through the forest, some piercing flesh, others implanting themselves in the stonework of the castle. As the forest continued to launch an assault on the dark army, a large chimera approached from the northern side of the castle grounds, spraying fire from its mouth and immersing each part of the forest it passed in flames.

As Takhi heard the distinct wails of a forest ablaze, she called upon her gods to send a torrential downpour. With her wings spread wide and her chin to the heavens, she felt relief in the droplets of water beading down her feathers. The momentary respite was shattered when Takhi was infused with the familiar sinking feeling of aggression aimed in her direction. The chimera, angered by Takhi's thwarting of its destruction, locked eyes on her and charged through the battlefield, igniting a trail of death straight to her. Takhi, now backed into a corner of fight or flight, had a moment of clarity as the bodies stacked up around her. To her left, Misha battled several vile creatures at once, his knives clanging and slicing in an almost rhythmic dance. To her right, Headmaster Vogel summoned white light in an attempt to shield the normies from the volley of incoming spells. His light spared several soldiers, but was not enough to spare them all, and the bodies began to cover the forest floor like a patchwork quilt of sacrifice. Death surrounded Takhi, and the empath within died a little with each extinguished life. Now within reach, the chimera drew in a deep breath, its throat glowing hot with amber light. Takhi closed her eyes in preparation for her untimely end.

"Takhi, no!" Misha screamed, sprinting to her with all of his might. The chimera unleashed a massive fireball directly at Takhi. Intercepting the fireball with his body, Misha became engulfed in flames, dropping to the dirt, screaming in agony. Misha's screams tore through Takhi's heart like a barbed arrow. The chimera now recharged to unleash another ball of fire at Takhi. Takhi flapped her wings vigorously, amassing a huge gust of wind and extinguishing Misha while blowing several members of the dark army into trees—snapping their necks and bashing their heads against boulders and large tree trunks. It was too late. Misha lay charred and bloodied on the forest floor, lifeless. Takhi raised herself like a phoenix from the ashes and flew at the chimera with all of her might, ripping through the throat of its lion head with one talon, and gouging the eyes from the goat head with the other on her second pass. As Takhi ripped the throat from the creature, the fireball that was forming was unleashed from its womb and engulfed the creature itself. The pained shrieks were ear-piercing as it blindly stumbled, igniting other dark mystics in the final moments of its life. Takhi flew back to Misha's charred remains and yelled for a healer. Headmaster Vogel approached, his hand on her right wing.

"Oh, Misha, no." Headmaster Vogel's eyes welled up, and his right hand shook as he kneeled down, touching Misha's neck to check for a pulse. "He is gone, Takhi. There is no healing to be done. He died a hero, but we have no time for grief. Ze time for mourning is when ze danger has passed. To honor his memory, so his death is not in vain, we must fight. It is time to fight, Takhi."

Tears rolled down Takhi's cheeks as the ash of Misha's remains ran from his body down into the dirt with each raindrop. Slowly raising herself up, her eyes still fixated on the crisp remains of Misha, a once fearsome warrior, Takhi was only able to mutter four words: "I am so sorry."

Headmaster Vogel nodded with a pained look on his face. Wiping the grief from his cheeks, he returned to battle, transmuting the profound pain of his loss into new protective energy for the military forces who had now dwindled down to a mere hundred able-bodied Marines.

Takhi called to her gods once more, requesting a hailstorm to center over a mass of dark mystics who had formed a shield wall and were moving as a singular unit, mowing down everyone they encountered. As the bowling-ball-sized hail rained down on the group, some of their skulls were crushed; others fell to the ground as their bones snapped and protruded from their flesh. Takhi once again called upon her gods, this time requesting an earthquake to the north of the castle, which created a chasm and slowed the trickling of the dark army's reinforcements. Takhi continued to suffer the pain of each and every soul she snuffed out as their bodies plunged into the crevice, screaming with terror as the earth enveloped them. A marine platoon leader turned to Takhi and thanked her. Takhi silently nodded in acceptance of his gratitude, but she felt no pride in what she had done—for Takhi knew she would never quite recover from this day.

Nineteen

The Fickleness of Fate

T he crisp winds caressed Antje's face, chilling the tip of her nose as she sat on the same summit she'd visited once before. Freezing fog swirled around the mountaintops in the distance, and snowflakes danced through the air. The serenity she felt in that moment had entirely separated Antje's soul from her body; a sense of oneness with everything washed over her.

"Antje, you are here?" Odin's voice gently approached from behind her, his footsteps getting closer. "You are supposed to be fighting a battle right now. You are in the wrong place."

Antje flashed a melancholy smile at Odin as he sat next to her and grabbed her left hand, holding it on his knee as his rough, thick fingers interlocked with hers. "I failed. The Dark Queen killed me. I failed you, Cole, Eír, the nine realms, and most of all, I failed my entire team." Antje closed her eyes, pinching a tear from each as she pulled a deep breath into her lungs, exhaling as if she were blowing out birthday candles.

Odin turned his head, and with furrowed eyebrows, he replied, "No, Antje. You are not dead. You are unconscious, but you are not dead. You must return."

Antje opened her eyes and stared blankly at the fog off in the distance. "What if I don't want to? What if I want to stay here forever? The things I've seen, the things I've felt...I don't want to go back there, Odin. Life is nothing but suffering."

Odin squeezed her hand gently. "We must all make sacrifices, daughter."

"Daughter?" Antje asked, turning to Odin with wide, glassy eyes.

"Yes—I called you my daughter, because you are." Odin placed his left hand on top of Antje's, now enveloping her left hand in both of his.

Antje suddenly looked less bewildered. "Oh, right. You're the All-Father."

"Yes, but—not in the way I am to you. I am your father, and Frigg is your mother. Eír is our daughter. I sent her to Lyfjaberg after she was born, to serve as Menglöð's handmaiden—a peace offering to the Jotuns. It has managed to keep the peace in our realms—to some extent, anyway. You have always been a peacekeeper of the realms, Antje—even from birth."

Antje remained silent, unable to comprehend how what Odin revealed could possibly be true. "No daughter of mine leaves a battle halfway through. I am the God of War, the God of Death, and you...you are a valkyrie. Antje, you must do your job, even when you do not want to. As I said, we all make sacrifices." Odin lifted his left hand and tapped under where his right eyeball once lived.

Antje shook her head, her eyebrows furrowed with incredulity. "I'm sorry. I'm... I'm your daughter? But I have a father..." she trailed off, pinching her temple with one hand and dragging her fingers down the side of her face, as if to wipe the disbelief from it.

"You have a father I chose for you; one with all of my shortcomings, so that you would not be disappointed when you found out the truth about who your father really is. I knew if you could love him with all of his flaws, you could love me the same—and you loved him in spite of what he did, just as Eír loves me."

"So, what does this mean, exactly?" Antje said, her foot tapping against the stone beneath her.

Odin let out a muted chortle. "It means you are the child of two Norse Gods, and as such, right now, it is your duty to protect Midgard and its inhabitants, at all costs. If Midgard falls, all of the realms will fall with it. You must keep the balance and the peace, Antje. As you know, I see all. The Norns, the weavers of fate, this is what they have woven for you. You can bargain with the Norns, but some threads are fixed; this is one of those. You must return to Midgard." Odin patted her hand and again enveloped her hand with his.

Antje stared off into the distance, her hair fluttering in the wind as the ebb and flow of air changed directions. "My fate—but, how do I go back?" she answered, slowly turning to Odin, still processing the revelation of being the offspring of two Gods.

The tides of war were decisively moving in a direction that neither the military nor Cisterne's mystics desired. The bodies of their dead now lined the edge of the forest like a wall, and the remaining marines used said wall for cover, often staring into the lifeless faces of their future before meeting their untimely end.

Mathias and Mikono had been battling in the forest on the eastern front of the battle, Mikono and her band of mystical beasts picking off the few remaining dark mystics that Mathias hadn't slain. Cerberus bit the heads from enemies and snapped dark mystics in half like brittle chicken bones, their frothy mouths dripping with rainbow-colored spittle infused with the blood of their victims. As the last of the dark mystics in reach fell to Mathias's axe, he turned to Mikono, pleased.

"Let us move south and westward and meet William Henry!" Mathias yelled to Mikono.

Nodding with a quiet smile, Mikono's eyes bulged in horror. "Mathias! Turn around!" The point of a spear pushed through Mathias' chest, puncturing a lung. Mathias turned around to find a half-dead goblin, whom he used his remaining strength to cleanly behead, before pulling the spear from his chest, inch by inch—his hands dripping with his own blood. Mathias collapsed to the forest floor as Mikono dashed to his side.

"Mathias! Mathias, no! Please stay with me. Mathias! Healer! I need a healer!" Mikono turned to a trusted ally, a kamaitachi named Kaze. Mikono instructed Kaze to fetch help. His claws, resembling scythes, moved so quickly that the weasel-like creature now appeared as a whirlwind of dust to the naked eye. Practically vanishing into thin air, Kaze took off to the southwest.

"Mik—Mikono, do not cry. To Valhalla I go, to eat and drink with my gods. This is a happy day for me, but you must keep fighting, for Antje—for our people. You must..." Mathias fell unconscious as Mikono applied pressure to his chest, crying and sniffling as the blood seemed to boil through the cracks of her fingers, no matter how hard she pressed.

"How do you go back?" Odin's chest bounced with laughter. "You are a valkyrie, Antje. If anyone knows how to traverse the path between life and death, it is you, daughter." Antje once again stared dead ahead, still stunned by hearing the word "daughter" roll off Odin's tongue.

"Antje! Is that you?" a familiar voice rang out. Antje and Odin simultaneously turned around and looked up, only to find Mathias towering over them. Antje jumped to her feet.

"Mathias! What are you—"

"No time, Antje. Why are you here? We are dying down there. We are losing the war, and you're meditating!" Mathias looked down at Odin and dropped to one knee, bowing his head. "Forgive me, All-Father."

"I'm not meditating—the Dark Queen got the drop on me, and I guess I'm in some sort of unconscious state. If you're here, you're also unconscious?"

"I'm dying, Antje—on the battlefield like a dog. Go save our people!" Mathias demanded.

Antje, with fire renewed, looked to Odin and Mathias. "I'm going back. Mathias, I will see you again one day. Odin, come fight with us," Antje said in a tone that suggested it was more of a demand than a request.

"I cannot, daughter. This is your battle, not mine. The Norns have woven the fate of this battle, and I cannot intervene without risking... *everything*. Call upon your brother when you return—Thor has taken a liking to you," Odin said before once again shoving Antje off the cliff. "Breathe, Antje! When you hit the ground, you must be ready to fight!" he screamed.

Freefalling, Antje turned her head and looked up at the rock face to find Mathias and Odin peeking over the edge. Mathias grinned and flashed a thumbs-up before she hit the ground with alarming force.

Headmaster Vogel, ragged and weary, looked to Kenny as he surveyed the carnage on the battlefield below. "We have to kill ze Queen. We will all be dead within ze hour if we don't take her out."

Pulling his binoculars down from his face, Kenny sighed. "Agreed—I don't think we have another option. I'm going to send in my special ops team, but they will need cover to get into the castle, where I'm assuming she's holed up."

The General looked at his cellphone, and without his gaze wavering from the screen, said, "Why don't we just call in air support and put an end to this? My losses are becoming untenable."

Kenny's head whipped to the left as he glared at the General. "With all due respect, sir... we can't do that. We have people inside the blast zone. My superior is inside, as is Antje, who is the entire reason we even knew where the Dark Queen was," he snapped back.

"We all have to make sacrifices, Agent Davis," the General casually mumbled, still fixated on his phone.

Kenny clenched his fists and shook his head with exasperation before turning to Headmaster Vogel, who winked and flashed a soothing smile.

"General, these are not normal enemies. Some will survive ze blast, and then we will have disabled one of our greatest weapons," Headmaster Vogel explained.

Looking up from his phone, the General's curiosity was piqued. "What weapon? And if our enemies can't be bombed, then what good will his 'special ops team' do?"

"Antje—she is not a normal mystic. She is a valkyrie with far more power than anyone on this battlefield—your aerial support included. We must give her a chance to end this. Ze ops team, and ze CIA have special weaponry that we helped to develop for just this occasion. Their bullets are not ze same as your men's bullets."

"A valkyrie? As in, the Norse angels of death? That's a myth," the General scoffed.

"So is ze three-headed dog down on ze field to your right. Does that mean it isn't really there? Are we all hallucinating? You are not fighting a normal war here, General." Headmaster Vogel placed his hand gently on the General's shoulder. "Please trust me—we need her, or in ze end, we all die. Everyone on Earth, not just ze people here today. This is bigger than today."

"What say you, Agent Davis?" the General asked, turning to face him. Headmaster Vogel dropped his hand from the General's shoulder and clasped them behind his back, winking again at Kenny.

"I'm in agreement with the Headmaster. Antje cannot be sacrificed, and neither can Cole for that matter—we need them. Let's get the special ops team inside to support them and kill the Queen. If that goes sideways, we can try your plan."

The General faced the battlefield and answered, "Very well. You have thirty minutes before I call in air support. I need to call the President and warn him about the gravity of the situation. None of us were aware this was a global threat that could not be neutralized by normal weaponry."

As Kenny gathered his special ops team, Headmaster Vogel closed his eyes and telepathically contacted Takhi, who pulled herself back from the battlefield and answered.

"Headmaster, it's horrific down here," Takhi said with a gulp.

"Takhi, we need to retrieve Antje immediately. Are you up to fighting still?" he asked gently.

"Yes, Headmaster. What is done is done, and at this point, losing is not an option. I will do what needs to be done in order for us to win."

"Good. We need to kill ze Dark Queen and you're ze only one other than Antje who might have a fighting chance of doing so. Meet me on ze western edge of ze forest, but Takhi? Steel yourself, or this might be ze end of all of us."

Upon her crash landing, Antje heard the sound of Katya's spit-laden voice carrying through the room's walls. "She promised me that I would rule all of Europe when this is over. Prime Minister Katya—I like the sound of that," she snorted.

Antje cracked one eye open, her chin resting on her chest. Her feet were tightly fastened to the legs of the chair she sat on, her arms bound behind her back. To the right of her chair lay Shields, who groggily attempted to wriggle loose from his bindings and muzzle. Antje couldn't see inside the casket to check on Cole without lifting her head, but what Antje did see, was the white transformation reversal potion she had stuffed into her bra earlier that day—and it was just within reach of her lips. Grabbing her shirt and lifting it with her lower lip, she used her tongue to slide the vial out from the edge of her bra and into her mouth. As Katya and the two draugrs in the room started a new conversation and turned their backs to her, Antje slowly tilted her head, gripping the cork with her teeth and opening it inside of her mouth. The liquid spilled from the vial onto her tongue, and she curled it upward to create a vessel to contain the potion. As the draugrs began to argue over who got to keep Daggert, Antje quickly lifted her head and spit the transformation potion onto Shields.

Exploding from his bindings, Shields' teacup-muzzle fell to the floor as he transformed back into his rightful body. Turning around, Katya and the draugrs jumped backward, readying themselves. Shields, now as large as a lion, barreled through the room with his fierce jaws poised to attack.

Cornering one of the draugrs, Shields began lunging and snapping at him. The draugr holding Daggert charged Shields, his long arm swinging down and stabbing Shields in the side. Shields let out a pained whimper but continued to rip at the grey, rotting flesh of the other draugr he had cornered. As the second draugr swung his arm upward in preparation for another assault, Shields quickly turned his head, biting the Daggert-wielding hand clean off his assailant's arm. Antje stretched her neck as far as she could and checked the empty casket for Cole with no such luck. Still bound, Antje hurriedly wiped the potion from her ring with her other hand until the ring transmuted itself back into a sword, which Antje then used to free herself.

Katya grabbed Daggert from the greedy draugr's uncoupled hand and squared off with Antje. Shields continued ripping the trapped draugr limb from limb until the putrid being retreated into the corner and curled into a ball. With his first foe subdued, Shields turned his aggression on the remaining one-armed draugr. Cowardice washed across Katya's rotund, green face as she dropped Daggert, turned, and sprinted down the hallway as fast as her tree-trunk legs could carry her.

Retrieving Daggert from the floor and slipping it into her boot, Antje turned around and swiftly decapitated the one-armed draugr with her sword before plunging it through the second one's undead heart. Shields dropped to the floor on his belly, panting and exhausted.

Antje carefully examined Shields, her hands sticking to his blood-drenched fur in the area surrounding the puncture. Using his oversized paws, Antje maneuvered him onto his side.

"Trust me, buddy. You'll be okay, I promise." Shields gave Antje a concerned look before flopping his head haphazardly onto the floor. His tongue hung from his mouth as he panted, brushing the ice-cold marble beneath with each labored breath. Antje stroked his fur gently, using her hands to pull his energetic body above his physical one. A red ball appeared, and she slowly pulled at the red thread of injury until it exited Shields' body. Antje pressed the red energy into the marble, and gradually lowered the energetic body back into Shields' physical one. With a large exhale, Shields' head popped up and jerked around to where his stab wound once was, but could no longer be found. He licked Antje's face from chin to forehead.

Antje smiled, wiping away the slobber with her shirt. "You're all healed up, bud. Let's go find Cole."

As Antje and Shields exited the room, Antje began screaming Cole's name repeatedly as she made a second round through all of the rooms she'd previously searched. Entering a southern-facing room, Antje looked out the window, only to feel her heart sink through her boots. It was apparent at just a glance, that Mathias' report was unfortunately accurate. Bodies of good souls littered the castle grounds, and a horde of dark mystics gathered in what was once the immaculate garden and surrounding meadow but now looked more like the scene of a cataclysmic event. Antje grabbed her Mjolnir with one hand, opening the window with the other as she closed her eyes.

"Thor, God of Thunder, I need your help. Help me send a chain of lightning through this crowd of my enemies."

Thor's booming voice coolly replied, "You have three charges, sister. That's all your body could absorb right now. Use them wisely." Antje opened her eyes to witness her fingertips crackling and snapping with a blue, energetic light. Focusing on a group to the east, she shot a thin bolt of lightning from her fingertips. It traveled through the air with ease and ping-ponged around the crowd of dark mystics, transferring from one body to the next, killing the majority of the throng, but leaving several only incapacitated. The second charge was sent to the western group, again killing most, while only stunning others.

As the last charge left her fingertips and sailed toward the center of the pack, Antje spotted Headmaster Vogel and Takhi approaching the castle with a platoon of men dressed in black tactical armor. The last of Antje's energy rippled through the center mass of loathsome creatures, electrifying their bodies and dropping most of them immediately. Antje yelled to Headmaster Vogel, but the sound of battle drowned out her voice. No one took notice of Antje's screams—with one exception—the Dark Queen. Glaring at Antje with a most evil smirk, the Dark Queen stood at the doorway directly ahead of the path Headmaster Vogel and Takhi forged.

"Oh, no...Oh, no, sh...she's going to kill them." Antje panicked, launching herself from the room with Shields not far behind. She was willing to slaughter anything and everything that stood in her way as she maneuvered through the castle hallways—and she did.

"What the hell was that?!" the General exclaimed, witnessing the blue lightning easily defeat the enemies that had so effortlessly slaughtered his men.

"The weapon Headmaster Vogel was telling you about." A warm smile crept to Kenny's lips. "She's alive. There's hope."

The General continued to marvel with his mouth agape as he pressed the binoculars against his eyes so tightly that it seemed as though he was trying to meld them into his sockets. "She can shoot lightning from four stories up?!"

"She can do things you can't even fathom, General. We're witnessing the power of gods right now. It's incredible, isn't it?" Kenny replied, still grinning and unable to peel his eyes from the scene unfolding below. Raising his comm to his mouth, he pressed the button with his thumb. "Team Norse, come in. Remember, code word is Sahira. Antje is alive, and inside the castle. Do not engage and protect her at all costs. Over."

Immediately, Special Agent David received an answer: "Kssshht. Affirmative, sir. Over."

With his binoculars still fused to his face, the General announced, "I have to call the President. Looks as if the tides have changed. My men are now able to take these monsters down." The General continued to observe as his marines beheaded the remaining dark mystics where they stood, stunned and unable to move. Kenny looked to the General, knowing full well what would become of Antje if the President of the United States was made aware of her abilities. A pit grew in his stomach, and he began to sweat as he wore a path in the dirt beneath his feet.

The Dark Queen snarled with delight as black, wispy energy gathered in her hands. Takhi scowled at the Dark Queen and opened her wings to shield Headmaster Vogel and the special ops team in formation behind her. Calling upon her gods for gale-force winds, Takhi unleashed a violent airstream on the Dark Queen, who struggled to hold the dark energy in her hands, let alone launch it as she normally would have.

Frustrated by the change of tides, the Dark Queen let out a deafening and shrill scream as she began to gather red energy in her hands instead. Headmaster Vogel saw this over Takhi's shoulder—he knew that red energy was not impacted by the physical world or its laws. Crawling under Takhi's wings, he stood in front of her and summoned a white, protective energy bubble that encompassed the entire group. The Dark Queen unleashed the red energy orbs, and as they collided with the Headmaster's bubble, it disintegrated. Headmaster Vogel froze with shock for a split-second as his protective bubbles typically held through several volleys of spells—not merely a single strike. Snapping out of his disbelief, he began to summon another protective shield, but the Dark Queen was skilled, and an expedient summoner; she launched another red orb directly at them. Takhi, as if time had slowed, looked to Headmaster Vogel, pulled her wing in, placed it in front of him, and flicked it backward—knocking the Headmaster behind her. Takhi braced herself, and as the red ball made impact, it singed her wings, burning them to the bone before consuming her bones and traveling across her body in its entirety.

Headmaster Vogel again projected a protective bubble around the group. Rattled by the sight of Takhi's disintegrating body, he closed his eyes and sent a telepathic communication to Philomena. The leader of the special ops team signaled to begin firing, as Takhi was down and they now had a clear line of sight to the Dark Queen. Several gunshots popped, and an anointed bullet hurtled through the air, piercing the Dark Queen's shoulder.

The Dark Queen looked down at her bloodied shoulder with feelings of dubiety. "Impossible. I put a protective spell on the castle. I'm inside the spell's boundary..." she trailed off, now holding her shoulder with her opposite hand and retreating quickly inside the castle door.

"Takhi! Takhi, you are going to be okay. Philomena will be here any moment with a healing potion. Stay with me, you brave, foolish girl," Headmaster Vogel assured Takhi, his hand holding her face as tears welled in his eyes.

"I think I'm done, Headmaster. Thank... thank you for loving me like a daughter," Takhi gasped, as loss of consciousness punctuated her sentence. Headmaster Vogel again closed his eyes, unleashing tears down his weathered cheeks, and he sent one more telepathic message.

"Hurry, Phil, we are losing her."

Antje finally slaughtered her way to the door where she'd seen the Dark Queen previously, only to find Takhi's mottled and disfigured body down less than fifty feet away, with Philomena and Headmaster Vogel kneeling at her side. The familiar feeling of rage burning inside bubbled up to Antje's face as the special ops team approached Antje with rifles aimed straight at her.

"Sahira!" she yelled. Their weapons lowered simultaneously. "Where is the Dark Queen?" she yelled to the special ops team through her clenched teeth.

The lead answered respectfully, as if he were speaking to a superior officer. "She has been wounded and retreated inside the structure. We're headed in to find her now."

"Give me one of your comms. I had eyes on Cole. He's alive, but in a coma or something and then I lost him again. I need Kenny and Leif, right now. We need to find Cole before it's too late, and then—I am going to make that bitch suffer for what she's done," Antje snarled, staring at Takhi's skeletal body as Philomena scrambled to tend to her.

Leif and William Henry mopped up what was left of the bodies on the southern edge of the battlefield. Both Leif and William Henry had stayed toward the rear of the assault, acting as snipers and providing suppressing fire, which had shielded them from any damage. Using his seax, Leif jabbed through the heart of a human-salamander hybrid, whose slimy tongue twitched as it limply hung from its mouth. "What the fuck is this thing?" he asked, repulsed.

"It's dead. That's what it is," William Henry answered, wiping black, viscous blood from his rapier. "One day, you really must come to the Cisterne, so you can understand what it is you've seen here today."

"I would like that. I have so many questions. But, how awesome was Antje with that lightning! Surely that was Thor! The gods smiled upon us today! That's why we're victorious!" he proclaimed. Suddenly, a marine tapped Leif on the shoulder; Leif jerked and put his knife to the man's throat. "Oh, sorry!" Leif quickly removed his knife. "Battle jitters...you know," Leif laughed, sheepishly.

"I have orders to inform you of a change in position. You will meet Antje and Kenny at the western entrance of the castle." The Marine pointed at the castle door and quickly returned to his duty of mopping up the last of the dark mystics. Leif continued to blankly stare at him, not saying anything in return as the Marine walked off.

"Go, I will take care of things here," William Henry instructed. Leif nodded and turned toward the castle, jamming his seax into the forehead of a dead body next to him, which let out a slight gurgle.

Turning back to William Henry, he grinned and shrugged one shoulder. "Just in case it has some magical resurrection ability... I don't know how this shit works."

As Kenny made his way to the meeting point Antje requested, he heard a "Pssst" from the side of a large tree to his left. Kenny immediately pulled his pistol from his holster and aimed it at the tree—finger not yet on the trigger. A scantily clad woman stepped out from behind the tree, and Kenny's gun followed. It was Katya in her human form.

"I have a message for you from the Queen," Katya said, putting her hands up. Kenny kept the sight of his gun pinned on her and nodded silently—signaling to continue.

"The Queen wants to barter a trade. Cole for her life. If you and your team will retreat to the southern side of the property and allow her to escape through the catacombs under the castle, she will not kill Cole. He is under a stasis spell, and in the catacombs waiting to be rescued as we speak. I have been instructed to undo the spell after she has surfaced, and I've confirmed her escape. Do you agree?"

Special Agent Cole digested her words for a moment and then demanded, "Let me talk to the Queen."

Katya nodded, and her pupils rolled into the back of her head, her body becoming motionless for several seconds. "Hello, Kenny. What a momentous day for you. You have somehow managed to best me this time. What say you of our deal? Do you want Cole alive or not?" Katya's mouth moved, but it was the Dark Queen's voice that spoke through it.

With his gun still pointed at Katya, he gruffly replied, "How do I know you won't kill him anyway?"

"I'm a lot of things, but a liar isn't one of them. You'll just have to trust me. The alternative option is that I kill him and leave anyway—or maybe I turn him into one of my mindless zombies and unleash him on you? Hah—that would be delightful. Your choice."

"Fine. Deal—but if there's so much as a bruise on his body, I will hunt you to the ends of the Earth with Antje, do you understand me?" Kenny stepped two steps closer to Katya with his gun still aimed at her head.

"I would expect no less. Quite the team you guys make. I must admit, I was not expecting Antje to be able to shoot lightning from her hands. What a show! I'm going to miss her. She's so *thrilling*."

Kenny ground his teeth. "I'm restraining and taking your lackey as collateral. If anything happens to him, or if he doesn't wake up, she'll be sent to a black site and tortured until we find you."

An amused laugh spilled from Katya's mouth. "Do what you will, but here's my second condition: Antje is not to come with you. I need to secure an escape through the catacombs, and we both know there is absolutely no way she's going to allow that. Bring as many men as you want, but no Antje. If I see her approach, I will kill him instantly."

"Fine. No Antje. I'm headed that way now." Kenny took two more steps forward and then side-stepped his way behind Katya and handcuffed her. "Know this, Queen. No funny shit. No surprise spells, no traps... I know you're injured and you don't want me unleashing Antje after the loved ones she lost today. We pulled the blueprints of the castle. We know where the tunnels lead to, and I have aerial support just waiting for my call."

"Yes—yes, I know, her ridiculous human attachments. I will never understand why someone with so much power suffers such idealistic notions. We have a deal."

Katya's eyeballs rolled back to where her irises once again showed, and she struggled with her handcuffs, hissing at Kenny.

"Careful, this gun is loaded with special bullets that will put you down. That's not what you want, is it? Show me to the catacombs," Kenny ordered, walking behind Katya, his gun target-locked on her head. Begrudgingly, Katya began to trudge through the forest, grumbling under her breath the entire way to the western castle door.

As Katya's eyes caught Antje's, daggers shot from them. Antje smirked, her arms crossing her chest.

"Well done, Kenny. You caught the Dark Queen's lapdog," Antje sneered as Shields let out a low growl, glued to her side. "Oh, sorry—that's an insult to dogs." Shields' growl ceased and his furry chin lifted in superiority.

Kenny looked down at Takhi as her motionless body was placed onto a stretcher, Mikono now present and sobbing. Sighing, he looked at Antje; his gun still pointed at Katya's head as Leif arrived and stood next to him. "Antje, you're not going to like what I'm about to say, but I need you to trust me." Antje stiffened and gave a quick, singular nod to Kenny. "The Queen has bartered Cole in exchange for her escape, and I've accepted the deal."

Antje's stern disposition flipped into one of elation. "He's alive! That's great! Let's go get him—we'll deal with her later. She's injured and her army is debilitated. As far as I'm concerned, the threat has been neutralized for now...why wouldn't I like that deal?" Antje asked, grinning from ear to ear.

"Because the terms of our deal are that you aren't to be on the premises when the exchange happens," Kenny somberly replied.

"You're right—I don't like that. It's too risky, Kenny. She's planning something, I just know it." Antje's brain whirred with scenarios.

"I'll go!" Leif raised his hand, looking to Antje and Kenny before slowly lowering it. "What? I don't even have a scratch on my body from today. I will go...as a representative for Antje." Antje smiled at Leif, tilting her head affectionately as Kenny continued the conversation with no acknowledgment of Leif's offer.

"I don't think she is, Antje. She knows—we all know—that if you were allowed into the area she's using to escape, you would pursue and kill her. That puts Cole at risk, and I don't see the benefit in that risk. My team has already injured her; she's on her heels. We can take things from here. I hate to do this, but on behalf of the CIA and the US government: this is an order to stand down, Antje. Head back to camp, where we have trailers set up now. Go shower, try to relax, and wait. I promise you will be the very first person to see Cole once we return. You have my word."

Antje paused for a moment, committing her thought process to being brutally honest with herself and replied, "Okay. I see your point. You didn't have to pull rank on me, Kenny. I want Cole returned to me alive; whatever plan has the greatest chance of that outcome, is the plan we need to go with. You're right, and I don't think I'd have the self-control not to hunt her down. She's not meant to be alive as she is right now, and I don't always have control over my compulsions when it comes to who lives or dies these days." Antje uncrossed her arms and took in a deep breath, exhaling her frustration loudly.

"Valkyrie thing, huh?" Kenny replied, his lips curling into an empathetic half-smile. "I know this is hard for you, Antje. Trust me, I will bring him home."

Antje's eyes watered up, and she nodded, her lips pursed tightly, fighting back tears. "You better." Antje stepped off the stone stairs and began walking toward the woods, Shields by her side.

"HUNGRY. SHIELDS HUNGRY."

"I know, boy, let's go get cleaned up, and I'll get you something to eat," Antje answered, stepping over the minefield of decayed, rotting bodies as if they were merely fallen logs on a forest trail.

Leif turned to Kenny and drew an X across his chest with his index finger, "No extra paperwork, I promise."

"Fine. Load your rifle with the bullets my men will provide you, and follow my orders to the letter, understand me?" Kenny replied as Leif's face lit up with enthusiasm.

"Yes, sir!" Leif yelled, saluting and straightening himself as Kenny let out a slight chortle

TWENTY

PASSAGEWAYS AND PROPOSALS

K enny reconvened with his team inside the castle, giving implicit instructions to protect Cole at all costs. Pushing his gun between her shoulder blades, he urged Katya to show them where Cole was being held hostage. Katya led the team into the kitchen and walked up to a large, wooden, freestanding pantry.

"Move the pantry," Katya drolly instructed. Kenny motioned to Leif and one of his men to push the hulking cabinet to the side as the remainder of the team kept their rifles fixed on the pantry. As the pantry feet slid across the icy floor beneath, it unveiled an entrance guarded by a heavy oak door. Using the butt of his rifle, Leif knocked the chain lock off the door and kicked it open. The slamming of the door against the stone wall echoed through a series of stairs that were absorbed by the darkness on the other side of the doorway. The tapping of Kevlar could be heard, and a bright, cold, white light shone from the helmets of the special ops team; with a path illuminated, their journey deep into the catacombs beneath the castle began.

Upon reaching the bottom of the twisting and turning stairwell, the team spilled from the narrow passage into an empty, cavernous room with a casket in the center. Kenny again motioned with hand signals for Leif and one of his men to approach and open the casket as the rest secured the area. Leif carefully removed the lid as the agent looked down into the casket, and swiftly turned to Kenny. "Affirmative. It's him, sir. He appears to be in a coma."

Kenny jammed the gun deeper into Katya's back, as her eyes rolled and she let out a low-energy hiss. "You're up. No funny business. I promise you: I won't lose any sleep over killing you and leaving you to die in the dark, alone."

Pausing for a telepathic confirmation of the Dark Queen's escape, Katya approached the casket and whispered into Cole's ear. A loud gasp for air caused Leif to jump back a step before Cole's upper body practically ejected itself from the coffin. Kenny handed Katya to Leif and outstretched his hand to Cole.

"Good to have you back, sir. You're going to be okay." Cole grabbed Kenny's hand and stepped out of the casket. "Where's Antje? Is she alive? I could hear everything while I was under. The Dark Queen, I think she killed Antje..." Cole rambled, out of breath and panting as panic took over.

"Deep breaths, sir. Antje is fine. She escaped and is back at camp waiting for you."

Cole unleashed a massive sigh of relief. Grabbing Kenny's gun, without a single thought, Cole shot Katya directly between the eyes. Before her body had time to crash to the floor, Cole buried two more bullets into her skull—just for good measure.

With his face drenched in brown blood, Leif's eyes lit up with excitement and he outstretched his hand to Cole. "I'm Antje's representative. My name is Leif. It's good to meet you."

Silently, Cole nodded his head at Leif and headed for the stairwell. Kenny, whose eyes were still parked on Katya's dead body, shrugged at his team and motioned for them to return to formation; the last two brought up the rear as they scanned the catacombs with their rifles, walking backward to ensure a safe exit.

In the trailer, Antje found a few MREs tucked in the kitchen cabinets and poured the contents of them all into one bowl and filled another with a bottle of water from the mini fridge. As Antje set the bowls on the floor of the micro kitchen, Shields descended upon them as a wolf does on a fresh kill. Antje giggled and patted the top of his head.

"You did *so good* today, buddy. Thank you for saving me, but—slow down, Shields; you'll get a tummy ache. I'm gonna take a shower. Be good." Antje disrobed, setting her weapons across the small sink and stepping into the claustrophobia-inducing shower in the trailer's bathroom, the floor shaking as Shields' feet pranced around excitedly during his supper.

The shower felt heavenly, and as the hot water ran from her body, it turned greenish black, cleansing her from the viscera of the day. Antje closed her eyes and focused on the feeling of the droplets individually hitting her skin and rolling down her face all the way to her toes. It was the reset she had so desperately needed for days. Flashes of battle played like a silent film in her mind's eye, including Cole's lifeless face in the casket. The film was interrupted by the sound of Shields' growl from the other room. Quickly exiting the shower, Antje wrapped herself in a towel and grabbed her sword, bursting through the door, ready to fight.

Upon exiting the bathroom, she found no one to fight; Cole walked through the front door, with Kenny following behind. Kenny quickly pulled his hand to his forehead, as if he froze mid-salute, and pierced the floor with his eyes.

"It's okay, Shields! Take it easy, boy," Antje said, dropping her sword and walking up to Cole slowly with tears in her eyes.

"Is it really you?" Antje asked, choking back the overwhelming emotions that were saturating every molecule of her being.

"It's me. I'm here, Antje. I'm so sorry I left you to fight this all alone. I am so sorry, darling," Cole replied, rushing to Antje and wrapping her tightly in his arms. He leaned back, cradling her head with his hands, her dripping-wet strands of hair weaving themselves between his fingers. Staring deeply into her eyes, Cole whispered, "I'm so sorry," and kissed her forehead, wiping the tears from under her eyes with his thumbs.

"I never stopped looking for you," Antje sobbed. "I was ready to burn the whole world down to find you."

"I know. I heard everything while I was under. I knew you were coming. Thank you for finding me, babe. You're unlike anyone I have *ever* met, and I love you so damn much." Cole's eyes were now glassy as tears formed in the corners. Leaning in, Cole gently kissed her pillowy lips once more.

"I love you so damn much, right back," Antje replied through her sniffling, letting out a nervous laugh as she wiped her nose with the towel. "Sorry. I'm snotty."

Cole laughed. "Well, I love snot. So—give it to me!" he playfully replied, kissing the tip of her nose and the apples of her cheeks.

As tears continued to roll down Antje's face, Kenny turned his back to the happy couple. "Friends, I don't want to ruin your moment, but we have a massive problem brewing and it needs to be addressed immediately. Antje, can I ask you to please put on some clothes?"

The couple both laughed, easing the tension in the room.

Turning around and looking to Kenny, Cole replied, "You act like you've never seen a woman in a towel before, Davis. I knew you were a virgin."

Kenny rolled his eyes and let out a mocking laugh. "Good to have you back, sir. My self-esteem was getting out of control with you gone," he replied as Antje walked into the bathroom, reemerging fully clothed. Using the towel to dry her hair, Antje sat down on the tan-colored loveseat opposite the kitchen. "What's this problem you needed to talk about?" Antje asked, as Cole sat down next to her, wrapping his arm around her shoulder.

"The General called the President of the United States after you unleashed that lightning with your hands," Kenny replied. Cole stiffened and removed his arm from her shoulder, sitting up and leaning forward with his hands clasped between his knees.

"So, the President knows who I am now? Is that the problem?" Antje asked, not fully following.

"That's not it, Antje," Kenny continued as Cole put his head in his hands, tufts of hair poking between his fingers. Antje looked at Cole and put her hand on his back, her head ducking down to look at him.

"They're going to take her to a black site and experiment on her like a lab rat, and even if they don't manage to catch her, they'll hunt her indefinitely," Cole lamented with anger spilling from the space between each word.

"Affirmative," Kenny replied. "I overheard him talking to the President, and from the parts I heard, that's exactly what they're planning. They'll want me to bring her in since they know fighting her is a terrible idea—especially with today's losses—and they know she trusts me."

Antje leaned back into the loveseat, flabbergasted. "So, I help save his men and the world—and the thanks I get is to be kidnapped and turned into an experiment? That lightning wasn't even my power—it was Thor's."

Cole's hand grabbed Antje's knee gently as he turned and looked to her. "It doesn't matter. All they see is a new weapon to develop, Antje."

Kenny put his thumb to his chin and his index finger on his upper lip, the wheels of his mind spinning a solution. "Unless..." he trailed off.

"Unless what?" Cole asked, clinging to a newfound thread of hope.

"What if you and Antje got married immediately, and she joined the CIA? If she offered to willingly give blood and tissue samples, while continuing to be a part of the agency... They might agree to that. Strategically, it makes no sense for them to pick a fight with someone they think can shoot lightning from their hands on demand—especially not if she's useful in hunting down the Dark Queen."

Cole stood up and began pacing the space in front of the loveseat. "You're right. If she's one of us, and they get what they want, they won't take her to a black site, especially not as the wife of the head of the CIA's supernatural division," he replied, his tone less somber than before.

"Wait—what?! You're the head of the CIA's supernatural division? I just thought you were some agent?" Antje replied, astonished by this revelation.

Cole stopped mid-stride and turned to Antje. "Your response to me even being in the CIA didn't leave a lot of room for me to share that with you, babe. Do you have that necklace I gave you?"

Antje nodded and pulled the broken necklace from her pocket. "It's broken. I think I used all of the power in the jade, I'm sorry," she said, handing it to him by the chain, the empty setting dangling in mid-air.

Receiving the necklace in his hand, Cole laughed quietly. "It did its job then. Don't be sorry. I gave it to you to make sure you didn't get hurt—and here you are, in one piece." Lowering himself onto one knee in front of Antje, Cole presented her with the necklace once more. "Antje, I love you—I have since the moment I met you. Our relationship has been...r ocky, through no fault of our own, but you are unlike any woman I've ever met. You literally saved my life and risked everything in the process. Will you marry me, and let me spend the rest of our lives loving and protecting you like you have loved and protected me over the last couple of months?"

Antje's eyes again filled with tears. "Just to be clear, you're actually asking me to marry you, right? This isn't just an 'on paper' thing so that I don't end up with electrodes implanted in my head...right?"

Cole laughed, his head lowering toward the floor as he attempted to compose himself. "Yes, Antje. I am really asking you to be my wife. I would have liked for this to happen in a completely different way, several months from now, after we've gotten a chance to hopefully have some form of a normal relationship... But it seems like that's not what fate has planned. So, will you be the love of my life, and also allow me to protect you from our government as the secondary reason for us getting married?" Cole grinned and locked eyes with Antje.

Almost frantically, Antje nodded. "Yes! Yes, I'll marry you!" she cried, tears again streaming down her cheeks. Launching herself into his arms, Antje and Cole kissed once more.

"You guys are the weirdest, but most perfect couple ever. Congratulations, you two. I'm really happy for you both," Kenny announced before rifling through the mini fridge. "There's no champagne, but I can shake up this bottle of lemon-lime soda and spray it on you if that helps?"

Antje and Cole turned and laughed, hand in hand, as Shields wrapped his large mouth around the plastic soda bottle in Kenny's grasp, slobber now coating his hand in its entirety.

"I think he likes you, Kenny!" Cole joked, kissing Antje's hand. Releasing the bottle and slinging the mucous-like slobber from his hand, Kenny watched as Shields lay down on the floor, puncturing the bottle and licking furiously at the streams of soda erupting from each hole.

"I think he likes *soda*," Kenny chuckled.

TWENTY-ONE

TRANSITIONS AND TRUTH

Cole and Kenny exited the General's trailer, Antje observing from her trailer window in suspense. As the General stepped off the last step, he turned and shook Cole's hand, his other on his shoulder. Antje exhaled a large sigh of relief, as it was clear he had accepted their terms.

Cole's feet hit the ground in tandem with Antje's heartbeat as he approached her, beaming. He opened the door and cheerfully announced, "Crisis averted, my future wife." Picking her up, he pulled her close to his chest and spun her around once, setting her down while planting a long, tender kiss on her lips.

"I like the sound of that. *Your wife.*" Antje pulled her head back and gazed deeply into Cole's amber eyes.

"Well, here's to hoping you also like the sound of this: we need to stay in this region until we've found the Dark Queen. I know you have a job back home, and a life there, but to keep you from spending the rest of your days in a black site, and to keep me from being charged with treason for trying to break you out...you'll have to quit your job and work for the CIA in my division. Now that the Dark Queen is on the government's radar, and they know the mystical threats that exist beyond just reading about them in my reports, the situation escalated to the President's desk. His acceptance of our plan hinges on both of us continuing our work here. Are you okay with all of that?" Cole's body was tense with concern, and Antje felt it.

Running her fingers through his hair, the curls passing between them one by one, she kissed his forehead, giggled, and replied, "*Oh no*, I'm going to miss that shitty job so much! Honestly, I knew my old life ended as soon as I stepped foot in the Cisterne, Cole. I'll call and resign today. I'm good with staying here—other than my Uncle Isaac, there's not much reason for me to return, and I really need to check in on the Cisterne and all the people who came to our aid. I need to check on Takhi; last I saw, she was in really bad shape, even with Philomena administering potions."

Cole's eyes dimmed. "That's the other thing I need to talk to you about. Sit down, babe." Cole led Antje to the loveseat and sat down next to her, his hands forming a clamshell around both of hers, as if they were a pearl. "As you know, we had a lot of losses today. We lost over a thousand Marines, and I don't know how to say this..." Cole trailed off.

"Who died?" Antje asked, a lump of grief growing in her throat.

"Mathias and Misha didn't make it, Antje—I'm so sorry. They both died heroes. According to the report I received from the field, Misha died saving Takhi's life, and Mathias single-handedly terminated hundreds of dark mystics."

Antje began to sob, her chest heaving as soundless screams eked through her constricted throat. Cole pulled Antje into him, her face buried in his chest as he too choked back tears—the loss was hard enough, but Antje's heartbreak was unbearable. Antje regained some semblance of control as she regulated her breaths, and through her sobs, she asked, "...and Takhi?"

Cole pursed his lips, the corners turning down. With brows furrowed, he replied, "Still alive, but her prognosis is guarded."

"I have to try and heal her!" Antje tearfully exclaimed, jumping up from the loveseat and staring at the floor as she frantically paced back and forth. "I'll explain more later, but I have to try. I asked them to come here—this is literally all my fault—their deaths are all my fault. Mathias, Misha, Takhi...I practically killed them myself. Mathias was dying when I saw him with Odin. Why didn't I go heal him? I should have healed him. I was just so focused on finding you and the Dark Queen. I should have—I didn't even get to say goodbye." Antje's body trembled, the tears flowing freely once more as the depth of her guilt consumed her.

Cole stood up from the couch and grabbed Antje's shoulders, stopping her in place and forcing her to face him. "Antje, look at me. Remember when I was having a hard time at the bar about Afghanistan, and you told me that it wasn't my fault—that I just happened to be in a hard situation with no good choices? Apply that to yourself. Take a few deep breaths and really look at me." Antje's bloodshot, glassy eyes locked on Cole's, her chest quivering as she drew in a deep breath. "*This is not your fault, Antje.* I know you feel responsible, and I know how crushing the weight of that is—but this was not your fault. We can go to Takhi. She's been airlifted back to the Cisterne for medical treatment, and I can get us transport there, but I need you to know, none of this was your doing. You helped save me and the world today, as did Mathias and Misha. We took down her army; their deaths were not in vain—they died heroes. You're a valkyrie, Antje. You of all people know that death comes for all of us at some point. You can't bear the burden of fate's decisions, or you'll drive yourself insane. Trust me—I know."

A renewed wave of grief crashed into Antje like a freight train, and she collapsed into Cole's embrace. Her tears staining his shirt as he pressed his cheek against the top of her head. When Antje was done expelling her sorrow, she looked up at Cole, sniffling. "I'll grieve later. We need to get to the Cisterne immediately."

Cole leaned in, wiping the tears from Antje's face and kissed her forehead lovingly. "I'll call for transport."

The puddle-hopper Cole chartered managed a sketchy landing on the long stretch of meadow outside the castle. Kenny checked the identification of the pilot and gave an "all clear" as Antje and Cole approached with Shields following like a shadow. Prepared to board the eight-passenger plane, Antje and Cole stopped dead in their tracks as Leif bolted across the lawn, screaming, "Wait! Antje, wait!"

"Leif! I can't tell you how happy I am to see you! We're headed to the Cisterne. I'm not sure when or if I will be back, but I will be in touch. I owe you for *so many* reasons." Antje hugged Leif with her one free arm, the other occupied with holding her bag. Kenny approached and stood next to Cole. Leif tensed. "Can—can I come? I've seen things this week that I can't explain, and William Henry extended an invitation for me to visit earlier. I need this, Antje. I—I need answers." Leif's expression was solemn and serious. Antje looked to Cole, whose tilt of the head and casual shrug expressed it was her decision.

Antje smiled at Leif and wrapped her arm around his shoulders. "Of course, Leif. I know that feeling well. We don't have time for you to run home and grab clothes though. I hope that's okay. You can stay at my rental in Copenhagen."

"We'll get you new clothes, Leif. You're a CIA consultant now, and we take care of our own. Kenny brought me up to speed on the invaluable work you've done for the agency, and for my fiancée this week. I also owe you. Anything you need, you just let Kenny know," Cole answered, reaching his hand out to shake Leif's. A smile crept across Leif's drained face, and he shook Cole's hand, some of his signature exuberance returning.

"How did I go from second in command to Leif's errand boy? I saved your ass today, I might add. Candidly, sir, this is bullshit," Kenny jokingly chided, jabbing Cole in the ribs with his elbow. "Welcome to the team, Leif. Thanks for not getting yourself killed—you should see the stack of paperwork I have sitting on my desk right now." Kenny flashed his signature smirk that Leif now knew as his expression of fondness.

Leif placed his hands on his hips. "Gods forbid you'd have to do any paperwork. That was what I kept repeating as I was dodging bullets and spells—let's not create paperwork for Special Agent Davis, Leif. We must not!"

Laughter erupted, and Cole replied, "You fit right into the family already, Leif. Let's get going."

As the trio climbed into the plane, Kenny cupped his hands around his mouth and yelled, "Don't go getting married without me! I'll never forgive either of you!"

"We won't, Kenny! Yours will be the first invitation that I write!" Antje hollered back from the open door to the plane before taking her seat next to Cole. Cole turned to Antje with his eyebrow raised.

"You guys sure got close while I was gone." A look of uncertainty washed across Antje's face, as she couldn't discern whether this was jealousy or Cole just being himself. A grin grew between Cole's lips. "Relax, Antje," Cole laughed. "I'm not the jealous type. He's my brother, and I'm relieved you two not only got to know each other, but seem to actually like each other. Honestly, you've effortlessly slid into my world like the missing piece of a puzzle I didn't think I would ever complete. The whole valkyrie, Gods, and supernatural part of this aside—if I didn't believe in fate before, I do now."

Antje smiled, her eyes welling up with joyous tears; the emotional roller-coaster continued. Reaching across her and buckling the seatbelt, Cole leaned in and delicately kissed Antje on the cheek. "Precious cargo," he said, winking at her and smiling before grabbing her hand and wriggling himself into a comfortable position in his seat. As he tilted his head back and closed his eyes, a deep breath of contentment escaped Cole's lips.

Antje stared adoringly at Cole, her gaze shifting to Shields, who lay in a full sploot at their feet, snoring, his hind legs stretched across the aisle, nearly touching Leif's feet. Despite the bliss buried in the day's otherwise dreadful events, Antje's heart was heavy, and the weight only intensified with each passing moment. Closing her eyes, Antje enacted the breathwork that had served her so well on this adventure and stared at the back of her eyelids.

Once sitting in the stars, Antje asked, "Eír, are you there?"

Eír approached Antje from the left, her wispy green gown and ethereal face aiding Antje to let go of her earthly attachments and fully shift into the frequency of the astral plane. Eír beckoned Antje to follow as she opened a doorway in the stars. Stepping through the portal, Antje and Eír were now in a large hall filled with hefty wooden tables, lined with benches, that nearly spanned the length of the room. The tops of the tables were set with roasted pheasant, stuffed whole boars, and all of the accoutrements that even the most discerning patron could possibly desire. Raucous laughter clashed with the drunken, incoherent yelling of hundreds of men, golden liquid splashing from their drinking horns as they swayed.

"Welcome to Valhalla, Antje," Eír said, her voice unexcitable but teeming with warmth. "Our father would like a word with you." They approached Odin at the head of the room, whose oversized carved wood and silver throne sat atop a patchwork of various animal hides.

"Daughters! You are here! What a victorious day!" Odin exclaimed, his mead spilling onto his fingers from the top of his oversized white and tan-tipped horn.

"Victorious in some ways. We lost a lot of good men today, including some who I would call family," Antje lamented, looking down at the ground as the familiar sting of tears occurred.

"On the contrary, my child, we gained many good men today, including one of your family members. Turn around, daughter."

Antje turned around to find Mathias hunched down, with his face uncomfortably close to hers, a large grin plastered across it. Mathias let out a deafeningly joyous, "Ahh!" and dropped his drinking horn, mead splashing everywhere as he lifted Antje with both arms in a back-cracking hug. "Antje, my darling niece!" Antje's eyes watered up with a flood of conflicting emotions, and Mathias's face quickly turned from crazed playfulness to quite serious. "Why are you crying? Stop that."

As her feet touched the ground, Antje replied, "I'm crying because I thought you were dead, and here you are." Grabbing his hands, she examined him from head to toe with astonishment.

Mathias looked to Odin and back at Antje. "How are you a valkyrie that doesn't understand death?" Mathias chuckled, hugging her once more—this time with tenderness rather than aggressive enthusiasm. "My body in Midgard is dead, Antje. For my soul, I live here now. Death of the body is not a real death—it is just a transition to another level of your soul's journey. It's like, you drive the truck your parents bought you, then one day it breaks down and no one can fix it, so you send it to the car graveyard. You didn't die, but your truck did. That's all the body is—a vehicle for transporting your soul. Thanks to you, I died an honorable death in battle this lifetime, and now I've received the honor of serving in Odin's army." Antje released Mathias, wishing their embrace could have lasted indefinitely, and collected herself.

She pulled her shirt down and pressed her hands to straighten any creases. "So, this was your fate then?"

"Always has been!" Mathias was handed another horn of mead by a woman familiar to Antje; the woman's ethereal gown trailed behind her, catching on the small bursts of air created by the lively men's gestures. A realization hit as the woman walked past Antje—she was the valkyrie Eír had healed during Antje's visit with Freya.

"Yes, that's who you think it is," Eír responded.

"Holy shit, you can hear my thoughts? I can't even hear my thoughts—how does that work?" Antje asked, a little unsettled by the lack of sovereignty.

"You are me, and I am you. I know everything that passes through that beautiful brain and heart of yours—silent or not," Eír said. Antje audibly gulped. "Don't worry, I don't judge. Your struggles are my struggles and vice versa. We think and feel identically—I just have a much bigger piece of the puzzle completed, which gives me a different perspective at times."

Fidgeting, Antje let out a nervous giggle and looked around the room, scanning the men's faces one by one. "Mathias, is Misha here?"

"Misha belongs to Yahweh, daughter," Odin butted in. "He is in Yahweh's afterlife, not our realms."

Disappointed, Antje replied, "That makes sense. Am I limited to only the Norse realms?"

Odin and Eír laughed. "No, daughter. You are a valkyrie. You are welcome among all the realms—except for Helheim; Hela is particular about the company she keeps, and you will have to be invited by her or sent by me each time you visit. For the most part, she is reasonable, as you have already seen. You will have plenty of time to learn about this in the end—now is a time for celebration, not work!" Odin lifted his drinking horn as he rose to his feet from the throne. The boisterous symphony of sounds that echoed in the great hall quickly subsided as several men, still in their marine-issued uniform, made their way to the front of the hall where Mathias stood, his chest proudly puffed, and his chin raised.

Frigg appeared from behind Odin's throne and kissed Antje on the cheek, gently pushing stray strands of hair from Antje's face and gazing at her lovingly as Odin proclaimed, "A toast, to my daughter, Antje, for her victory, and a toast to the newest members of our army! To die in battle is to die with great honor! We, the Gods of Asgard, salute you! Skol!"

Once again, the hall erupted in rowdy cheers, the tips of horns now pointed at the large timber ceiling above as the mead within emptied into the mouths of fearsome men and the occasional woman.

"Hello, daughter," Frigg greeted Antje. "You're here for advice on healing your friend. Trust in your abilities, my love—you know how to heal her. That knowledge has always been a part of you, as you are a part of Eír." Frigg tucked Antje's hair behind her ear and kissed her on her forehead, flashing a proud smile afterward.

Frigg's presence comforted Antje in a way she could never have fathomed. Like a warm towel swaddling a hypothermic body, her words made Antje feel safe—and understood. It was in that moment that Antje realized she had never known the genuine love of a mother until Frigg. Antje loved her mother and always would, but realized that she loved her the same as any of her fellow humans; the love Antje shared with Frigg was different—it was deep, sacred, and unconditional.

Eír smiled and put her hand on Antje's shoulder, "She's lovely, isn't she?" Antje nodded silently, her cheeks flushed with the embarrassment of someone having access to her head—even if they were the same soul.

A handsome man snuck up behind Eír, wrapped his arms around her waist, and picked her up. Eír squealed and slapped him on the arms playfully to put her down. "Antje, this is my husband, Vatn."

Antje examined the man's face, she felt incredibly connected to him, but knew she had never seen him before. From his curly brown hair to his cleft chin, and his honey-colored eyes reminiscent of a warm summer day—Antje was mesmerized. A fur shawl hung from his shoulders, accentuating their broadness, and the impressive breadth of his muscular chest.

"Antje! *Finally*!" Vatn shouted, hugging her as though they were childhood friends. Pulling back after feeling the discomfort in Antje's body, Vatn chuckled. "Oh, you don't know yet! I'm Cole's higher self," he explained, wrapping his arm around Eír's waist and shining a grin at Antje.

Like the final scene of a murder mystery, the full picture finally clicked for Antje, whose face broadcasted her recent epiphany to the entire room; her circle of spiritual family guffawed in concert. "That's why Cole and

I immediately knew we loved each other—because our higher selves are married? We *actually are* soulmates..." Antje reasoned out loud.

"Fate, daughter. You can petition to change it, but some things are set in stone. You and Cole...Eír and Vatn—stone," Odin explained. Suddenly, Antje saw her consciousness pulled backward from the halls, as if she were being pulled up into outer space. Antje attempted to cling to her vision as she ascended, and it faded into blackness.

"Antje? Babe? Wake up, we're landing," Cole's voice rang through her ears as her eyes opened. "I know you must be exhausted, but we're in Copenhagen."

The plane's tires kissed the tarmac as it spastically jumped about, the whooshing sound of landing gear overtaking the noise of the engine. Shield's tongue curled into a yawn as he stretched every muscle in his body, his paw tapping Leif's foot, who then snapped out of his sleep with a startle.

Cole kissed Antje's cheek. "I'll grab your bag. I've been sleeping for months, and you still seem pretty groggy," Cole said, unbuckling both of their seatbelts as the plane came to a halt. Antje intensely stared at Cole.

"Cole—you're my soulmate," Antje said, still processing what she had just seen, shock painted across her face.

Cole cocked his head and chuckled. "You don't seem too excited about that, babe." Antje leaned in and kissed Cole passionately, her hands gripping his face on both sides. Pulling back, Cole flashed his signature boyish grin. "I take that back. I guess I still need to learn your facial expressions."

Antje beamed as she reached into her bag and poured the last of the transformation potion onto Shields—this time whispering the word 'Pit-bull.' Leif looked into the aisle, expecting to see Shields in his gargantuan shisa form. In his place lay a blocky-headed, stocky white pit-bull with grey brindle markings and adorably floppy ears; drool strings hung from his jowls, landing on the industrial blue carpet below. Shields looked up at Leif and said, "HAPPY. SHIELDS LIKE NEW BODY. HAPPY."

Leif looked to Cole, who was unfazed by the speaking dog. "Sir, at what point do you get used to this shit?" Leif asked, brows furrowed with the look of confusion radiating from his eyes.

"Never, Leif. You will never get used to this shit. I've gotten used to the violence of war, the crushing guilt of my decisions—I've even gotten used to seeing grown men wearing skinny jeans, but I have never gotten used to magic. It still blows my mind, just as much as the first time I witnessed it," Cole answered, squeezing Antje's knee with a chortle.

Leif turned his head straight forward and blankly stared. "I need a stiff drink—or ten."

TWENTY-TWO

MIRACLES AND MISSED MOMENTS

The sight of two glass pyramids with a fountain at their side was a welcome one for Antje as she, Cole, Leif, and Shields made their way across the lush landscaping of the park, and down into the Cisterns. Shields jumped and splashed about in the runoff, his large tongue and jowls slapping against each other as Antje and Cole chuckled quietly amongst themselves. Trailing not far behind was Leif—silent with curious eyes, and a face filled with excitement as they waded through the water.

"You two first." Antje motioned to Cole and Leif as she turned around, raising her selfie stick.

"First for what?" Leif questioned, looking around him to grasp what she meant before his gaze returned to Antje. Only this time, the column behind Antje had been replaced with an elevator. Leif, now permanently living in a state of disbelief, circled the column, examining the surface with his eyes and his hands. "My gods. There is a magic school under Copenhagen...my whole life is a lie."

"Get in the elevator with Cole, Leif. It's safe, I promise," Antje instructed, snapping Leif out of his skepticism.

Joining Cole in the elevator, Leif felt the need to apologize for his impertinence. "Of course, it's safe. I trust you. I'm sorry, Antje."

With a warm smile, and a flashback to her first visit to the Cisterne, she turned her head over her shoulder and replied, "Nothing to apologize for, Leif. It can be a lot to take in at first. I'll see you in a few minutes." The doors closed, and to Antje's surprise, as she'd never had to wait before, a new elevator followed just seconds behind the last. Shields playfully hopped inside the elevator and shook the water from his entire body, his ears clapping as they slapped his head.

"Gross, Shields! You couldn't have done that outside?" Antje wiped the dog-tinged water from her face and slung it from her bare arms. Shields sat at attention, panting.

"SORRY. SHIELDS SORRY."

Antje laughed and patted Shields on his water-logged, enormous head, which immediately tilted up so he could lick her hand several times before staring at the doors with anticipation.

Minutes passed, and the doors opened. Antje waved at the security guard, expecting to be ignored once more, but this time, he stood and bowed his head to her.

"Welcome back, Miss Antje. Special Agent Stalvey and his guest await you inside." Antje gave an awkward but friendly nod to the man and opened the entry door. Bounding through the doorway with zero hesitance, Shields ran to Mikono, who stood in front of him in the atrium, tackling her small frame and furiously licking her face. Mikono giggled with delight as they rolled on the floor together. Antje stood alongside Cole, who watched Shields and Mikono with a content grin on his face. Leif, too awestruck by the Cisterne to say much of anything, remained entirely unaware as a friend approached.

"Leif, old chap—you came!" William Henry called from down one of the corridors, his demeanor warm and exuding copious amounts of emotion by his standards. Leif's head whipped around, and his face lit up at the sight of William Henry.

"There he is! This place is amazing. Show me around, will you?" Leif replied, with his arms outstretched to William Henry, whose body tightened but quickly relaxed when he received a slap on the back rather than an embrace. The two wandered down the hallway as Shields' enthusiasm tapered off enough for Mikono to get back onto her feet.

"How's Takhi, Mikono?" Antje asked anxiously.

"She's alive. We've got our best healers with her now, but—her improvement isn't going as quickly as we had hoped." Mikono's quiet disappointment was deeply felt by Antje who grabbed one of Mikono's hands and said, "I've learned a lot in the time since I was here last. As it turns out, I can also heal. Can you take me to her, please?"

A small flame of hope glimmered in Mikono's eyes as she nodded quickly and turned, walking down the hallway opposite from the one William Henry and Leif had disappeared into. Cole and Shields followed behind Mikono and Antje silently. The familiar scent of herbs became so pungent that Antje knew they were close—and signaled that Jinpa was tending to Takhi. Relief ran through Antje's veins knowing Takhi was receiving the very same treatment that had once saved her life—and by a healer whom she had come to greatly respect. The foursome arrived at a large wooden door with a yin-yang symbol carved on it. Mikono took a deep breath and lowered the door handle slowly, knocking quietly on the door as she opened it.

There lay Takhi, who looked more like a pin-cushion than the Takhi Antje had hoped to see. At her side were Headmaster Vogel and Jinpa; the Headmaster's face was solemn as Jinpa approached Antje and gently linked arms with her. "We go outside, okay?" Jinpa requested. Antje nodded. Exiting the door, Jinpa released Antje's arm and faced her. "She no heal. Medicine stop progression, but she no heal."

Antje grabbed his hands with tears welling up in both eyes. "Mange tahk, Jinpa. Mange tahk for everything. Do you mind if I try something I learned from my gods?" she asked. Jinpa's face changed from a look of concern to intrigue. "You find you healing valkyrie, huh?"

Antje tilted her head and asked, "How did you know?"

"You energy very different when I heal. I know you healer. You help Takhi and I watch." A sweet smile crept across Jinpa's face as he again linked arms with Antje. "I happy you alive. You important soul."

"Less important than the one who saved me from the edge of death not too long ago." Antje affectionately grasped his arm with her opposite hand and squeezed it gently as they walked back through the door.

"Headmaster Vogel, do you mind if I try to heal Takhi?" Antje asked.

Headmaster Vogel stood up and slowly approached Antje with his shoulders rounded downward. "I am willing to try anything, Antje. Please, do what you have to do to bring her back to us. I can't bear ze thought of losing her."

Antje hugged Headmaster Vogel and nodded. "Mikono, can you please bring me a container with soil in it?" Antje requested, turning to Mikono.

"Of course." Mikono nodded and quickly exited the room.

Takhi was unconscious, and her breathing labored as Antje approached her bedside. Closing her eyes, Antje visualized Takhi's energy body. Her fingers spread as far apart as she could, she pulled the green energy print above Takhi's broken body. Opening her eyes, Antje witnessed a captivated audience gawking at Takhi's energy body, which was riddled with glowing red orbs. In that moment, Antje realized her new normal wasn't normal to anyone else—not even other mystics.

Mikono entered the room with a sizable terracotta planter filled to the brim with soil and presented Antje with the pot. "Will this work?"

"That is absolutely perfect, Mikono. Can you place it on the bedside table next to me, please?" Antje asked, keeping one of her hands in place as the other reached into the red orbs and dismantled them by pulling at the fiery red strands and pressing them into the soil. After clearing every red orb from Takhi's body, Antje slowly pressed Takhi's energy body back into her physical body and took a step back, holding her breath for any sign of improvement.

After only a few moments, Takhi's breathing began to normalize, and her eyes slowly opened, her head turning to Antje.

"Did we win? Is she dead? Is Headmaster Vogel okay?" Takhi asked Antje, who now had tears rolling down both cheeks as she kneeled next to the bed, her eyes level with Takhi's.

"Yeah. We won." Antje smiled. "She isn't dead yet, but don't worry about that. I'm just so happy to see you awake. You saved so many lives and helped us win that battle. Thank you, Takhi. I know that was so hard on you in every way," Antje managed to articulate through her tears.

"Takhi, my precious Takhi," Headmaster Vogel sobbed, placing his hand on Takhi's forehead, and locking eyes with her. "You scared me. I thought we'd lost you."

Antje backed away from Takhi's bedside, stood up, and took the terra-cotta pot with her to the door. She waved her hand for Cole and Shields to follow as Jinpa checked Takhi's vitals. Mikono sat on a chair in the corner of the room, wiping joy-saturated tears from her eyes.

As they exited the door and it closed behind them, Cole grabbed Antje's arm and turned her toward him in the hallway. "So, in addition to being a killing machine, you also know how to heal? I believe that's what the gamer kids call 'overpowered.' When did that happen?" Cole asked, both tickled and amazed by this discovery.

"Like I said before, a lot has happened since you were taken. I'm the incarnation of the healing valkyrie Eír, and the child of Odin and Frigg. Let's talk and walk; I've got to get this soil into the garden to release the energy of Takhi's wounds," Antje explained, Cole's face still painted with astonishment. It was a long walk from one side of the Cisterne to the other, and Antje updated Cole on what he had missed during his time as a captive. As she opened the French doors leading into the garden, Cole's bewilderment evolved into adoration. Kneeling to pour the soil from the pot onto a small plot on the edge of the walkway through the garden, Antje broke down in tears, the salty drops leaving divots in the fresh soil. Cole dropped to his knees and drew her into a warm embrace, holding her as he gently stroked her hair.

"They're tears of joy. I'm just so relieved that Takhi is going to be okay. I may have to heal her a few more times, but I know she's going to live," Antje sniffled.

"Antje, you are magnificent. Every time we've been in this garden, you've done something that my brain can't comprehend. First, it was killing Kitt and saving a baby from permanent death on your first day of exposure to this insanity, and now you've pulled Takhi back from death's door—I'm in awe of you and everything you can do. I'm also questioning why the gods would put someone like you with a normie like me."

"You're not a normie, Cole," Antje corrected, pulling back from his chest and wiping the last drop of relief from her face. "I met your higher self. He's Eír's husband."

"Wait...*what*?" Cole's eyes widened as he looked at Antje's face.

"When I said we are soulmates, I meant we are *literally soulmates*. Our higher selves are blissfully married in Valhalla, and judging by the fact that he is Odin's son-in-law, I don't think that he's just some guy who lucked into marrying Eír. You are not a normie; you just haven't been woken up yet."

Cole stared past Antje, over her shoulder, deep in thought. "If she's the valkyrie of healing, what is he?"

"I don't know what Vatn is yet. I met him on our plane ride over here, and it was a very short interaction."

Cole looked back at Antje's face and grabbed her hands, forcing her to stand up with him. "Vatn? That's my higher self's name? What a weird name."

"I think it's a nickname. Anyway—the reason I am sharing this with you is that Odin told me that you could sometimes change your fate, but other things are set in stone. He told me that we are set in stone, just like Eír and Vatn are set in stone. We are literally soulmates—it's not the peonies." Antje grinned at Cole, hoping to balance out some of his tension around the unknown.

Cole laughed, his emotions spilling from his eyes as he pulled Antje into a hug and pressed his lips against her forehead. "Honestly? I'm relieved. These feelings I have for you, they've been freaking me the fuck out. I've been rolling with it because I felt compelled to love you... But, I didn't know if it was a spell or something else I didn't understand, and that was always lurking under the surface for me. So, to hear this feeling is because it's fate, and we're literally soulmates—oh God, I'm relieved." Cole paused for a moment. "I love you, Antje...and I love that I can finally say that without it feeling weird about it."

Antje giggled, her eyes also saturated with emotional overflow. "I love you too. I'm sorry we haven't had time to really just be together. I'm hoping we get some time before the wedding to just...be in love." Antje gently planted a kiss on Cole's lips.

"Where and when do you want to get married?" Cole asked. "It needs to be sooner rather than later thanks to our favorite General." Cole returned Antje's kiss, and snugly wrapped his arms around her waist.

"Can we get married back home? Do you think they'll let us leave here for that long? I've always loved one of the national parks near Moab, and I had a vision the first time we kissed that we were standing in Canyonlands National Park. I recognized it from the colors of the cliffs."

"Canyonlands sounds great, my darling. I would happily marry you anywhere. I'll make sure they okay it. The powers that be would probably see it as a more legitimate marriage if it occurred on US soil, anyway. Is two months long enough for you to plan? I know that's not very long, but three months from now is when the next presidential election happens, and I don't want to risk that our fickle government changes its mind about our deal. I'm really sorry that this is even a consideration for our big day—but it's just the reality of it." Cole sighed, still holding Antje in his arms.

Antje squeezed Cole as tightly as she could with her arms. "I'd marry you tomorrow next to a dumpster, Cole. Two months is perfect."

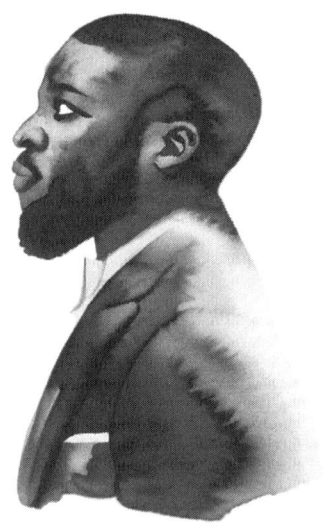

Twenty-Three

Prosthetics and Preparations

Two months had passed—some of which Antje spent at the Cisterne with Takhi, working to regenerate her wings and help her regain her strength; Takhi's progress was slow, but steady. The remainder of Antje's time was spent with Cole; their days dedicated to tracking down the Dark Queen, and their evenings spent in the throes of pre-marital bliss as Antje and Shields now called Cole's government housing their home. They'd become inseparable, and apart from her time with Takhi, the only time Antje spent without Cole was at her standing appointment with Kenny and his weaponry development team—which both Antje and Kenny dreaded. These sessions were spent examining her abilities and administering biological testing. Wanting to fill the day's appointment with something other than the collective irritation of Antje being exploited by the government as a science experiment, Antje requested Cole's company.

"You brought Cole. Nice to see you, brother!" Kenny beamed as he leaned into Cole, shaking with one hand, and leaning in for a half-hug, which Cole heartily reciprocated.

"Antje asked me to come today, for...some...reason," Cole said, both men turning to Antje.

Antje flashed an omniscient grin and placed a large container of soil on a portable steel table next to the operating table. "I'm going to show off my healing abilities for you, Kenny. The government can't use it as a weapon, but I'm sure they'll try to find a way." Antje's eyes rolled as she laughed and motioned for Kenny to lie on the table that she'd spent dozens of hours on over the last two months. Kenny shrugged his shoulders at Cole and lay on the table.

"I know you've gotten used to your bionic leg, but how do you feel about having your old leg once again, Kenny?" Antje asked, putting her hand on the cold metal of his mechanical leg.

Kenny's eyes doubled in size. "Antje—are you for real right now?"

"I am. I think I can bring your old leg back. No promises because I've never had to heal or regrow an old injury—but Takhi's wings regrew in one of my healing sessions this week, and it made me think that maybe we can regrow your leg."

Kenny thought for a moment and expressed his concerns. "I mean, I'm not going to end up with a tiny baby leg, or a tentacle, or something weird, am I?" The room erupted in laughter.

Antje tapped on his bionic leg. "I hope not, but truthfully...I don't know."

"You know what? Fuck it. Let's do it." Kenny became resolute in his choice as he wriggled into a somewhat comfortable position on the medical table. Antje pressed the call button next to the entry door, and requested the development team come in to disconnect his leg.

Cole approached the table and looked down, grabbing Kenny's right shoulder with his left hand. "If it does come back as a baby leg, I hope you know that I'm never going to let you live it down. I'm going to call you 'Special Agent Baby Leg,' and when Antje and I have a kid, we'll use you to model its shoes before buying them." Cole flashed a smile and a wink at Antje before she turned her face away from Kenny and giggled quietly.

Kenny let out a chuckle and fired shots back over the bow. "Careful, Sleeping Beauty. I saved your comatose ass, and I will still give you the beatdown of a lifetime, then I'll stick my baby leg right where the sun don't shine!"

"Boys, boys. Less negativity in my operating room, please," Antje scolded with a smile.

Cole squeezed Kenny's shoulder once more, patting it affectionately before taking his seat on a doctor's stool and wheeling himself backward until his back pressed against the wall.

Two laptop-toting members of the development team entered the operating room, and with a nod from Kenny, they unpacked a kit of small hand tools, readying themselves to remove his electromechanical leg. One of the team members reached for a syringe of sedative, his hand stopped by Antje's who gave him a quick shake of the head. Antje placed her hand on Kenny's forehead, putting him into a dreamlike state. After the team members concluded their removal, they too pulled up chairs and sat next to Cole, with bated breath.

Antje spent an hour carefully unraveling the softball-sized mass of calcified, garnet-red string from his leg. Cole obsessively checked his emails as his foot shook like the death wobble of a steering wheel at high speed. Mesmerized by something they truly didn't understand, the two team members furiously typed reports, barely glancing at the screens on their laps. As Antje pulled the last strand from his leg and placed it into the container of soil, Kenny's leg began to slowly regrow. Over the span of six hours, where his cybernetic leg had once connected, a full-grown leg now appeared. Antje placed her hand on Kenny's forehead and whispered into his ear, "Kenny, wake up."

Kenny's eyes opened; groggily, he looked down at his leg.

"Holy shit! My leg!" he yelled, sitting up way too quickly. Light-headed, Kenny laid back down onto the table with the aid of Antje's arm supporting his upper back.

"Easy there, Kenny. Do me a favor and curl your toes upward?" Antje watched with glee as Kenny's big toe wiggled. "Let's get one of the facility's physical therapists to come work with you—" Antje motioned to one of the team members who quickly rushed out the door, "But I suspect you'll be up and ready to walk at our wedding next week."

With tears of joy in his eyes, Kenny squeezed Antje's hand. "Thank you, Antje. Thank you.... Thank you." Antje leaned down and kissed Kenny's cheek. "Anything for our best man, and the guy who brought Cole back to me. We love you, Kenny."

Cole appeared over Antje's shoulder. "Kenny, are you crying? Antje, turn this man's leg into a baby leg. He's a big baby!" Cole gave a shit-eating grin to Kenny.

"Man, shut—up! You really know how to ruin a moment, Cole." Kenny's scowl turned into a grin as he sat up and bumped fists with Cole. "You sure are my favorite pain in the ass, sir."

Cole finished typing something into his phone and pocketed it. "Ehhh, you like it. Glad to have you, and your leg, back with us," Cole smirked as the sound of an email sending emanated from his phone. "Oh—I just requested physical therapy for you, three times a week, along with a cane to be brought to you immediately. You know what this means, right? No more excuses—you'll have to be smack-dab in the action with me again, Kenny."

Kenny looked at his former bionic leg sitting on a counter to the left of his bed and exclaimed, "Antje, put that thing back on—I don't wanna die. This fucking guy is always running toward death, not away from it!" Once again, the room filled with laughter.

Wedding planning had been tedious and thwarted the week of relaxation Antje had planned in Moab for Cole and herself. Antje's head rested on Cole's chest, his fingers tracing her shoulder and arm as they lay skin-to-skin in their hotel room bed.

"Today's the big day. You ready?" Cole asked.

Antje lifted her head from his chest, propping herself up on one arm, and looked Cole in the eyes. "I've been ready for today since the day we met," she replied, kissing his neck before staring back into his warm, chestnut eyes.

"Me too, babe." Cole kissed Antje's lips. "Are you sure you're okay with not having your Mom and Dirk here? I know how you feel about them, but still—it's family, you know?"

Tracing circles in his chest hair with her index finger, she replied, "I'm absolutely sure. Family is who you choose to love, and who chooses to love you...Not just some people that fate threw you into a home with." Lifting her head once more, she stared into his eyes. "I've got you, Isaac, Kenny, Shields, and all of my Cisterne people here—that's all the family I need." As Antje finished her sentence, a thunderous knock on the door startled them both. Cole grabbed his gun off the nightstand and put his index finger over Antje's lips, pausing for a moment before dropping his hand from her mouth.

"It's Phil, ye love birds! Rise 'n shine—it's gettin' hitched time!"

Cole and Antje both laughed as he released his gun and kissed Antje's forehead. Antje rolled out of bed, dressing herself quickly as she replied, "One moment, Philomena! I'm coming!" Antje blew a kiss to Cole, who still lay naked in bed, and she exited the room, carefully closing the door behind her as she pulled on her second shoe.

"Ah, young love! Off ye go!" Philomena sighed, handing a full champagne glass to Antje and shuffling her into a room several doors down. As Antje crossed the threshold, elated faces greeted her. Mikono was the first to greet her, with both hands palms up. In her palms lay a handkerchief with blue embroidery on it. "I researched American wedding traditions. Here is your something blue." Mikono smiled as Antje received the dainty lace-trimmed cloth and leaned in to embrace her.

"Thank you, Mikono—for everything. For giving me Shields, for teaching me ways to ground myself, and for being such an amazing friend. I appreciate you so much."

Kari stepped to the side of Mikono, towering over her. "Something new!" Kari chirped, handing Antje a satin garter belt, and hugging her. "You saved Karl, and I will forever be indebted to you. Anything you need, I will always be here."

Antje began to cry and squeezed Kari before responding with, "You held my hand and walked me into this world, a world which gave me the man I'm marrying today, and my purpose in life. The debt is honestly mine." Kari and Antje both released each other and wiped the tears from under their eyes, giggling in slight discomfort at their collective release of emotion.

Takhi approached as Mikono and Kari stepped out of the way. "Antje..." Takhi trailed off, tears streaming down her face.

Tears continued to leak from Antje's eyes. "Don't even. I'm going to start sobbing more than I already am! Takhi, I love you," Antje said, embracing Takhi as they both unsuccessfully attempted to halt their tears.

"You saved my life, Antje. Something borrowed." Takhi plucked a large feather from her wings and handed it to Antje. "May this feather remind you that we are family—forever. You can return it to me once one of us moves on to our next life."

Uncontrollably sobbing, Antje's shoulders bounced as every woman in the room, Philomena included, surrounded her and hugged her. Philomena covertly wiped her eyes and said, "Alright, 'nuff of the sappy stuff! We've gotta get ye ready for yer weddin'!"

Ragnar yelled through the hotel room window as he stood outside in the parking lot, "I see you crying, old lady!"

"Feck! He's never gonna let me forget this!" Philomena said, swiftly jerking the curtains closed as laughter filled the room. "Oh! I fergot to tell ye, Leif sent me with his own weddin' gift." Philomena shuffled over to her bag and removed a phone charger. "He said ye might be needin' this, and that he's sorry he and William Henry couldn't make the trip. Yer stupid government is makin' him do an intensive course on mysticism in order to keep his job. Those feckin' cabbages are ruinin' yer big day after forcin' ya' to have one! They're cracked, I say!" Philomena rambled, handing Antje the phone charger.

Antje received it and let out a small laugh. "Oh, Leif. Always making sure my phone is charged," she said, blotting her eyes with her sleeve.

"Ah feck! We fergot to give ye somethin' old!" Philomena paused for a moment and plucked a hair from her head, winding it around her finger and knotting it into a loop. "Here ye go: somethin' old!" Philomena handed

Antje the small loop of her silver hair and jabbed Antje in the ribs with her elbow. "Anyhoo—when are ye and Cole gonna give me a wee little lad to bounce on me knee?"

Antje chuckled. "One step at a time, Philomena."

Twenty-Four

"I Do's" and Dastardly Deeds

The resonant harmonies of a string quartet rode the winds as guests took to their seats, the notes gracefully carving through the airwaves as a kite does on a blustery day. Set on a plateau overlooking the deep canyon walls, the ceremony boasted views of the rock face below, each layer of golden yellow, deep purple, and burnt sienna containing a geological tale of times long since passed. The herbaceous scent of sagebrush outcompeted the symphony of guests' designer perfumes and colognes, evoking the unbending and wild spirit of the western lands they stood upon.

Cole stood under an arched trellis of thoughtfully curated flora, debonair as ever in his timeless, fitted tuxedo—a single lock of his wavy hair kissing the top of his forehead. To his side stood Kenny in a dapper, Aegean-blue suit and bowtie, opposite Takhi. As her sage-green gown danced in the wind, the petals of flowers woven into her antlers flitted about with each gust. Philomena, centered at the head of the ceremonial space, was adorned in her finest ritual gown with a tawny, white-spotted, deer-skin shawl draped across her hunched shoulders.

Antje's Cisterne family sat in the right front row, Ragnar taking the seat closest to the aisle, while Mikono and Shields were seated at the opposite end of the row; Headmaster Vogel and Kari sat in between. The left front row was filled with various aunts, uncles, and cousins from both familial sides, with a single empty seat bordering the aisle.

As Isaac prepared to walk Antje into wedded bliss, Cole's eyes illuminated at the spectacle of Antje in her form-fitting, satin wedding gown—his face bursting with adoration that could surely be seen for miles. Antje's eyes locked with Cole's as she lovingly smiled at him, despite the crippling sensation of concurrently feeling every guest's heightened emotional state. She took in a single deep breath through her nose, exhaled through her mouth, and carefully stepped onto the runner of river pebbles blanketing the aisle.

"Are you ready, Antje?" Isaac asked, his bright, noble eyes beaming with pride as he presented his arm to her.

Antje hooked her hand around his upper arm. "I am. Thank you for walking me down the aisle, Uncle Isaac. I can't tell you how much I love and appreciate you...it's literally impossible to put into words."

A doting smile crept to his aged lips. "I love you, my adopted daughter. Forever and always. I am so proud of you for everything you've done and accomplished this year... and I love Cole. You've picked a great spouse. I couldn't be happier for both of you." Antje's eyes welled up. Isaac quietly chuckled. "Oh, Antje, don't cry. You'll ruin your beautiful makeup." Pulling a handkerchief from the chest pocket of his suit, Isaac blotted Antje's face where a single tear landed. Kissing her on the cheek, he smiled once more and asked, "Shall we?"

A crowd of familiar faces, some welcome—some not, filled Antje's line of sight as she walked down the aisle. From the General, to her loved ones, to not so familiar faces—everyone stood, their eyes fixed on Antje in her champagne floor-length gown as it trailed behind her. Over Antje's shoulder, Cole noticed a few tourists gawking curiously from the road. Cole's gaze quickly shifted back to Antje, his eyes magnetized to his picturesque bride, whose hair fluttered in the wind as the afternoon sun bathed her in a soft, golden light, illuminating her blue-green eyes.

Uncle Isaac shook Cole's hand. "Welcome to the family, Cole—my son."

Cole flashed his pearly whites and cupped Isaac's hand affectionately. "Thank you, Isaac. I want you to know, I'll take great care of Antje. I'll protect her with my life if I have to."

To which Isaac replied with a smile, "I have no doubt about that, Cole." Isaac kissed Antje on the cheek and took his seat across the aisle from Ragnar, who had, despite his best efforts, not cleaned up to Philomena's liking—a fact made apparent by her steely glare.

"'Ere ye, 'ere ye!" Philomena yelled as the string quartet finished. "Ope! Wrong ceremony." The entirety of the wedding party laughed. "We're gathered 'ere today to witness the marriage of these two beautiful souls: Antje Valason and Cole Stalvey. The couple has prepared their vows, and there's nothin' this old crazy coot could say that'd be any better, really. Cole, ye go first," Philomena instructed, extending her right arm to Cole as the pagoda sleeve of her dress swayed in the breeze. Kenny detected movement from the corner of his eye and watched as nosy tourists filled the last few empty chairs scattered about the rear and middle rows on both sides of the aisle.

Cole cleared his throat nervously and gulped. "Antje, where do I begin? We all know that our relationship has been... unconventional." Again, chuckles filled the air. "But, there is not one single thing I would do differently. From the moment I laid eyes on you, my heart just—knew—you were the one for me. And since that moment, I've only become more and more convinced that there is no one else in this world I'd rather spend the rest of my life with than you. I promise to love you in sickness and in health—and to protect and love you for the rest of my life. Thank you for choosing me—for continuing to choose me—every day...it's the biggest honor of my life." Cole slipped a black diamond ring onto Antje's finger, followed by a white diamond band. Kenny sniffled. Antje, still barely managing to hold it together, locked her glossy eyes with Cole's. He smiled, knowing his words had been truly heard.

Philomena chimed in quietly, "Antje?"

Takhi handed Antje a tungsten band. Turning around, Antje took in a deep breath, giggling on the exhale and pinching her lips together as she smiled. "Cole, I never believed in love at first sight, or in soulmates, or that I'd ever even find someone that I didn't want to kill after spending five hours with them." Muted chuckles rippled through the crowd. "But here we are. You are literally everything I could have ever dreamed of...and more. From this day forward, it's no longer me, facing the world alone—it's us—us versus the world. You've shown me unconditional love and support through some of the craziest moments of my life, and I couldn't have imagined that someone like you would love me like you do, with all of your heart. I promise to protect and cherish that heart forever." Antje began to cry, whimpering through the last sentence of her vows. "Our love surpasses all time and space, and I will love you until the heavens fall."

The concinnity of gentle sobs trickled through the wedding as Philomena reached across Cole and Antje's entwined hands and heisted the handkerchief from Cole's pocket to blot her eyes, haphazardly tucking it back in when she finished. Cole and Antje quietly chuckled through their tears.

Philomena flattened her dress with her hands and composed herself. "See what I mean? Who could've said it better than they? If anyone believes these two soulmates shouldn't be married, speak now or forever hold yer peace!" Philomena announced, surveying the crowd of glassy eyes and sentimental smiles, until a woman in the back row stood up, her blonde hair thrashing in the wind.

"I object!" she yelled. The onlooking tourists began to descend upon the wedding; concomitantly, the other tourists rose from their seats.

"Everybody, get down!" Cole screamed as the tourists' hands began clapping and conjuring spells. Cole quickly pulled his gun from inside his tuxedo jacket, desperately searching for a clean shot as he took great care not to shoot members of the wedding party in the crossfire; there was no such clean shot to be had.

Headmaster Vogel stepped to the outside of the right grouping of seating and conjured a protective shield while yelling to his staff and the guests to get behind him. Panicked guests screamed in terror and fled from their seats, knocking their chairs over onto those who chose to hunker down between rows. The quartet's instruments fell to the ground, making a discordant racket upon landing.

The General lay himself flat on his stomach between the row of chairs, his face pressed into the compacted, dusty ground as he shielded his head. The cacophony of gasps, terrified screams, and dark mystics chanting continued as Antje motioned for Philomena, Takhi, and Isaac to take cover. Takhi flew to the left side of the seating and motioned for various family members and guests to get behind her wings. Takhi invoked the help of her Gods to create a small protective tornado around her and the group of bewildered guests, including Philomena and Isaac. The winds of the tornado flung and deflected spells as they collided with its violent winds.

Kenny kneeled behind the front row of chairs with Ragnar. With his gun in his hand, and his phone to his ear, Kenny called for backup. He dropped his phone from his ear as he fired a shot at one of the dark mystics—barely missing. Kenny ducked as a spell whizzed past his head and hit the flower-adorned arch above Antje. Cole pulled Antje into his body as the arch toppled onto his back. Throwing the arch off of him and pulling her behind him, Cole shielded Antje as she reached for Daggert, only to realize—she was completely unarmed. Her stomach dropped as she frantically searched the area in her direct vicinity for a makeshift weapon. Antje broke a large piece of wood from the fallen arch, the thorns of roses bloodying her fingers as she ripped them from the wood before breaking it into two sharp stakes over her thigh.

Antje and Cole took cover behind the left front row of chairs along the aisle. As Cole landed shots on several dark mystics, Antje kissed his cheek and shuffled to the chair on the far-left side of the row. Leaping from the chair, Antje cleared a third or fourth cousin in the second row who was crawling on her hands and knees, attempting to flee. Antje landed one of the stakes right into the heart of a summoning dark mystic in the fifth row, his blue blood erupting like a geyser as Antje ripped the stake from his chest. Her gown drenched in blood, Antje crouched down on the ground as she surveyed her next victim.

An enormous man with black hair and piercing green eyes stood in the same row across the aisle from Antje. His steely gaze locked on her as he cast offensive spells in rapid succession, flinging sparking yellow orbs at Antje, one after another. Witnessing this, Shields broke free from Headmaster Vogel's protective bubble and charged the dark mystic, latching onto the monstrous man's rear end. Dodging the first three, Antje used the power of her intention—the same power she had once used to kill Kitt—to stop the last one in mid-air and flung it back at him. Too occupied with Shields, the dark mystic was unable to block Antje's volley and as the orb absorbed into his chest, the man clutched his heart, his body crashing onto the ground as though it were a felled sequoia tree. Antje huffed, exhausted from the massive expenditure of energy. She placed her hands on the wooden chairs around her, and her hands began to glow green. Shields bounded across the aisle and stood next to her, snarling and growling at something over her shoulder—ready to attack. Antje whipped around to find a female dark mystic summoning a spell from the outside edge of the row. Just as the dark mystic was about to release the spell, Ragnar broke a chair over her head, knocking her out; he then drove one of the chair legs through her chest and crouched down with Antje.

"Hey, bride. You didn't think I was going to let you have all the fun just because it's your big day, did you? I didn't bring any weapons—I don't think any of us did except the CIA guys. This is going to be an interesting battle," he said, standing up and punching another dark mystic in the face as they approached, entirely unaware of Ragnar and Antje's presence in the next row. Shields leapt from one of the chairs, landing on the dark mystic and ripping their throat out. With purple goo dripping from his jowls and staining the white fur surrounding his mouth, Shields proudly turned to Antje and Ragnar.

Ragnar chortled. "Brutal. What a good boy!" he playfully said, patting Shields' head and tousling his fur. Antje sighed in relief.

"This fucking bitch—my wedding day of all days, and she didn't even have the balls to show up as herself. I've gotta get closer. I'm going to kill her. Do you think you and Shields can handle the ones on this side?"

Ragnar grinned and pulled a black potion from his pocket. "Philomena gave this to me to use on belligerent, drunk guests later on... it's a knock-out potion. Shields and I can handle it."

Antje hugged Ragnar tightly and kissed the small indention between Shields' eyes. "I love you both. Be careful."

Shields licked Antje, spreading purple sludge across her cheek as Ragnar chuckled and replied, "Go kill her, bride." Launching the knock-out potion into the crowd, Ragnar and Shields began clearing the throng of dark mystics, one by one.

Antje took a deep breath, pulling in more energy from the wooden chairs, and dove across the aisle. She leapt over one row of chairs, tackling a small, male dark mystic with greasy hair and a fanny pack. After tumbling to the ground, he headbutted her in the nose; primal fear tensed in his face with the realization that he had simply angered Antje rather than incapacitated her. Antje raised the stake in her right hand, blood dripping from her nose as she plunged it through his heart. Antje poked her head above the chairs quickly, noting she was only three rows from the Dark Queen. Under her breath, Antje muttered, "I'm going to end your reign of terror—once and for all."

Still squatting behind the front row of chairs with Kenny, Cole picked off several more of the remaining henchmen. With each bullet zipping over the heads of trapped guests, Cole systematically terminated the touristic threat while he dodged the barrage of orbs and magic arrows being unleashed at his head.

Kenny aided Cole, killing two dark mystics. With a skillful snipe, he managed to shoot the blonde woman in the thigh. The woman's appearance glitched, her face now split in two by a long scar; she looked at her thigh, seething. The woman continued to summon the largest red orb Kenny had ever seen, and although the Dark Queen didn't look like this woman—every bone in his body told Kenny this was indeed her. Kenny fired a few more bullets at her—which she then froze in place and tapped back toward Kenny with the flick of her hand. Ducking behind the chair, two bullets narrowly missed him—the third hit a wedding guest who made the deadly decision to attempt an upright escape from the chaos.

Hunkered down, his veins coursing with adrenaline, Kenny looked over at Cole and yelled, "Cole, shoot the blonde woman in the head! She's the Dark Queen!" Cole nodded and jumped up to get a clear line of sight as he quickly aimed his gun at the Dark Queen, firing the last bullet in his magazine as she launched a bowling-ball-sized red orb over the top of the crowd at Cole.

Time again stood still for Antje as she saw the narrow gap between the red orb and Cole. Antje jumped into the aisle and sprinted as fast as she could to Cole, time slowly returning to normal speed as the orb approached. With no time to remove him from its path, she stepped in front of Cole and kissed him on the lips, heartache flowing steadily from her eyes—for this was a stolen moment she knew would be her last.

"I'll love you forever, Cole. I found you in this life, and I will find you in the next. Please forgive me," she tearfully whispered as the red orb smashed into her back, time catching up as Cole's bullet burrowed into the Dark Queen's chest. Her face transformed—a scar now revealing itself down the center of her face as her motionless body hit the ground.

Antje fell forward into Cole's arms, her body limp as Cole fell to the ground, holding her. Confounded by how she had blinked into his arms, but fully aware of her sacrifice, Cole clung to Antje with tears streaming down his face as she mouthed, "I love you."

"No! Antje, no! Healer! No, no, no...Antje, please no!" Cole screamed, clutching Antje to his chest and rocking her as Philomena, Isaac, and Kenny lunged toward them. Antje's body began to disintegrate into ash, and grief washed across their collective faces as they realized Antje's fate was sealed.

"Antje, please...please no. Stay with me, my love. Please don't leave me," Cole pleaded, his heartbreak radiating from every pore. Antje's lifeless eyes stared back at Cole as the last of her body—her tear-stained face—disintegrated into white ash. As Antje's ashes fell through his fingers, a single gust of wind carried her over the canyon's edge in a swirl, before dissipating and falling into the canyon itself. The skies darkened as two ravens flew overhead, announcing the death of Antje to the natural world.

Backup arrived and slaughtered the last of the dark mystics with the aid of Ragnar and Shields as Cole bellowed in agony, his screams echoing through the canyon, birds and animals fleeing in groups as his shockwave of loss hit them. Kenny held Cole to his chest as Cole sobbed uncontrollably, sporadically screaming to the point of his voice cracking between sobs. Uncle Isaac stared off over the edge of the cliff face, silently crying.

"Until later, my dear daughter," he whispered to the winds before turning around and placing his hand on Cole's forehead—Cole went limp in Kenny's arms.

TWENTY-FIVE

THE AFTERMATH OF ABHORRENT ACTIONS

A s Kenny stood near Cole, he watched as the Dark Queen's wrists were confined by the agency's magic-binding cuffs—her body strapped onto a stretcher as Philomena approached him.

"It's unfair, innit? That evil shite lives while our precious Antje dies. Feckin' fate and its bullshite," she scowled, wiping her tears on her sleeve as she stood by his side.

Blankly staring, Kenny replied, "What's about to happen to the Dark Queen is a fate far worse than death. We have a black site for destructive mystics where she will live out the remainder of her days, however long that may be, as a lab rat in solitary confinement. Death would have been too kind for what she's done."

Philomena sniffled, lowered her head, and patted Kenny's shoulder before shuffling over to Ragnar, who enveloped her in a heartfelt hug. Philomena and Ragnar sat on either side of Takhi in the left front row seats that had been joyously filled just a half hour ago. Takhi sat with her head hung low, sobbing into her hands as Ragnar wrapped his arm around her wings and pulled her into his chest.

"It's okay, Takhi. She is in Valhalla with Odin now, and he will welcome her with a most glorious celebration. Her fight will go on—you know that is our way," Ragnar quietly assured, tenderly stroking the side of her face as tears continued to saturate her fur.

Headmaster Vogel and Kari kneeled beside Cole, who was still anesthetized but had been propped up against Mikono and now had Shields laying across his lap—refusing to leave him. "We need to get him out of here before he wakes up. Ze last thing he needs to wake up to is ze aftermath of ze worst day of his life. Let us take him to ze Cisterne if that is okay with you, Kenny?"

Kenny turned his head around and silently gave a nod before returning his bloodshot gaze to the armored vehicle. The General entered into the rear of the vehicle and sat on a metal bench, sandwiched between two CIA special ops members as the Dark Queen's stretcher was hoisted into the space in front of him. The General caught eyes with Kenny and saluted him with a heavy heart as the doors to the armored vehicle closed.

Isaac walked up on the other side of Kenny. With tears trickling down his face, Kenny turned to Isaac, extended his hand, and said, "I'm so sorry for your loss, sir. Your niece was unlike anyone I've ever known. She was strong, kind, smart...she was incredible. She made my best friend the happiest I've ever seen him, and she gave me my leg back. Honestly, I don't know if either of us will ever recover from losing her."

Isaac wrapped his arms around Kenny, who returned and savored the embrace. Still holding him, Isaac patted his back and quietly replied, "I'm heartbroken too, Kenny—but we are at the mercy of fate in the end, and this was her destiny. I didn't know today was the day, but her ascension has been the plan all along." Releasing Kenny from his arms, he handed him the handkerchief from his coat pocket. Isaac turned and observed the trail of dust kicked up in the armored vehicle's wake as it drove off. "She has far more important duties to tend to now than keeping our hearts whole."

Twenty-Six

Voyage to Valhalla

C ole's eyes opened to an unfamiliar scene—he stood in the midst of a battle. Swords clanged, and blood poured from the bodies of unknown people around him. Cole took a step back, bumping into the bulky chest of an old man adorned in full metal armor, who carried a long spear at his side. Shocked, Cole immediately recognized the man. "Odin," he blankly stated, his mouth agape.

"In the flesh, Cole. You've come at just the right time," Odin answered.

Cole, forced to come to terms with what he had just experienced, seethed with rage. "Why would you let her die, Odin? Why? Your own daughter, and you let her die!"

"Calm yourself, son. This was her fate, just as now, you have met yours. You want to see her again, do you not?" Odin outstretched his arms and loudly cracked his knuckles.

"Of course I do—what kind of fucking question is that?" Cole sneered, crossing his arms across his chest.

Odin, amused by Cole's anger, pointed at a man at the far end of the battlefield. "Watch that man over there, and when it is done, I will explain."

"When what's done?" Cole asked. Still perturbed, Cole witnessed a fearsome warrior carve his way through a sea of his opponents effortlessly, dropping bodies as if they were composed of paper rather than flesh and bone.

"Just watch," Odin instructed, his eyes fixed on the formidable soldier. Cole sighed and followed Odin's directive, locking eyes on the man whose face was drenched with the blood of fallen foes.

An enemy charged the man from behind, taking advantage of his occupation with the three men to his front and sides. Suddenly, a woman with strawberry blonde hair and broad, onyx wings flew over Cole and Odin's heads. Cole ducked his head slightly, looking upward and catching the iridescent shimmer of her feathers in the sun.

Agog for a moment, Cole mumbled, "A valkyrie." Mesmerized, Cole couldn't take his eyes off the aerial angel of death and watched as she released her bowstring and fired an arrow through the charging man's head from above—dropping the man like a hailstone.

Odin beamed with pride. "Correct. Not just *a* valkyrie—one of my most cherished, and also my daughter." His gaze now shifted to Cole, who turned to face him, his eyes wide with curiosity.

"Is that Eír?" Cole asked.

"Correct."

Turning back to the man on the battlefield and squinting to get a better look, the dots connected internally for Cole. "That man is Vatn. That's my higher self."

Odin grabbed Cole's shoulder and leaned in toward him. "Yes, son. That is Vatn, my son-in-law, and the leader of my army." Swinging his arm up, Odin placed his arm around Cole's shoulders. "Do you know why he is called Vatn?" Odin asked, shaking Cole with excitement. "Vatn means water in the old tongue. He is called Vatn because he carves through the battlefield as water carves through the earth. He is an unstoppable force, as are you. Come, I have something else to show you."

Cole blinked once and found himself in the great halls of Valhalla alongside Odin. They stood on a side wall as Odin's past self sat on his throne, carefully watching something in the herd of boisterous men. Cole followed his eyeline and caught a glimpse of Eír serving Vatn mead as they coquettishly chatted.

"This is the first time Vatn and Eír met with both of their bodies in the higher realms."

"I...don't understand what that means," Cole admitted.

Odin chuckled heartily. "Your body is in Midgard right now, but your consciousness is here because Isaac put you into a hypnagogic state and I pulled you through the astral plane. In this memory of mine that you are witnessing, Eír and Vatn are both physically in Valhalla. Vatn has just died in battle in Midgard, and Eír carried his soul to Valhalla. She now serves him mead—our tradition—to welcome him into our ranks. He wasted no time in proving he was meant to marry my daughter and lead my army."

Intrigued, Cole observed Eír and Vatn flirting before Past Odin called both of them over to his throne. After witnessing a conversation that Cole couldn't hear, he turned to Odin and asked what was happening.

"I am asking Vatn if he wants to go back to Midgard to be with Eír. Come, let us get closer." Odin motioned for Cole to follow as he walked up behind his own throne and rested his elbows on the back of it, just over his past self's head.

"I don't want to return to Midgard. I hate it there. It's nothing but misery and pain, Odin. Please don't make me go," Eír pleaded, clasping her hands and pulling them to her chest.

Past Odin stood from his throne and wrapped his hands around hers, "I am sorry, daughter—we all make sacrifices to keep the balance."

Downtrodden, Eír touched her forehead to Past Odin's as he leaned down and grabbed her head gently with both hands. Kissing her forehead, Past Odin lifted his head and turned around, releasing Eír from his hands. "Vatn!" he hollered loudly. "Vatn, come. I have a mission for you."

Vatn quickly traversed the room and took a knee in front of Past Odin, "All-Father, anything you need."

Past Odin extended his hand to Vatn. "Stand up, son. You do not bend a knee to anyone—ever." Taking his hand, Vatn rose to his feet and curiously looked at Past Odin, who grabbed his shoulders with both hands and locked eyes with him. Past Odin flashed a grin and continued, "Good. Vatn, I need you to return to Midgard as Eír's spouse. Protect her, love her, but above all—keep her on her path, so that she can heal the wounded, extinguish the darkness, and help wake the souls around her to meet their fates." Past Odin released his shoulders. "What do you say?"

Vatn straightened himself, gave a stern nod, and reverently replied, "With honor."

Past Odin reached one hand into the chests of both Eír and Vatn. His hands emerged holding two small, glistening shards resembling glowing quartz crystals. Vatn rubbed his chest as Eír tapped her heart with a melancholic look on her face.

Two ravens appeared and landed on Past Odin's shoulders. Odin lifted both of his hands to the birds, who each grasped a shard in their talons before flying out of the great hall's main entryway.

Before Cole could ask, Odin began to explain, "Those ravens are Huginn and Munnin. I tasked them with taking Vatn and Eír's soul shards to the Well of Urd, where their souls will be taken to Midgard and given bodies."

Cole stared at Odin with befuddled eyes. "None of that was ever in the Edda, Odin."

Odin guffawed. "I am aware. The Edda was written by humans, not gods. You don't really think it has captured everything, do you? Humans can't even relay messages to each other in the same existence with precision. Do you really believe they are capable of capturing communications from the higher realms with any real accuracy? That is funny." Odin slapped Cole's back as he continued to chuckle, almost knocking Cole off his feet. "Anyway, those two soul shards are you and Antje. Which leaves us with today...I am sympathetic to your heartache, son—but this was part of both of your fates. Are you ready to meet your fate and live alongside my daughter again?"

"I will do whatever I have to—to be with her again," Cole said earnestly.

Odin placed his hand on Cole's shoulder and squeezed before patting him on the back affectionately. "Good. You will have to fight your way through all of the nine realms to prove that you are capable of being the leader of my army and the husband of my daughter. Valkyries cannot marry mere men—I won't allow it, nor will the Norns."

Cole cocked his head slightly. "The Norns...the weavers of fate? The nine realms as in...the Norse nine realms?"

"Yes—to both. Your body will stay in Midgard, but you will battle your way through all the nine realms. Only then will your body be brought to Valhalla, and you may be reunited with Antje." Odin's expression became serious as he locked eyes with Cole once more. "There is one catch, Cole. If you die in any of the nine realms, your body will die in Midgard, and Vatn will die along with you. If you succeed, Vatn will become a god, and you will become the leader of my army. Do you still wish to meet your fate?"

Cole paused, taking a moment to mull over this proposition. But, no matter what thought passed through his head, all he could think about was being with Antje once more.

Cole pursed his lips and asked, "If I succeed, I will get to live an eternity with Antje, correct?"

"Yes—assuming your incarnations perform as well as you undoubtedly will. Do you agree to these terms?"

"I do." Cole gave a firm nod. "I agree under one condition—I get to visit with Antje before I embark on this journey."

Odin practically howled with laughter, slapping Cole on the back. "You are just like Vatn. I accept your condition. Go."

The stone walls of Antje's room were bathed in the soothing, golden light of autumn. Her eyes slowly opened, and as she gradually took in her unfamiliar surroundings, Antje glanced down at her hands—noticing the scars that once adorned them had vanished and left dainty, well-manicured ones in their stead. She looked to the doorway where Cole leaned against the arched frame, his signature adoring smile painted across his face. Springing from the bed, Antje ran to Cole, wrapping her arms around him and kissing him passionately as their bodies tangled into each other's.

Confused by her surroundings, and sensing Cole's internalized pain, she leaned back and looked deep into his languid eyes.

"Cole... where are we? I had the most insane dream that we were at our wedding, and the Dark Queen showed up, and I—I died."

"That wasn't a dream, my darling." Cole paused thoughtfully, brushing the hair from her face and tucking several strands behind her ear as he kissed her forehead. "We're in Valhalla... and you *are* dead, my love."

A Love Letter to Readers

Hey there. Thank you so much for reading my work. I truly do appreciate you supporting an unknown author. I poured my heart and soul into this book, and I'm elated it isn't sitting as a file on my laptop any longer. Don't worry...I have no intention of leaving you hanging with that ending (I know you cursed me a little). Book two of nine is done and will be released shortly if it hasn't been already, by the time you read this.

I hope this book entertained, brought up some uncomfortable stuff to confront, and ultimately left you feeling a zest for the hidden aspects of life that we become numb to in adulthood.

If this book left you wanting more in the meantime, feel free to head on over to my website, where I have many short stories and poems that were previously published for your perusal at **esoliver.com** Be sure to sign up for the newsletter—there's a lot of fun stuff boiling in this brain of mine that I can't wait to share with you.

You can also find me on social media on **Facebook & Instagram**

And lastly... A shameless favor to ask: It is insanely hard for new authors to find their readers, and one of the best ways you could help me find others who will enjoy this book like you did, is via reviews. If you could head on over to GoodReads and/or Amazon and leave me a review, that would be very kind of you.

Made in the USA
Columbia, SC
22 July 2024

a89203d7-a3fd-416b-b6fa-96afe9419cffR02